T0038454

Everything for You

A BERGMAN BROTHERS NOVEL

CHLOE LIESE

BERKLEY ROMANCE
NEW YORK

BERKLEY ROMANCE
Published by Berkley
An imprint of Penguin Random House LLC
penguinrandomhouse.com

Library of Congress Cataloging-in-Publication Data

Names: Liese, Chloe, author.
Title: Everything for you: a Bergman Brothers novel / Chloe Liese.
Description: First Berkley Romance edition. | New York: Berkley Romance, 2024. |
Series: The Bergman Brothers
Identifiers: LCCN 2023031475 (print) | LCCN 2023031476 (ebook) |
ISBN 9780593642436 (trade paperback) | ISBN 9780593642443 (ebook)
Subjects: LCGFT: Romance fiction. | Gay fiction. | Sports fiction. | Novels.
Classification: LCC PS3612.I3357 E93 2024 (print) |
LCC PS3612.I3357 (ebook) | DDC 813/.6—dc23/eng/20230714
LC record available at https://lccn.loc.gov/2023031475
LC ebook record available at https://lccn.loc.gov/2023031476

Everything for You was originally self-published, in different form, in 2022.

First Berkley Romance Edition: February 2024

Printed in the United States of America
1st Printing

Book design by Kristin del Rosario

This is a work of fiction. Names, characters, places, and incidents either are the
product of the author's imagination or are used fictitiously, and any resemblance
to actual persons, living or dead, business establishments, events,
or locales is entirely coincidental.

For anyone who's been scared or hurt,
who's loved and lost.
You're brave.
You're enough.
I believe in you.

Dear Reader,

This story features characters with human realities who I believe deserve to be seen more prominently in romance through positive, authentic representation. As a neurodivergent person living with chronic conditions, I am passionate about writing feel-good romances affirming my belief that every one of us is worthy and capable of happily ever after, if that's what our hearts desire.

Specifically, this story portrays a main character who lives with chronic pain and a main character who has anxiety, including two on-page panic attacks. No two people's experience of any condition or diagnosis will be the same, but through my own experience and the insight of authenticity readers, I have striven to create characters who honor the nuances of those identities. Please be advised that in one scene a queerphobic slur is directed at one of the main characters, but it is not named on page, and it is vehemently condemned by me and in the narrative.

If any of these are sensitive topics for you, I hope you feel comforted in knowing that loving, affirming relationships—with oneself and others—are championed in this story.

XO,
Chloe

I have no notion of loving people by halves; it is not my nature.

—JANE AUSTEN,
Northanger Abbey

ONE

Oliver

Playlist: "Capsized," Andrew Bird

I will be the first to admit that I am not my best self when intoxicated. A generally upbeat, sociable guy, I don't seek alcohol for its loose-limbed, easygoing buzz, and after throwing back a few, I don't get it. I simply turn, for lack of better words, into a highly unfiltered emotional mess.

Which is why I will not be drinking this weekend. Nope, not a drop. Not when I've just started to feel like myself again, months after getting my heart crushed. Not when I'm about to spend spring break celebrating my brother's marriage alongside my still-very-much-in-love parents and my six siblings, four of whom are also happily partnered.

Drinking would be a bad choice. Not only because, as I've said, I'm no peach when drunk, but because it won't take much to send me spiraling into the bleak thoughts that have plagued me since my breakup.

"Oliver."

My brother Viggo, so close to me in age and looks that we operate like twins, turns off the rental car's stereo, bathing us in silence.

I glance his way from where I've been staring out the window. "What?"

"I'm *talking* to you."

"So keep talking."

Viggo sighs and rakes a hand through his unkempt brown hair, our only discernible difference, compared to my dark blond. Same angular jaw and faint cleft chin as our dad, same high cheekbones and pale blue-gray eyes that we inherited from Mom. Same tall, lean bodies, except I've started putting on more muscle, thanks to weight training so I can hold my own on a D-I soccer field.

"I could keep talking." Viggo throws a concerned glance my way, eyes on me much longer than they should be for how fast he's driving. "But I don't think you've been listening."

"I'm listening," I tell him so he'll keep his eyes on the road and not get us killed before we even make it to the party.

"Uh-huh." Thankfully, he trains his gaze ahead even as he leans my way, wrinkling his nose.

"What are you doing?" A smile I can't help tugs at my mouth. Viggo drives me up the wall, but he's just about the only person who both indulges my rare foul moods and can pull me out of them.

"I'm sniffing you," he says, throwing on his turn signal and passing a slowpoke in front of us.

"Sniffing me."

"Mm-hmm. I smell the angst wafting off of you."

"Shut up." I punch his thigh. He twists my nipple. I yelp in pain. "Dammit, Viggo! That hurt!"

"Serves you right," he says. "That's my gas leg you hit. I could have caused an accident."

I slouch down moodily in my seat and stare out the window. Sharp lemon-yellow sunlight slices through the slate-blue sky marbled with clouds. It's early spring, and—unlike our family's current home base of Los Angeles—Washington State, where Mom and Dad first lived and started their brood of seven Bergman kids, feels like it fights for every fragile blossom and green shoot that muscles its way through the cold, hard earth. In the Pacific Northwest, there are edges and effort. Here, hope feels hard-won.

That's how hope feels inside me, too.

Lowering the window, I suck in a gulp of midfifties, wet air—petrichor and the promise of full-blown spring just around the corner. God, I love this place.

"So . . ." Viggo clears his throat, yanking me from my thoughts. "I know you're dreading seeing everyone in their coupled bliss."

"Coupled bliss?" I snort a laugh, trying to deflect how on the mark Viggo is. Annoyingly, this is typical, his confident and freakishly accurate emotional intuition. After reading hundreds of historical romance novels, my brother considers himself an expert on the human heart.

"I'll be fine, Viggo. I'm over it."

Mostly.

For once, my brother lets it go and stays quiet, though his skeptical arched eyebrow speaks volumes as he takes the hairpin turn preceding the entrance to our family's getaway home, a lakeside A-frame nestled in the woods.

Well, we call it "the A-frame," but it's actually been expanded extensively. As Viggo pulls into the drive, the view hits me like a direct kick to the chest. Dark wood and steep roof, tall glass windows across the front, the sprawling addition that made it spacious enough for all of us looming to the left, smoke curling from the chimney. Tiny green leaves and pink buds kiss wet black branches, forming a canopy over us.

It's a view so bittersweetly beautiful, it hurts. A lump forms in my throat.

"I have a plan to cope, okay?" Viggo slows as we roll over a pothole.

"A plan."

He nods. "So, Axel and Rooney are already married—"

"I do remember being informed of that last month. Sort of

hard to forget, along with the sight of your face when you found out."

Viggo scowls. He hasn't recovered from the devastation that his romance-reading radar didn't pick up on our brother Axel and Rooney's covert marriage.

He mutters darkly, "I'm still salty about that. A secret marriage! An elopement! How did I miss it?"

"Because they weren't speeding off in a horse-drawn carriage to Gretna Green?"

"Shut up."

I pat his back to console him as Viggo mutters under his breath about emotionally constipated siblings. "Even if you did read romances postdating the nineteenth century," I tell him, "you weren't going to have a clue what was going on until Ax was ready to tell us. That's just how he is."

My oldest brother's a man of few words. Deeply loving but intensely private and quiet, Axel lives on the family property here, in his own cabin, so we see and hear from him less often, and when we do hear from him, it's frequently via the written word.

Axel's on the autism spectrum and finds writing the easiest way to tell us personal things. Which is why, when he told us how twisted up he was over Rooney this past Christmas—when I saw how long they spent alone on the porch after she showed up, how close they seemed while she spent the next few days with us—I wasn't *terribly* surprised to receive a beautiful handwritten note from Axel last month explaining that he and Rooney had been together since the fall and they were now married. The letter also said that he was sorry he hadn't been able to make us a part of their wedding, but he still very much wanted to celebrate their marriage with us.

The only thing that made getting that heartfelt letter written in Axel's tall, sloping scrawl even better was watching Viggo's dawning horror as he read his letter, too. Not because he disapproved of Axel's methods but because he'd been clueless about what was going on.

"As I was saying." Viggo sniffs, maneuvering around the other vehicles parked in the clearing. "My plan to cope. It's a low-key party. It's not like you'll have to see them get married. Knowing Axel, it'll be chill. Practical. Relaxed. We'll pound some delicious food. I'll get you good and liquored up, tuck you in, and you'll sleep it off. Tomorrow it'll be back to the same old family shenanigans, and you can blast me in the face with a soccer ball when we play pickup."

"For the hundredth time, it was an *accident*."

He rubs the bridge of his now slightly-less-than-perfectly-straight nose. "Uh-huh. And it had nothing to do with the fake snake I put in your bed the night before."

"If it *did*," I say testily, throwing my phone, water canteen, and snacks into my carry-on bag between my legs, "it was subliminal. And you deserved it."

Wrenching the car into park, Viggo turns and looks at me. "Listen, something I tell myself regularly, as I wait for my one true love—"

"Here we go." I slump back in my seat and scrub my face.

"—is that someone's romantic gain does not equate to my loss. Most of our siblings are happily paired off, and while I wish I was, too, I can be happy for them while I wait. Our time *will* come." He sets a hand on my shoulder and gives it a squeeze. "Until then— well, more like for the next seventy-two hours—let's be the untethered man cubs and have some fun. Got it?"

I sigh and throw open my car door. "Fine."

———

Well. I'm intoxicated. Thankfully I haven't veered into shit show territory.

Though I think I might be on my way.

Stashed in a shadowy corner of the A-frame's wide back deck, I'm outside the golden reach of countless twinkly lights strung overhead. A cool late-March breeze weaves through the small gathering, and as I nurse my who-knows-what-number beer, my gaze travels my family.

Mom and Dad sway to the music, eyes only for each other. Mom slips her hands through Dad's copper hair, which is threaded with white, and smiles softly up at him. Dad's eyes crinkle as he grins at her, wrapping his hands tighter around her waist.

They look so in love, and I love that my parents are still gone for each other, but I don't need to see them kiss, which they're about to. So I look away just in time and catch the oldest of us, my sister Freya, with her arms around her husband Aiden's neck—*ack!*—kissing him.

I shut my eyes briefly, and when I open them again, there's Axel, next in birth order, swaying his wife, Rooney, to the music's rhythm. He's the tallest of us, which makes him gigantic, seeing as no one in the family is under six feet. His hair, chocolate brown like Viggo's, falls over his forehead as he stares at Rooney, her spun-gold waves adorned with a crown of flowers. He kisses her forehead, eyes shut, his world nothing but her.

Then there's Ren, so much like Dad, with his broad build and ginger hair, and just a little like Mom, with her pale blue-gray eyes and sharp cheekbones. I try not to watch him make his girlfriend, Frankie, flash a rare wide smile and laugh as he whispers in her ear.

I was hoping I could count on my grumpy lumberjack-looking brother Ryder—with Dad's feisty green eyes and penchant for provoking the woman he loves—to cut me a break, but even *he's* being romantic. A heated grin plays on his mouth as his girlfriend, Willa, smiles up at him and sinks her hands into his dirty-blond man bun, tugging him down for a deep, hard kiss.

My sister Ziggy, the only one younger than me, sits happily curled up on a deck chair, a lock of long red hair twirled around her finger, smiling to herself as she reads one of her thick fantasy romances. I know that look, her green eyes darting down the page, a fiery blush heating her pale skin—she's being swept away by another dark-haired, sardonic villain who'll somehow be redeemed and turn into a love interest by the end, if the past few stories she's gushed about are anything to go by.

Among a few other close friends are Rooney's parents, too. And though they're divorced, they share what seems like an amicable dance between friends now, their loving gazes directed at their daughter.

In short, I'm surrounded by all kinds of happy endings, which is lovely . . . but also terrible.

"Okay." Viggo plops beside me and swaps out my beer for a glass of water. "I didn't know Axel was going to surprise Rooney with renewing their vows in front of their families and closest friends."

I rub my chest, where it still aches with the knot of joy and sadness that's been there since I watched them promise themselves to each other again just a few hours ago. "You told me it was only gonna be a party."

Oh boy. My words are sloppy. I sound very drunk.

Focusing on my diction, I try to sound more sober as I tell my brother, "They already got married. It was just supposed to be a *party*."

"I know, bud," Viggo mutters, cupping my neck, an affectionate, steadying gesture that's common in our family. Tipping back his beer, he takes a long pull. "But it seems our surly, silent oldest brother turned into a full-fledged romantic somewhere in the past three months and had the swoony idea to invite the most important people in their lives for an intimate gathering so they could share a wedding with us after all."

I glance back at Axel, who's holding Rooney. He kisses her so long, they stop dancing, until their rescue dog, Harry, bounds up and breaks them apart with a cheerful bark.

I shut my eyes again. "I'm happy for them," I whisper.

"I know you are," Viggo says. "It's still hard to see, though, and that's okay. You and me, Ollie, we do nothing by halves. You fell in love, and you fell hard. Healing from heartache takes longer for big hearts like ours."

As I open my eyes again, they land on Axel's close friends, Parker and Bennett, who dance with their daughter, Skyler, nestled between them. That's what I used to think I'd have with Bryce. What I dreamed about.

I know I'm young, and I know not everyone finds their forever person when they're a sophomore in college. But I was so sure I had. We had everything I thought you were supposed to—we talked easily and got along right away. Bryce was all play and fun, which balanced my brutally disciplined work ethic both on the field and in the classroom. It was easy with him, straightforward. Wasn't it supposed to be easy? When did I miss the signs that my boyfriend was losing interest? That his eyes had started to wander?

My chest tightens as those unanswered questions, those obsessive worries, shout over each other in my brain until the familiar, anxious noise inside my skull threatens to make me scream.

I suck in a breath and exhale steadily, coaxing myself to focus on sensations around me—the cool air on my skin, the sound of soft music nearby. A trick my therapist taught me since I realized those "anxious days" I'd been having were every day, that anxiety wasn't just a by-product of my busy, high-pressure schedule, but a reality of my brain, my body, my life.

While I was learning to cope, while I started trying antianxiety meds, Bryce was my fun, lighthearted person. My happy place. I thought I knew that so fully, so completely. And then with one sweep of remorseless infidelity, down came the house of cards.

"I never wanna feel like this," I mutter. "*Never* again."

Viggo's quiet for a moment. "I know. I don't want you to either."

I shut my eyes. The world's starting to spin as I say to Viggo, "Why's he have to play on the team and be in half my classes? I'd be fine if I could just . . . get away from him."

"And to address that, my offer still stands."

I snort a drunken laugh, blinking open my eyes. "While I 'preciate your offer to prank Bryce so bad he'd leave UCLA, I'm pretty sure two-thirds of what you have planned is felonious, and I don't want you to go to jail."

Viggo scoffs. "I'm a stealthy guy. I could get away with it."

"Or I could say yes to the Galaxy's offer and get away from it all."

His head whips my way. "What?"

I tuck my lips between my teeth. "*Shooot.* I said that out loud."

Viggo turns to face me fully. "I'm not surprised they want you. I'm surprised you're considering it. You've always said you wanted to complete your degree, no matter what."

"I did." I feel unsteady, so I lean back against the house. The world's spinning even faster now. I hiccup drunkenly. "I wanted—I *want*—my premed degree."

At least, I think I do.

Do I?

My brother's quiet for a minute. "Why do you do it, Ollie? Work *so* hard? You know how good you are at soccer, how much you love it. When was becoming a doctor ever a real plan for you, when going pro was inevitable?"

"It wasn't inevitable." I try to sip the water Viggo gave me and mostly miss my mouth.

Viggo rolls his eyes. "Yes it was. And I've never understood why you've been busting your ass since freshman year of *high school* to prepare for something you never really intended to pursue."

I laugh emptily. I can tell Viggo almost everything, but not this. How hard it is to be the fifth son, to live in the shadow of a decorated military veteran and physician father and four older brothers who, each in their own way, are profoundly capable and talented and confident. How difficult it's been to find myself amid all of that, to feel seen and . . . maybe just a little admired?

Axel's a brilliant, successful artist. Ren's a professional hockey player, an NHL darling. Ryder's fast building an accessible wilderness-experience-and-outfitter-store empire. And Viggo's so damn good at everything he tries, even if he doesn't seem to stick with his interests very long, he could literally do *anything* he wanted.

Then there are my sisters. Freya, the eldest, a physical therapist who's already managing her practice, for God's sake. She's just barely in her thirties! And Ziggy, who's always known what she wanted and singularly pursued it: soccer. She's the beloved baby, the adored and wanted second daughter, the perfect bookend to our family.

Then there's me. A hard worker. A diligent student athlete. Someone who got swept up in medicine because it was fascinating but most importantly because it was something Dad and I could always talk about. Someone who aced every test because that was the one thing I did that made Mom smile and hug me hard with relief that I wasn't getting into trouble again or making mischief with Viggo.

Being on a premed track, getting good grades, I've derived pride and satisfaction from it. I've always liked doing well, knowing I've exceeded expectations, pleased the people who matter to me in doing so. If soccer weren't the one place I felt freest, most joyful, most myself, I would like to be a compassionate, competent doctor. But soccer is my heart, and the opportunity I've wanted for so long is finally here, begging me to be brave, to give up these familiar, safe places of validation and straightforward reassurance, to take a risk and grab this opportunity with both hands.

"I think . . ." I lick my lips, which feel tingly, almost numb. "Med school was my backup plan."

Viggo snorts. "Only you would have medical school as a backup plan."

"Will they be proud of me?" I mumble.

His amusement dies away. He leans in, his hand slipping down the middle of my back. "Who?"

"Mom and Dad. All of you."

"Ollie, of course. We're already proud of you. If you did nothing but exist the rest of your life, we'd be proud of you. Because you're ours and we love you."

I hiccup a laugh. "Sure."

Viggo frowns. "What's ever made you doubt that?"

I shrug off his arm. "You wouldn't understand."

"Then tell me so I will."

Drunkenly, I lean my elbows on my knees, burying my face. One elbow slips off. "I'm gonna do it. I'm gonna tell the Los Angeleeees Galaxy yes."

There's a thick pause. "Maybe," Viggo hazards, "this decision should wait for daylight. And sobriety."

"Pff." I wave a hand and lose my balance so badly, I nearly fall on my face. Viggo wrenches me back up. "Who needs sobriety?"

"You do, my brother. Now, c'mon, let's get you to bed—"

"No way, José." I stagger as I stand. Viggo wraps an arm around my waist, and I use his steadying influence to reach into my pocket for my phone. "Gonna get on my Gmaaaaails and tell them my answer *right* now. 'Yes, please, Galaxy! Signed, sincerely, yours truly, Oliver Abram Bergman.'"

"I'll just take that." Viggo plucks the phone from my hand. "You're not emailing anyone right now."

"Good*byeeee*, Bryce," I sing as Viggo starts us toward the deck stairs, away from the party. He's going to sneak me around the side of the house, in through the front door, so I don't embarrass myself around the family, and in some dim, not-as-drunk part of my mind, I'm grateful for it. "Good*byeeee*, collegiate soccer," I croon. "I was better than you anyway."

A quiet laugh rumbles in his chest. "This is my favorite part of your drunkenness. You finally find your ego."

"I am fast as a panther," I sing to the sky. "And excellent at organic chemistry! And I have a great ass! Hear that, incorporeal celestial being, up there? Ooh, I think I see the Little Dipper. He's my favorite." I hiccup. "Oh dear. I think I'm very drunk. How did that happen?"

Viggo laughs again. "You had a lot of beer, Ollie. What did you expect?"

What did you expect? That sentence. It sends me hurtling back to earth from my stargazing as the world's spinning worsens, memories blurring across time and space. That's what Bryce said to me when I walked into his place and caught him with someone on their knees, his dick down their throat, and asked what the hell was going on.

What did you expect?

As if we hadn't been exclusively together for months. As if expecting my boyfriend to be faithful was an absurdity. As if I wasn't *worth* his faithfulness. Or his remorse.

My stomach heaves. I groan, "Gonna puke."

Viggo seems to have anticipated that, because he's ushering me across the lawn, where the light doesn't reach and there's a row of hardy rhododendron bushes. Just as we round them, we both stop. My sister Freya's bent over, doing exactly what I'm about to.

I open my mouth to ask if she's okay, but vomit comes out instead.

Freya takes one look at me, then turns and pukes again.

"Okay." Viggo lifts his hands, backing away. "I love you both. Deeply. But I—" He gags. "I do not have your medical-people iron stomachs. Be well. Call for help if you need it, but I'm sending in reinforcements if you do."

Then he bolts back up the steps of the deck.

After another wave of hurling, Freya moans and sinks to the grass, flopping onto her back. I feel one last surge of alcohol churning up my throat, retch it out, then turn and face my older sister. She looks like hell, starfished on the grass, eyes shut.

I, however, feel eight thousand times better already after having puked up my liquid bad decisions. I have a hankie in my pocket that I use to dab my mouth. Then I crouch and offer Freya my backup from my other pocket. She takes it listlessly, wiping her sweat-beaded brow, then her mouth, before she shoves it in her cleavage and winces.

"Hit the wine too hard?" I ask.

She sets a hand over her mouth. "Please don't talk about alcohol. The thought of it makes me nauseous."

"What's wrong?" I flop down beside her and lie on my back. Side by side, we glance at each other, same pale eyes and Mom's blond hair, though Freya's is still white blond, while mine's darkened, like Ryder's.

Sighing, Freya glances up at the dusky sky glittering with silver stars. "My boobs hurt," she whispers, wiping a tear from the corner of her eye. "And my period's late."

Discussing this topic isn't taboo in the Bergman household. When each of the boys got the puberty talk, that included my dad sitting us down and saying, "You don't turn into a juvenile jerk about your sisters' periods. You ask them if they need anything, and if they do, you go to the store and get them pads, tampons, pain meds, comfort foods, whatever they need to survive, then thank God your body doesn't do that to you every twenty-eight days."

"Last month's was light, too," Freya says, her voice soft. "Almost like . . . not a real one."

I push up on one elbow. "Wait. Are you—"

"Pregnant," she whispers, smiling so wide up at the sky, tears streaming down her face. "I've been so scared. It was too good to be true, after waiting and hoping . . . I couldn't take a test yet."

I clutch her hand because I know her. I know when Freya's emotional, she doesn't need you to fix anything for her; she just needs a hand to hold. So I hold it tight.

"Does Aiden know?"

She bites her lip. "He knows I'm a few days late and feeling wiped out. I promised him I'd take a test tomorrow morning if I still felt this way when I woke up, but . . ." She shakes her head, wiping away more tears. "I didn't have high hopes. I didn't think it could finally—" A half sob, half laugh jumps out of her. "I *never* puke. And my boobs never feel like this. It has to be a baby, doesn't it?"

I laugh softly, but my throat's tight with emotion. "Yeah, Frey. I think so."

My sister's smile widens. She starts to laugh through happy tears, and then I'm laughing with her, like I haven't in months. My heart feels full, its cracks and bruises bandaged by hope.

The clarity of this moment feels surreal. How sure I am, how free I feel having made this decision—albeit under the influence of alcohol, but *in vino veritas*, the saying goes—to move on, to be brave, to step into this new season, believing in myself and the possibilities awaiting me.

No more brushing shoulders with Bryce. No more relationships complicating my happiness or risking my joy in soccer. My friends and family, playing the beautiful game, that'll be enough for me. And soon, there'll be a tiny Bergman baby to adore and pour my love into.

I'll protect my heart, keep my head down, work my ass off. Those will be my worlds, two distinct ones—the people I love and the game I love. As I glance up, hope burning as bright and hot within me as those stars lighting up the sky, I make a promise to myself: I will never let them be one and the same again.

TWO

Oliver

Playlist: "Simplify," Los Coast

Four years later

"Tiny terror incoming!" I yell outside the training room.

The moment she hears the familiar rehearsed screams of fear, my niece, Linnea, slips through the door, a blur of youth Galaxy jersey and soccer socks, a size-two soccer ball glued to her feet.

"Watch out, folks." I mime a sportscaster's voice through hands cupped around my mouth. "She's three—"

"And a third!" Linnie yells.

"Three and a third," I amend. "Three foot three, and she's here to make you—"

"Pee!" she yells.

Preschoolers are strange. Still speaking inside cupped hands, I tell her, "I was going to say 'weep.'"

Linnie's dark hair, which she inherited from Aiden, is braided back, her tongue stuck out in concentration. Those pale Bergman eyes Freya gave her narrow as she runs at Ben, one of our defenders. He stands with legs wide open for her, and she nutmegs him, sending Ben tumbling in exaggerated defeat to the floor.

"She's unstoppable," I boom as she does a step over, which Santi feigns falling for spectacularly, wailing in despair as she beats him.

Next, she throws a shoulder into Carlo's thigh and cuts past him, closing in on Amobi, our goalie. "And she's going for the—"

"Kill!" Linnie hollers.

Amobi lowers into position, blocking off the entrance to the next room, which is filled with treadmills. Linnie does a tiny rainbow, and Amobi lets it sail right through his open hands.

"Actually," I tell her, "I was going to say—"

"*Goal!*" Linnea screeches, wide-eyed with adrenaline, fists high in the air. The room explodes in celebration.

Laughing, Amobi rolls the ball back to Linnea and tells me, "I'm scared, man. If I'd had moves like that at three—"

"And a third," Linnie says, dribbling off with the ball.

"She legitimately got me last week," Carlo says from behind me. "Maradona-ed my a—I mean, butt—straight to the floor."

"Yeah, I did!" Linnie yells. Everything she says is at FULL VOLUME. Wiggling her eyebrows, she grins up at me. "I'm gonna score on *you*, Uncle Ollie."

I flick my hands in a *give me your best shot* gesture. Which Linnea does. She completes a few step overs, pulls back the ball, then cracks it straight into my nuts.

"Oooh." A collective groan of sympathy echoes in the room.

I drop like a sack of flour. "Son of a biscuit."

"Sorry, Uncle Ollie!" Linnie hollers, throwing herself on me.

Yanking her onto my chest, I tell her, "Good thing I know just how to get you back."

Linnea shrieks as I tickle her, then quickly climbs off of me, shoves me onto my stomach, and gets my arm pinned behind my back. "No tickles!" she yells.

I spin, gently rolling her off of me, and give in to our typical wrestling match. As usual, the entire locker room starts cheering on my niece.

"Linnie! Linnie! Linnie!"

"Ack!" I'm in a choke hold that's pretty impressive for someone so tiny when the noise abruptly dies away.

Slowly I glance over my shoulder. Linnea flops off, scrambling behind me as I sit up.

Coach stands, arms folded over her very pregnant stomach. And next to her stands Gavin Hayes. World's best player in recent memory, grumpiest grump, curmudgeonly captain, and once upon a time, my idol.

After a stunning fifteen-year career playing exclusively for England's most prestigious clubs, he moved home to the States two years ago to play for the Galaxy. Ever since then, he's either ignored me or scowled at me, like he does now, eyes dark with disapproval.

I flash a dimpled smile.

His scowl deepens.

This is how it goes. Because the man I once looked up to—whose public coming-out as gay inspired me to come out to more than my friends and family, to be openly bisexual in my professional public life—is an asshole of epic proportions. Life's too short to be a jerk, especially when the media always has an eye trained on you, and the repercussions of a few harmless Bergman pranks could blow up in my face, so I've opted to kill him with kindness instead.

Linnie gapes at Gavin, looking intimidated. She hides behind my shoulders. To her credit, he's intimidating. I remember being similarly gape-mouthed when I first saw him in person. I remember my throat working with a rough swallow, my gaze sliding up his body. He looks the same today as he did two years ago when he joined us: towering height, a broad, powerful body. Suntanned skin, coffee-dark eyes, a tight beard, and thick hair—cropped on the sides, a bit longer on top, the same rich, bittersweet chocolate color.

Gavin looms over us in that aggressive stance that I've watched him take before every free and penalty kick since I was in grade school and he was a young hotshot teen who'd ascended to the highest level of soccer before he could even legally drink. His eyes never leaving mine, he flicks Linnea's ball up into the air with his foot and catches it, palming it in his hand.

"Bergman," Coach says, her black box braids swaying as she bends to see past me. "And Linner the Winner, of course."

Linnie peeks out from behind my shoulder. "Hi, Coach."

"Keeping these boys in check?" Coach asks her.

She nods.

"Good. Well—" Coach clears her throat, dabs her forehead and the sheen of sweat glistening on her dark brown skin. Like Freya, Coach seems to be experiencing one of advanced pregnancy's not-so-pleasant symptoms of being unbearably hot *all* the time. "I was looking for you, Bergman. Mind escorting Miss Linnie back to her mom so we can have a quick chat?"

I stand, setting a reassuring hand on Linnea's shoulder when she wraps her arms around my leg. "Sure thing, Coach."

"Uncle Ollie," Linnie stage-whispers, because she's incapable of speaking softly. "Can you get my ball from the grump?"

"Oh shit," someone mutters.

Gavin glares down at her. He's massive. Six four, built like a linebacker. For his size, he defies physics with how fast his feet are, and they aren't even as fast as they used to be, not that I'd say that to his face—I like my limbs intact, thank you very much.

As I stare at him, debating the most diplomatic way to tell the crank to give the kid her ball back, his gaze meets mine for just a moment. Then he blinks, drops the ball, spins, and storms out of the room.

Coach glances over her shoulder as he whips open the door and disappears, a sigh gusting out of her.

"Uncle Ollie." My niece taps my shoulder. "I have to pee."

"My office in five," Coach says. "And don't forget the goods."

I smile. "I got you covered, Coach."

"Uncle Olllieeee," Linnie whines, starting to do the *I have to pee* dance, hopping from one foot to another, clutching her shorts.

"Okay, bud. Let's go find Mommy."

As per usual for these Linnie visits, I left Freya talking shop with our physical trainers on staff, Dan and Maria, who's a friend of hers from her college days. If the past is any indication, Dan and Maria will be in their swivel chairs, sipping the coffees I brought them, Freya with her feet up on a massage table, hands propped on her stomach, which is currently home to Bergman-MacCormack baby number two.

Crouching, I give Linnie my back, and she hops on, soccer ball clutched in one arm. "Bye, Coach! Bye, guys!" she calls. "See ya next time when I beat your butts!"

They laugh, saying their goodbyes as we exit the locker room.

"Hurry, Uncle Ollie!" Linnie yells. "I'm gonna pee my pants!"

———

After handing off Linnea to Freya, I'm halfway to Coach's office when I stop and backtrack, remembering what I need. At my cubby in the locker room, I open the cooler and grab the container holding one of Viggo's homemade *semlor*. With a quick jog back down the hall, I'm at Coach's office. The door is cracked, so I step in, then shut it behind me.

"Oh, thank God," Coach says, rubbing her hands. "You're the best."

Smiling, I set down the dessert that makes her eyes light up— *semla*, a cardamom-infused bun bursting with marzipan whipped cream, a sliver of the bun resting on top, dusted with powdered sugar.

Gavin watches this transaction with his usual unreadable, albeit chilly, expression, but I can imagine what he's thinking: *Kiss-ass. Brownnoser. Suck-up.*

When, really, I just like making people happy. I like that Viggo gets sales for his baking side hustle, and Coach gets the sweets she's craving. It makes me feel good to give people what they need and put a smile on their faces.

But I'm long past expecting Gavin to understand where I'm coming from. He's made it clear since day one that he can't stand me.

It stung when he first joined. I'd hoped we could at least be friendly teammates—that is, after I got over being starstruck. And maybe it's because I looked up to him *so* much that his disdain cut so badly. He's not only the world's greatest player in modern history—he's one of the first and few openly gay professional soccer players.

His coming-out, given in that low, authoritative growl at a press conference with so much succinct confidence and poise, inspired me to be out everywhere in my life. It emboldened me to talk openly about being queer with my college and then professional soccer teams, about my hopes for the game to become safer and more accepting—whether players were questioning, out just to themselves, to their families, to their friends, or to the public.

I hoped as two openly queer guys on the same team, we could have each other's backs in a sport that has failed me many times over the years. Toxic masculinity. Blatant and subtle homophobia and biphobia. In locker rooms, on the field, at tryouts, in the media.

But no. Ever since he joined us two years ago, all Gavin has done is act like he sees this career move as a thoroughly unpalatable demotion. All he's done after scoring each one of those beautiful goals is scowl at the camera, shower off after the game, growl his way through interviews, and walk out.

"So," Coach says around a bite, gesturing for me to sit down. "Bergman. I have some good news."

Good news sounds promising. I should be excited, but I have no idea what it's about, so anxiety and my mind's pervasive tendency to worst-case-scenario everything I don't have clarity about clouds over the moment. Somehow, my brain twists "good news" to "good news *but*."

I swallow nervously as Coach sets down the semla and dusts off her hands.

"In your three seasons," she says, "you have demonstrated true leadership and incredible work ethic."

Nerves clench my stomach. "But . . . ?"

She frowns, swiping her finger through the cream filling and popping it in her mouth. "But nothing. I'm giving you a compliment."

"Uh. Okay." I shift uneasily on the chair. "Well, thank you, Coach."

"You're welcome. And it's because of that dedication and leadership you've demonstrated that you're our new co-captain."

My eyes widen. My gaze snaps toward Gavin, who's boring holes into Coach's head with his stare. "What?" I whisper.

Coach leans in, flashing a wide, bright smile. "You're. Our. New. Co-captain. Congratulations."

"B-but, no. Wait. I—" Clearing my throat, I shift to the edge of my seat and lean in. "I'm not. That is, Hayes is—"

"An incredible presence on the field," Coach finishes, smiling at Gavin, whose only tell that he's two seconds away from flipping the desk she's leaning on is a vein pulsing furiously in his temple. "Brilliantly skilled. But so are you. You two have . . . complementary technical strengths, leadership styles, and field presence."

Now his jaw is twitching.

Her gaze meets Gavin's calmly, then slides my way. "Given that, management and I agree our team will be better for *both* of you leading it, our team's rising star and our illustrious veteran player. The pressure's on. We won our first MLS Cup in years this past December. Now we've got to keep that momentum, pick up in this preseason right where we left off at the end of last year, and do it all over again. I'm counting on you two to get us there."

I'm stunned. And honored. It's the kind of opportunity I've wanted for as long as I can remember. And yet my stomach's a knot of worry. What if I mess up? What if I get it wrong? What if I fail the team? What if—

"You don't look as happy as I thought you'd be." Concern tightens Coach's features as her eyes search mine.

"You kidding?" I sit back in my chair, lacing my hands behind my head and smiling my breeziest smile, hoping I hide my terror well. "Happier than a polar bear after the UN committed to taking concrete action to prevent global warming from exceeding two point seven degrees."

"They haven't done that," Gavin grumbles, staring resolutely ahead. His voice is gravel, his speech crisp and neat, betraying that while he's American, up until two years ago he'd been living in England since age seventeen.

"True," I tell him. "But what do we have if we don't have hope!"

Coach's mouth quirks. "It's okay to be nervous, Oliver."

"Who, me?" I wave a hand. "Psh. Cooler than a mini cucumber shoved all the way back in the vegetable crisper. You know what I'm talking about? Those little ones that get *so* cold they're practically tiny veggie Popsicles. That's how chill I am. Cucumber Popsicle coo-ool."

She smiles, eyes narrowed. "Mm-hmm."

For a second, I could swear I feel Gavin's eyes on me, but as soon as I glance his way, they're trained over Coach's shoulder. Bored, annoyed, already beyond this moment, this threshold we're about to cross.

Becoming co-captains.

Taking a slow, deep breath, I force a smile. Then I say, "Coach, I'm honored."

She smiles back. "I know you are. One of the many reasons you deserve this. You don't see yourself as entitled to captaincy. You'll treasure the opportunity for what it is—an honor. It is an *honor* to be a leader."

Is that somehow meant for Gavin? She throws him a sharp glance and tears off a corner of the bun, then another, topped with marzipan whipped cream, and offers one to each of us. "It's also a responsibility."

Gavin shakes his head. I take the piece of semla and tell her, "I understand."

"You don't know what you're missing, Hayes," Coach says as she tosses back the bite he declined.

As I pop the bun in my mouth, I feel Gavin's eyes on me again. I glance his way, licking the whipped cream off my thumb, and Gavin stands so abruptly, he sends his chair scraping across the floor.

"Excuse me," he says.

"Excuse you where?" Coach says, arching an eyebrow.

Gavin clutches his lower back. "Ow," he deadpans. "Back needs treatment. Common ailment, for an old *veteran player*," he snaps, before throwing open the door, then slamming it shut behind him.

Groaning, Coach shoves another bite of semla in her mouth. "That went well."

"Due respect, did you expect it to?"

She smirks, offering me another bite of semla. "No. But at least there's the world's best cream-filled buns."

"True. Semlor can fix almost anything."

"Except poorly timed due dates," she mutters.

"Aw, Coach. It'll be all right. We get you for the preseason at least. We'll manage a few regular season games, then you'll be back here, whipping us into shape again before you know it."

"I know. It's still annoying that I can't just snap my fingers, pop out a baby, and get back to it. However, I suppose you're right—it's just a few games. Not the worst. And I've been told this kid's cuteness will make the professional inconvenience completely worth it."

A smile warms my face as I think of how Linnea upended not only Freya and Aiden's ordered world, but our whole family's, beyond our wildest dreams. How superhero capes and Play-Doh and miniature soccer nets, tiny sticky handprints and finger-paint pictures and endless photographs of a perfect dark-haired, ice-blue-eyed baby, then toddler, then preschooler, fill our homes, cover our refrigerators and walls. "I don't believe you're being misled."

Sighing, Coach sits back and sets the semla in its container on her belly. "You and Hayes will work it out," she says. "I'm confident. And with you two leading the team together, along with Rico and Jas, you'll be fine without me."

Our assistant coaches are solid, good people and excellent at their jobs. I have no doubt we'll be in good hands until she comes back. The part about Gavin and me leading *together*, that's what I'm not so sure about.

"He barely talks to me, Coach. It's all grunts and *fuck*s."

She laughs. "He does swear like a sailor."

"I'm ready to work with him . . ." I rake a hand through my hair. "But he does not seem to share my willingness."

"Now, come on," she says, taking another bite of bun. "Don't act like you're *entirely* innocent."

I gape. "*Moi?*"

"Uh-huh. *Toi*. I'm onto you. You put it real sweet, but everything you say to him is like it's specially designed to get under his skin."

I blush. Scrub the back of my neck. "I'm the second youngest of seven kids. It's in my DNA."

"Mm-hmm, well, you may just have to alter that genetically predisposed approach." After a beat, and another bite of semla, she says, "Hayes has a . . . tough shell. And, yes, he's intimidating. Stubborn—"

I laugh quietly. "No kidding."

"He's old and set in his ways," she concedes. "I mean, old for soccer. Who knows, this may even be his last season."

I hadn't considered that. Gavin's thirty-four, and he's been playing world-class soccer since he was seventeen. A lot of players retire by this age, especially after playing as physically and sustaining as many injuries as he has. That said, I can't imagine Gavin retiring, or that *he* can imagine retiring either, for that matter. At the end of last season, when a reporter asked him about the possibility, he glared at them so long and viciously, they ran out of the room crying.

Coach pops the last bite of semla in her mouth and snaps the container closed. "There's more to Hayes than meets the eye. You just have to . . ." She grimaces, stares up at the ceiling. "Hell, I don't know. It's hard to explain. I've barely seen that 'more' myself, and I've known him for over a decade."

Coach and Hayes played around the same time, and both made appearances for the US national and Olympic teams, though she was further along in her career than he was and a bit older. I knew this, but it's funny to think about them as peers. Gavin's never acted like he's her equal, never referred to their history. He listens to her, respects her, even if his eye twitches sometimes when she's barking orders that include him.

"I know this is hard," she says. "But you two won't be co-captains forever. While you are, why not try to . . . give him another chance, make the best of it, right?"

I contemplate what this is going to look like. The monumental task ahead of me to find a way to share leadership with the man who loathes me to my core.

Meeting her eyes, I force my widest smile yet. "Right."

THREE

Gavin

Playlist: "Lo/Hi," The Black Keys

"Damn, you're playing dirty tonight." Mitch, my accuser, throws his cards onto the table as I rake in my chips.

"I'm playing poker, Mitchell. It's a dirty game."

He grumbles under his breath along with the four other men around the table as they toss in their cards. My poker companions are all in their seventies and couldn't care less that I'm a world-famous professional soccer player. As soon as they figured out that I didn't play baseball, basketball, or American football, I was chopped liver. More than fine by me after living over a decade in a place where soccer players are royalty, hounded by the paparazzi, constantly under the microscope. Compared to that, the poker guys are a breath of fresh air.

I met them through Mitch, who's my neighbor—not my immediate neighbor, but he lives in the neighborhood. And I met Mitch when I was seeing a specialist about my forever fucked-up back and he was there for his knee replacement follow-up, both of us sitting in the waiting room. I drove him home after his appointment since he mentioned he'd used public transportation to get there, and when we realized how close we lived, there was no damn sense in him taking a bus when I could drive him. By the time I'd dropped him off, somehow I'd gotten myself roped into not only weekly poker nights with his buddies, but hosting them, too.

The table's littered with snacks, sweets, and seltzer cans. You think teenagers eat a lot, watch out for five septuagenarians. They'll clean out your pantry in one night.

"I need a drink," Lou grumbles, his silver Afro swaying as he shakes his head and scowls at Jim.

Stacking my chips in order, I tell him, "I'd be glad to oblige if the alcohol police here didn't ban all the fun."

"It's contraindicated for my meds!" Jim snaps. "If I can't have fun, none of you assholes get to either."

Collective grumbles fill the room as Jorge deals.

Itsuki pokes my bicep. "What's on your mind? You're particularly bad-tempered tonight."

I glare down at him. He smiles back. He's not remotely frightened of me. None of them are. It's strange. Everyone else is scared of me. I'm six four, big-boned; my voice sounds like gravel-laced ice, and my sentences are 85 percent profanity. These guys don't care. They simply roll with how I am, and tease me along the way.

I know if anyone would hear what turned my day to shit and not judge me for it, it's them. I'm just too used to holding my cards close, in every sense of the word.

"Nothing," I mutter, sweeping up my cards from the table.

"Nothing," they all mock-grumble.

"Oy." I glare at them.

"C'mon," Jorge croons, rearranging his cards. "Just get it out. You'll feel better. Less constipated."

"I'm not constipated, you pink-haired troll."

Jorge pats his rose-gold-dyed hair, which—while annoyingly bright—I will concede complements his warm golden-brown skin rather nicely. "Emotionally, you are."

"Am not."

Itsuki, Jorge's partner, gives me a long, serious look. "Oh dear."

"What?" Jorge hugs his cards to his chest and leans in. "What is it?"

Itsuki sets a hand over mine. "I think our boy's been bitten by the lovebug."

The room erupts.

"Who is he?"

"Tell us about him!"

"What's he like?"

"Have you kissed?"

"Oy!" I yell.

They fall silent.

"I have *not* been bitten by the fucking lovebug. I . . ." My voice dies off. Mitch gives me an encouraging nod. I clear my throat roughly, glaring down at my cards. "I . . . may have experienced a . . . professional . . . setback . . . today."

Jim wrinkles his nose, feigning thought. "What the hell do you even do again?"

Mitch tuts disapprovingly. "Go easy on him."

"Man, I'm still mad about that," Lou says. "Mitch reels us in with some shit about you being a big-deal professional athlete. I'm picturing seats behind home plate at Dodger Stadium, a nice, toasty box at the arena. I'm seeing courtside with the Lakers, the fifty-yard line at SoFi Stadium, and what do you do? Kick a bathroom-tile-looking ball around and run so long you make *me* tired."

Itsuki snorts a laugh, then schools his expression. "That wasn't nice, Louis. Besides, I like soccer. It's very calming."

"You're watching the wrong kind of soccer, then," I tell him.

"Back to the matter at hand," Mitch says. "What's going on?" He leans his elbows on the table, offers a nod of encouragement. His hair's a soft cloud white, his matching mustache neat and trimmed. He reminds me so much of Fred, the one person who ever saw something in me, whose kindness changed my life.

Maybe that's what makes me momentarily shed my typical armor as I gruff, "I have to team up with someone at work who I don't want to team up with *at all*."

A chorus of *hmm*s and *ooh*s echoes around us.

Itsuki asks, "Why not?"

"You don't get along?" Lou offers.

"I hate sharing *air* with him," I snap.

It sounds vicious, but God help me, it's true. I hate sharing a team, a field, a practice space, a locker room, meetings, you name it, with Oliver Bergman. Sharing *captaining* is the straw that broke the camel's back.

Jorge frowns at me in curiosity. "Why?"

I bite my cheek, remembering vividly how it felt the first time I saw him two years ago. Like I'd taken a direct kick to the gut. Tall, fast. All long, lithe limbs and easy smiles. He's everything I once was and more. Young. Happy. Healthy. The world at his feet. Untold possibility on the pitch.

It stung like a thousand paper cuts doused in vinegar. It hurt in so many ways. And the last thing I need in my pain-riddled life is one more thing to make me hurt. So I've made it abundantly clear to Oliver Bergman that I want nothing to do with him.

"Dispositional differences," I mutter. "Now can we play some fucking cards?"

"Nope." Jim stands slowly, hands braced on the table. His gaze travels his fellow card sharks. "Gents, you know what we need to do."

Mitch sighs, scrubbing his face. "I'm going to have to call in sick tomorrow, aren't I?"

"You're retired, asshole," Lou grumps. "*I'm* the one who's gonna be hating himself in the morning."

"Oh dear," Itsuki says quietly.

"What?" I bark. "What the hell is going on?"

Jorge pats my hand and smiles. "It's best not to ask questions and just go along for the ride."

My tongue is sandpaper. My head pounds.

"Fuck." Groaning, I blink open my eyes, hating the existence of daylight. I'm on my bed, still wearing last night's clothes, reeking of sweat, fried food, and syrup-sweet tiki drinks.

A vague memory of the night flashes through my mind. The poker guys piled into my Land Rover, commandeering my sound system, dragging me to some hole-in-the-wall that Mitch promised me "nobody who's anybody knows about."

I groan again as I slowly roll to my side, then sit up. My body screams in protest over how I slept—my sore knee bent off the bed, my always-aching back twisted sharply.

Breathing slowly, I shut my eyes and try to piece together the rest of the night as pain pulses through my body. I remember karaoke. I definitely didn't sing. I never would. But the poker guys did, especially Jim, who stuck to mocktails and brought down the house with his version of Kelly Clarkson's "Stronger."

Clearly I drank a metric shit ton of tropical drinks with those damn tiny paper umbrellas to survive the experience.

Gingerly, I ease off the bed and stand.

"Shit. Fuck. Shit. Shit." Each step toward the bathroom is agony. My knee hates me. So does my back. So does my neck. Waves of white-hot pain radiate through my body, so intense my stomach churns.

Or maybe that's the alcohol talking, too.

I vomit, and the pain of my torso contracting, engaging my spasming back muscles, nearly makes me vomit again.

Cursing under my breath, I flush the toilet and gingerly ease myself upright. I avoid my reflection in the mirror, knowing it'll show me something I don't want to see, and rinse out the taste of last night's poor choices.

Fuck, I should not have drunk like that.

After gingerly peeling off my clothes, I step into the shower, hissing as the hot water hits my skin. Once I've showered, changed, and gulped down my usual complete-meal breakfast shake, I grab my practice bag, wallet, and keys, pocket my phone, then head out the door.

Which is when I realize my car is nowhere to be seen.

"Fucking hell," I growl, dragging down my Ray-Bans. The sun's trying to fry my retinas right out of my head.

"Morning, neighbor!"

My jaw clenches at the sound of his voice. Yes, this is the worst part. Not only do I have to *see* Oliver Bergman nearly every goddamn day, January through December; I live next door to him.

That's right. He's my fucking next-door neighbor.

We live in mirror-image bungalows in Manhattan Beach, a few blocks inland from the beach itself. It's not entirely surprising he's in the neighborhood—a lot of players for LA's professional sports teams live in Manhattan Beach—but of all the houses I had to pick, it *had* to be this one. Right next to his. I wish I'd known. I'd give anything to have known that he'd be next door before I bought this place after I signed with the Galaxy. I could have avoided so much misery.

"Mighty fine day, isn't it?" he says, smiling brightly.

"Glorious," I deadpan.

Oliver frowns thoughtfully, glancing at the empty spot where my black Land Rover is normally parked. "Hmm. You seem to be missing your typical mode of transportation. I don't see that beautiful gas-guzzling beast anywhere."

My teeth grind. I don't respond. Nothing I say will paint me in a favorable light.

Oh, well, you see, Bergman, I was out getting shit-faced with a handful of seventy-year-old men, and I got so plastered, I had to leave my car at a questionably hygienic tiki-slash-karaoke lounge. Then I woke up this morning smelling like an overworked deep fryer and bottom-shelf bad decisions, and here I am.

"You, uh—" He scrubs the back of his neck and smiles, pale blue-gray eyes squinting against the sunlight. "Want a ride?"

"No."

He frowns again. A thoughtful frown. Not sour or sullen or glum, because he's constitutionally incapable of it. "*No*," he repeats. "Hmm." Sniffing, he peers up at the sun and smiles even wider. "Well, enjoy the walk!"

How he knows that I hate any chauffeuring system—being placed in the back of a vehicle with some rando in control, capable of fuck all, while they engage in small talk and make me wish for a swift, merciful death—is beyond me. But he does. And that means he knows, right now, I'm screwed.

"Fine," I grumble, storming toward his absurdly compact hybrid car.

"Hop on in," he says, as if he expected this, which just makes my teeth grind harder. After unlocking the car, he pops the trunk. "It only took you twenty-four months and three weeks to accept my carpool offer, but who's counting?"

"I like personal space," I grumble.

"The environment likes lower emissions." He points to the sky. "But what's a colossal carbon footprint to the personal preference for solitude on a twenty-minute, twice-daily commute?"

"Exactly." I throw my bag in the trunk, then walk to the passenger side. "God, man. I can't fit in there."

"You're only an inch taller than me, and I fit fine," he says with another one of those infuriating smiles before he drops into the driver's seat and shuts his door.

Cursing under my breath, I ease into the passenger seat and slide it back until I bump into something. I glance back to see what it is, barely holding in a groan as my neck burns from the movement. I'm so fucking tired of hurting already, and I've been awake for only thirty-five minutes.

"Sorry about the car seat." He smiles, tracking my gaze as he presses the car's "Start" button. "Gotta keep the little niece safe on Uncle Ollie days."

I grunt in response.

We're in the car for all of fifteen seconds before he turns on what sounds dangerously like a Broadway musical, so loud the bass rattles his speakers. My skull's still pounding, and I need silence like I need a cup of coffee. Very badly.

I turn off the music. Oliver throws me a smile, but it's a little tight at the edges. He turns it back on. I turn it off.

"Now, Mr. Hayes," Oliver says. An odd *something* zips down my spine, hearing him call me that. "I'm a simple man with a simple need to start his day on the right foot: sunshine filling the sky and the best of Broadway filling my ears as I cruise in my environmentally conscious vehicle."

"And I have a raging headache. The music stays off."

Oliver stares ahead, exhaling slowly. Sixty seconds pass in blissful silence. Until he starts whistling.

It sounds like the trill of songbirds, Bing Crosby in *White Christmas*, whatever shit is so perfect it's unnatural. In fact, it's lovely. At least it would be if my head didn't have a jackhammer rattling inside it.

"Bergman," I snap.

"Hmm?" He glances my way. "Oh. I was whistling, wasn't I? Sorry about that."

I glare at him.

"Pit stop time!" he says brightly, making me wince.

"Jesus Christ."

"Nope," he says, turning into a coffee shop drive-through. "Just Oliver Bergman, reporting for caffeinated-beverage duty."

"God, strike me down."

"Good morning, Ms. Bhavna!" he says cheerily to the woman at the drive-through window. "You look radiant today. Still getting good sleep?"

The woman beams at him, warm brown skin, wide smile, black hair threaded with silver spun into a bun on her head. "Aren't you sweet, Oliver. I am. Ever since I tried that white noise machine you recommended, my wife's snores haven't bothered me a bit!"

I wish I could say that was the end of the torture. But it's not. Oliver places seventeen—*seventeen*—highly specific beverage orders, then, as we wait, proceeds to make incessant small talk with the cashier, Ivan—with whom Oliver is, of course, on a first-name basis—not limited to their forthcoming vacation plans, how their dog's responding to its antibiotics, and whether or not they've tried the new Chinese place down the road.

I'm about to throw open my door and limp my way to work when Oliver finally rolls up the window and sets an elaborate multi-tiered beverage carrier system in my lap.

"Whew," he says. "Thank goodness you're here today! You should see me try to drive while keeping those puppies safe. I buckle them in, but let me tell you, the stops and starts of Los Angeles morning traffic are *not* conducive to spill-free passage."

I glare at him as he finally pulls out. "Remind me never to get in a car with you ever again."

"Aw, this isn't that bad, is it?"

"Says the man steering a car rather than holding a beverage carrier holding seventeen coffee drinks, the bottom tier containing a disturbing medley of both hot and cold liquids that I can assure you are not a pleasant experience for my groin."

"You love Icy Hot, though," Oliver says, throwing me a smile. "Or no, it's that natural stuff—Tiger Balm, right?"

"How very observant." I lift the carrier slightly to give my dick relief from the highly unpleasant sensation of being part frozen, part steamed. "However, never in a million years would I put Tiger Balm or Icy Hot on my cock."

Oliver turns bright red as the word rings in the car, his gaze resolutely trained on traffic. That's shut him up. And for some inexplicable reason, my gaze remains fixed on him, watching with fascination as a blush creeps up his throat and stains his cheeks. He sinks his teeth into his bottom lip, and my dick twitches.

Shit.

I glance away, out the window.

Looking at him was a bad idea. Looking at him while he blushed and bit his lip was the height of self-sabotage.

Because on the most ordinary of days, let alone when he's blushing and sinking his teeth into that bottom lip, Oliver's the kind of beautiful that's undeniable—a face for sculpture. High cheekbones, strong jaw, the smallest cleft in his chin. Fair, sun-kissed skin. Hair the color of wheat at sunset, pale blue-gray eyes, cool and striking as moonlit ice.

Fuck, I've got to stop reading poetry. Just listen to me.

As traffic slows to a stop, Oliver glances my way. And for a moment something . . . snags. Like catching my toe on the curb. Hitting a pothole while in the car.

I glance away and rub my temples, which pound mercilessly.

After a light throat clear, Oliver says, "Heads up, seven up."

Before I can make a biting remark about juvenile phrases, his arm brushes my thigh as he reaches across my lap, around the beverage carriers, and opens the glove compartment.

"Aspirin, naproxen, ibuprofen, acetaminophen," he says, pointing to a slim black pouch with a red cross symbol on it. "Help yourself."

"What?"

Traffic resumes. He pulls his arm back, once again brushing my thigh to navigate around the beverage carriers. "You said you've got a headache, and I'm assuming it's pretty bad since you're staring at the sun like it's the devil itself. Oh, and this one here," he says, eyes on the road, yet tapping a short cup in the top tray with *GG* written on the side. "Wash down your pain relief of choice with that. Aspirin and acetaminophen chased with caffeine will get that headache under control lickety-split."

I swallow, desperately trying to ignore the heat blazing up my thigh after such faint contact. Clearing my throat, I unearth the cup he pointed to. "GG," I read. "What's that stand for? Ginger green tea? I hate that shit."

"Nope," he says.

"What is it, then?"

"A very fancy breve," he says after a beat, staring resolutely at the road.

I blink at him. "How the hell do you know I prefer breves?"

"Hayes, everyone on God's green earth knows you drink a breve. Anytime we're in public, you order one."

"What's the GG stand for, then?" I ask.

Oliver flashes me one of those aggravating, dazzling smiles. "That's between God, me, and Bhavna at Deja Brew."

After holding seventeen specialty coffee drinks reeking of a stomach-twisting medley of flavored syrups including, but not limited to, hazelnut, strawberry, mint, and pumpkin, while Oliver hummed under his breath the rest of our drive, I'm on the verge of losing my ever-loving shit.

"*Buenos días*, Julio!" Oliver belts like we're on fucking Broadway instead of in the lobby where we enter the sports complex.

Julio, who's head of security—middle-aged, built like a house—smiles, a wide grin lighting up his face. "*Qué tal*, Oliver?" His brow furrows as Oliver extracts a to-go cup from the beverage tower he's holding and hands it his way. "Oh, man, is that what I think it is?"

"Your Mocha Mexicana, and this time I triple-checked they didn't forget the cayenne," Oliver says, beaming as Julio pops off the lid and breathes in the aroma of his drink.

"*Gracias*, Oliver. This is just what I needed."

"*De nada*. I'm glad," Oliver says. "Have a great day, Julio! And you let me know how Paulina's surgery goes next week, all right? I'll be thinking about her."

"Will do, man. Will do."

Oliver turns back to me and hands me a beverage carrier. Then another. "Be helpful if you're just gonna stand there looking grumpy."

"I—"

"*Hasta luego*, Julio!" Oliver calls.

Gritting my teeth, I turn and give Julio a polite nod.

Julio lifts his coffee in greeting and smiles faintly, nothing like the wide, warm grin he had for Oliver. "Have a nice day, Mr. Hayes."

"*Gavin*" leaves me before I can stop it.

What the hell's wrong with me? Someone's hijacked my brain and mouth this morning. That's the only explanation for why I willingly got into a car with Oliver Bergman, held his damn specialty coffee drinks, and am now making sure I'm on a first-name basis with Julio in security.

Maybe I concussed myself last night at the bar. Wouldn't be my first head injury, and the doctors warned me I can't afford too many more before they start worrying about long-term neurological impact.

Julio lifts his eyebrows. "Sorry?"

I clear my throat, glancing down at the beverage carriers and wedging a cup more securely in its holder. "Just call me Gavin. Unless you'd prefer to be called Señor Rodriguez."

Julio's deep chuckle starts in his barrel-sized chest. He looks a little surprised that I even know his last name. "Nah. First names is fine with me . . . Gavin."

I nod, picking up my head and glancing after Oliver, who's whistling his way down the hall. "Right. Well." I jerk my head that way. "Beverage duty calls."

Julio lifts his cup again in a salute, his smile wider, friendlier. "*Chau.*"

"Chau."

My strides are long, if a little uneven, because my knee is still pulsing with pain that I'm deeply used to pushing through. Soon I'm close behind Oliver, who's once again whistling merrily and making me wish I had a pair of earplugs.

I blame exhaustion, maybe even being a little drunk still, the weird spell that being forced into a morning with Fucking Ray of Songbird Sunshine Oliver Bergman has cast on me, for what I allow to happen:

I let myself look at him like I did in the car.

Like I absolutely shouldn't.

Starting with his bright yellow sneakers that have a cobalt-blue stripe, up the length of his legs, which are wrapped in snug-fitting blue joggers that hug his tight ass and sit low on his narrow hips.

God*damn*.

"Enjoying the view?" Oliver calls over his shoulder.

Shit. "More like wondering how you can breathe in pants that tight."

"Considering my respiratory system is located beneath my ribs and not in my lower extremities, quite easily, Mr. Hayes."

"Stop calling me that," I growl.

Oliver comes to a halt so fast, I nearly bodycheck him. Instinctively, I grab his waist to steady him as I rotate away so we won't fully collide. We knock shoulders, so close that I'm inundated by his scent. Fresh laundry, line dried by a sea breeze and sunshine. Soft and warm and clean.

I snatch my hand away, because it's burning.

Oliver stands with his back to me, head bent over the beverage carriers as he steadies the cups. "Sorry about that," he says, much quieter than normal, before clearing his throat. "Forgot my turn signal."

I'm stunned, as if it's a hit from behind—brutal, swift, blacking out the world around me. The feel of him, lean and hard beneath his clothes, the delectable scent of his body. My brain's flooded with an image I can't stop. Warm, sweaty, sun-gold skin. Crisp white bedding. My hands pinning down those hips as my mouth teases him, as he fists the sheets, gasps, begs—

"Good morning, Maria! Morning, Dan!" Oliver hollers as he enters the training room.

I exhale roughly, willing the heat that's roared through my body to dissipate. Begging my body to cool down.

Fuck. Just . . . *fuck*.

Ignoring me, thank God, Oliver hands the next two beverages to our athletic trainers. Their conversation hovers outside my awareness.

This cannot be happening. I won't let it.

Without another word, I set the beverage carriers I was holding on the desk right inside the room, nodding politely to both our trainers while Oliver prattles on with his back to me.

And then I leave.

Heading straight for the world's coldest pre-practice shower.

FOUR

Oliver

Butter-yellow sun pours down on us. A crisp January wind whips across the field, carrying Santi's beloved banda music, which blasts from the speakers as we scrimmage. I've got everyone in the habit of taking turns playing their favorite upbeat tunes to keep the mood light, and boy, have we needed our mood lightened today.

There's a lot of pressure when we first come back and try to get our legs under us. After a few months off, trades and new contracts, we're a fresh group, rusty and a bit unused to each other. There's a hold-your-breath phase when we pick up preseason training, a sense of pivotal importance. If we can't get synced up and confident before the season starts, we're likely in for a string of draws and losses until we find our rhythm.

Because soccer, more than any other game, is a collective effort, a truly collaborative game. The more attuned we are to each other, the more comfortable and connected, the better our play will be. We can field eleven elite athletes, but we'll get our butts handed to us by less-skilled players *if* that team plays cohesively and we don't. Soccer is as much of a team sport as you can get, and its victories rely on unity.

Which seems to be something Gavin's forgotten. Because he's huffing and stomping like a raging bull right now, yelling at the guys for minor mistakes, playing way harder than necessary when we're just scrimmaging each other and getting back into the groove.

I glance at Coach, who stands on the sidelines, her gaze critical, razor focused. Rico and Jas stand beside her in identical postures. Jas's black hair is pulled back, revealing their shaved undercut, late afternoon sunlight bouncing off their polarized lenses and dark brown skin as they frown at the field. Rico frowns, too, arms bearing golden skin and colorful tattoos folded across his chest.

"Coach," I mutter between gulps of water from the sidelines.

"Hmm?" She narrows her eyes at Ben, who sprawls after Santi fakes him out and cuts toward the goal.

"You, uh, gonna tell Hayes to simmer down before he breaks something?"

"Or someone," Rico mutters.

Santi rips a shot low in the corner of the net, one that Amobi had no chance of saving, and dances in celebration across the field in rhythm to the music. Gavin glowers at Ben.

Jas clears their throat, then says, "I concur, Coach. Hayes is in the danger zone."

I lift my water bottle to them in salute. "Thank you."

"Bergman," Coach says.

I glance her way. "Yes, Coach."

"How about I coach and you play?"

Ouch.

I exchange glances with Rico and Jas, but they're unwaveringly faithful to her. They nod in agreement, trusting Coach to handle this however she's planning to.

On a groan, I drop my water bottle and jog back out onto the field.

"Get your fucking ass up, Benjamin," Gavin yells at Ben, who's still sitting on the ground, head hung, after Santi beat him. "You forget which team you're on today?" he barks.

Ben sighs as he stands.

I clap him encouragingly on the shoulder as I jog by. "Shake it off, B. Next time, you'll get it."

"Ollie!" Santi dances my way, smiling wide. *"Bailemos!"*

I laugh and dance toward him, mirroring his movements, until we high-five. Gavin's eyes narrow at me, his jaw tightening furiously.

It's the first time he's acknowledged my existence since our hallway collision right before I delivered coffee to our trainers. He was MIA when I turned around after giving Maria and Dan their drinks, ready to head to my next stop.

Which was probably for the best.

Actually, definitely for the best.

Because on our little stroll down the hallway leading up to that delivery, I was a tad—well, *very*—distracted. I couldn't shake the full-body flush of heat that hit me in the car when Gavin looked me dead in the eye and said the word *cock*.

For the first time, I worried I'd given myself away.

The fact is, while I think he has the personality of a rusty freezer, I can't deny that Gavin's hot as hell. Thankfully, I've found that his crappy attitude toward *everything* helps me suppress the crush I've harbored since my teen years, long before I knew him.

Freya grew up lusting after David Beckham. I grew up lusting after Gavin Hayes. As a horny teen discovering his sexuality, I stroked off so many times to the mental image of what I'd seen on his televised games. Thick, chiseled thighs, the memory of his broad bare chest after he ripped off his shirt in victory—dusted with dark hair that swirls around his nipples, then slides down his stomach, past his waistband, leading to a thick heavy outline in his shorts.

It's helped, how much of a jerk he is. It's made it much easier to stick firmly to the promise I made myself years ago: lust, sex, romance—none of that is going to infiltrate my professional life ever again.

But in the car? That resolve simply . . . melted away. It was just me and Gavin and his growly voice saying *cock* and the sound of it waving through my bones like a low-level earthquake.

And then I felt him looking at me as I strolled down the hallway. After two years of the evil glares he throws me when he thinks I'm not looking, I've learned what it feels like to have Gavin's eyes on me.

And they were right on my ass.

Which, you know, is understandable. I have a great butt. He's got eyes in his head, and they were naturally drawn to the pleasing view in front of him. But it felt like sunlight warming my skin on a cool day, like a hot trail of slow kisses down my spine, hands gripping my hips, tugging me back against—

Yep. No. That's where I can't let my mind wander again. Because that's how I got carried away with daydreaming and nearly walked right past the trainers' room.

That's what made Gavin almost slam into me, both of us saved by his large body's unnatural agility. His shoulder brushed mine, his hand wrapped around my waist, and sweet Jesus, I breathed him in, which was *not* wise but was sadly unpreventable, because he smelled so damn good. Clean and spicy.

A shiver runs down my spine as Coach blows the whistle for another kickoff. I huff a breath, set my shoulders, rein in this nonsense. I can't do it—start thinking about Gavin in a way that once came so naturally, a way I swore to myself would never again have a place anywhere near my soccer career. I learned that the hard way in college, and I'm not making that mistake twice.

I focus on my surroundings. My happy place. The field. The sun in the sky, the ball at my feet, a breeze kissing my skin. At least, I try to, but it's hard when all I can think about is what's made Gavin Hayes nastier than he's ever been.

Is he *that* mad about the co-captaining thing?

Dropping the ball back to Carlo, I sprint up the field, getting into place at the top. I'm distracted as I watch Gavin bark orders from his command center in the midfield, the wind whipping his dark hair severely to one side, the sun casting the tips of his thick eyelashes bronze, catching the auburn in his beard.

He glances my way and scowls at me just as the ball arrives at my feet, a snappy pass from Andre, who's running wide up the midfield. I turn with the ball, fake out Stefan, who's defending me, then cut toward Nick, our backup goalie.

Ethan does just what he should and steps in to mark me after Stefan left me open. Stefan scrambles to cover Andre for him so I can't do a give-and-go and send it back Andre's way for a shot on goal.

As Ethan steps in closer, I cut the ball and throw my weight into him, harder than I normally would, my frustration with Gavin pouring into the physicality of my play. Ethan's thrown off-balance by that, stumbling, his foot slipping forward and inadvertently tripping me. I hop over it, take one more step, and shoot, nailing the ball into the upper ninety of the net.

Turning toward Ethan, I offer him a hand. "Sorry about that," I tell him.

"Me too," he says. "All good?"

"Just fine."

He takes my hand and lets me hoist him up before we clap each other on the back.

Gavin's voice cracks like a gunshot over the grass. "Bergman!" he bellows. When I turn and look at him, there's fire in his eyes.

I clear my throat and force a friendly smile as Ethan wisely jogs away to take his place for kickoff. "Hayes."

He's stalking toward me, quickly closing the distance. "What the *fuck* was that?" he snaps.

I lift my eyebrows. "Uh. A goal. Did you miss it?"

A chorus of chuckles that quickly turn to coughs dances across the field. Gavin ignores them, eyes glued on me. "You don't help up someone after they fucking tripped you."

"It was incidental." I shrug. "I shoved him first. Besides, he's my teammate."

"Not right now he's not. Right now, he's your opponent."

"Hayes, it's just practice."

"Exactly." Gavin steps closer, until our chests almost touch, exploiting the full inch he has on me to glare down his nose. "And it's called *practice* for a reason. What you do now is what you do in the game. And you do *not* fucking help them up."

My jaw clenches. Fire fills the pit of my stomach, burns up my throat.

"Last time I checked, Hayes," I tell him, taking the final step, elongating my spine to erase the gap in our heights as I look him dead in the eye, "you weren't my coach. I will play to the level of sportsmanship that I value. I will help up whoever I damn well please."

Silence rings around us. Everyone's watching. And I'm too fed up to do what I have for two years: make myself smile, brush it off, and move on.

A vein pulses in Gavin's forehead. His eyes glitter dangerously, fiery amber in the sunlight. "Your 'sportsmanship,'" he says, low and menacing, "conveys a tolerance for being mowed down that makes *all* of us look like pushovers. I won't stand for that to be the example. They push us, we push back. They fall on their asses, we run by. This is a brutally competitive fucking game, not recreational lawn bowling."

"Aw, thanks for the reminder. But I think I know what I'm doing." I lean in, my voice nearly as low and just as even. I'm so far past the point of no return, I couldn't shut my mouth if I tried. "Or have you forgotten who had the most goals last season?"

His eyes widen. His nostrils flare.

I know it's a sore point for him. He has an incredible record with every club he's ever played for—leading scorer, year after year, truly a feat for a central midfielder whose goals come from far out on the pitch, those Hail Mary shots in the dwindling minutes to tie up the game, during high-pressure set pieces. The moments that make or break a player are the ones Gavin has broken under his will, time and again.

Until last season. When I outscored him by nine goals.

"You think that's everything there is to it, hmm?" he sneers, his chest nudging mine. I can feel the barely contained rage thrumming inside him. "Finishing open-net goals? Looking good and flashing that toothpaste-commercial smile of yours when you score, simply enjoying what the fruits of good genetics and youth have to offer you?" His lip curls. "You're their fucking captain now, not their friend. They need a leader, someone who's hungry for better, demands more, not someone who's late to practice because he's kissing ass with the staff, who tolerates sloppy shots and shit defending and half-assed breakaways. But you're too obsessed with pleasing every fucking person in this place."

Every word is a blow to the chest, knocking the wind out of me.

Rage boils through my system as I set my hands on his chest and shove him violently away. Gavin's eyes widen with surprise, then narrow, fury burning in their depths as he takes an involuntary step back to steady himself. But then he steps forward and shoves me harder. I shove back, harder yet.

"Hey!" Coach blows her whistle. I glance over at her, breathing like the raging bull I accused Gavin of being not five minutes ago. "Both of you, get off the field and cool down!"

Seething, I jog off the pitch, through the tunnel, and into the locker room, ripping my jersey over my head and throwing it into my locker. It's suffocating me. Or maybe that's the pressure of my anger, the weight of everything I've set on my shoulders, everything I've bottled up inside for too long.

I hear Gavin's cleats on the concrete, infuriatingly calm, his gait slightly uneven. He's in no rush. He won. He got under my skin, got me to fly off the handle and lose my cool in front of the team.

Is that so bad? a voice inside me whispers. *For them to see you as a flesh-and-blood human being, someone who has limits and struggles and bad days?*

The thought of that . . . exposure, that vulnerability, it makes me shudder. That's not who I am here. I'm the reliable one, the always-okay one, the unstoppable optimist who takes his problems home and drowns them in twenty-seven-dollars-a-pound French cheese.

Gavin strolls in, ignoring me, heading for the toilets. He goes into a stall, pisses, then comes out. I watch his reflection in the mirror as he methodically washes his hands, eyes on his task, his expression smooth and detached. I want to scream.

I want to grab him by the shirt and shake him until *I* have a hold on him like he does on me. A fist around his guts like he has around mine, the need to earn his approval, his professional respect, his decency on and off the field.

Why won't he give it to me? Why has he *never* given it to me?

That old, wounded fear curls its way through my thoughts and whispers, *Why am I not enough?*

"What did I ever do to you to make you hate me like this?" I spit out the words, air sawing from my lungs.

Slowly, Gavin glances up until our eyes meet in the mirror. His gaze rakes down my bare chest, then drifts back up to my face. His expression is flat, unreadable. "Who says I hate you?"

An empty laugh jumps out of me. "How you've acted for the past two years says plenty."

Calmly, he dries his hands, then strolls toward his cubby. "Disagreeing with your choices in leadership is not hating you. Expecting more of you on the pitch is not hating you—"

"That's not what I'm talking about, and you know it." I rake both hands through my hair. "It's every glare and disapproving look. It's your inability to offer me a polite greeting or engage in civil conversation in all the hundreds of hours—"

"Thousands," he mutters.

"*Thousands* of hours we've spent on the same team, in the same locker room, in the same—"

"Enough," he snaps, air heaving out of his chest.

He turns toward his bag, roughly searching it, then pulling out a prescription bottle that I can see from here is a high-dose NSAID. He pops open the bottle, throws back a pill, and swallows it dry. "Go back out there," he says. "We're done talking."

"No, we're not." I close the distance between us, standing right behind him. "Answer my question. Why can't you be civil to me? How the hell are we supposed to be co-captains when you can't even treat me decently?"

He's silent, that vein pulsing in his temple as he rips open a tub of Tiger Balm from his bag and rubs it on his knee, then his neck, then his temples. He won't look at me.

Like a beam of light slipping beneath a closed door, the words leave me, quiet, unstoppable: "Why can't we be friends?"

I wish I could rewind time, take back those words I've thought so many times and refused to humiliate myself by saying. But it's too late.

The Tiger Balm drops. Gavin turns and faces me, setting us toe to toe, face to face. Our eyes lock. Suddenly, I'm keenly aware of the brush of his hard body against mine, the fabric of his jersey scraping my bare chest, making goose bumps bloom across my skin, the spicy scent of what he's rubbed into his skin wrapped around us like a spell.

We're so close. I breathe him in, feel his body, warm and hard and just *barely* touching mine. Our chests. Our hips. Our thighs.

Gavin swallows, his breaths fast and unsteady as he stares down at me, as his gaze lowers to my mouth. I lean in, the faintest sway of my body toward his. Now he's closer, too. So close our mouths share air, our lips nearly brush.

What the hell is happening?

Time suspends, everything turns soundless, weightless. Nothing exists but the pound of my heart, the swift and brutal impulse to taste him, to sink my hands into his hair as his mouth falls open for mine, to scrape my nails down his scalp and make him beg. To pay him back for all the pain he's caused me by torturing him with such unbearable pleasure, it brings him to his knees.

My eyes fall shut. I can't believe this is happening, but I'm powerless to stop it, helpless to avoid something I know I'll regret. Except what comes next isn't a brush of lips, the taste of his mouth on mine.

His voice is low and dark, the heat of his body pouring over me as he says, "We are *never* going to be friends."

My eyes fly open and lock with his. I'm speechless. Stunned.

A banging fist on the door shatters the moment, jolting us apart. "You two!" Coach barks. "My office. *Now.*"

FIVE

Gavin

Playlist: "Believer," Imagine Dragons

"What the *hell* was that?" Coach shuts her office door behind us. At her pointed finger's direction, we sit in the chairs on the other side of her desk.

I'm reeling. It's been so long since I lashed out like that. Granted, I swear up a storm and bark orders at my teammates, but it's always measured, intentional. I learned long ago that soccer wasn't the place to lose control—it was the place I found it. Even when I'm on the field, my aggression is precise and controlled, reserved for the unfortunate souls I play against, not my teammates.

Then there's what happened in the locker room. That's *never* happened before.

And it never will again.

As I sit, my knee bends too sharply, too fast, pain knifing down my leg. A sobering, agonizing jolt back to the present moment. At least, until I glance over at Oliver, who's biting his lip. And then I think about how fucking close I was to dragging that lip between my teeth, earning his breathless gasp—

I straighten my knee, knowing the pain of extending it will be worse, nearly unbearable, before I have relief, an agony that turns my vision blurry. But not long enough. Because once it's cleared, he's still there, looking as unsettled as I feel while he stares down at his feet, silent. I'm hit with a terribly unwelcome gut punch of guilt. I see it all over again, the pale blue–flame flicker in his eyes dimming as I told him the truth: *We are* never *going to be friends.*

I compress that unwelcome feeling back down inside me. There's no room for guilt or softness or regrets. There's room for this game, and not a fucking thing is coming between me and playing it for as long as I have it in me.

"Anytime," Coach says, plopping down into her chair and parking both elbows on her desk. "Anytime you want to explain why, one day into being named co-captains, you're acting like children on the field. What kind of message are you sending the team? What if there'd been press covering practice?"

Oliver's head snaps up. "Was there?"

Coach arches an eyebrow, tipping her head. "Could have been, for all you knew. You two weren't thinking about the press. Or the team. Or the shitty publicity that would come out of brawling. You weren't thinking at all, and that's exactly what a captain is *not* supposed to do. You're the ones who keep your heads, who keep your cool."

Fury emanates from her in waves. There's something dangerous in her expression, a warning. Time to defuse the situation.

"Bergman and I talked," I reassure her. "It won't happen again."

Oliver cuts me a skeptical glance.

"Damn right it won't," she says, sitting back, arms folded across her stomach. "'Cause if it does, you can both say goodbye to your captaincy."

I barely stop my jaw from dropping. "You're not serious."

"Dead serious."

"Lexi—"

"*Coach*," she reminds me. "December to January you get to call me Lexi because I'm not bossing you around a field and because what we went through when celebrating the 2012 Olympic gold went south, and however the hell you got us out of that scrape, secured you lifelong first-name status privileges, but then and *only* then."

"But the US men's team didn't even *qualify* for the Olympics in 2012," Oliver says, blinking innocently my way.

I cut him a scathing glare. "And you were doing what in 2012, Bergman? Still getting your ass wiped?"

"Hey." Coach points a finger my way, then his. "That's what I'm talking about. Be nice."

"He started it!" I tell her.

She rolls her eyes, then directs herself to Oliver. "Bergman, you are correct. The men didn't qualify. But Hayes was there being classy with some of the guys from the men's team, cheering on the women."

"Back to the matter at hand," I say through a clenched jaw.

She turns and looks at me. "Proceed."

"*Coach.* I've been captain since I signed. You're not honestly threatening me with loss of *my* captaincy, when this complication's only arisen after this—"

She clears her throat. Raises her eyebrows. "Proceed with caution, Hayes."

Oliver sits back and folds his arms across his chest, staring at me. Waiting for what I'm going to say.

"I'm simply pointing out . . ." I studiously avoid Oliver's eyes. "If anyone should be on probation for this, it's Bergman."

Air rushes out of him. Like I've stunned him. Which just goes to show how naïve he is, how little he knows me and the desperation with which I cling to every moment I have left in this world.

Because after this? I've got nothing. Soccer is it for me. And when I'm too old for it, too broken too many ways, I honestly cannot say what life will hold, but I can tell you I'm not going to fucking like it. Oliver Bergman sure as shit isn't coming between me and every remaining moment I get leading a team, starting each game, playing every fucking minute.

Coach stands, palms on her desk as she leans in. "Your captaincy is just as on the line as his, Hayes. It's earned on an ongoing basis. Because being a captain is more than being an incredible player or charismatic or—typically, at least—in control." Her gaze dances between us. "It's about showing your team that you have their best interests at heart, that your every moment on that field is for them, that your love of the game and the club you represent is what guides your behavior on and off the field."

I glance down, my gaze traveling the scars on my body from so many matches that ended in a new injury, a new source of pain. This game is everything to me. I've literally broken my body for it. It's my life. Being lectured on this is acid poured in a gaping wound. It stings like hell.

"You two," she says quietly, making me glance up. "You make better partners than you think, or you *would* if you gave each other a chance. But you've got chips on your shoulders, both of you, and they've got to go. If they don't, I don't want to replace you, but I will."

Oliver nods. "Understood, Coach."

I don't say a word. But I nod tightly.

"Excellent." She straightens slowly, rubbing her lower back. "Well, at least you waited until we were winding down practice for this nonsense. Now go home, get some rest, and when you come back tomorrow, I expect to see nothing but complete professionalism."

After throwing her bag on her shoulder, she opens the door and points toward the hallway. "Go. Shoo. I'm hangry, and you're pissing me off."

Oliver holds the door, gesturing for her to go first. "Please."

Coach practically melts, throwing him a tired, grateful smile. "Thanks, Bergman." She cuts me a narrow-eyed glare. "Hayes."

I nod again and say pointedly, "*Coach.*"

We follow her on a lag in some mutually understood self-preservation instinct, giving Coach a wide berth to more or less waddle down the hallway and turn the corner, before proceeding that way ourselves. Oliver drags her door shut until it clicks closed and locks. That's when something else clicks, too.

Unless I'm willing to endure a taxi—and I'm not—I need someone to drive me to pick up my car at the dive bar the poker guys dragged me to last night. I stroll into the locker room and glance around as I gather up my things. Everyone's gone for the day. It's just me. And Oliver.

Mother *fuck.*

"Well, Bergman," I say, throwing my bag onto my shoulder. "If we're going to play nice, why don't we start with you giving me a ride?"

If I gave a shit about awkwardness, the car ride would be really awkward.

Thankfully, I don't.

I don't care that Oliver drives me in absolute silence to the tiki lounge, which, in the late afternoon daylight, looks even less likely to pass a health inspection than it did last night. I'm not bothered that he cracks not a single joke or pun about a place named the Leaky Tiki.

In fact, after Oliver pulls out the moment I exit his car, I'm completely beyond the weirdness of the day, from our unfortunate and never-to-be-repeated carpool-turned-coffee-run escapade to the fumbling hallway collision to losing my absolute shit on the field to the moment in the locker room when I was inches away from Oliver's mouth, thinking very specific and inappropriate things about what I'd like to do to it.

By the time I pull in front of my house, I have one thing on my mind: a scalding-hot shower involving a fast and furious wank to the mental image of some faceless man who absolutely does not resemble Oliver, then going the fuck to sleep.

Then waking up tomorrow resolved to keep myself together for the next ten months while I have to co-captain with Oliver Bergman.

"Fucking hell," I mutter, slamming my car door shut. I glance up to the sight of Oliver on the phone, pacing outside his house next door. Yelling.

Not that it's any of my business or concern that he's doing something so abnormal. I'm just intrigued. I didn't know he was capable of it.

Eyes on my feet as I walk toward the door, I try very hard—and fail completely—to ignore what he's saying.

"I don't *care* if you're sorry!" he yells into the phone. "Being sorry doesn't get me back in my house!"

He's either too pissed to notice that I'm nearby or he's ignoring me. Oliver spins and makes another turn in his circuit, stalking the length of his house toward the back entrance. "Yeah, well," he hisses, "I know I did. But this is *not* a proportionate response, Viggo. I'm locked out of my house, and you're in Escondido!"

I wince. Escondido's a two-hour drive south, and that's if traffic's behaving. Stopping outside my front door, I check the mail, because it's been a while since I last did, not because I'm eavesdropping on the oddity that is Oliver Bergman angry enough to actually yell. Even today on the field, he didn't yell.

What does it take to provoke him into acting like this? Hand tangling in his hair, chest heaving, heat high on his cheeks, his voice loud and uninhibited.

"I want in my *fucking* house!" he yells into the phone, holding it away and squeezing so hard it just might crack. A man's voice sounds from the phone faintly before Oliver brings it to his ear. "You're in for a *world* of pain!" he yells before jabbing the "End Call" button on his phone, turning, and hurling it into the grass.

I'm unreasonably delighted by this.

"Locked out?" I ask, leaning against the front of my house.

I watch Oliver shut his eyes slowly before opening them, as if summoning calm from a place deep inside himself. "Yes."

"Lost your keys?"

He groans, scrubbing his face with both hands. "Not exactly. No offense, Hayes, but I really don't want to talk to anyone right now."

"Hmm." Stepping off my porch, I start down the side of my house. I lift my chin toward the lock on his back door. "Too bad you don't have a code program like mine; you'd be able to simply reset it from your phone."

Oliver's nostrils flare. His hands turn to fists as he lowers them from his face. "Yes. So helpful right now. Thank you."

This is a new, fascinating side of Oliver Bergman. Anger crackling off of him like ungrounded electricity. He looks like Thor, evening sun turning his hair liquid gold, his eyes the glowing color of cool morning light lancing across the sky. He's impossible to look away from.

And now, I realize with a sinking feeling, he's also going to be impossible to *keep* away from.

So far I've dealt with Oliver by avoiding him at all costs. But now that we're co-captains, with Coach breathing down our necks to mend fences, what am I supposed to do? I can't make friends with him, but I sure as shit can't make hell with him either when my captaincy's on the line.

"C'mon," I tell him, jerking my head toward my house.

Oliver's still breathing heavily. He blinks at me, like I've stunned him. "C'mon what?" he asks.

"Come inside, until your locksmith shows up, or whoever has a key."

His jaw twitches. Turning, he searches the grass for his phone, scoops it up, and brushes it off. "I'll just go . . . wait at my brother's place. He's close."

I shrug, ignoring the odd sting that throbs through me in the wake of his brush-off. "Suit yourself."

Opening my back door, I'm about to walk in when he says, "Wait!"

Can you be both relieved and filled with dread? I am.

I turn back, holding open the door as Oliver sweeps up his bag and bounds across the yard up to my porch. Stopping right at the threshold, he hikes the bag higher on his shoulder. Like me, he's still in practice gear, sweaty, his hair mussed, sunlight sparkling on the scruff of his beard. "Thanks," he says tightly before stepping inside.

I stare up at the sky, knowing I'm tempting fate. That more than one threshold is being crossed, and none of them are wise.

Oliver walks carefully into my house as I shut the door behind me. I drop my bag and kick off my shoes, watching him take in the place.

"So . . ." He glances around, toeing off his shoes. "Apparently, you've got a thing for gray scale."

I glance around my house, seeing it from his perspective. Dark wood floors, white walls, cool metallic finishes on the white kitchen cabinetry and modern light fixtures. Black-and-white photographs, charcoal sofa, heather-gray club chairs. A silvery area rug. I shrug. "It's calming."

He points to Wilde, my black-and-white cat, who jumps off the couch and, like a traitor, slinks across the room, curling around Oliver's legs. "You even got a cat that matches. Would a little color hurt ya? Maybe just a splash of green to match . . ." He nods toward the cat.

I swallow, watching him crouch and scratch my cat's chin. "Wilde," I tell him reluctantly.

He smiles as the cat purrs. "*Wilde*. How about a little mint green to match Wilde's eyes? Some rose pink like his nose. What do you think?" he asks Wilde as the cat presses up on his knee and meows, reaching toward Oliver for a harder scratch of his head. "I don't know what the color wheel ever did to piss him off either, but clearly, he has not gotten over it."

Wilde purrs louder. Traitorous bastards, cats.

"Not all of us want our homes to look like the inside of a Froot Loops cereal box."

Oliver shakes his head and sighs like I'm hopeless. If it weren't for his phone, which has started buzzing, he'd probably pet Wilde and flat-out ignore me until his locksmith came. Standing reluctantly, he unearths his phone and mutters something under his breath that sounds distinctly not English. As I watch him, something awful snags inside my chest.

Cheeks flushed, jaw tight, thumbs dancing across his phone screen, he stands framed in the archway, his bright yellow practice jersey and gold hair lighting up the space like spilled sunshine.

I stare at him, panicking as everything turns kaleidoscopic—colorful, off-kilter, dizzyingly bright—and I have the frantic urge to throw open my door, then shove him out until my world is once again small and monochromatic and manageable.

He catches me staring. I look away, turning toward my cabinets and banging one open like a scrambled fool.

"I'll be able to get back into my house in about two hours," he says. "But I really can go let myself in at my brother's place. I don't want to impose—"

"You're not." I find a glass, smack on the water to fill it. "You, uh . . . want a shower, I imagine. We left before we showered—you showered, that is—"

Fuck me.

I drag in a breath. I can*not* look at him.

Oliver clears his throat. "I mean, yeah, I wouldn't mind a shower."

"Help yourself." My voice is gravel. My blood is on fire. My traitorous imagination can't stop picturing him stepping under the water, rivulets slipping down his lean, suntanned body. The ridges of his stomach, that tight angular V at his hips. His long legs with their fine golden hairs.

"Sorry?" he says.

"I said help yourself to a shower. Go on."

After a thick beat of silence, he says, "Okay."

When the water turns on, I slump forward and bang my forehead into the cabinet. "I need to get laid."

———

My lust-soaked body is in no better shape when Oliver reemerges, clean, wet hair slicked back into one of those tiny little ponytails, wearing a white T-shirt and bright red joggers that are snug on his long legs.

Heat rushes through me. This is what I get for being abstinent since I moved here, for not taking advantage of the ample interest that's a given when you're a decent-looking celebrity athlete. I'm a miserable beast when I'm sexually frustrated, but I couldn't stand the thought of being wanted for what I've felt slipping through my fingers every time I walk onto the pitch any more than I could stand the vulnerability of trying to find someone who'd want me for who I am otherwise, given *I* don't even know what the fuck that is.

I stare resolutely at my phone, which has zero messages from anyone except my PA, Angela, badgering me as per usual to actually show my face at the nonprofit I founded, publicly share my relationship to the nonprofit, and consider whether I'd like to take a more hands-on approach, should the Event That We Do Not Name Involving a Jersey Being Hung Up for Good happen to occur. To which I reply, No, no, and fuck no.

"Your water pressure is better than mine," he says.

"The things money can buy."

He steps closer, into my field of vision. "Listen, about what happened—"

"I'm answering an email."

A pause. "And here I thought you were just trying not to acknowledge my existence."

"Pretty hard to do that when you're standing in my kitchen, looking like a human ketchup bottle."

He rolls his eyes. "You wouldn't know a ketchup bottle if it slapped you in the face. You probably put salt and pepper on your fries and call it a day because God forbid you enjoy something bright and delicious like the wondrous culinary mystery that is ketchup."

Fuck, he's aggravatingly funny sometimes. I don't give him the satisfaction of seeing my annoyed amusement, though; I stare at my phone, refusing to look up.

I will not do this, lust after someone whose capacity to piss me off is unparalleled, whose very existence grates and rankles and reminds me that the best part of my life, the part that awaits him, is almost gone for me.

"Hayes, seriously, though, we should talk about this," he says, sitting at a stool on the other side of the counter, which serves as a breakfast bar. His stomach growls loudly.

I point to the bowl of fruit in front of him and the basket of protein bars. I'm not cooking for him. That's a bridge much too far. "Go on," I tell him.

He snatches a banana and peels it.

"Thanks," he mutters around the bite, his throat working in a thick swallow that makes my body heat.

"Mm-hmm." Doing everything I can to not focus on him, I stare at my phone again.

Already, the banana's gone. "So about that meeting," he says, setting the peel on the counter, then folding it into neat thirds, like a weirdo.

"What about it," I grit out.

He leans in a little, sending that sunshine-and-sea-breeze scent my way. "Well, I was under the impression you were there and heard us threatened with losing captaincy if we don't get over our . . . differences."

"There's no getting over our differences, Bergman."

He tips his head, curious. "I'm not following."

My jaw sets. I glance up at him and immediately regret it, because our eyes lock and I can't look away. "We're not getting over our differences. We're not being friends."

He folds his arms across his chest. "No."

"Excuse me?"

He lifts his chin. "I said, *no*. That doesn't work for me."

My eyebrows lift. Slowly, I stalk my way around the counter. Oliver pivots in his seat so he's facing me as I close the distance between us. I tower over him, standing as he sits, but Oliver looks entirely unfazed.

"I meant what I said in the locker room," I tell him. "I'm not riding in your car. I'm not picking up coffee with you. I'm not even going to acknowledge you beyond as a teammate on the field that I send a ball to, *if* you get your ass where it's supposed to be and earn it. You will smile your flashy smile and make sure Coach knows everything's fine. And I will tolerate sharing that armband with you. That's how this is going to go."

Oliver's pale eyes flash and darken to blue flames. He stands, placing our bodies once again nearly flush, our faces millimeters apart. "You seem to be forgetting one small thing, Hayes."

"And what is *that*?" I growl between clenched teeth.

He smiles, but it's different. New. In fact, it might just even be . . . sinister. He leans so close our mouths almost brush before he pulls back, his eyes meeting mine. "You're not the only one calling the shots anymore."

I stand there, stunned, as he steps back, sweeps up his bag, and strolls right out the back door.

SIX

Oliver

Playlist: "Let It All Out (10:05)," COIN

Two days. I've spent two days fuming. Being civil with Gavin, who's watching me like I'm a bomb that's about to go off and that he'd like to punt into the next universe. I'm seething. And I'm done. I'm done being shit on by someone who needs me as much as I need him. Gavin loses his captaincy if we don't smooth things over, and I'm *almost* angry enough at him to sabotage us both.

But the bigger part of me loves this honor too much, cherishes this opportunity too deeply, to ruin it simply to spite him, knowing what it would cost me, too.

I'm going to save this captaincy. And I *will* have my spite. Somehow. Some way.

I just haven't figured it out yet. So, beneath the lemon tree that dominates the backyard of Freya and Aiden's Culver City bungalow, I sit, stewing. Which is not what I should be doing. I should be happy, celebrating. I have a brand-new nephew. My sister had a smooth, uncomplicated delivery.

Which kicked into gear right after I stormed out of Gavin's house, got in the car, and was about to call Ren, who lives nearby, about crashing at his place while I waited for Viggo to come and let me into my own damn house. I'd just plugged in my phone when I got Aiden's text that Freya had gone into labor (a few weeks early, though not so early to cause major concern).

So, instead, I went over to their house and distracted Linnea while Freya made really intense groaning noises and swore a *lot* as Aiden helped her out to the car. I was the only one available to watch Linnie, and I wasn't complaining about spending the evening coloring, making lemonade from the lemons we picked out back, jamming to the *Encanto* soundtrack ("We Don't Talk about Bruno" lives rent-free in my head).

My mom met Freya and Aiden at the hospital because Freya wanted Mom there for support while she labored. Dad, while finally retired from practicing medicine, still has his hands in a dozen health-related organizations and was at some board meeting up at Stanford and was trying to get the first flight home.

Both Ziggy and Ren were traveling with their teams, for training and away games, respectively. Frankie, Ren's fiancée, was flying back after a visit out east to see her mom, sister, brother-in-law, and baby niece, who'd just been born. Ryder and his fiancée, Willa, and Axel and his wife, Rooney, all live up in Washington State, and while they've now flown down to meet the baby, they were a three-hour flight away at the time.

And Viggo, the asshole, was driving up from Escondido with keys to the new locks he put on my house after my latest move in our never-ending sibling prank war.

It probably sounds juvenile, and maybe it is, to be twenty-four and still doing things like sticking a turd-shaped Tootsie Roll in your brother's coffee or filling his toothpaste with sour cream—yes, that's as labor intensive as it sounds—but it's just how we are, and frankly, I need it, some sort of sinister outlet. I spend so much time with the team, being so good, being kind and positive, all while Gavin, the giant grump, craps on it left and right.

And I've reached my limit. I'm at the point that not even juvenile antics with Viggo and expensive cheese indulgences can defuse my anger. My frustration with Gavin, my resentment toward him, it's poisoning everything.

Like this evening. Right now. I want to be relaxed, present, positive. My sister's home, feeling good. Baby Theo is here, safe and beyond precious. My mom's cooked up a Swedish smorgasbord (her specialty, since Sweden is where she's from) for all of us to eat, and the freezer is filled with meals we all brought so Freya and Aiden have one less thing to worry about while they get used to being parents of two.

Now that everyone's grown up, our lives full and busy and spread across the West Coast, it's not often that we're all in one place, gathered over good food and for such a happy occasion. I want to soak it up, the comfort of being together, the soothing sounds of my family's voices and laughter through the open windows as we drift in and out of the house.

But all I can do is glare up at a lemon tree, legs wiggling, something building inside me that feels dangerously explosive.

"Okay, Honey Bunches of Oats." Viggo slaps my thigh as he sits beside me. "What's going on?"

I don't answer him. I'm so close to yelling or crying or both, I don't trust myself to open my mouth.

"Dude," Viggo says. "Don't you think I've paid enough without getting the silent treatment? I still look like an Oompa Loompa."

I slant him a glance and feel a smile unwittingly crack my mouth. The orange tint of his skin is mostly faded, but against his brown hair and pale blue eyes, what remains of the color tingeing his complexion still jumps out. "What good is a half-finished biochem major," I tell him, "if I can't use it for the ultimate prank revenge?"

Viggo grumbles to himself before biting into his sandwich.

Willa plops down across from us at the outdoor table, brown curly waves tangled up into a bun that bobs as she tucks into

Mom's Swedish meatballs. "Goddamn, these are good," she says around a bite. "They may actually be a *smidge* better than Ryder's, but don't tell him."

"You're secret's safe with me," I reassure her.

She flashes me a smile before her gaze dances over to Viggo and she chokes on her bite.

He rolls his eyes. "Laugh it up."

Willa cackles and says to me, "He looks like he took a bath in beta-carotene."

Frankie eases down next to her, setting her smoke-colored acrylic cane between her legs and smoothing her dark hair into a pony-tail. "He looks like he took a nap in a tanning bed and forgot to wake up."

Willa cackles harder, clutching her stomach.

"Wow," Viggo says around his sandwich. "Who needs six siblings to bust your balls when you've got their significant others to do it for them?"

"Anybody need refills on their food?" Ren calls from the door-way. The sun turns his hair bright copper as he flashes a beaming smile. My older brother has the kind of purehearted goodness I aspire to. There isn't a gentler, sweeter guy in the world.

The truth is, I've tried to take notes from what a class act Ren is as a professional athlete, now captain of his hockey team, the LA Kings. How composed he always is, how warm toward the media, how gracious toward fans. He's so good at it. I've done what I can to follow his example.

And in some ways, I think I've found my stride. I'm all too happy to chat with fans, especially kids, do the PR circuit, partici-pate in humanitarian initiatives. I love my biweekly coffee blitzes for the staff, making them feel seen and appreciated. I enjoy being the voice of encouragement to my teammates, keeping things up-beat, believing in us when belief feels a little hard to come by.

But I'm also tired. Because ever since Gavin showed up, it's become harder and harder to maintain that positivity. I'm tired of being good and friendly and endlessly patient with his miserable, pervasively negative presence. I'm tired of his relentless grumpiness. And I'm tired of the fact that every time I shut my eyes, I feel his hips brushing mine, his mouth a whisper away, heat burning through me.

"We're good, Zenzero!" Frankie tells Ren, snapping me from my thoughts.

"You okay, Ollie?" Willa pushes back her clean plate. The woman eats faster than me, which I really didn't believe was humanly possible.

I force a smile. "Just a little worn out."

Axel slips past Ren in the threshold and walks across the yard, a plate of food in hand, squinting against the evening sun.

"He's not worn out," Viggo says. "He's working through something. Just get it out, Ollie. You always feel better when you do."

"I'm fine," I mutter.

"Uh-huh." He rocks onto the back legs of his chair, one hand flying on his phone, the other combing through his mangy beard, which he refuses to cut. I should have never made that bet with him. "Sure you are."

Frankie and Willa exchange glances.

"Actually," Willa says, nudging Frankie gently, "turns out I do want seconds."

Frankie stands slowly and grips her cane. "Me too."

I sigh miserably as they leave. I know what a mass exodus of significant others means: an influx of Bergman brothers.

Axel plops down in the chair Willa just vacated. Rooney's halfway across the yard, in conversation with my sister Ziggy, both of them poised to join us, but they stop as Willa and Frankie say something to them. After a quick quiet conversation during which all eyes dart my way, they spin and slip back inside.

"What's wrong with him?" Axel asks Viggo, direct as ever.

Viggo clears his throat, patting my back. "Ollie's got some feelings to get out, and he's being stubborn about sharing with the class."

"Please drop it," I say between clenched teeth.

Viggo makes an exasperated noise in the back of his throat as he removes his hand, then focuses his attention on Axel, who's best to catch up with when the group dynamic is small and you can chat with him one-on-one.

Hoping that maybe I've avoided a full-on brotherly intervention, that the ladies making an exit was just to give me some space, I zone out, leaning back in my chair, staring up at the lemon tree, until a shadow is cast over me.

"Aiden." I drop back to earth in my chair.

My brother-in-law stands with his back to the low, glowing sun, shielding baby Theo from its light. He looks wiped and also dreamily happy. His thick black nerd-frame glasses do nothing to hide his exhaustion, the half-moon shadows beneath his vivid blue eyes. Unshaven, he has dark wavy hair just like Linnea's, though streaks of silver now sparkle at his temples. His hair's a little flat on one side, like he fell asleep on it that way and never fixed it when he woke up.

He smiles tiredly. "I had a feeling you could use another round of baby snuggles."

I smile back, opening my arms and accepting Theo, who's swaddled tight in a soft cream-colored blanket, a matching cap snug over his fuzzy white-blond hair. He fusses for a moment, then settles as I tuck him inside the crook of my arm and sway him with a steady rhythm. Aiden plops down in the seat beside me with a groan and slouches until his head falls back.

"Good night," he mutters.

"Uh-huh," I tell him. "Your true intentions are revealed."

His eyes slip shut. "Just, like, five minutes. That's all I need."

Aiden's snoring within seconds, which makes Viggo chuckle. He stands, grabs a piece of lettuce from Axel's plate, and is about to tickle Aiden's nose with it, but Axel slaps the lettuce out of his hand.

"Sit your ass down, Carrot Man," Axel tells him. "Leave him alone. He's exhausted."

Viggo pouts. "But it would be so good—"

"Viggo." Axel arches an eyebrow. "Sleep-deprived parents of newborns are off-limits."

"You joining the ranks?" I ask, half-teasing, half-curious.

Axel throws me a sharp glance. "I can barely stand to share Rooney with the dog, let alone a baby. Give me some time."

"No one's fun anymore," Viggo grumbles, throwing a sour glance at Axel, then drawing a mass-market paperback historical romance from his back pocket when he glances my way and I don't back him up. I'm too busy staring down at Theo, his perfect, tiny face scrunched in a thoughtful frown. Or maybe he's about to unload in his diaper.

Either way, he looks adorably grumpy.

Which reminds me of another grump, though one who is far less adorable. More like aggravating. And there goes my mood, in a nosedive.

"Stop scowling at the baby," Ren says around a bite of roll as he joins the table. After dusting crumbs off his hands, he reaches toward me. "C'mon. I want a turn."

"Fine," I sigh, letting him take Theo.

Viggo drops his book long enough to glance over at Ren, who's the biggest baby-lover ever.

Ren strokes a finger along Theo's cheek and sighs wistfully. "He's so tiny."

"Something I think Freya is very grateful for," Viggo quips, eyes back on his book.

Ryder shows up next, carrying his stainless-steel water canteen and a plate piled high with food. He plops next to Ren and peers down at Theo, smiling.

I glance around. And realize my fears have been confirmed.

"Viggo Frederik Bergman."

Viggo doesn't look up from his book. "Present and accounted for."

"You sent the Bat Signal, you asshole."

Ren gasps and cups a hand around Theo's ear. "A child is present. Watch your language."

I glower at Viggo. "I told you I didn't want to talk about it."

"Huh?" Ryder says, pointing to his ear. Since his freshman year of college, when he came down with bacterial meningitis, he's had severe and moderate hearing loss in his left and right ears, respectively. While his hearing aids allow him to hear much more, and we've learned as a family how to communicate considerately and effectively with him, it's still not uncommon for Ryder to ask us to repeat ourselves.

I tell him, "I was saying, I told Viggo I don't want to talk about it."

Ryder leans in, looking confused. "Talk about what?"

"About my pain-in-the-ass teammate and neighbor Gavin—oh *shit*!" God, I'm so gullible. Groaning, I slump down in my seat and scrub my face.

"Ollie." Ryder clucks his tongue. "Sorry, my brother. You walked right into that."

Viggo beams at him. "I bow down to your greatness."

"You're such dicks," I mutter inside my hands.

"Actually," Ren says diplomatically, "they're just being resourceful.

We don't have much time before we all go our separate ways, and you're clearly in need of—"

I groan as they say in unison, "A Bergman Brothers Summit."

———

The backyard is silent but for a few birds chirping up in the lemon tree and Aiden's rhythmic snores.

I just told them what happened on the field with Gavin, the gist of our confrontation in the locker room, and the details of what Coach said in her office. I left out the part where our mouths were millimeters away in the locker room *and* later on, in his kitchen, when things went from bad to worse on that front.

I simply cannot stand to admit that I almost kissed someone who's been such an ass to me.

Ren paces the yard, bouncing Theo because he started fussing and the movement keeps him asleep. "That son of a—" He stops himself as he peers down at the baby, then pivots to his usual swearing alternative, Shakespearean oaths: "Pigeon-livered canker blossom!"

Ryder folds his arms across his chest. "He sounds like a jerk."

"Agreed," Axel mutters.

"The damage I could do . . ." Viggo glares into the middle distance, wearing the familiar expression of a man plotting deep, terrible mischief.

I smile faintly, buoyed by their heartfelt defense of me. "He's not the easiest person to play with . . . or co-captain with. But I'll figure out how to handle it."

"How?" Ryder asks honestly. "He sounds impossible."

"Your coach shouldn't have roped you into that ultimatum," Ren says, keeping his voice quiet so as not to wake Theo. "Gavin's the one who was out of line."

"I mean, I did shove him first."

"After he's been awful to you for two years," Ryder points out.

Ren nods in agreement, a rare flash of anger in his eyes. "Coach shouldn't tolerate that kind of behavior."

"That was the first time he's ever gone off on me like that, though. Generally what she sees is my kill-him-with-kindness routine and his grumpy gruffing. In her eyes, our antagonism has been mutual, rather than his responsibility, which . . ." I sigh. "Is sort of fair. He definitely started it, but I've done my best to make him just as miserable when I realized he didn't like me. He's never humiliated me in front of the team. Usually, he plays fair, leaves me alone—basically ignores me—but it's just that when we *do* interact, one-on-one, he's so—"

"Cold," Viggo says thoughtfully.

"Yeah."

"Ollie." He turns toward me. "Obviously, much as we'd like to, none of us can afford the legal fees for beating up this guy who's treated you like crap."

"Though it's awfully tempting," Ryder grumbles.

Axel nods.

Aiden snores loudly.

Ren lifts Theo's little fist, which has worked out of his swaddle, and mimes a right hook.

"I know that," I tell them all. "I appreciate the sentiment."

"But," Viggo says, eyes lighting up as he sets his hand on my neck and squeezes gently.

"But . . . what?"

"You want the dynamic to change," he says. "Right?"

I glance between my brothers, no idea where this is going. "Yes," I say slowly.

"And being nice hasn't changed anything, has it? Your kill-him-with-kindness method, it's almost like it's backfired."

Ryder's eyes widen. "Oh shit."

"Hey." Ren covers Theo's ear again. "Language. But also, yes, Viggo. You are absolutely right."

"Right? What?" I blink at them, confused. "What are you talking about?"

"Viggo's logic," Axel says, "is that if being kind hasn't changed how he treats you, perhaps being *un*kind will."

Viggo beams at our oldest brother. "You read that enemies-to-lovers that I sent, didn't you?"

Axel sniffs, fiddling with a loose button on his plaid flannel shirt. "I might have."

"What are you *talking* about?" I half yell.

"Shh!" they chide me, gesturing toward Theo, who squawks at my noise, then settles back in Ren's arms.

"You refuse to read romance novels anymore," Viggo says. "So you wouldn't understand."

"Well, then that's supremely helpful."

Viggo shrugs. "I don't know what to tell you. Everyone else here has seen the light and followed in my path of romance-reading brilliance."

Axel rolls his eyes. "*Brilliance* is a bit of a stretch."

"I'm sorry, is or is not your life undoubtedly richer because of the books *I* gave you to read?"

Axel grumbles under his breath and bites into a roll.

"No offense," I tell them, staring down at my hands. "Romance novels just aren't for me. I'm happy they make you happy, but . . ."

Viggo leans in, elbows on his knees. "But what?"

They're too painful, I almost tell him. *They hit too close to home, to what I've always wanted. They make me feel and hope for things that are too scary, too risky to try to share with someone again, only to have them ripped away, only for them to be used against me, to make me feel the worst things I feel about myself.*

"They're not a good fit for me," I tell him. "I've tried. I'll watch a rom-com on TV till the cows come home, but romance novels just aren't my vibe."

"Explain this to me," Viggo says. "Clearly you're not averse to the idea of romance. Why the movies but not the books?"

"I . . ." Staring down at my hands, I sigh. "You know how bad Bryce messed me up."

My brothers are quiet, patient.

"I just . . . haven't figured out how I can try to have a relationship differently, how to be more careful, more guarded. Those novels, Viggo, they're so intense. It's like I'm there, like it's in my heart, and it's just . . . kinda hard to not have it and not know if I'm ready to have it."

Viggo nods, gently pats my thigh. And for once, he stays quiet, too.

"Movies," I tell them, gaining momentum, like a dam inside me has burst, "they're so obviously not real, ya know? It's just feel-good entertainment, actors playing parts. It indulges the romantic in me but lets me keep my eyes wide open, reminds me this is all pretend.

"But your romance novels, they always felt so . . . real. I don't know if it's because I picture them, their voices are clear in my head, they feel like . . . part of me. And before I got my heart broken, I used to love them for that. But since then? I don't know, man—it hurts to read it, to *feel* people love each other the way I've always wanted to be loved, only to get to *The End* and realize it's over. That my life looks nothing like that and I'm honestly not sure if I want it to, because shit, is it scary to fall in love."

"That makes a lot of sense, O," Viggo says. "And you take as long as you need to sort out what you want, what you're ready for. No one's rushing you here. We just want to understand where you're coming from. Thanks for telling us."

I nod, taking a deep, steadying breath. "So, what does my lack of romance reading have to do with my problems with Gavin?"

My brothers frown, exchanging inscrutable looks.

"What?" I ask.

Viggo glances up to the sky as dusk rolls in and paints the world moody mauve tinged with tangerine. "I mean, romance novels, while focused on romantic relationships, also spend a lot of time excavating the main characters' interiority—their past wounds, how those drive their present behavior and motivations, what fuels their dynamic with their love interest and the rest of the characters. I was simply going to use a certain trope to illustrate my point, but speaking plainly will do.

"I know when you signed with the Galaxy, you saw it as . . . turning over a new leaf. A fresh start. Take two."

"Yeah," I tell him. "And?"

Axel clears his throat. "And sometimes we worry about you." He glances toward Ren.

"You've changed, Ollie," Ren says, quiet for Theo's sake. "Some of that is good, of course—growing up, maturing."

"But you've gone so far," Ryder adds, "we worry you've buried a fundamental part of yourself."

"What part?" I ask warily.

"The wild child," Viggo tells me. "The mischief-loving man cub."

"The kid who plays ruthless, brilliant pranks," Aiden says, startling the hell out of us.

"Jesus!" Viggo hisses, hand slapped over his heart. "When did you wake up?"

Aiden eases upright, scrubbing his face. "When my kid squawked. I'm hardwired to hear him, no matter how tired I am." Gently, he takes Theo from Ren and holds him like a football in his arms. "I'm gonna go give this guy a fresh diaper and let Freya nurse him."

But first he stops, gently ruffling my hair. "Ollie, no matter what, just like you told me years ago, you always have us. We love you, okay?"

I swallow, unexpected emotion knotting my throat. "Okay."

"What we're trying to get at," Ren says, joining us again at the table as Aiden slips inside the house with Theo, "is that maybe this frustration you're experiencing with Gavin is just as much about *you* as it is about him."

"Exactly." Viggo nods. "Not only is he getting under your skin, but you're also taking it lying down in a way the Ollie we know never would. That's bound to wear on you."

"So what am I supposed to do? I told you, if Coach sees us fighting or in any way at odds, she'll fire us both as captains."

"Ollie." Viggo shakes his head. "Listen to yourself. Of course she can't *see* you fighting. And she won't. She also won't see you getting even with him."

Ryder leans in, elbows on the table. "But that doesn't mean you *won't* get even with him."

"Do it Bergman-style," Axel says. "Stealthy as hell. You're sneakier than all of us. If anyone can get revenge on a guy and put him in his place while looking like an angel, it's you."

I shake my head. "I can't."

"You can," Ryder says. "Let off some steam. You aren't someone made to take bullshit with a smile, Oliver. Give it back to him. Set him straight."

God, I'd love to. But I can't . . . Can I?

I look to Ren. "You understand. It's different—the stakes are higher when you're in front of all those people, when you know anything you do could end up in some tabloid."

"I do know," he says. "So be your sweet, charming self to him when you're in front of Coach, the fans, the team. But he's your *neighbor.* I mean, it's like God's handed him to you on a silver platter to do with what you will, O. When it's the two of you, stop trying to mend fences with someone who doesn't want to. I've had to deal with teammates like that before, and trust me, I kept my cool, but I had to find ways to vent so I could handle it."

"You did?"

Ren laughs. "Heck, yes. I'm no saint, Ollie. Sure, I carry myself a certain way publicly, and you'll keep doing that, too. But privately? I'm a loudmouthed goofball with you guys—you know that. I beat the life out of a punching bag pretty much daily. I nerd out, act like a weirdo with my Shakespeare club, throw back more than a few beers on the porch with Frankie some nights until we're giggling like fools. You have to blow off steam sometimes. You have to let yourself be a little bad when you spend so much time being so good. No one expects you to be perfect."

"Except . . . *you*," Ryder says gently.

Those words, they're like a lock that clicks open something inside me. Something that's been held back for years. My throat feels thick. My vision blurs with tears that threaten to spill over.

"Ollie." Viggo sets a hand on my back. "You can't do this to yourself. And that's why you've got to start doing things differently. Hell, this Gavin guy might be exactly what you've needed."

I laugh emptily, staring down at my hands, which are knotted so hard my knuckles are white. "For what? To drive me off the deep end?"

"Nah." He leans in, wearing a familiar conspiratorial smile that I know all too well. "To remind you of exactly who you are."

"What does that mean?"

Viggo throws a sly glance toward our brothers, then back at me. "It means you, my dear Oliver, are long overdue for some mischief-making."

SEVEN

Gavin

Playlist: "Personal Jesus," Johnny Cash

"Anytime you want to tell me why I'm really over here, I'm all ears," Mitch says, staring up at the stars from my back porch. "I'm not getting any younger, sitting around, waiting."

I sigh before taking a sip of seltzer. "Can't a man take pity on his neighbor who won't nourish himself properly, and feed him a home-cooked meal?"

Mitch throws me a withering glare. "I'm seventy-eight. Whatever damage I did, living a good life, drinking, smoking, eating delicious high-cholesterol foods, is done. Let me eat my Lean Cuisines in peace."

"They're pure sodium. They're a heart attack wrapped in plastic."

"You're worse than my wife was!" he says, crossing himself, then blowing a kiss up at the stars. "Miss you, baby."

"You're here because you couldn't say no to my chicken piccata."

Mitch scoffs. "Sure. Okay."

My chest tightens. It's worse today, the crushing weight bearing down on me, expanding inside me, to the point that I feel like I can barely breathe. "I'm fucking losing it," I blurt out.

Mitch glances my way, one silver-white eyebrow arched. He

shifts his chair until it faces me directly. I decide to inspect the inside of my seltzer glass.

"Go on," he says.

Clearing my throat, I give the stars an inspection next. Just as I
left them last time. "The guy I was . . . The other night, the guy I
was frustrated I had to team up with . . ."

Mitch is quiet, waiting for me.

"Coach made us co-captains, *and* she said we have to get along."

"And?" he says after a beat.

"I can't," I mutter. "I can't be friends with him."

"Why not?"

Because one moment, that disturbingly honest voice inside me
says, *of letting down my guard, and I nearly crashed my mouth to
his, to shut him up, to wipe the wounded, stricken look off his face
and replace it with pleasure.*

"Because he's intolerable."

Mitch rolls his eyes. "Let me guess. He's happy. And good-
looking. And kind."

I glare at him. "If he was, that would be irrelevant. Seeing as we
work together. And we're fucking teammates. And he's *ten years*
younger than me."

"And you like him. And it scared the shit out of you. So you bit
his head off."

"He's fucking irritating! He whistles like a goddamn Disney
character. He smiles *all* the time. He's unnervingly upbeat. Biting
his head off is all I *can* do."

"Not true. You can apologize."

I tug at my hair. "Fuck's sake, Mitchell. It's not that simple."

"Yeah, it is," Mitch says while hacking one of his wet, former-
smoker coughs. "You're just so used to making things complicated,
Gav."

"What the hell does that mean?"

"It means you're lonely, but you won't let anyone close. You're miserable, but you won't open your arms to happiness. You're scared—"

"I'm not scared."

"—and you won't let anyone comfort you or help you figure out how it's going to be okay."

Because it's not going to be.

I swallow roughly. "Bit harsh, Mitchell."

He shrugs. "I'm too old to prevaricate. Now, listen here. I don't know much about you beyond what you let me see. I know your folks never come around. I know you left an entire life in England—friendships, a home, maybe a relationship—that you'd built for over a decade. I know you're hurting in more ways than one, and you hate for people to see it. So you snarl and growl and put up your big cold walls to keep them from getting too close, from seeing the cracks in your armor."

My throat thickens.

"But I got news for you, Gav." Mitch sets his folded hands on his belly, his wedding ring, which he's never taken off, glinting in the moonlight. "And I hate to sound like a Hallmark card, but the cracks *are* where the light shines through. You can deny it until you're blue in the face, but everyone wants to be loved somehow, someway, for their little bit of warped, jagged light, for those cracks that have shaped who they are—not just their joy but their pain. Everyone wants to be seen." He pauses, smoothing down his mustache. "Some folks are just very good at denying themselves that. And you are an expert."

I blink at him as silence stretches between us. A car door slams; a dog barks. Inside, my cat, Wilde, meows about something, then thumps to the floor from his window bed.

"So," Mitch says, holding my eyes. "Whenever you're done living in denial, I'm here to listen. Or better yet—" He juts his chin in the direction over my shoulder. "Talk to that tall, cool drink of water who lives next door."

I jolt like I've been electrified, head whipping so fast, a muscle pops in my neck and burns. "Fuck me," I hiss, clapping a hand over it.

There he stands, Oliver Bergman, wheat-at-sunset hair falling in his face, just long enough that he tucks it behind his ears, frowning at the lock on his back door. The floodlight turns the tips of his eyelashes to tiny glittering stars, bathes his head in a halo of light.

How appropriate. There he is, angelic, whole, dazzling in the light. While I sit in darkness, broken, scarred.

"Well, probably time I hit the road," Mitch says loudly. So loudly, Oliver glances our way.

"I'm going to murder you," I growl.

"I'd like to see you try." He flexes a Navy-tattooed bicep as he stands and pats it, then says to Oliver, "Evening!"

Oliver glances between us, wearing a confused frown before his expression smooths and that familiar, sparkling smile warms his face. "Evening!" He waves.

"Mitchell O'Connor, at your service," Mitch says, making his way across the yard.

Oh, God. It's a train wreck. I can't stop it. I can't stop watching. My worlds are about to collide.

So far, I've managed to avoid introducing the poker guys to Oliver, to avoid meeting anybody who matters to him either. It's simple enough, seeing as I've always pretended Oliver isn't my neighbor at all.

When the guys come for poker, I rush them inside like I run a speakeasy, desperate for them not to see him, positive they'll know there's some kind of connection, let alone one that I resent so deeply. And whenever Oliver's small yard, a mirror of mine, is packed with people laughing, shouting—the sounds of family, the smell of home-cooked food and belonging wafting toward me—I close my windows, lower the blinds, and turn up the stereo until it's drowned out.

It was only a matter of time until those evasion tactics failed me. I should have been prepared. I was not.

"Oliver Bergman," he's saying as Mitch shakes his hand. "Nice to meet you."

I throw back the rest of my seltzer, wishing it were something stronger.

"Ollie," Mitch says, patting his hand, "a pleasure to meet you. Gavin's said great things."

The fizzy water rushes down my windpipe, making me cough.

Oliver flashes him an amused smile. "I doubt that highly."

"You kidding?" Mitch claps a hand on Oliver's arm and glances back at me. "Says you're a real rising star that he's honored to share the field with—isn't that right, Gav?"

My eyes are watering as I smack my chest, but I still manage to glare murder at Mitchell.

Oliver doesn't buy it, and he shouldn't. Our eyes meet, and the hairs on the back of my neck stand on end. Something's different. That infuriatingly upbeat smile, that dogged optimism oozing from his pores, is gone. In its place are a blue-flame fire in his eyes, insouciant posture, a sinister edge to his smile.

Is that fucker smirking at me?

Mitchell clears his throat, wrenching me from my thoughts. "Well, I better be going."

"I'll drive you." I stand out of my chair so fast it flips back.

Mitch glances from the chair to me and raises his eyebrows. "No, you won't."

"Yes, Mitchell," I say between clenched teeth, "I will."

A honk sounds out front. Mitch grins. "No, you won't. I've got plans. And my ride is here."

"Plans!" I yell, indignant. "What was dinner with me, then?"

"Ah." Waving a hand, Mitch starts walking toward the front of my house, where the poker guys are piled into Lou's '55 Chevy. "You don't want to spend all night with a bunch of old guys who can drink you under the table."

Except Jim, at least, who honks the horn and hollers out the front passenger window, "Hurry up, slowpoke! I've got a Shirley Temple calling my name!"

"Ollie," Mitch says, throwing him a wink. "Great to meet ya. Don't be a stranger, okay?"

"You too," Oliver says on a smile.

Jorge catcalls from the back. I flip him the finger. "Tossers!" I yell.

I get a bunch of shit hollered my way for that. Oliver bites his lip, hands in his pockets, as he watches them pull out. I turn back, and our gazes collide.

"Who are they?" he asks, jutting his chin toward Lou's Chevy as it takes the bend and disappears. "They seem like fun."

I shove my hands in my pockets. "I play poker with them."

His brow furrows. "You play poker with a bunch of grandpas?"

"They're feisty grandpas," I grumble defensively.

He smirks again—that damn smirk!

"What?" I snap.

Oliver shrugs. "Just didn't picture you as a poker player. Or a hang-out-with-fun-senior-citizens type. Then again, I can't say what I *do* picture you as, other than miserable."

My eyebrows shoot up. "Did something . . . *rude* just come out of your mouth?"

"Is it rude if it's the truth?"

A surprised laugh bursts out of me, deep and rusty. I can't remember the last time I laughed. "Wow. Okay."

Oliver leans against his house, arms folded across his chest.

"Just because I haven't *said* it doesn't mean I haven't been thinking it, Hayes."

Well, welcome to that club. I clear my throat and stare down at my shoes. "Fair enough."

There's a thick quiet between us. I watch him inhale a deep tug of air, like he's about to say something. But he doesn't.

And he shouldn't.

Because *I* should. I'm the one who owes him an apology. An explanation. I know this. I'm a fucking jerk sometimes, but I'm no fool. It's been one thing to create distance, be aloof, demanding, terse—to use my seniority as an excuse for holding everyone at arm's length. But I know it got away from me. I took it too far on the field the other day and at my house. I lashed out at him. I lost control, snapped, spoke like an overbearing ass. And I shouldn't have. I should have kept my cool.

Instead, the warning voice inside me whispers, *you burst into flames and came so fucking close to pinning him against the wall and kissing him until neither one of you remembered your own names.*

"Bergman, I—" My voice catches. I clear my throat. "I realize I was . . . a bit high-handed the other day."

It's quiet but for the faint roar of the Pacific a few blocks away, a stray bird singing its night song. Slowly, Oliver pushes off the side of his house and steps out of its shadow. In moonlight, his eyes are eerily pale, the sharp planes of his face sharper as they cast shadows on his skin. "'A bit'?" he says.

I grit my teeth. "Yes, *a bit*. However, in a nutshell, I meant what I said. We're not getting chummy, but I'll keep my temper in check with you. I have the last two days, haven't I?"

"You've been okay, I guess." He takes another step. Then another. A foot stands between us, mirrors of each other. Hands in pockets, gazes locked. "So, that's what we'll be . . . civil."

"Yes."

"And that's it."

"Yes," I grit out.

He tips his head, examining me. "Why?"

That's the question I can't answer. That I *won't*.

I'm not telling him that I've had my fill of learning how little I mean to people beyond what I can do with a ball at my feet and the world it can buy me. I'm not telling him that soon I'll be an always-in-pain washed-up former athlete, and he'll be where I once was, the world before him, and I cannot let one more person, let alone someone who has everything I'm about to lose, decide that I'm not worth much at all, certainly not worth keeping around when his life and career are soaring into the stratosphere while mine crash and burn.

"I don't have friends here," I finally tell him.

"Except the poker grandpas."

"They forced themselves on me. And *friends* is a generous term. I endure them. That's all I do with anyone here, and that's what I meant when I said that to you," I lie. "Even if I said it . . . a tad . . . harshly."

"But you meant it," he says. "You'll never be my friend."

I stare at him, knowing down to my bones that's impossible. "No. Not your friend."

My gut twists. I don't like hurting people, believe it or not. I've just accepted that many small cuts are better than one large gaping wound. To avoid much worse hurt down the road, these brief, sharp inflictions are necessary.

I brace myself for that stricken expression again, like in the locker room, the one that cut straight through me like a knife to the gut. But it doesn't come.

"You got it," he says, staring down, toeing the grass.

I blink, surprised. "I . . . what?"

He glances up, and there it is—fire in his eyes, that devious smile as he backtracks toward his house. "On practice days, you pack a change of clothes, right?"

My eyes narrow. "Yes. Why?"

Oliver slips into the shadows of his house, his expression hidden as he says, "Just wondering. Good night, Mr. Hayes."

Just wondering, my ass.

Seething, I walk into the locker room the next morning, rainbow confetti stuck to my hair.

And clothes.

And skin.

And other places I'm not going to mention.

I'm going to murder Oliver Bergman.

Santi, whose cubby is beside mine and whose sunny disposition gives Oliver a run for his money, turns to say his usual good morning but comes up short on a gasp.

"*Buenos días*, Santiago." I drop my bag, making the entire room startle. They stare at me warily.

Santi swallows, his gaze darting nervously over me. "*Capitán.* What happened to your . . . hair? And clothes? And—"

"My entire fucking body?" I wrench off my sparkling shirt, sending a plume of rainbow confetti bursting into the air overhead.

Santi jumps back to avoid it. "Uh . . . yes?"

Oliver walks in, whistling cheerily, bag on his shoulder, the top half of his hair tugged back into an irritating little spurt of golden hair that makes him look deceptively innocent.

His eyes dance over me. He bites his lip. Hard. An infuriating cocktail of rage and unwelcome hot-blooded awareness spills through me, reminding me of that mouth I came so close to tasting, those fast, sharp breaths as our bodies drew close. *Too* close.

Fuming, I stand there and brush glitter off my chest. Oliver looks away as he clears his throat, heading for his cubby.

"Well, Santiago, I'll tell you what I know." Storming over to the sinks, I run my head under the water, then my face, rinsing off as much glitter as I can. "I was minding my own business this morning, opened my car door, sat myself down, and when the sun hit right in my eyes, I pulled down the visor." I cut a seething glance at Oliver, who's started changing, his back to me. "Imagine my surprise when a glitter bomb of confetti baptized my fucking car."

"*Ay, Dios mío.*" Santi cringes. The rest of the team makes sympathetic sounds.

"Damn, Cap." Ben grimaces. "That's a nasty prank."

"Kids these days," Amobi says wearily. "They have no shame."

Carlo nods in agreement. "At least they didn't—"

"Put it in the vents, too?" I offer. "Oh, they did." I glare at Oliver's back. "I have confetti in my fucking sinuses."

Oliver coughs, then clears his throat. He turns, shirtless, skin gleaming, his jersey balled in one hand. "Damn, Hayes, that's rough. Whoever's bad side you got on, I sure would want to mend fences with them, if this is what they're capable of." Strolling by, he lowers his voice and says, "Especially when they're just getting started."

EIGHT

Oliver

Playlist: "It Ain't Easy," Delta Spirit

Well. It seems I underestimated Gavin Hayes. Who knew he had it in him?

"Oliver," Santi says as he steps up behind me at the airport. "*Tu pelo*. How do you get it so . . . soft?"

Gavin stands ahead of us, eyes down on his phone, expressionless as always, a statue named *Innocent Disinterest*.

Even though he's *anything* but.

I silently wish him a swift, violent case of diarrhea the moment we board the plane, then I turn to face Santiago. "Nothing like a deep-conditioning treatment, Santi. Does wonders for it."

Santi reaches for my hair, then stops. "May I touch?"

"Be my guest."

He slides his hand down my hair, which after five home washes last night has only just begun to feel like it's not shellacked with butter. After I realized Gavin—and it was undoubtedly Gavin—swapped the conditioner and shampoo in the dispensers of my favorite shower stall at the facility (I tried not to think about how he even *knew* which one was my favorite), my head looked like I'd dipped it in a bowl of oil.

Such a dirty move. Then again, I'd forked his yard the night before and coated his outside doorknob with peanut butter that looked very much like poop after I'd added some cocoa powder and red food dye, so I should have seen it coming.

He just seemed way too curmudgeonly to be the retaliatory-pranking type.

"Wow," Santi says in awe, stroking my hair some more. Andre joins him. Then Ben.

"Oy," Gavin snaps. They all look at him, dropping their hands like kids caught with their hands in the cookie jar. "We're in an airport, not a petting zoo."

I shrug. "We're modeling a healthy departure from toxic masculinity, wouldn't you say, fellas?"

Their heads swing my way.

Gavin's jaw tightens, his left eye twitching as he glares back down at his phone. He may not be looking right at me, but he's paying attention. I smile my widest, sweetest smile.

"Men," I say, loud enough for him to hear from his few feet away, "are taught touching each other without roughness, reasons deemed socially acceptable, like a contact sport, is a sign of weakness or— heteronormative patriarchy forbid—having *feelings* for one another."

"Ah, yes," Gavin drawls, eyes still on his phone. "If anyone needs a lecture on homophobia's inherency in patriarchal constructs, professional sports, and broader culture, it's me."

"Not a lecture. Just saying, would a few pictures on the internet of the guys touching my hair be the end of the world? Would it maybe even be . . . a good thing?"

Slowly, Gavin glances up from his phone, eyes searching mine.

"Beautifully said," Carlo mutters. "Ollie, you should write a book. You speak so . . . inspirationally."

"Nah. But that's nice of you, Carlo."

Ben blinks, sniffling. "Man, that really hit a chord with me."

Amobi pats him on the back in reassurance. Ben turns, throwing an arm around him, and says, "I love you, man."

"I love you, too, but get off." Amobi shoves him, smiling. "Just because we're unpacking our embedded patriarchy doesn't mean I like unsolicited hugs."

———

Unlike lots of other professional sports leagues, the MLS, up until last year, flew its teams almost exclusively commercial. This year, after basically a decade of back-and-forth with the powers that be, we've been guaranteed at least eight chartered flights, and the cross-country trek for our first preseason game, against New England, has been deemed a solid candidate.

So rather than packing onto a regular old Boeing 747 along with everyone and their grandmother, we're stepping onto a private plane. No screaming babies or awkward rubbernecking to sneak pictures of us. No legs squished in a seat whose row doesn't begin to accommodate my six-three frame. No layovers lasting hours on end.

I should be ecstatic.

Instead, my chest is tightening in an invisible vise named *anxiety triggered by new environments* meets *general fear of flying*.

"Bergman. Hayes." Coach points to the pair of wide leather seats that compose the lone first row on the plane. "Seats of honor." She raises her eyebrows, her expression loud and clear: *I'm watching you. Play nice.*

Without waiting for us to answer, she walks past us and joins Jas in the next row, who's already tugging on their headphones to tune out the team's noise.

Gavin exhales a slow, measured breath, turns, and pops open the first compartment, then throws his bag in there before easing down to his seat. I follow suit, lifting my bag to stash it in the overhead compartment, but my hands are so shaky, I drop it.

The bag lands right on Gavin's knee. The one that seems to bother him most.

"Fuck's sake," he growls under his breath. He glances up, angry coffee-dark eyes pinning mine.

"Sorry." My voice comes out hoarse and tight, but it's the best I can do. Clearing my throat, I pick up my bag. My heart pounds in my ears. I'm a clumsy mess, but I manage to get my bag in the overhead compartment and shut it before more or less collapsing into my seat.

I want nothing else than to slip in my earbuds and tune out the flight with my favorite Best of Broadway playlist I always listen to, but I realize my earbuds are still in my bag, and I think if I try to so much as stand up and go back to my bag, I just might pass out before I even get there.

Gavin slants a glance at me, brow furrowed. "What's wrong with you?"

"I'm fine," I mutter, focusing on breathing. Or trying to.

My heart's a snare drum in my chest, its frenetic beat reverberating through my body. I shut my eyes, clamp my hands together over my stomach, and focus on feeling my breaths. Extending my legs, I do everything I can to luxuriate in the rare pleasure of being able to stretch them fully, rather than fly with my knees wedged against the seat in front of me.

Dimly, over the roar of blood in my ears, the rapid thud of my heart, I hear the chief stewardess explain flight safety, the captain come over the intercom and tell us we're in for a smooth cross-country flight.

"Bergman," Gavin says. "What's going on?"

"Can't." It's all I can manage, shaking my head. I'm too focused on doing everything I know to cope with my escalating anxiety.

I suck in a breath through my nose as the plane begins to roll forward and turns onto the runway, as the engines begin to roar. The plane picks up speed. Momentum pins me against the seat, exacerbating the compressed sensation in my chest.

My anxiety's such a frustrating conundrum. It ebbs for stretches, lulls me into a sense of calm. Days will go by that I feel like I finally have the best medication, the right balance of comforting routine and mood-boosting variety and excitement, and then this happens—I wake up, my chest tight, my breathing short, my stomach knotted so hard I can barely eat, because of something that just a few days ago I felt would be completely manageable.

Gripping the edge of my seat, I sink my fingers into the cool, buttery leather and beg the choking sense of dread tightening my throat, tearing through and around me like a tornado, to release its grip.

"Oliver." Gavin's voice cuts through the chaos like a hot knife through butter.

And now I'm melting.

My name. He's never said my name. Let alone like that—like the blackness swallowing me up is an immaterial veil his voice has rendered, a wisp of smoke cleared with one sweep of gravelly sound: *Oliver.*

I'm on the precipice of a full-blown panic attack. I recognize that now, scrambling at the edge, and then—

A hand. *His* hand. Warm, rough, heavy. It settles over mine. Air rushes out of me before I suck it in, stuttering as if I've surfaced from too long underwater, as if my lungs were about to burst.

"You're okay," he says. His hand is so heavy. So strong. Wrapped around mine, squeezing it tight. "You're safe."

I'm too desperate for the lifeline to try to make sense of who threw it, the last person I ever expected to give me kindness, let alone comfort. I spin my hand and clutch his, because I'm still there on the ledge, panic whistling around me like a violent wind that's about to send me over into a terrifying free fall.

For long moments, as the plane climbs in the sky, I count my breaths, grounded by Gavin's hand clutching mine so hard I feel my pulse in my palm. A pulse that's slowing, steadying.

My breaths come easier, oxygen flooding my system, bringing me back to my body.

"S-sorry," I mutter.

He squeezes harder, his thumb sliding along the back of my hand. Something cracks inside my heart and spills through my limbs.

"You should apologize," he says, his voice low and quiet, "for glitter-bombing my car. For forking my yard and sticking shit-looking peanut butter on my doorknob, but not for this."

My mouth tips into a faint smile. But it doesn't last. I'm so tired. I'm always tired after this happens. And I slept like hell last night because I was nervous. About the game. The flight.

Him.

As the plane finally levels, the bands of my anxiety start to loosen around my ribs. And when sleep wraps around me, heavy, peaceful, I feel it still—

His hand. Warm. Strong. Holding mine.

———

I have a feeling Viggo would have something to say about this.

I stand just inside our hotel room.

Gavin's and *my* hotel room.

And there's only one bed.

Something niggles at the back of my brain. It's been years since I've read a romance novel, back when we were in high school, when Viggo left them lying around Mom and Dad's house and I'd pick them up once he'd finished. In one of those romance novels, I remember there being some situation like this. A couple at odds, newly married but strictly for convenience, pausing their travel by carriage to sleep at an inn, only to realize there was only one room for them and only one bed.

That they had to share.

And then sharing a bed led to sharing much *more*.

Which is definitely not going to happen. Especially since my skin is still warm, my palm tingling with the memory of Gavin's hand wrapped around mine.

The. Whole. Flight.

When I jolted awake as we touched down, Gavin slowly released my hand, then used it to wrap his old-school earbuds around his phone like it was nothing. I didn't know what to say or do. So since then, I've said and done nothing except move like a zombie, going through the motions. Deplaning, getting on the bus, staring out the window as we rode to our hotel, then accepting my key. Riding the elevator with Gavin.

Walking down the hall with Gavin.

Stopping outside the same room as Gavin.

"Fucking hell," he grumbles, tossing his bag aside and heading for the bathroom.

Which has only one shower.

Not that I'm thinking about sharing a shower with Gavin Hayes like I'll be sharing a bed.

"I call window side," I say to his back, trying to defuse the massive tension in the room.

He lifts his hand, and a long, thick middle finger, before disappearing into the bathroom with a *thud* of the door.

"Warm and cuddly as ever," I mutter, crossing the room and setting my bag on the dresser. I pull back the curtains and glance around, trying to distract myself with the view of Foxborough and Gillette Stadium, but it's pointless.

I can't shake what happened on the plane.

Worse, I don't want to.

NINE

Gavin

Playlist: "Come a Little Closer," Cage The Elephant

There's a lot about my life that's felt like a downgrade since I signed with an MLS team. That probably sounds arrogant and spoiled, and maybe it is, but after playing for some of the most cash-rich, prestigious teams in European football—soccer, that is—it's been an adjustment. At least it was at first. I've gotten used to it after two years: sharing commercial flights with passengers, sharing stadiums with the other local professional teams, sharing hotel rooms.

Not sharing a bed.

Hiding in the bathroom, I pull out my phone. This is exceptionally unprofessional, Alexis.

Three dots appear. Then Lexi's—Coach's—response, which makes my phone chime quietly. Not that I'm agreeing to your assertion that making co-captains share a room *is* unprofessional, but who says I made you two roommates?

Not just roommates, I write. There's only one. Fucking. Bed.

Yikes, she texts. Best hope Bergman doesn't hog the mattress.

"Jesus Christ." I drop my phone on the counter, splaying my palms across the cool quartz surface. With a glance up, I lock eyes with my reflection. Dark eyes. Darker smudges beneath them. I look exhausted. Because I fucking am.

In so many ways.

I cannot stop replaying what happened on the plane any more than I can stop the ache in my chest that pounds in time with my heart.

Or maybe it *is* my heart.

It fucking hurts. It's a festering, nagging ache that wants me to do something foolish, like hold Oliver, crush him to my chest, and make him tell me where the hell that came from and how the hell I can make it never happen again.

Which is . . . a problem.

This is why I've kept my distance. *This* is why I've held him at arm's length.

Because I knew this is how it would be. The moment I let him punch through those icy walls I've built around myself, I'll melt faster than a dropped ice-cream cone on a Los Angeles sidewalk in July.

And I cannot do that. Except I can't seem to fucking help myself.

"Goddammit." I grip the counter harder, then push away, scrubbing my face. With a flick of the handle, I flush the toilet to make it seem like I was doing my business instead of losing my fucking mind in our bathroom. Then I turn on the faucet, run cold water, and splash my face.

Right. I've got this.

I look at my reflection. "You've got this."

My reflection does not look convinced. Which is why I turn away from it and whip open the door.

Oliver leans against the windowsill, pinning the curtain between his shoulder and the wall. He stares out at the view, which from here I can see includes the stadium. When he senses me, he glances over his shoulder, those glittering pale eyes meeting mine.

For a moment that holds an eternity, he doesn't say anything.

Neither do I. The world is nothing but the warmth of sunlight spilling across his face, casting one side in sharp shadow. The faint whir of forced air from the vents, the distant sounds of guests shutting doors, their suitcase wheels crushing plush carpet, the ding of an elevator.

I drink in the moment like a magnificently tall glass of ice water after a run in brutal heat. I'm hot, and as I absorb what I'm doing, fierce coolness works its way through me, a shock, a warning: *This is not wise.*

And yet I couldn't look away if my life depended on it. I stare at sunlight sparkling off his lashes, slipping down his long, straight nose in a whispering warmth like a lover's caress, over sharp cheekbones and soft lips. An intimacy I'll never have with him.

Not that I want it.

Too much.

Because I haven't let myself. I haven't let myself look and linger and think and dream. It's pointless. Futile. His life's just beginning. Mine's coming to a fucking end—at least the meaningful part of it. He's young. I'm old. I'm a miserable, pain-riddled misanthrope, and he's a perennially happy ray of fucking sunshine.

Or so I thought.

I see it again, his hands clutching the seat, air sawing out of his lungs. I swear I heard his heart flying from where I sat beside him. Perhaps he's not so fine, then. Or happy. As much as his always-the-optimist, upbeat demeanor grates on me, the threat to it makes me infinitely angrier.

"What was that?" I ask sharply.

Oliver blinks away, stares down at his bright yellow sneakers, toeing the carpet. "A staring contest? Which I lost."

I sigh impatiently. "That's not what I'm talking about, and you know it."

"Yes, Mr. Hayes. I know."

"I told you to stop calling me that."

He glances up and pins me with those moonlight-pale eyes again. A faint smile tips his mouth. "And I never told you I would."

Anger flares inside me, hot, agitated. I want to cross the room, fist his shirt, and kiss that coy fucking smile right off his face. I want to throw him down on the bed, press my body into his, and show Oliver what happens when he insists on provoking me, smiling at me, holding my eyes so long I want to fall into those ice-blue pools and never resurface.

"Answer me," I demand. "Stop provoking and prevaricating. Answer me, dammit."

He lifts his chin. "Why?"

My teeth grind. I don't say what I'm thinking. I don't tell him, *Because I'm worried. Because you fucking scared me. Because I hate what being near you does to me, but I hate whatever's hurting you more, and I have to know what that is. So I can bend it in the iron grip of my will and protect you from it.*

"Because I have a right to know." I stand to my full height, legs wide, arms folded across my chest. My most authoritative stance. "As your co-captain, what happens on team time is fair game."

Oliver's eyes flash, his smile slips, but for just a moment, before that coy charm is back, sparkling in his eyes. "Fair game, eh? Pun intended?"

"Fuck off, Bergman. Tell me."

Slowly, he pushes off the wall, then strolls my way. He stops with a foot between us, stance natural, feet shoulder width apart as he slips his hands into his grass-green joggers' pockets. Like a fool, I let my gaze drift up from those heinously bright yellow sneakers and green joggers to his gold-and-blue Galaxy hoodie, which drapes frustratingly loose around his torso.

Oliver clears his throat. "How about I tell you when you're done undressing me with your eyes."

My gaze snaps up and meets his, fear and heat flooding me in equal measure. His eyes twinkle. His grin widens. He's teasing me.

"I am *not* undressing you. I'm struggling to understand how a grown man can dress so terribly."

His mouth drops open, stunned at my insult. "I wear color like a pro."

"You look like a disorganized crayon box."

He tips his head, giving me a slow, appraising once-over that sends a fresh wave of heat searing through me.

"No offense," he says. "But coming from a guy who wears three colors—black, charcoal, and heather gray—your fashion critique doesn't hold much weight."

"Horseshit." I pluck at my zip-up jacket with the team's embossed logo. "I wear other colors. Blue. Yellow. That's five."

He rolls his eyes. "Hayes, you're *obligated* to wear those colors. You don't voluntarily wear them."

"Awfully aware of my wardrobe, aren't you?"

"Hard to miss it when you walk around dressed like a storm cloud."

We are wildly off topic. I grit my teeth. "You're distracting me."

He grins. "You're catching on."

I close the distance between us, and his smile evaporates; his breath catches in his throat. I stare at his mouth, then meet his eyes. And then, sweet God, a faint pink blush creeps up his cheeks. It's as satisfying as it is torturous. "You're playing with fire, Bergman. Mind you don't get burned."

All humor vanishes from his face. He swallows roughly, and I watch his Adam's apple roll. I barely suppress a groan. I can see it so easily, his head thrown back, his throat working as his eyes scrunch shut, his face tight with agonizing pleasure.

"Tell me," I say quietly, holding his eyes. "Tell me what happened." I bite my tongue so I won't reveal any more than I have already. How worried I am. How much I care.

He searches my eyes for a long, silent moment. "I had a panic attack."

As I thought. But it's not enough. "What triggered it?"

Something flickers in his gaze, but he steels himself, stands tall. "A combination of things," he says slowly, carefully.

"These happen regularly?" I've never noticed. I'd remember if this happened to him before.

He nods.

"You hide it."

He hesitates, then says, "They don't happen often, and generally when they do, yes, I'm able to isolate myself and deal with them privately. I see a therapist. I know what to do."

"But they still happen."

His nostrils flare. "Yes, Hayes. They still happen."

"And what caused this one?"

He shrugs, agitated. "Like I said, a combination of things. I didn't sleep great and it wasn't our normal way of flying, and I hate flying to begin with. It's our first game of the season, my first time being co-captain, let alone with someone who hates my guts—"

"I *don't* hate you. I told you that."

"Your actions, however, indicate otherwise."

My teeth are clenched so tight, my jaw should have cracked by now. "What have I done for two years that's so egregious, hmm? So I don't kiss your ass and indulge your playful antics. I haven't asked you over for a Sunday barbecue on the back porch simply because we're neighbors. After two years of biting my tongue, I gave you hell for the first time on the field at practice. And frankly, that was long overdue. You know why? Because you hide who you really are behind that sunshiny shit, and I'm tired of it. You're suffocating someone inside you who is capable of so much more than you give yourself credit for, and I demand that greatness, for your sake and the team's."

"Who the *hell* do you think you are?" Oliver says, anger hardening his features. "You don't know me, Hayes. You don't get to hold me at arm's length for years, then try to speak into my life—"

I lean in until our noses nearly touch, and it's the locker room and my kitchen all over again, except, God help me, I'm so much closer to giving in, to taking what I want, damn the consequences, but I can't. I won't.

"I know you better than you think," I tell him. "And I see straight through the illusion you've so deftly crafted. I've told you I don't hate you, and I mean it. If I hate anything, it's the lie you make yourself live and force everyone around you to maintain."

Silence rings between us. Oliver stares at me, eyes wide, mouth parted like I've stunned him. I should stop. God, I should stop. But I can't.

I close the distance between us, my mouth nearly brushing the shell of his ear. I breathe him in because I can't help myself, and the ache inside me knots so tight, I have no choice but to bathe in the scent of him, trapped in my lungs. Until air finally leaves me on a slow, pained exhale. "Actions speak louder than words—isn't that the saying? I held your hand across a fucking continent, Oliver Bergman. Do with that what you will."

Before I can give in and crush my mouth to his, I step back, grab my room key, and storm right out the way that I came.

TEN

Oliver

Playlist: "Young & Sad," Noah Cyrus

The door snicks closed at the same moment I realize my jaw is hanging open.

"Holy shit," I whisper to the room.

I plop onto the mattress like I've been knocked there. I think I have been. By shock.

"Shit, shit, shit." I fumble in my bag for my phone and call Viggo.

"You rang?"

Standing, I pace the room and tug at my hair. "What did you do?"

"I mean, I've done lots of things since I last saw you. Which one—"

"Viggo." I make a fist with my empty hand, wishing it were the front of his shirt and I could give him a good shake. "Something is . . . something's going on with Gavin and . . ." I exhale heavily, scrubbing my face.

"Gavin and . . . ?" he prompts.

I sigh miserably. "And me."

"Hmm." He sniffs. I can see him leaning against the kitchen counter at Mom and Dad's house, which is where he's living right now. Next comes the crunch of an apple between his teeth. Around his bite, he says, "Why would you think I've done something?"

It sounds ridiculous, but that doesn't make my suspicion that he and my brothers have wreaked some kind of covert havoc on my psyche any less unprecedented. "Because ever since we sat out in Freya and Aiden's backyard and you dipshits forced a Bergman Brothers Summit on me, things have completely changed between us."

Another crunch on his apple. "Isn't change what you wanted?"

"Dammit, Viggo, not this kind of change! I did not want to escalate my antagonism between my now co-captain and myself beyond the level of mutual juvenile pranks, to holding hands across the goddamn country, then being stuck in the same hotel room WITH ONLY ONE BED!"

There's a brief pause. "Did you say only one bed?"

"Viggo!"

"What? I'm asking a question!"

I groan in frustration, dropping my head back and staring up at the ceiling. "Yes," I mutter bleakly. "Only one bed."

"And you . . . held hands?" he asks carefully.

I glare up at the ceiling. "I had a panic attack during the flight. He held my hand and talked to me, helped me calm down before it got bad. Then I fell asleep and woke up and he was still holding my hand, and now we're in a hotel room together and he was acting all intense and concerned about what happened on the plane, and then he said something really cryptic, and it freaked me out, because this makes no sense. He's a giant asshole who hates me and who I frankly cannot stand either, but holy shit, we keep getting really in each other's personal spaces, and now he drops this, like, poetic bomb on me!" I barrel on, sucking in a sharp breath. "'I held your hand across a fucking continent, Oliver Bergman. Do with that what you will.' That's what he said!"

Finally, I'm done. The other end of the line is silent for a moment, until my brother lets out a long, slow whistle. "Wow. That *is* poetic. He really said that?"

"Yes." My chest is tight again. My legs itch with the need to pace. Stalking across the room, I step into the bathroom. A faint trace of Gavin lingers—clean and warm and a little spicy. I don't breathe in deeply to catch every trace.

Because that would be creepy.

I just take a . . . little whiff.

"You okay over there?" Viggo asks. "Doing your deep-breathing exercises?"

"So I don't bodily harm you when I get home," I mutter, staring at my wonky plane hair and trying to do something with it. It's in this weird grow-out phase where it's just past my ears but barely long enough to tug most of it into a ponytail. "Viggo, what's going on? What did you guys do? What the hell is *happening*?"

"Ollie-bo-bollie." Viggo crunches on his apple and says around his bite, "First of all, I'm sorry you had a panic attack. Those are zero fun."

"Zero fun," I agree, giving up on my hair, spinning, and parking my butt against the sink. "Thank you. I'll be okay. It's just . . . a lot."

I can't see it, but I feel his affirming nod. "Cross-country flight when you hate flying."

"Yeah."

"First game of the preseason," he adds.

"Yep."

"Seeing your dirtbag ex from college who plays on the opposing team."

"That, too," I agree.

"Co-captaining for the first time with a guy you've been infatuated with since you were a teenager."

"God, yeah—whoa!" I scramble off the sink as if escaping the room where Gavin's scent still lingers will somehow distance me from what I've just admitted. "I didn't—you tripped me up with that."

"Oliver."

Dammit. Now I can see his arched eyebrow. The one that says, *I see your bullshit, and I buy none of it.*

"Dude, I grew up with you, remember?" he says. "I know how hard you crushed on him when we were teens. Shit, *I* crushed on him when we were teens. Gavin Hayes is hot and competent. Beyond competent. He's a goddamn legend. He will, beyond our lifetime, be remembered as one of the greats."

"He's not dead," I say defensively. "Or retired. Stop talking about him in the past tense."

There's a thick, heavy pause. Without a doubt, he's biting his lip, trying not to smile.

I flop back on the bed, groaning in frustration. "I hate that I know you so well, I know exactly what you're doing *and* thinking right now."

"Am I so predictable?"

I stare up at the ceiling. "You're trying not to smile, totally failing, and you've got that conniving glint in your eyes."

"Damn, you're good. Okay, back to what I was saying, point number two: Do you think maybe you two are . . . into each other? I mean, are there feels? Just really—"

"I do not have feels!" I jackknife up on the bed. "I have a massive hard-on for him. That's it. He's hot and, as you say, competent. And he's . . . bossy and intense, and that's my catnip. But he's also a giant, high-handed, cold, snarky jerk who I cannot stand."

"Who held your hand," he reminds me.

"An outlier."

"And dropped the poetic bomb," he adds.

"Okay, so another outlier."

"Ollie, you can ignore that poetic bomb, but if you do, you're in denial. He has some kind of feels for you," Viggo says.

"Yeah. *Feels* of frustration and annoyance. He's probably just doing all of this to mess with my head and make me feel bad for pushing his buttons."

"Or he held your hand because he cares and asked about your panic attacks because he's worried about you, and he almost kissed you when you had your fight in the locker room the other day because he's been into you and he's running out of the strength to hide it."

I roll my eyes. "You really read too many romance novels."

"No such thing, Oliver. No such thing."

"I'm telling you—wait." I frown. "The almost kiss." Well, almost kiss*es*, not that I admit that to Viggo. "I never said anything about that."

"Ollie, Ollie, Ollie. It was written all over you. You don't read as many romance novels as I have and not learn the signs of a good almost hate kiss."

"Stop it with the romance novels," I beg. "This is what I'm talking about. I don't *want* to start looking at him with rose-colored, happily-ever-after glasses. Life is not a romance novel."

"One of my biggest beefs with life." *Crunch.* Once again he's back at the apple.

Sighing, I rub my temples with my thumb and forefinger. "What am I going to do, V? I feel like I'm all turned around and upside down. Much as I hated how things were before this co-captaincy threw a wrench in everything, at least he was predictable. Now I don't even know what to expect."

Viggo's quiet for a moment except for the last crunch of his apple, the slap of the composter lid opening before I hear the core drop with a *thunk*. "Does something need to be done?"

"It's a pretty stressful existence right now. I can't maintain this."

"So talk to him during your little sleepover tonight. See where things go. Let passion take you where it may—"

"Viggo, no. Not that I think anything close to romance is possible between us, but even if it were, I promised myself I would never do that again—fall for someone who's in my profession."

"Who said anything about falling?"

I narrow my eyes. "You know what I mean. Going there with someone in my professional life, even if it were only casual."

"Who said anything about casual?"

"Stop being so darn Socratic. Stop repeating what I've said."

"Fine." Viggo clears his throat. "Ollie, while I love a good romantic journey on the road to the HEA, you know your best way to happiness. You know if you're ready for romance or not. You don't have to take this anywhere with Gavin, even if my personal hunch is there may be somewhere to take it."

I frown, suspicious. "Do you have a fever? Have you swapped personalities with someone?"

He laughs quietly. "O, if I've learned anything by now in my twenty-five years of meddling existence, it's this: you can lead a horse to water—and I am *very* good at leading a horse to water—but you can't make them wear swimming trunks."

"What the hell does that mean?"

"It means," Viggo says patiently, "that you will make your own decision about how to proceed on the path before you, even if your brothers steered you to view it from a slightly different angle. And maybe a little further down the path than you were before."

"'A *little* further down the path'?"

"Oliver, you have to admit you were at the end of your rope. What were we going to tell you when clearly what you'd been doing wasn't working? I stand by our advice, and I'll be honest: our primary concern was your well-being. Sure, my romance-loving heart saw the potential for a combustible connection, but as a perk, not the point." He clears his throat. "At the end of the day, we just want you to be happy. And maybe in his ass-backwards way, Gavin wants you to be happy, too. Why else would he care about what's going on with your panic attacks? Why else would he comfort you on the plane?"

I swallow nervously. "I really don't know."

"Well, I think it's a good sign. Maybe you and Mr. Grumpypants will end up at least being friends. Man, I really love nothing more than a good friends-to-lovers romance. The longing. The high stakes of risking an enduring friendship for a new kind of love that might not last. The angst. The pining. The will-they-won't-they—"

"Viggo."

"Sorry. I digress. What was I saying? Oh, yeah. Friendship between you two—"

"Trust me, I've broached the subject. The friend part *only*. He didn't like that idea."

"Hmm." Viggo sighs, sounding thoughtful. "So you've got the hots for him, but you don't want to fall for him. He seems . . . invested in you, but he says he doesn't want to be your friend. And being at odds is no longer allowed, if you want to keep your captaincy."

"Yes."

"Shit, son. This has even me stumped."

My phone buzzes with a calendar reminder. I need to get downstairs to take the bus over to the facility so we can get our training in. "Viggo, lovely as this chat has been, I have to go do my job."

He feigns a long, drawn-out snore. "Jobs are overrated."

"Says the guy who has five."

He laughs. "All right. Go. Love you."

"Love you, too."

"Text me whenever, okay? You got this, Ollie."

Viggo hangs up before I can confess that I'm really not sure I've got this at all.

Thankfully, I have plenty to keep me distracted the rest of the day. We spend the late morning doing light technical training. Then we break for lunch, during which Gavin sits as far away from me as possible, avoiding me while scrolling through what history dictates is sports news on his phone. After that comes an afternoon spent scrimmaging, which, like the morning, we keep on the light side.

Dinner is more of the same: a catered healthy meal we all share. Normally, I'd enjoy it, except (1) it's the night before our first game of the season, which makes me a nauseous, anxious mess, and (2) I'm so viscerally aware of Gavin and the fact that we're about to go back to a room with only one bed, I barely taste the food I do manage to get down my throat.

Taking the elevator with a good portion of the team, I force a smile, throw out a joke that lightens the mood and makes the guys laugh. No one knows that inside, I'm freaking the hell out.

When Gavin unlocks the door with his key and shoves it open, he turns and acknowledges my existence for the first time since he stormed out of our room this morning. "I discreetly inquired about empty rooms with the manager," he says. "There are none."

My stomach drops. He's that eager to put distance between us. I shouldn't be surprised, shouldn't feel like I've taken a point-blank-range kick to the solar plexus. But I do.

"Ah, c'mon, Hayes," I tell him, breezing by, then turning, walking backward as I open my arms wide. "It'll be fun."

"*Fun.*" He lets the door fall shut behind him with an ominous thud and tosses his keycard onto the table. "Sure."

"Listen . . ." I plop onto the mattress, searching for the right words.

Gavin avoids my eyes, setting a container of food and plastic-ware on the table beside his keycard.

"I think it's fair to say things have . . . gotten out of hand the past few days," I tell him. "I admit that I've been juvenile with those pranks."

He still stares down at his feet. His jaw twitches. He rubs the bridge of his nose. "And?"

"And . . ." I sift through what Viggo and I talked about in our meandering way, what I pushed aside while I focused on drills and scrimmaging today. "I propose a truce. I'll try to chill out with the provocation. You'll try not to be a ginormous dick."

Gavin clucks his tongue and shrugs apologetically. "Can't help what nature gave me."

My mouth falls open. "Did you just crack a joke? And a *dick* joke?"

Silence hangs between us for a long, tense moment. "Seems so," he finally says, strolling over to his bag.

I watch him, stunned and intrigued. The faintest hint of pink is on his cheeks. Holy shit, Gavin Hayes is blushing. And I know I just promised not to purposefully get under his skin, but that was before I knew I could make him blush.

"Did you know," I ask him, "that, in absolute terms, the blue whale has the largest penis, *but* relative to its size, it is far outstripped by the barnacle, whose penis can stretch up to eight times the length of the barnacle itself? Pretty nifty evolutionary trick, if you think about it, given barnacles have to fix themselves—"

"Bergman, for the love of God, stop."

He's banging around in his bag. His cheeks are now *bright* red. "Whatcha looking for in there?" I ask.

"Something to gag you with," he mutters.

I lean back on my palms. "I'm not into gagging, Hayes. Blindfolds are more my thing."

He nearly drops his bag, saving it at the last minute with those freakish reflexes. "You," he says, "are a nuisance. A horny, inappropriate nuisance."

"You're the one who led with a dick joke," I point out.

He sighs as he turns with an armful of clothes in his hands. "Trust me, I regret it. Had I known it would lead us here, I never would have said a word. Now I'm going to shower. And while I'm in there, you're going to eat."

He grabs the container I noticed him carrying in, slaps the package of disposable plasticware on top of it, and shoves it into my hands. "You barely ate anything at dinner, and you'll be useless tomorrow if you don't carbo-load tonight."

"I was going to eat a high-carb bar," I mutter, hearing how peevish I sound as I open the container and unwrap my fork.

He arches an eyebrow. "Inadequate. Eat that. Then, when I come out of the shower, you're going to go in and shower next. After that, we are going to put all the pillows we don't need between us on that mattress, and not talk about penises belonging to anything on land or sea, and get some fucking sleep. Understood?"

I peer up at him, a massive bite of grilled chicken and pasta arrabiata giving me chipmunk cheeks. It tastes so much better now that my stomach's not knotted with nerves. "Anyone ever tell you you're bossy as hell?"

He smirks. "All the time. Now eat."

ELEVEN

Oliver

Playlist: "Lay Down," Son Little

Turns out eating a real meal makes me feel a lot better. So does a bit of teasing with Gavin, who emerges from the bathroom in one of his grayscale outfits—charcoal joggers, black T-shirt, dark hair dripping wet and curling at the ends.

My whole body tightens, an ache settling deep and low in my groin. Looking at him now, replaying when he told me to eat with the kind of concerned command that absolutely turns my crank, I spring off the bed and rush toward the bathroom before Gavin has the chance to notice how worked up I am.

I haven't had sex in years. I went through a phase that first year I was with the Galaxy when it felt like all I did was have sex, soaking up the attention, the appreciative gazes and touches and kisses. It felt good. I needed it. I needed to wipe away the sadness I associated with sex because of Bryce. I needed to have sex that was fun and carefree and simply for pleasure's sake, no feelings, no repeats. But then—and no, I'm not going to analyze the timing—by the time my second season started, it began to feel unsatisfying. What once made me happy started to hurt. I knew why. I was ready again, not for the rush of anonymous release and relief, but for familiarity, comfort, and cuddles . . .

Intimacy.

I've wanted it. I just haven't known how or where to find it. The team and all the publicity I do for it is time-consuming. I spend nearly the whole year training or playing. And unlike for most other folks, meeting and falling in love with a coworker is off the table for me. I won't risk anything imploding my joy in my profession or compromising its stability like I let my relationship with Bryce mess with my college career, even if it did end up leading me to make the best choice I could have in signing with the Galaxy rather than staying with UCLA and finishing my degree.

It makes sense, knowing this loneliness inside me, that I'd feel drawn to Gavin after such a long day, after he witnessed my vulnerability and actually showed me compassion for it.

But just because in a way it makes *sense* doesn't mean it's anything I'm acting on. Or acknowledging. I don't even rub one out in the shower, because I know what I'd fantasize about if I did. And that's exactly the direction I can't let my mind, body, or feelings wander.

Despite leaving me uncomfortable in the erection department, my chaste shower makes me feel otherwise pretty damn incredible, the hot water soothing my tense and sore muscles. Full of chicken and pasta arrabiata, blissed out from a steamy shower and my comfy clothes, I'm whistling happily to myself when I exit the bathroom.

Then my whistle dies like the sound of Wile E. Coyote plummeting to his doom.

My insides resemble that moment when poor Wile E. runs right off the ledge and hovers in the air, suspended in time, before he realizes he's in seriously deep shit.

Gavin sits on the bed—*our* bed—legs crossed at the ankles, bare feet, long, thick legs tight in his charcoal sweatpants. A book rests on his flat stomach as he frowns down at the page, then turns it. "Look your fill?" he asks without glancing up.

"Couldn't tell if that was you or your shadow," I quip.

He snorts. "At least I don't look like Rainbow Brite."

I'm wearing a lime-green shirt and navy-blue joggers. "I don't know who they are, but by name alone, they sound like a good time."

"A TV character from my childhood," he says, turning the page again. "Which is obviously before *your* time."

"There was color television back then?"

He rolls his eyes. "Piss off, Bergman."

"I want to hear about Rainbow Brite. Clearly, they have a great eye for color, since I remind you of them."

He peers up at me, eyebrow arched, before his expression blanks. His gaze darts halfway down my body before he refocuses on his book. "Go to bed."

My stomach knots as I stare down at him, as I remember what Viggo encouraged me to do.

Talk to him.

"First, we need to talk," I tell him.

Sighing heavily, he closes his book and tosses it onto the nightstand. "Let's have it, then."

I sit on the edge of my side of the bed, the middle of the mattress divided by a row of pillows Gavin must have lined up while I was in the shower. "I know you said we can't be friends. I know things are . . . strained between us."

He shifts slightly on the bed, then clears his throat. But he doesn't say anything.

I peer up to find him staring right at me. "I can accept that we won't be friendly, only civil. But this tension . . ."

Our eyes hold.

Gavin swallows thickly. "Yes," he says. His voice is low and rough.

Heat slips through my veins, warms me. I tamp it down, remind myself what I'm trying to do. "This tension is wearing me out. It's distracting and exhausting, and believe it or not, even though you think I'm a big old softie on the field, I don't want distractions or anything draining me, Hayes. I want to win. I want us being co-captains to make this team even better. I want to crush New England tomorrow, and I want to tear through our preseason undefeated. I can't do that when we're like this."

His eyes search mine. "Meaning?"

I lift my chin, steeling myself. "I want honesty and respect between us. No more games."

"No more games, as in, no more shit-looking peanut butter on my doorknob?"

"Or conditioner in the shampoo dispenser," I fire back.

He tips his head, his expression infuriatingly inscrutable. "Honesty when it comes to what?"

"Whatever's affecting our performance, our ability to be our best for the team. Any baggage we're bringing to the field, anything that's preventing us from having the united front that our team deserves."

Quiet holds between us. His jaw clenches. "Agreed."

"And respect?" I prompt.

"I'll respect you on the field." His mouth quirks. "But off it, I'm still going to bust your ass."

"Likewise. However, in front of the team, any and all public appearances—"

"Yes. We'll be respectful."

"Okay . . ." I stare down at my hands, picking at a cuticle. "Then, in the spirit of honesty and counting on your respect, I'm just going to . . . get this out."

He shifts again on the bed, facing me more fully. "I'm listening."

"I'm nervous," I admit. "I'm nervous to wear a captain's armband alongside one of the greatest players of all time. I'm nervous I'm going to fail to be a leader on the field. I'm nervous I'll disappoint everyone who's counting on me, and that I'll do it in front of a guy who really messed me up."

His expression sharpens. "What?"

"What do you mean, 'what'?"

He leans in, hands clasped between his legs. "Who messed you up? When?"

I'm taken aback by the intensity of his voice, the fire in his eyes. "Uh . . . one of the guys on New England's team. It was years ago, though. Water under the bridge, except when I play against him and it seems to kick up stuff."

"Name, Bergman. I want a name."

I search his eyes further, wishing he wasn't difficult to read. "Why?"

"Because you promised honesty, and I deserve to know."

I cross my arms over my chest. "I want some honesty from *you* first. A little *quid pro quo*, if you please."

He glares at me. I glare back.

Sighing, he leans against his pillow and peers out the window, the stadium's lights and streetlamps twinkling in the darkness. "I'm dealing with a few . . . chronic issues that didn't resolve in the off-season that have affected my play since we started and will affect my play tomorrow . . . indefinitely, really."

Pain, is what he's not saying. He's in pain. And if he's admitting it to me, if he's admitting it's affecting his performance—his speed, his agility—that means he's in agony.

My heart twists. For once, though, I stay quiet, listening, waiting. I can tell he's not done, that he needs time to say whatever else he wants me to know.

"I won't be terribly fast," he says, gaze pinned on the view outside. "When we're counter-attacking, on breakaways, don't count on me being right behind you."

I force an easy smile and lean on an elbow. "You like bossing from the command center anyway. I don't need you up top, cramping my style."

He gives me an *I see right through you* look. "And let me take the fucking set piece kicks. You shank the shit out of them, and becoming co-captain hasn't suddenly made you better outside twenty yards."

My mouth quirks. "Fair enough."

"Now," he says sternly. "A name, as promised."

I swallow, debating lying, but what good would it be to tell him the wrong name? Finally, I tell him, "Bryce Burrows."

"Bryce Burrows?" He grimaces. "That fucking diving wanker?"

I bite my lip. "He does tend to dive."

Retrieving his book from the nightstand, Gavin opens it to the dog-eared page. "Can't believe you were with *Burrows*. Christ."

"Well, that makes two of us." I now recognize what a waste of time Bryce was. I just wish I hadn't been a lovesick wreck after he cheated on me. I wish I could have had the perspective I have now so much sooner. And I wish the thought of seeing him again didn't kick up my insecurities, didn't wound my pride all over again.

But I'm not going to wallow in those negative thoughts. I'm going to remind myself what my therapist said—that cheating reflects the character of the cheater, not the cheated on—and I'm going to distract myself with comfort TV.

Scooping up the remote, I sink onto the bed and stretch out.

"Burrows," he mutters again, disgust painting his face. "Of all the people—"

"It was college," I say defensively. "I was young and—"

"Delusional?" he offers, flipping the page of his book a little roughly. "Indulging in a particularly masochistic phase?"

"He was charming and cute. I mean, he seemed like it back then."

Gavin snorts, shaking his head as he flips another page. "Whatever."

"I definitely had on rose-colored glasses when it came to him. I saw what I wanted to instead of what was there." Staring down at the remote, I slip my fingers across the buttons. "He's the last person I dated, actually. I don't really trust myself not to make the same mistake twice."

Gavin goes still for a moment before clearing his throat and focusing back on the book in his hand.

I turn on my side, still looking at him. "Who was the last person you dated?"

Sighing, Gavin glares down at me. "Really? Pillow talk?"

I shrug. "I'm just asking."

"Yes, well—" He turns the page in his book again and sniffs. "Seeing as I agreed to honesty only as it pertains to the team and our co-captaincy, I'm going to not so politely tell you to fuck off and go to sleep."

"Aw, c'mon. Let's bond. Swap heartbreak stories."

His jaw twitches. "I'd rather not."

"So you *do* have a heartbreak story?"

"Everyone has some kind of heartbreak story," he says gruffly.

My stomach flips. There's something wounded and guarded in how he's said that. Something raw in how tight he holds his book. I don't push the topic. I can recognize when someone has been hurt and doesn't want to hurt anymore by talking about it.

"What are you reading?" I ask, switching gears.

He lifts the book, showing me the cover. "Poetry. Carl Phillips."

"Is he any good?" I ask.

He turns the page again, eyes darting left–right. "Very."

"Is he queer?"

"Very," he says again.

"Nice." I drum my fingers on the bed and sigh, recognizing I've hit a wall with Gavin. Then again, we got a lot further than I thought we would. We still don't exactly get along or feel too happy about these close quarters, but at least some of that tension's gone. A swell of relief crests inside me. I feel calmer than I have in days.

That is, until I realize how warm I've gotten. I'm sweating. Gavin is, too.

"Is it blistering hot in here?" I ask. "Or is it just me?"

Gavin clears his throat. "No, you're right."

"Mark it down, folks. Gavin Hayes said I'm right about something."

He rolls his eyes. "I tried turning down the thermostat after my shower. I'm guessing it didn't work."

I hop off the bed and stroll over to the thermostat. "It's blinking. Is that bad?"

Gavin groans as he tosses aside his book. He eases off the bed stiffly, then stalks my way.

I peer closer at the thermostat. "Think it's broken."

He nudges past me to get a look for himself. "Fucking hell."

Sweat drips down his temple. It beads along my throat. It's so damn hot.

"We can ask them to come fix it," I offer.

Gavin turns away, shaking his head. "It's late. And even if they could get someone in here to fix it, I told you already, there are no free rooms. We'll be stuck, sitting up and waiting for the HVAC guy to leave, and we'll lose out on sleep."

"Well, I got news for you, Hayes—I won't be sleeping much in heat like this."

"We'll be fine," he says, sinking onto the bed, on top of the blankets again. Gavin rips off his shirt, and my mouth runs dry. Massive, round shoulders. Thick torso. Muscles rippling in his back as he tosses his shirt aside.

"Get that blanket off," he orders.

I'm too hot and bothered, in every sense of that phrase, to complain about how bossy he's being. While I drag the blanket down and off the bed, he rearranges the pillows along the middle of the bed again, then tugs the chain on the bedside lamp, bathing the room in nothing but moonlight and the glow of the stadium, painting the room pearly white.

"Are you taking off your pants, too?" I ask as I yank off my shirt.

"No. I thought I'd poach myself to a meaty boil in my sweat-pants all night, get no sleep because I'm so miserably hot, then play like shit tomorrow. Yes, I'm taking off my pants."

"Oh, thank God." I tear off my joggers and launch them into the air, where they land on my bag. Gavin's lying with his back to me, the sheet tucked neatly along his hips. "Want to tell ghost stories until we cool off?"

"Go to sleep, Bergman."

"I'm not tired."

"Jesus Christ," he growls.

I slip under the sheet, kicking one leg out on top of it to help me cool down. "I was gonna watch a little *Hamilton* until my eyes got tired. It's sort of my thing the night before a game. You mind?"

He sighs. "Be my guest. Just keep the volume down."

"You got it."

I turn on the TV and adjust my pillow behind me, careful not to disturb the fluffy pillow fort between us as I navigate my way to the recorded live performance. Picking up the little notepad they leave on the nightstand, I fan myself. Heat blasts from the radiators. It's stifling.

Just a few minutes into the opening number, Gavin turns gingerly onto his back, frowning at the TV. I hold my breath. If he says something snide about *Hamilton*, I'm going to lose it. I recognize I might be slightly keyed up about his potential critique of a favorite musical, but I'm sweaty and unsettled. Talking with Gavin was supposed to make me feel better, and while it eased the tension between us to a degree, now what I've gained has somehow made it worse.

Personal knowledge. A little trust. Now I know someone broke his heart and his body hurts and he reads poetry and he's begrudgingly watching *Hamilton*.

And I want to do something ridiculous. Like curl up next to him and tangle my legs with his, breathe in that spicy scent of his soap and the heat of his skin.

Gavin snorts derisively at something Aaron Burr says, and a fresh wave of annoyance crests through me. I hit the remote, turning the TV off.

"Oy!" he yells. "I was watching that."

I turn it back on, our eyes meeting in the TV's glow. "This is my happy place. No laughing at it. No condescending remarks. Got it?"

Gavin scowls at me. "C'mon, that line was a bit—"

"Not a word, Hayes, or off it goes. I'll watch it on my phone if I have to."

His eyes narrow. He flicks his gaze to the TV, then back to me, before settling into his pillows. "Fine. Carry on."

After the opening number finishes, I ask him, "Well?"

He shrugs. "It's surprisingly . . . poetic."

"That's because Lin-Manuel Miranda is a *genius*. Shakespeare and Sondheim in one body. It's all poetry."

"Shh," he chides as the next number starts, eyes not leaving the TV. "I'm trying to listen."

The familiar twisty blend of satisfaction and annoyance tangles inside my ribs. I grab a pillow and hug it to my chest. It's that or slug Gavin in the head.

TWELVE

Gavin

Playlist: "Animal," Neon Trees

Pain is as familiar to me as pulling air into my lungs, as opening my eyes when the sun breaks the horizon. What's far from familiar, what's been absent from my life for so long that I've forgotten its shape, its texture, teasing my senses, is pleasure.

For the first time in too long, pleasure is a glove wrapped around the bare-knuckle fist of my pain. It's in my hands, settled against warm, smooth skin. In my face, buried in sunlit softness, the scent of a sea breeze kissing my skin. In every inch of me, hard, hot, aching where I'm nestled against a firm, tight home.

God, it's been so long. So long since I felt anything but hurt. Gnawing in my joints, screaming in my muscles, a never-ending reverberation in my bones. My eyes prick with tears as pleasure floods every corner of me, a deluge of hot sunlight that thaws the icy edge of my pain, softens the raw-nerve throb that scrapes my senses each day until I collapse from exhaustion at night.

Now it's all pleasure. My hands, tangled tight with warm strength. My mouth, brushing velvet hot softness. My cock, nestled in snug. Oh, God. I'm going to come. It builds, deep inside me, tightens my body, makes it move. My breath sticks in my throat until it bursts free in a hoarse groan.

And then I hear it echoed back to me, softer, rasped. A moan that tugs at my awareness, draws me closer to the surface of wake-fulness.

Not yet. Not when it feels so good. Not when I'm so close.

I pant, helpless, desperate. But I'm not alone in those sounds. It's a symphony, a wave of crashing breaths, rushing gasps, and it drags me toward consciousness, cresting to a brilliant view as I open my eyes.

Sunlight floods the room. Sheets twisted around long limbs that are tangled with mine, golden hairs, suntanned skin, flexing muscles—

Fuck!

I snap upright. Well, I try to, but my back burns in protest, wrenching me down to the mattress along with the white sheet twisted snugly around my torso.

Oliver is asleep, head nestled on my forearm, golden hair spilled on the pillow like a halo. I stare down at us in horror. Thank fuck our underwear is still on, not that it's helping much. Oliver's boxer-brief-covered ass is nestled against my hip. His hand rests on his stomach, which is, I realize, where my hand was until a moment ago.

"Jesus," I whisper. A prayer. A plea. I have to extract myself, leave him unaware. I can't stay tangled up here a moment longer.

And of course, because I've just made this resolution, Oliver takes that opportunity to sigh in his sleep and turn toward me. He slips his long leg over mine; his hand glides over my stomach, then lower, grazing my boxer briefs' waistband. Which just barely holds back the tip of my painfully hard erection.

My stomach jerks beneath his touch. My brain is short-circuiting, refusing to tell my cock to stand down, to stop responding to the nudge of his thigh, the whisper of his breath across my skin, the glide of his hand along my happy trail.

"O-Oliver." It comes out so hoarse, I barely hear it. There's no way he has. I shut my eyes against the sweet agony of his touch, knowing how wrong this is, how desperately I need to make it stop.

"Hmm," he mutters sleepily, his mouth brushing my skin.

Oh, fuck. Fuck.

I grit my teeth and try to sit up again, to slip out of this Gordian knot of sheets that there's no hope of untwisting.

But in doing so, I smack my head against the headboard. Hard.

"Fuck me," I growl.

Oliver's eyes snap open, then widen in horror. Slowly, his gaze slides up my torso, before his eyes meet mine. "Ah!" he yells, thrashing violently back.

We're so tangled in the sheets, it brings me with him, wrenching my back painfully, then my knee. "Fuck!"

"Shit," he says hoarsely, wiggling frantically. "I'm sorry. I'm so sorry."

"Bergman, stop." He doesn't stop. He's thrashing, tugging, spinning, and it's hell. It's agony, because the tighter he tugs, the closer we get, our hips, groins, thighs. "Wait. Just—fuck!"

We tumble off the bed. I land on him but catch myself with my hands. It does nothing to keep us apart except to stop us from bashing faces. The sheet is knotted around us so tightly now, I feel him, every inch of him, hard and long, wedged right beside me, the material between us horribly inadequate.

Air saws out of Oliver's lungs, hands over his head, his hair splayed out on the dark carpet, like a comet streaking across the night sky. His eyes are wide, a sweet, unfairly beautiful blush on his cheeks. "Jesus," he whispers, shutting his eyes.

I'm speechless. I'm afraid to move. One single rub of my hips or his and I am in serious danger of spilling my load. My cock pulses; my balls are tight and heavy. Oliver exhales roughly, moving his hips enough for me to slam a hand down on his wrist, to make his eyes snap open.

"Do. Not. Move."

He stares up at me, frozen, mouth parted. Looking at him, I know that if God himself laid a new body before me, the cosmic forces of time to bend and reverse at my will, and made me choose between that and one taste of this man's lush mouth, I honestly cannot say that I would have the strength to make the sensible choice.

"Gavin," Oliver whispers.

I stare down at him. My name. On his lips. It's my undoing. "What?" My voice is hoarse. Breathless.

"We're . . . really stuck," he says quietly.

"I know. I just . . ." I shut my eyes. "Give me a minute."

He's silent for two pathetic seconds before a smoky laugh bursts out of his chest.

My eyes fly open. "What the fuck are you laughing about?"

His nose wrinkles, and he clutches my shoulders, smiling so wide as he laughs, it fucking wrecks me.

I stare down at him, tears leaking out of his eyes as his hands, warm and strong, clutch me, his throat rippling as he throws his head back and laughs even harder, so hard it curls his legs up, pins our hips even tighter.

A growl of annoyance rumbles out of me as Oliver laughs so hard he's shaking.

"S-sorry," he says between spasms of laughter. "God, you're heavy. I—" He laughs even harder.

"You are fucking useless," I grumble.

Oliver bursts out another laugh, but it cuts off abruptly as I brace myself on either side of his head, then wrench him with me, so that now *I'm* on my back, a movement that hurts like hell but is entirely worth it because now Oliver's on top of *me*.

His laughter dies off. His eyes search mine.

I stare up at him, my hands slipping between us to the tightest knot of fabric, stuck low between our hips. "Not so funny now?"

He laughs nervously. "It's, uh . . ." He swallows, tries to shift, which rubs our bodies together again. I hiss in a breath as his eyes snap shut. "Maybe not as funny as I originally thought."

"Exactly," I say through clenched teeth, attacking the knot between us. "Now be still."

For once, Oliver does as I ask, quiet, hands braced on either side of my head, as my hands make slow progress on the sheets, my knuckles brushing his flat stomach, making it jerk. Our breaths echo in the room. I glance up and watch his throat work in a swallow, fresh sweat beading down his skin.

Peering back down, I keep my eyes on my task and scour my brain for something horrible to knock down my erection, but nothing—*nothing*—is working. If Oliver's trying what I am, he's just as unsuccessful.

We're both as hard as when all this started, which I try very much not to think about.

Unfortunately it's all I can think about.

Finally, the knot gives. And then Oliver Bergman moves faster than I have ever seen him go, flying with a tangle of white sheets streaking behind him as he races toward the bathroom. "First dibs on the shower!" he yells.

The door slams.

I lie on the floor, willing my dick down, praying my body can forget what just happened.

It's absolutely hopeless.

I'm dressed and ready when Oliver reemerges from the bathroom, a towel slung low on his hips, his cheeks flushed. I tell myself that's from a hot shower, though the chances he took a hot shower when it's still sweltering in our room and he had an iron-hard erection are virtually nil.

I turn away, giving him privacy while pretending I'm actually reading the emails that roll in on my phone.

And then a few minutes later, he's there, close behind me, that familiar clean, warm scent wafting from his skin as he chews the last of a banana.

I turn around as we both say, "Sorry."

Oliver shakes his head, tossing the peel in the wastebasket. "It's okay. It was an accident."

I nod. "Right."

He glances away, cheeks heating, an infuriating smile on his face. He snorts a laugh.

"It's not funny." I grab the keycard and my bag, then wrench open the door.

He hikes his bag higher on his shoulder, strolling past me out into the hallway. "It's kinda funny."

"We're never talking about this ever again. It didn't happen."

He wrinkles his nose, staring up at the ceiling and completely ignoring me. "What I wanna know is, how did we move *that* many pillows? I mean, you had a veritable pillow Fort Knox between us."

"Bergman. Drop it."

He lifts his hand in surrender, and we stroll down the rest of the hallway in silence. When we get to the elevator, there's music playing, a funk song that Oliver starts shimmying to before he transitions to the chicken dance and uses his elbow to hit the button.

"What the fuck is wrong with you?"

"Lots," he says matter-of-factly. "But while using my elbow might look funny, it is good hygiene. Buttons, handles, doorknobs are germ central."

The elevator door opens with a ding, and I gently shove him in. "Captains of professional soccer teams don't do the chicken dance."

"This one here does. And the moonwalk." Oliver slides backward across the elevator. I am dangerously close to smiling.

"I'm embarrassed for you."

"C'mon, Hayes." He starts doing the floss. "It's the only way we're going to get past the awkward. We gotta dance our way there."

"Absolutely not."

He spins on his heels and starts the running man.

I bite my cheek and stare up at the ceiling. "You're a menace."

"But a smooth-moving one," he says on a wink. The door dings, and he moonwalks his way out of it, then promptly spins and straightens up professionally, a breezy smile in place. "Good morning, Donald!" he calls to the guy at the front desk.

"How the fuck do you know his name?"

"He's got this thing he's wearing called a name tag. You need spectacles, Hayes?"

I squint at it. The name tag's a blur. "The fuck you can read that."

"Believe it, my friend. Believe!"

"Bergman." I yank him by the collar toward the breakfast room. "Food first. Football later."

"Ah, right."

From there, the morning is a merciful blur of a bus ride and my pregame ritual of Tiger Balm and ice, wraps and braces, then warming up at the stadium.

Oliver is incorrigibly upbeat by the time we're out on the field, making the guys laugh, even putting Coach at ease long enough to smile at him before she returns to huddling over her clipboard with Rico and Jas.

Out of habit, she looks my way when it's time to round everyone up.

I'm about to holler my usual and get the team together, but watching Oliver, I pause. And then I call his name instead.

He glances up, then jogs over. "What's up, Co-cap?"

I blink at him, searching his expression. That's when I see it, what's hiding beneath the wide smile, the dance moves, and the nonstop chatter. He's nervous.

"You okay?" I ask.

"Nope," he says between clenched teeth. "I think I'm about to puke up that second plate of scrambled eggs. I knew I overdid it."

I set a hand around his neck, steadying him. "You can do this. Go puke if you have to, then come back here and say a word to the guys."

His eyes widen. "What? But you . . . you normally—"

"Grunt something threatening about how I'll knock their heads together if they don't leave it all on the field? Yes, I do. But now you do this, too."

He swallows thickly. "Okay, now I'm definitely gonna go puke."

I squeeze his neck, sliding my thumb along his skin. He stares at me as I tell him, "C'mon now. You've got this."

"Promise?" he says quietly.

I gently shove him away toward the toilets. "Promise."

"What was that about?" Coach asks.

I stare after Oliver, itching to follow him, to hold his hair out of his face, to rub his back, to squeeze his neck hard in reassurance so he doesn't start hyperventilating over a toilet. "Just fortifying our captainly bond." I throw her a blank look, hiding everything.

I hope.

Coach searches my eyes for a long moment before she turns back to the team, who're doing their normal warm-ups. A faint smile tips the corner of her mouth. "About damn time."

While I shut my eyes and stretch all the places Dan gave me hell this morning for not stretching well enough lately, I try not to stress over Oliver, but by the time he's jogging back my way, I'm about to shake him for taking so long and making me worry.

"Okay," he says, smiling tightly, his skin damp from splashing it off. "Wasn't too bad. Just a few rounds of hurling, threw some cold water on my face, and now I'm ready to go."

"All good, fellas?" Coach asks as she joins us.

I ease upright from my stretch. "Bergman's going to say a little something before we start," I explain to her.

She smiles wide. "Very nice. They could use a little upgrade from 'Don't fuck up, or I'll knock your heads together until you forget that shit effort you had the audacity to call soccer.'"

"Hey, it worked," Oliver says, "considering where we ended up last season."

"Mm-hmm." Coach flicks her braids over her shoulder. "Yet I'm sure Gavin would tell you that what works at one point in your career does not always work. Change is inevitable. And all good things come to an end."

I stare at her. She throws a fleeting glance at my wrapped ankle. And knee. My back, which is still periodically spasming from electrostimulation and is wrapped beneath my jersey, too. I decide I'm going to ignore what I know she's saying without saying.

"Oy!" I yell, calling the men in.

Once they're gathered around, Oliver throws on his widest, most reassuring smile. A twinge of guilt hits me. His optimism, his blithe always-all-right-ness—I gave him such shit for it, called it a lie. But I realize now it isn't a lie. It's . . . coping. It's how he survives.

I bend my knee slightly as my leg spasms, and a white-hot bolt of pain snaps up my leg. I peer down at my bandaged body, registering the aching soreness that's only about to get much worse, focusing on that instead of this fervent rush of *something* I won't name, won't admit, softening me, drawing me closer to Oliver as he clears his throat, stands tall, and addresses the team.

"Well, folks," he says. "This is it. We've got to start all over. We ended on the highest high last season. Feels pretty logical to think there's nowhere to go from here but down."

Coach gives him bug eyes.

He flashes her a smile. "But the truth is, we got ourselves to this highest height, and we can stay here." Glancing around, he clears his throat, sets his hands on his hips. "Where we get hung up is when we tell ourselves that we individually aren't at the level of play that we were last season. We fret that, personally, we aren't what we were, as fast as we were, as sharp with our shots, as quick with our reflexes."

Something twinges inside me. The words I confessed to him last night, my limitations, my weaknesses, it's like he's laying them in front of me one by one. And yet, glancing around, I'd say it looks like all of the men feel that way.

"Guess what, though?" he says. "That's the beautiful thing about soccer. Soccer isn't won by a 'me.' It's won by an 'us.'" He looks around. "You've got a weakness. Maybe a few. I know I do. But that doesn't matter. Because what I lack, he has." He points to me. To Ethan he says, "When you miss, who's got your back?"

"Andre," Ethan says.

He nods. "That's right. Amobi—" He turns to our goalie. "When it gets by you, what does Coach say?"

"It had to get past everyone else first," he says quietly.

"Yup." Oliver smiles wider. "I know you're nervous. I am. It's hard to start at the coveted height that everyone's hungry to get to so they can knock us off. Sports psychology tells us it's always easier to be the underdog than to be the one who's made it to the top and has to fight to stay there. Cool thing is, even though you're not where you were last season, someone else on this team is, and that game out there takes *all* of us, with all our weaknesses and strengths, to win." He glances around. "I have every belief we will."

Ben sniffles.

Carlo blinks away wetness in his eyes.

Amobi looks alarmingly emotional as he stares down at his big goalie gloves.

Oliver throws a panicked glance my way as he realizes his truly beautiful pep talk hit perhaps a little too close to emotional home.

I hold his eyes and hope he sees what I want him to. *Well done.*

"You heard him!" I bark, setting a hand in, watching more hands, every color and size, slap on top of mine. "Get your asses out there and get it done."

THIRTEEN

Oliver

Playlist: "Here We Go," WILD

Well. I talk a nice talk. Don't think it made much of a difference, though.

To say we are a tad ... out of sync would be generous. The game is in the eightieth minute, we're down 1–0, and we've messed up so many offensive opportunities, even *I'm* pissed, though of course I'm not showing it.

Neither is Gavin, and that's all you need to know. That's when you know it's bad—when Gavin Hayes is being quiet, eyes narrowed in fierce concentration, strategizing, racking his brain for what he can do to save this. He squints, black-coffee eyes sparkling with flecks of toffee as the sun hits them. A frigid wind flies through the stadium, whipping back his dark hair. He breathes out a puff of steam that I see as he backtracks in the midfield, receiving the ball, not even watching it roll to his feet as he stops it with one flawless touch that's as natural to him as that exhale from his lungs.

Finding me, he sends a pass that's perfect, threaded between two defenders, both of whom turn and run after me. They're fast. But I'm faster.

Unfortunately, they're onto me. New England's read our formation like a book and has every man marked. Santi's covered. Carlo, too. Ethan's fighting to give me something along the wing as he flies up from midfield, but his defender is right there, tight on him. I have nothing. It's just me.

That's when I remember what I told everyone. This game isn't won by one person. It's not all on my shoulders. It takes all of us.

Glancing back, I find Gavin, knowing exactly what I'm going to do.

I fake out my defenders and slip through them, pulling the ball in a Maradona and cutting central. I catch Gavin's eye, wishing we'd practiced this, wishing I'd said something when he told me not to expect him to be fast enough to be right behind me.

You can still get there, I should have told him. *I can buy you time.*

But then I realize I didn't have to tell him. He knows. Gavin knows exactly what I'm doing. No one's on him. He plays a commanding role that's pivotal in midfield but not the most vital position to cover when defending an offensive attack—at least, if that position's being held by anyone but Gavin. New England should know better, but they seem to be flying on autopilot, acting like he's some regular player who's not a threat outside thirty yards from the goal. Which he is. Oh, he is. And that's why I'm about to give him the ball.

I know Gavin Hayes's career better than I care to admit. I know his every goal, his every iconic game. I know the man has thighs like a goddamn truck for a reason. He might not have the speed that he used to, but he still has power; that man can crack a ball into the back of the net from here, easy.

As Gavin barrels down the field, I nutmeg my defender, cut past a guy chasing after me, and come face to face with Bryce. It's shocking how much *nothing* I feel as he bears down on me, as we hit bodies and I spin away with the ball, taunting him out of position, exposing the center of the field. I don't look at those russet curls of his and miss threading my fingers through them. I don't look into his bright blue eyes and remember staring into them as he touched me and begged me to touch him.

It's a sweet victory to feel nothing for someone who once made me feel everything I didn't want to—self-doubt, hurt, betrayal, loss. It's going to be an even sweeter victory when Gavin scores because of it.

And now he's here, having read me perfectly, exactly where I need him to be, as I send the ball in a lateral pass across the field, where it lands one step in front of him. I hold my breath, freeze as he plants his left foot and cracks the ball with one touch, a bullet through the air that hits its target at the top of the goal, rippling gloriously beneath the crossbar and down the back of the net.

Goal!

I sprint toward him—the whole team does, a crush of bodies throwing our arms around him.

As if he's soaking up the moment, Gavin's eyes are shut, his head bowed, as Amobi, the only one taller than him, ruffles his hair. But I see it when no one else does.

His smile. Small, private. The faintest tip of his mouth, but I'd swear if he'd shaved his beard down to scruff, I'd catch a deep dimple flashing in his cheek.

After he shoves the guys away good-naturedly, the group breaks apart. Gavin and I walk toward the center of the field.

I smile down at my cleats, watching them side by side with his. This camaraderie is what I dreamed might be possible when he first signed with the team. This is what I've been waiting for, for two long years.

We've scored together before; it's not the first time. But it's different today. Because of what he trusted me with, the way I knew where he'd be and what he needed, the way he leaned into my strength and leveraged it with his, and together we made something better than either of us could alone. Because of that trust, the kind of partnership I've wanted with him and almost gave up on having, we've tied up this game.

"Perfect pass," he says gruffly.

My head snaps up. I smile at him. "Perfect shot."

"That it was," he says, gaze trained ahead.

I roll my eyes. "Humble as ever."

"Nothing wrong with taking pride in what you can do, Bergman. You gain nothing by understating your abilities." He spins, stopping where I'll stand, just outside the circle, as we get ready for New England to kick off. Leaning in, he lowers his voice. "He's looking at you."

"Who?"

"That *wanker*."

"Ah. Bryce."

Gavin glances over my shoulder, locking eyes with him, glaring death. "Next time you have the ball, we do that play again," he says. "But this time you're going to keep running. I'll feed it back to you, and you do what you do best." He leans in, his mouth a whisper from my ear, the memory of this morning flooding my mind, his mouth against my neck, his breath warm and soft against my skin. His hand interlaced with mine.

I shiver.

"Put the ball in the back of the fucking net," he says quietly. "Remind that inveterate ass what he let get away and will never ever get back."

I stand there, speechless, at the top of the circle as he turns and strides deep into the midfield.

I'm still on a cloud as we walk to our cars in the parking lot back home in LA. After Gavin's goal to tie it up, I scored. We won. Not even another cross-country flight could bring my mood down.

"Will you ever stop dancing?" Gavin grumbles. There's amusement in his voice, faint, hidden, just like the smile after his goal.

I two-step my way across the parking lot, then spin, because there are honestly few things I delight in more than watching Gavin Hayes try to act like he doesn't enjoy the heck out of my dance moves. "Not anytime soon." I bounce to the rhythm of Carlo's music, which has started blasting in his car's stereo. To the beat, I tell Gavin, "Because there's no *I* in *team*, no *me* in *we*. You and I scored, got ourselves a victory!"

"And that's when you know you've watched too much *Hamilton*."

"Too much *Hamilton*?" I shimmy my shoulders while looking for my car. "No such thing."

Gavin rolls his eyes, brushing past me to unlock his gas guzzler. "Why the frown?" he asks.

I'm scanning the parking lot, and I don't see my hybrid anywhere. "Can't find my car." I pull out my phone as suspicion dawns and dread creeps through my limbs. My missing car has Viggo written all over it.

And there it is. A text as soon as I power on my phone, after having turned it off for our flight.

Viggo: Needed to make a long-distance bakery delivery and we both know my car is too delicate for such extended mileage, so I caught a cab to the parking lot and borrowed yours. Hopefully you can get a ride home! ;-)

Gavin opens his driver's side door but freezes when he sees me still standing next to him. "No lying about your car just so I'll give in to carpooling."

I pocket my phone, seething. Viggo's going to pay so bad for this. "It *would* give Mama Nature a little hug."

Gavin throws me a withering glare as he tosses his bag inside the Land Rover. "We played well together today—I'll give you that. Doesn't mean we're buddies, and it certainly doesn't mean we're carpooling."

"See, and here I was thinking, considering we woke up being big and bigger spoon this morning, a fifteen-minute car ride was peanuts in comparison—"

"Goddammit, Bergman." He pinches the bridge of his nose. "Fine. *Fine*, all right? We can discuss carpooling. But only if you swear never to bring that up ever again."

"You got yourself a deal." I beam a smile and offer him my hand to shake.

He glares down at my hand, then peers back up at me. "Get in your damn car and go home."

"Ooh, good idea. I'd love to caravan, except *my car isn't here.* My brother borrowed it."

Gavin sighs. "Well, then I suppose I'll have to drive you home. But we are *not* listening to any musicals."

FOURTEEN

Oliver

Playlist: "Fever to the Form," Nick Mulvey

I'm playing it cool with Viggo. I sent a nice No big deal text back while Gavin drove us home in silence and I stared out the window, fuming at my brother. I'm going to let Viggo think he didn't piss me the heck off, when he *knows* Gavin's my neighbor and he *knows* that taking my car meant Gavin would likely be the one to drive me home.

So much for his "you know your own path to happiness" bullshit. This was one of his "lead a horse to water" moments, and he might not have made me wear swimming trunks, but he certainly com- pelled me to carpool with my neighbor, who is also the guy I have a massive crush on, whom I was tangled up in bed with this morning and inadvertently rubbing hard-ons with while he extracted us and then made me promise never to talk about it.

And for that I will make Viggo pay dearly. I'm acting like I'm not upset with him only because revenge will be sweetest if he thinks I've let it go and he lets his guard down first.

After Gavin and I are home and have parted ways, I decide to try to lighten my mood with music, so I've got David Bowie's "Let's Dance" blasting in my house as I unpack my bag. Booty popping my way over to the hamper, I toss in my dirty clothes and freeze when I recognize a shirt that's not mine.

Not that it isn't obvious, given he and I were roommates, but I know by my senses alone whose it is. Black, soft. Clean and spicy.

Gavin's.

I stare at the shirt, weighing my options. I could wash it, then return it to him at practice, two days from now, since we have a rest day tomorrow.

Or I could take it over to his house . . . now.

I mean, sure, he might not miss it, but what if he does? What if it's his favorite shirt and not knowing where it is has him in agony?

Agony, listen to me.

I *suppose* I could simply text him and let him know that I have it. But then again, why waste the energy? Why make my cell phone work and contribute to the reckless waste of precious resources, when I can use my God-given legs, walk across the yard, bang on his door, and hopefully get lucky enough to see him in nothing but a towel and water dripping down his body as he scowls at me for having interrupted his post-flight shower?

Man, this is bad.

I'm a wreck. A horny, desperate wreck. I am six feet three inches of pure, unadulterated lust for that man, and this morning did nothing to help. His hands, his body, the persistent press of his cock along my ass, rubbing me. The way he groaned against my skin and clutched my hand tighter when I pressed back against him, when I was so sure it was a dream, everything I was feeling, how good it felt.

It's been a while—two years to be precise—but I can still remember plenty of what I've done sexually, the adventurous positions and explorations and wild marathon nights. I miss none of that the way I miss the pleasure of simply being touched by him, held by him.

And if that wasn't bad enough, this whole trip, from my episode on the flight to the end of our game, has made it worse, has made keeping my attraction to Gavin firmly contained in the box labeled *Very understandable but nevertheless a very bad idea to act on—DO NOT ACT ON!* even harder.

I know what I'm doing is a bad idea. But I can't seem to care. I can't stop myself as I slip on my sneakers, as I jog across his yard, as I stand at his back door, my fist hovering over the varnished wood . . . as I realize his door was left a tiny bit open, like he tried to shut it but didn't muscle it closed the whole way.

Well, good thing I came over here rather than calling. So there, universe. I made a smart decision after all.

Now comes the great debate: Do I tug the door shut, *then* knock? Or do I just go in and announce myself?

My choice is made for me when a pained shout emanates from deep in his house. I'm inside, the door slammed behind me, before I've made a conscious decision.

"Hayes?" I yell.

A groan sounds from a room to the right, past the kitchen. I make a guess and head to the end of the hall for what I anticipate is the primary bedroom, seeing as I'm pretty sure his house is a mirror layout of mine.

I open the door and stop short. Gavin lies on his bed, on his back. I got my wish, mostly, but I can't even enjoy it. Sure, he's in nothing but a pair of lightweight black pajama bottoms, hair wet, water beading on his massive chest as he scowls at me.

But he's obviously not okay.

"What in the *fuck* are you doing here?" he growls.

I lift his shirt, which is balled in my hand, and say intelligently, "Your shirt."

His gaze snaps from me to the shirt, then back to me. "Put it down, then leave."

I drop his shirt on the dresser beside me, which is—shocker—charcoal gray. "Not until I know you're okay."

"I'm fine," he snaps, pressing his palms into his eyes. His hands are trembling. He's in such terrible pain, he's shaking.

I'm fine.

Clearly he's not fine. And the fierce, unyielding part of me, the part Gavin rightly—much as I hate to admit—said that I hide and suppress so much to be my pleasant, friendly, easygoing self, will not be subdued right now.

"I don't believe you," I tell him.

He drops his hands, glaring at me. "Well, then even if I'm lying, it's still none of your business, is it?"

"Excuse me," I tell him, crossing the room, taking in the white walls, the black-and-white photos that are really beautiful, if not a little melancholy. "We promised we'd be honest about anything that affects the team—"

"A promise that I am swiftly and deeply regretting," he mutters.

I gesture to his supine position. "And this right here indicates that your body, which happens to be pretty pivotal to the team, is affected. So c'mon. Let's talk it out. Tell your old co-cap what's going on."

"Fucking hell," he groans.

I stop beside his bed. "Mind if I pull up a spot? We did a pretty good job talking this way yesterday."

He sighs, scowling up at me. "Fine."

Careful not to bounce the mattress and jostle his body, I ease onto the bed until I'm flat on my back like Gavin. Lacing my hands behind my head, I stare up at the ceiling, which is a boring cloud white, except for the textural swirls created when it was painted.

"I confess," I tell him, "that while I love a good skygazing, I don't quite see the appeal of the ceiling-gaze. But yours does have little swirly doodads adding texture, so I suppose I can work with that. Only thing is, I'm not one of those people who stares at the clouds and sees elephants and ice-cream cones and jellyfish, so I doubt I'll find anything of merit on your ceiling, but there's a first time for everything. When I look at clouds, all I see are big old cumulonimbus and stratus clouds, which, you know, are pretty cool on their own—condensed water vapor just floating up in the sky, waiting to let it all out and give Earth a good scrub-a-dub—"

"Bergman."

I glance his way.

Gavin's dark eyes hold mine, tight at the corners. "Why the fuck are you here?"

I swallow roughly, trying very hard not to look at his bare chest rising and falling, his hands clenched at his sides. "I told you, I had your shirt."

"Which you returned."

"And now we're gonna talk."

"You've talked. I've just talked. Now you can leave."

I search his eyes, knowing that I'm doing something I shouldn't. That staring at Gavin, feeling my heart crack open and flood my good sense with something dangerously close to affection, means I should leave. I should run out that door and just keep running and never look back. Because I swore to myself I wouldn't do this, wouldn't let myself care and want and long for anyone I played with or worked with, especially not him.

Pushing up on my elbow, I peer down at Gavin. "You've spoken, but you haven't talked, haven't said what needs to be said, and we both know it. Now listen, if embarrassment is stopping you, in this situation, you've got nothing to be ashamed of. Well, besides your stunning lack of appreciation for color in home decoration, but other than that—"

"It's my knee," he says tightly. "It gave out, and it burns like hell. Dan or Maria will sort it out tomorrow."

"Day after tomorrow," I remind him.

He sighs heavily. "Right."

"And until then?"

"I'll be able to stand in a little and hobble around until I can get a corticosteroid jabbed into it."

"Mmm, sounds lovely."

"The joys of aging." Slowly, he glances up at me.

I hold his eyes, examining them. Dark eyes flecked with gold. Thick dark lashes. His eyes seem to search mine, too. Something shifts between us, not unlike the moment the wind swirls in a new direction, replacing what was cool and bitter with a new, welcome warmth.

"You should leave," he says quietly.

He's right. I should. But I can't seem to make myself.

"I don't want to leave you alone to ceiling-gaze all by your lonesome."

"Being alone," he says, "is not the same as being lonesome."

"True. But sometimes it's nice not to be alone."

He stares up at me, those dark eyes unreadable, so frustratingly guarded. My heart slams in my chest. "You really should go," he says, digging his palms into his eyes again and exhaling slowly. I see how much he's hurting.

"Can I try to help first?"

He scoffs. "There's no help."

I have a few memories from growing up, when what was left of my dad's leg ached fiercely, phantom nerve pain, pain from his prosthesis chafing against his skin. I remember him lying on the sofa one evening, his head in my mom's lap, while the house swirled with chaos around them. Dinner waited. Extra TV time was allowed. I remember wondering, when it was his leg that hurt, why my mom didn't just focus on that. Sure, she massaged his spasming thigh muscle, the place where his skin and muscles had healed around severed bone.

But she spent much more time slipping her fingers through his hair, down his neck, pressing kisses to his face, his temple, whispering words we weren't meant to hear that made Dad groan and smile. I didn't understand why.

Now that I'm older, after having broken bones and sprained joints, after seeing the people I love hurt and heal, I understand. So often, pain isn't something we can cure or prevent, and that's not why we lean into the people we love. We don't need them to fix it for us or ask about all the things we could have done to avoid it or the ways we've tried to remedy it. We just need them to see us, to find ways to love us, not in spite of our pain, but through it.

Comfort was what my mom taught me to give and receive—not in an attempt to fix pain, but to love and be loved with humanizing touch, to give soothing pleasure where it could be had. The simple joy of having your hair played with, muscles that weren't on fire and bones that weren't broken stroked and kneaded and reminded: *Pain is part of you, but it's not all of you. You're hurting and you're here, and I am, too.*

"I know there's no fixing it," I tell him quietly. "That's why I only want to *help*. Helping is different." I lift a hand, reaching for his hair, wet from his shower, then stop myself. "Can I touch you?"

Gavin opens his eyes, then glares up at me. He's silent for a long, tense minute. "Yes," he finally says. "But lay so much as a finger on my knee, and I will rip your arm off."

"Ten-four." I scooch closer, then swipe my finger across his temple, over his nose, around his mouth. I trace his features, strong and sharp as if carved in stone. His eyes flutter shut, and a soft, slow breath eases out of him.

Next, I slip my fingers through his hair in slow, rhythmic strokes, scraping across his scalp, before moving on to massage his temples.

"Fuck," he groans.

I pause. "Of the good or bad variety?"

"Very good," he says hoarsely.

A smile lifts my mouth as I do it again. "Good."

After a few minutes of that, I drift my hands down his neck, kneading the tight muscles joining his shoulders.

A pleased groan rolls out of him.

Using one hand to scrape my fingers softly across his scalp again, I roll the other over his shoulder, down his arm. Air saws in and out of his lungs. His eyes scrunch tight. "What are you doing?" he whispers.

"Helping," I tell him, staring down at his severe features. Thick dark brows, lashes, beard—a beard that I'm still convinced hides a dimple. His nose just slightly off-center from when a player from Arsenal broke it with his elbow during a corner kick eight years ago.

I remember vividly watching the game, watching blood pour down Gavin's face, while he blankly stared ahead and they shoved cotton up his shattered nose. Like he felt nothing, like pain was the same as existing.

"Still feel okay?" I ask.

He nods slowly.

For a while, I keep my mouth shut and watch him for signs of what feels great and what doesn't. When it seems like I've exhausted all the places I can make him feel good without touching what will feel bad, I give his shoulders one last squeeze. "There."

Just when I'm about to pull away, his hand snaps up and wraps around my wrist, freezing me.

Time stretches. Our gazes hold. My pulse pounds in my ears.

His thumb strokes my wrist. "Thank you," he says quietly.

I need to leave. I need to run and keep running. But instead, Gavin's holding my wrist, then he's tugging me closer, and then my hand is cupping his face, my head bending.

Our mouths brush—soft, tentative. Light dances behind my eyes as I sigh against his mouth, as he sighs against mine. The sound of contentment. Sweet relief. Coming home.

His lips are firm and warm, his beard soft as I sip his mouth, as he releases my wrist and sinks a hand into my hair. A rough, deep moan leaves him as I sweep my tongue against his, wet, hot. I taste him and feel like I've swallowed sunlight. I need more. I need everything.

As if he's read my mind, Gavin wraps an arm around me, hauling me against him, pulling us close. He hisses in a breath as he turns fully and bends his knee.

I pull away, worried, glancing down at his leg. "Are you—"

"Shut up," he says hoarsely, cupping my head, drawing me tight inside his arms. "I'm fine."

I wrap my hand around his waist, up his bare back, my fingertips dancing over the terrain of hard, powerful muscles and smooth, warm skin. He shivers and exhales roughly in my mouth as I kiss him again, warm and slick, warring for control.

He kisses like I knew he would—harsh and hard one moment; then another, slow and tender. I kiss him back like he must have known I would, too, sweet and teasing, the next demanding and fierce. Gavin's hand slips down my waist and grips my ass, holding me against him. Our chests crush together, our hips move as we rub against each other, as our kisses build in speed and rhythm.

"Just this once," he says.

I nod. "Just once."

"Then tomorrow," he says between kisses, biting my lip, chasing it with his tongue, before he begins kissing my jaw, my neck. "At practice, we'll be what we were."

I moan as he grips my ass hard and moves me against him. "Day after tomorrow—"

"God," he says roughly, hauling me so tight against him I can barely breathe. "God, you feel so good, taste so good. So much better than I—" He kisses me harder, stopping himself, but it's not difficult to fill in the rest of that sentence.

I smile against his mouth. "Been thinking about this, huh, Hayes?"

"Piss off." He cups my jaw and holds it while he fucks my mouth with his tongue. "Like you haven't, too."

"Maybe just a little bit."

Groaning, he presses his mouth to mine, this time hard and slow. He holds my face, my hips. And that's when I realize what this is. A last kiss. A goodbye kiss. A no-more kiss.

On a slow, unsteady exhale, he cups my cheek, slides his thumb along my bottom lip as he stares into my eyes. And then he leans in, as if impulsively, for one more kiss, a bite of my bottom lip that he drags between his teeth, before he lets go.

I stare at him, hearing my uneven breathing, feeling heat flame in my cheeks. "Why did you—"

His finger stops my mouth. His eyes hold mine. "You're going to go home now. And I'm going to stay here."

"But—"

"And I will be fine."

I swallow against the knot of *something* in my throat, a bittersweet pang smarting against my ribs.

"And when I see you in two days," he says, "this will be behind us."

I stare at him. Hating that he's right. That as incredible as this was, it's the worst possible thing I could do. I have to be wise. I can't get sucked into caring about someone on the team and repeating the same mistake I made with Bryce.

Even though I know Gavin's not Bryce, it's too much of a risk. So what if we make out like champs? So what if at some point it snuck up on me—the mutual needling and provoking and smack-downs turning into something that turned me on? Even if we kept it to only off-hours, in our homes, even if we tried everything to keep it out of our minds and awareness when we practiced and trained and played games and did promotional stints, it could get away from us and compromise our captaincies, the team, the season. One of us could lose interest; the other could want more. We might slip up in front of the team and have to answer for breaking what I'm not even sure *are* the rules about players being together.

So much could go wrong. Gavin's right. This has to stop.

"C'mon." He sits up slowly, blanching with the pain as he swings his legs off the bed and stands. I scramble off his bed, following as he limps only slightly down the hallway before he turns into his kitchen and opens the back door.

I don't know how to exit this situation well. My insides are a blender of countless emotions, shredded by my anxiety until they're a messy, inextricable blur.

"Go on, then," he says quietly, slipping his hand around my back, low and gentle. "Go."

I glance from the view of his backyard, back to him, recognizing the moment as a threshold in more than one sense of the word. I want to stay and kiss him and ice his knee and draw him a bath and make him laugh and take care of him.

And I want to push him far away and pretend like none of this ever happened, like he didn't show me a different side of the sharp, harsh man he's been, revealing some of what's beneath that brutally cold facade.

Someone who cares. Who bleeds and hurts and fears.

Just like me.

I stare at him for a long moment. And he stares right back at me, his hand warm on my back, its pressure building every second that I stand there, pushing me where I know I need to go.

Finally, I force myself to do what I promised myself I would. I walk away. As I step onto his porch, I mentally congratulate myself. I've done what I failed to do before. I drew a boundary, put a firm stop to going where I shouldn't with a teammate.

I should be proud of myself. I should be relieved.

But when Gavin's door quietly slips shut behind me, I don't feel proud or relieved at all.

FIFTEEN

Gavin

Playlist: "Lonely Boy," The Black Keys

"Well, that was an experience," I tell Mitch. "Cough up the keys, old man. And let's pray the next time I fuck up my knee and need a steroid injection, it's the left one and not my gas leg again."

"You don't like my driving, that's your problem," Mitch says, slapping the keys into my palm.

I snort. "It's not a matter of *liking*. It was a matter of not wanting to die before I even got to the doctor's."

He waves his hand dismissively, helping himself to a glass of water from my kitchen. "Serves you right. You should have asked Oliver."

His name sends a bolt of heat searing through me. I shut my eyes, doing everything I can to block out the memory of kissing him, feeling him, tasting him.

I can't tell Mitch there was no way in hell I was asking Oliver after last night, when I made out with him on my bed, fucked his mouth with my tongue the way I wanted to fuck *him*, then kicked him out after telling him this was a one-time thing that we were going to put firmly behind us, and that, needless to say, keeping my distance is best right now.

So instead, I ask him, "Why do that when I have you?"

He sighs, scrubbing his face. "Because you need to rely on other people. Where's your family? Where are your friends?"

"My family? Exactly where I want them," I tell him dryly. "And friends?" I gesture to him, to the table where the group plays poker. "Right here. What more could I ask for?"

Mitch scowls at me.

"If you're that upset about driving me," I tell him, "you could have said no. Are you pissed about walking home? I told you I could manage to drop you off at your place and drive the short distance back to mine."

"No! That's not it." He drops onto a kitchen stool as I walk gingerly past him and toss my keys onto the counter.

"Then what is your point, Mitchell?"

"My point," he says sharply, "is that I'm tired of enabling your isolationist bullshit."

I stare at him. "Isolationist bullshit? You have no idea what you're talking about."

He nods. "You make sure of it. All I can do is read between the lines."

"You really want to hear my shit, Mitchell?"

He shrugs. "Yeah. But I'm not the person you should confide in. At least, not the only one, and certainly not the first."

I walk slowly into my living room, toward the sofa that's calling my name. "And to whom should I be confiding my deepest, darkest secrets?"

"People your own damn age," he says. "People who you build a life with. Friends. Family. Friends who become family."

Groaning, I ease onto the sofa and lift my leg, propping it on a pillow. Wilde meows at me like I'm supposed to do something for him when I'm laid up like this. "What do you want?" I ask him. "There's food in your bowl. Shoes I just took off for you to piss in."

He meows again, then weirdly bounds up the couch and settles on my chest, purring. He's a crotchety fucker, so he'll probably end up sinking his claws into me, but for the time being, I savor the rumble of his purr and scratch his fluffy black-and-white cheeks.

"Hardly any point in forming relationships," I tell Mitch, circling back to our conversation. "I'll be laid flat in a game one of these days soon and won't get back up. After that, I'll leave."

He arches a silvery eyebrow. "Nice to know you plan to split when shit hits the fan."

I glare at him. "I'll keep in touch with you when the time comes. Pay a visit here and there."

"Exactly." He bangs his fist on the counter. "Because I matter to you. And anyone else you built a relationship with here would matter to you, too."

It's on the tip of my tongue to explain myself, but to explain that would be to reveal just how badly I hurt, how deeply I already live in anticipatory pain, how much I dread.

But you're not part of the world that I'll have lost, I almost tell him. *You won't be a reminder of what I'll never have or be, ever again.*

"It's different with you."

He shakes his head, standing from his stool and strolling toward my front door. "I'm outta here."

"Mitch—"

"Nope. You're bad for my blood pressure when you're like this."

"Now, hold on." I try to sit up from the sofa, but Wilde sinks his claws into me just as Mitch shoves me back down with surprising strength. "Jesus. Now you're ganging up on me."

"You," he says, leaning in and jabbing me in the chest, "need to do some thinking. And stop being so damn stubborn."

I frown up at him. "I'm not stubborn. I'm practical."

He rolls his eyes. "See you for poker tonight, knucklehead. Rest up, because you have an ass-whupping coming your way."

"Where's the Skittles?" Jorge yells from the pantry.

"Well stocked at the mini-mart down the road," I tell him,

shuffling the cards. They land with a satisfying snap on the table. "But alas, not here."

Jorge pokes his pink-haired head out of the pantry and frowns at me. "I ask for one thing. *One* thing. Skittles."

I point a thumb at Itsuki. "Don't look at me."

Itsuki sits primly in his seat, sipping his lemon seltzer, and says, "I'm not driving you to the dentist again the day after poker because you managed to pull out another tooth on those things. They're too sticky."

Jorge levels a glare at him. "What's the point of having teeth if I can't eat what I want, hmm?" His rant switches to Spanish as he dives back in the pantry, searching for other goodies.

"It's not so bad," Jim says while stacking chips. "Let's think of some alternatives."

"There are none!" Jorge yells from the pantry.

"Sure there are." Lou sniffs, frowning in thought. "Strawberry applesauce."

Jim snorts. "Chocolate pudding."

Itsuki hides a laugh behind his hand, then says, "Prune juice!"

Jorge exits the pantry, slamming the door behind him and looking thunderous. "You're all dead to me."

"C'mon, now," I tell him, patting his place at the table. "Sit down and have your fancy pink lemonade and sort your cards. Takes you long enough."

"Speaking of taking long," Lou grumps, glancing at his wristwatch. "Where's Mitch?"

I fumble the cards slightly but catch them in time to shuffle them together. Parting on bad terms with the old man left me uneasy. I glance up at the wall-mounted clock in my living room, frowning. He's fifteen minutes late. Mitch is never late.

"Dunno," I tell Lou. "He said he'd be here."

Just as I finish my sentence, the back door opens.

And my stomach plummets to the soles of my feet.

There stands Mitch. And by his side . . .

Oliver.

"'Bout time!" Jim hollers. "Get your ass over here. We gotta start playing before Gavin shuffles the tits off the queens."

Mitch waves a hand dismissively, shutting the door behind Oliver, who's giving me a wide-eyed, deer-in-the-headlights look. I push up from the table with relatively more comfort and ease than I had this morning, thanks to that steroid injection, a result I can't always count on. Sometimes the pain is worse for a day or two after the injection before relief finally kicks in; other merciful, less frequent times, I feel relief much sooner. Thankfully, this is one of those rare times, and now the pain in my knee is muted to a dull, persistent but not incapacitating ache.

"Mitchell," I say tightly. "Why don't you join our friends at the table."

Mitch flashes me a wide smile, mischief twinkling in his eyes. "Look who I found outside. Isn't it great that Ollie could join us?"

I clap Mitch on the back and give his shoulder a good warning squeeze. "A delight."

"I'll just go get settled in," he says to Oliver. Then he turns to me and mimes tipping his hat.

Soon as he's out of earshot, Oliver says frantically, voice low, "I tried very, very hard to tell him no, but he's—"

"A goddamned bulldozer when he sets his mind to something."

Oliver nods. "I was just weeding out back, and he shows up in my yard, starts small-talking, which, you know, I'm cool with. He's a nice guy, easy to talk to. Then he pulls some wizardy conversational sleight of hand, and next thing I know, he's saying he's so glad I can come play poker with you guys. I kept trying to politely decline, said I had yard work, and then he *gets down on his knees and starts weeding with me,*" Oliver hisses. "Said 'With two of us working, we'll be done twice as fast, so you can join us!'"

I sigh. "Sounds like Mitchell."

"Who's this?" Jorge barges in, clasping Oliver's shoulders. He looks him up and down. "He is *lovely.*"

"*He,*" I tell Jorge, plucking his hands off Oliver's shoulders, "is a person who you are treating like a doll."

Jorge wiggles his eyebrows. "Well, look at him. He *is* a doll. Hel*lo.*"

I roll my eyes. "And he's *here.* Behave yourself."

Oliver clears his throat, then flashes his usual megawatt smile as he offers his hand. "Oliver Bergman. Nice to meet you."

"Jorge Delgado." Jorge crushes him in a hug instead. "So good to meet you, Oliver! Ollie! Oliverio! What a perfect name for a perfect man. Come in! Come in! Jim, make yourself useful and grab a chair."

"Already on it!" Jim calls, wedging a chair between his seat and mine. Of fucking course. I glare at Jim, who throws me an embarrassingly obvious wink.

Once Jorge's finally released Oliver and hurried off to rearrange the table so there's room for another, I tell Oliver, "You really don't have to stay."

He scrubs the back of his neck, eyes down on his dirt-stained sneakers. "I won't if you don't want me to."

God, if only it were that easy. I should tell him that I want him to leave. That it's best if he goes home and we keep our lives as separate as possible, even if in only these small ways, given how much practice, training, matches, co-captaining puts us together. I should tell him that what we did yesterday was a mistake that I regret and that we will never repeat. I should see him out, shut that door behind him, and shut out the memories of last night, the longing they unlocked, once and for all.

But I can't fucking make myself do it. I can't make myself keep pushing Oliver away when finally drawing him close last night felt so fucking good after months of nothing but pain and misery stretched together. I can't turn away someone who gave me comfort last night, even when I was snarling and snapping, whom I've held at arm's length for so long, fixated on the parts of him that are easy to resent him for—his youth, his health, his carefree happiness—instead of seeing what lies beneath: someone who battles anxiety's crushing pressure, who tries so hard to be good and helpful and hopeful and generous toward everyone yet is so mercilessly hard on himself.

Staring at him, I tell myself what I told us both last night—*Just this once.* Then tomorrow, we'll reset boundaries. Neighbors but not neighborly. Co-captains but not confidants. Civil. Tidy. Safe.

Just tonight, only tonight, I want to be reckless.

"Stay," I tell him. "If you want. But I'll warn you, we're a cutthroat bunch."

Oliver's head snaps up. His eyes sparkle as he smiles. "Duly warned."

"Get over here, Ollie!" Mitch calls. "You ever played poker? Need us to teach you the ropes?"

Oliver shrugs as he toes off his dirty sneakers and sets them aside. "It's been a while," he says, tugging his hair back into one of those tiny sunshine spurts of a ponytail as he walks through the kitchen. "I could probably use a refresher."

As he sits and joins the guys at the table, smiling and shaking hands, I have the most unnerving feeling that I've just made a very big mistake.

"Goddammit!" Jim throws down his cards. "What is this shit? He won *again*?"

Oliver rakes in a massive pile of chips, a coy smile on his face. "Beginner's luck."

"Beginner's luck, my ass." Lou snorts, sitting back in his seat as he folds his arms over his belly. "If you're a 'beginner' poker player, I'll eat my shoe."

Oliver's smile deepens. He shrugs. "Beginner-ish."

Mitch slaps his thigh and wheezes a laugh, downright delighted by this turn of events.

Jim reaches around Oliver and slugs my arm. "A little warning that I was about to get hustled out of my retirement would have been nice!"

"Honestly, Jim." Itsuki rolls his eyes. "We play for pennies."

"Pennies add up," Jim grumbles.

Oliver leans his way and says, "Don't worry. I'm a pretty reckless player. I'm sure I'll lose it all soon in spectacular fashion."

When he straightens, his thigh brushes mine for the eight millionth time since we all sat down, making a rush of heat blaze across my skin and settle low and hot in my groin. I fist a handful of chips and grit my teeth.

Mitch smiles across the table like he knows exactly why I'm suffering. I glare at him.

"Last hand?" Lou asks.

"Why, old man?" Jim says, accepting his cards as Mitch deals. "Past your bedtime?"

Lou throws him a colorful gesture. "Unlike you, I have a social life outside this vagabond crew. In fact—" He riffles around the trail mix I set out, then plucks an M&M from among the nuts and dried fruit. "I have a date."

Jorge's eyes widen. He smacks Lou in the chest. "And why are we just hearing about this?"

Lou shrugs. "It's just a first date. A cup of late-night decaf and a piece of lemon meringue pie at Betty's Diner. It may be a train wreck."

"Or it could be the start of something wonderful," Itsuki says encouragingly.

Lou shrugs again. "Could be."

"Well, at least *someone* here is living it up as he should," Mitch says pointedly, staring at me. If I wasn't worried I'd break his leg, I'd kick him under the table, right in the shin.

"Awfully fine talk coming from a man who refuses to date, himself," I remind him.

Mitch sniffs. "Who says I'm not?"

All our mouths drop open. For as long as I've known Mitch—and that's nearly two years now—he's only ever spoken of his late wife, Janie, in frankly reverent terms. He's never flirted with a soul, never given the faintest hint of interest in another person.

"Mitchell Thomas O'Connor." I set my elbows on the table. "Spill the beans."

"I have a pen pal," he says primly, adjusting his cards.

"It's cute you think that's all you're gonna get away with saying." Jorge taps the table. "Let's have it."

Mitch sighs, eyes still on his cards. "She and I grew up together, went to the same school all the way through high school, then lost touch once I joined the Navy. We bumped into each other at a reunion years ago, introduced each other to our spouses, parted then on friendly terms. I don't know who started it first, but we began sending Christmas cards, kept in touch that way. When she heard Janie had passed, she sent a very nice note. It took me a while to write back to everyone who'd sent their condolences, and ever since then, we've been writing to each other. And that's all I'm saying tonight."

Lou hoots as Jorge makes kissy sounds. Itsuki clasps Mitch's hand and says, "How romantic."

Jim stares at Mitch, looking deeply betrayed. "What happened to the Brotherhood of Wild and Winsome Widowers!"

I snort. "What a moniker."

Mitch shrugs. "The times, they are a-changin'."

"Great song," Oliver says as he sorts his cards. Quietly, he starts humming the Bob Dylan tune like he doesn't even know he's doing it.

Jim turns toward Oliver, eyes gleaming hungrily. "Do we have a music lover on our hands? One who actually appreciates *real* music? Not the crap kids these days listen to—the only exception being my queens, Adele and Kelly Clarkson, because damn, can those women sing."

Oliver smiles his way. "Ah, don't be too hard on modern music. There's lots of good stuff out there. But . . ." He scrubs the back of his neck. His nervous tic, I've recently figured out. I nearly have to sit on my hand so I don't cup his neck, soothe him the way that I did before he gave his first pregame pep talk.

What is *wrong* with me?

"Yeah," Oliver finally says. "I like music. All kinds. Plenty of oldies—no offense."

"None taken," Lou says, leaning in. "How oldies we talking?"

"Gershwin, Ella, Armstrong, Sinatra," Oliver tells him. "Big band's a great time. My little sister got me into it when she was obsessed with learning how to swing dance and wanted a partner to practice with, so that's got a soft spot in my heart."

My stomach knots. He has another sister. Not just the older one who comes to the complex with his niece. And I give a shit that I didn't know this. God, this is bad—no, ridiculous. I don't care if he has one sister or ten. I don't.

If I tell myself this enough, it will get through my thick skull.

"I think there's something to love about every music era," Oliver's telling the group as I tune back in. "It reflects what was happening at that time culturally, psychosocially. Music speaks to human experience and speaks for it. When we appreciate that, we appreciate so many people's perspectives on life. Know what I mean?"

Jim stands, throwing down his cards. "That's it, Ollie. C'mon."

Oliver glances up warily at Jim. "Um. Where?"

"See that TV?" Jim says, pointing to my living room.

Oliver peers that way. "Well, yes, I do, Jim."

"That TV," he says, "has a karaoke station hookup."

"Oh, Christ," I mutter. "No, James. No karaoke."

"Hush, you," Mitch chides as he scoots out his chair and ambles into the living room. The TV powers on. Mitch and Jim argue over the remote as they click through the programs to connect with the karaoke machine that I caved and bought last year when it became obvious Jim was going to serenade us, with or without a microphone in his hand and background music playing, so might as well indulge the man.

Oliver turns toward me, our knees bumping. The memory of when our knees last bumped, when his leg slid against mine on my bed, swallows up every other thought. I'm foolishly staring at his mouth, remembering how fucking good it felt to drag that bottom lip between my teeth, when he says, "I can conveniently receive a very urgent phone call and make my exit if you want."

"Ollie!" Jim calls. "Let's go! I got Sinatra cued up. You and me, kid, we're gonna bring down the house."

I glance among the group. Jorge and Itsuki have started doing the foxtrot as the opening bars of "Fly Me to the Moon" fill the speakers. Lou's on his hands and knees in front of the entertainment center, griping about how Jim plugged in the microphone wrong.

"Unfortunately," I tell Oliver, "when it comes to these pains in my ass, I am a giant, pathetic pushover. Better give them what they want and join them."

A smile breaks on Oliver's face. "This is your last chance to kick me out before things become very obnoxious."

I bite back a smile and settle into my chair, arms folded. "Go on, then. Do your worst."

SIXTEEN

Gavin

Playlist: "Fly Me to the Moon," Imaginary Future

Lou's Chevy lumbers down the road on a cheery trio of honks, hands waving out the windows.

"Thank God." I slam the door behind me and scrub my face.

When my hands drop, the view makes my heart trip, then lurch. Oliver, framed in the archway from my living room to the open-concept kitchen and dining area. He shimmies his way around the table while gathering plates, glasses, seltzer cans, and snack bowls. I recognize some of the same absurd moves he pulled at the hotel to try to dispel the awkwardness after the Great Bedsheet Catastrophe, as he circles the table and hums "Fly Me to the Moon."

I stare at him, fighting a smile as I remember him with Jim, those two serenading each other.

Oliver glances up and sees me, then nearly drops his armful. "Shoot." He saves it at the last minute.

I push off the door, forcing my expression into its usual blank inscrutability.

"You don't have to do that," I tell him, gathering what's left on the table. "I'll clean up."

"I don't mind." He turns and sets everything carefully in the sink.

I stare at him as he stands with his back to me, running water, squirting soap onto the sponge. It's infuriating that it's such a simple moment that holds the weight of the world inside it.

What I've feared and fought since the moment I first saw him is here, in front of me, as real as the heart beating in my chest, beating faster and faster, as I watch him.

This infuriating, aggravating, irksome man matters to me.

He more than "matters" to you, a dangerous, no-good voice whispers in my head. I silence it, bury it.

I can't let *matters* become more. Not when a lifetime exists between us, not when soon this team, this game, will be lost to me and it will be his whole world.

Better to keep what I feel to myself. To protect him. To protect us both.

But God, if I could just savor him one more time before I shut away this aching desire once and for all—

No. I shouldn't. It's not right to ask him for that, when lust and resentment tangle in my chest as I stare at him. It would be wrong to prey upon the impulsivity of what I'll concede seems to be a mutual, very intense attraction. It would be wrong to spin him around and pin him against the sink and kiss him slow and deep until we're both dizzy and desperate, until hands wander and the bedroom right down the hall lures us like a siren toward destruction.

"Thanks, by the way," Oliver says quietly, snapping me from my thoughts.

Stepping next to him, I add the last of the dishes I was holding to the sudsy water. "For what?"

"Asking me to stay."

I pick up a dish he's rinsed and dry it, leaning a hip against the counter as I watch him in profile. The long line of his nose. His mouth pursed in concentration. The play of light on the scruff of his closely shaved beard. "Technically, the others asked you to stay. I just indulged them."

He glances at me, a smirk on his face. "Of course. Well, thank you anyway. Despite you being a karaoke curmudgeon, I had fun."

My heart twists. I want to yank him by the shirt and kiss that smirk right off his face. I want to make him drop the dish in his hands and hear it crack like his resolve until he's touching me as frantically as I want to touch him.

But instead, I pick up another dish and dry it. "You really don't need to do this. You can go home. Get some rest. We're back at it bright and early tomorrow."

Oliver shrugs.

I grit my teeth, battling so hard for control, to stop myself from taking what I shouldn't. Abruptly, I slap my hand down on the faucet, shutting off the water. "You should go home, Oliver."

He stares down at the bowl in his hands for a beat of thick silence, then glances up at me. "Why?"

I hold his eyes when he peers up, feeling the last of my control slip away. "You know why."

Slowly, he turns, his hand trailing across the sink's ledge, stopping just short of my hip. "I want you to tell me."

My jaw tightens. I can't speak. If I open my mouth, it'll be to crash it down on his. I can't. I won't.

He takes another step closer and says, "We agreed what happened last night would be behind us."

"Exactly," I answer tightly.

He smirks. "But we said that would be effective starting *tomorrow*."

"Only because I hadn't factored in Mitchell taking you hostage in your backyard and dragging you to poker in my home tonight."

Oliver clucks his tongue. "Rookie mistake, Hayes. And you call yourself a veteran player."

"I don't call myself anything. I *am* a veteran player. I'm old and on my last legs, and you'd do well to remember that," I snap.

He frowns. That damn thoughtful frown. His eyes scan me. "What does that mean?"

I don't answer him. I glance out the kitchen window toward his home, wishing he'd take pity on me and go back there already.

"You think I care that you're older than me?" he says quietly.

"*Ten* years older," I tell him.

"Nine years, seven months, and six days."

My gaze snaps toward him. Oliver's cheeks are red. "Excuse me?"

He scrubs the back of his neck and stares down at the ground. "C'mon, Hayes. Everyone knows your birthday."

I narrow my eyes at him. "But have they done the math to know our age difference? For someone who doesn't care that I'm older—"

"I had a crush on you," he blurts. "As a teenager. Like, a sexual-awakening kind of crush. That's why I know your birthday and our age difference. I know every club you played for and every goal you scored, and I have a raging competency kink, and you have always, obviously, scratched that itch.

"So let me make myself clear," he says, closing the distance between us, so close I feel warmth pouring off him, smell the intoxicating scent of his skin. "I do not care that you're thirty-four. I care that you're a massive dick most of the time. And don't make a gloating size joke right now—I'm trying to be sincere. I care that while you're usually a growly, cynical grump, you're also sometimes a giant softie for the people you care about, even if those lucky people aren't many in number.

"I care that you showed *me* that care. On our flight. Before the game." His eyes drift to my mouth. "I care that you kissed me last night like you'd wanted to kiss me. Granted, probably not as long as I've wanted to kiss you, but—"

I yank him by the shirt and cup his cheek, my mouth whispering over his. "One last time," I tell him.

He smiles against the first brush of our lips. "Such a good song."

"Shut up. Kiss me back," I grumble, slipping my hands around his waist, pulling him against me. "Focus on this instead of *Hamilton* for one fucking minute."

"Aha!" he says against my mouth before I silence him with a deep, hard kiss. Warm and soft and wet. A groan rumbles in my throat as I suck his tongue. "I knew you liked it," he says, sinking his hands into my hair, cupping my neck.

"It's a frustratingly catchy soundtrack," I admit.

He groans. "Don't do this."

I kiss his cheekbone, the corner of his mouth. "Do what?"

"Make me want you even more. *Hamilton*'s my weakness."

"Lin-Manuel Miranda is your weakness," I growl against his neck, biting it, then soothing it with my tongue. "You hummed *Encanto* during our entire warm-up before the game. You called him Shakespeare and Sondheim in one person. And I don't appreciate being jealous of a musical theater dork who is, by the way, *actually* much too old for you."

He drops back his head, setting his hands on my hips, slipping them around my waist, and kneading my ass. I groan into his neck. "First," he says, "forty-two isn't that old. Second—*shit*." He gasps as I tug his earlobe between my teeth. "Humming happy music helps me stay calm when I'm nervous. So don't make fun of me for it."

I slip my hand beneath his shirt and rub his back gently, savoring those lean muscles, his warm, firm skin. "I would never."

He snorts a laugh that becomes a rough exhale when my hand wanders lower, along the waistband of his shorts, and I tease beneath the elastic, knowing I'm going somewhere I shouldn't. I slip my hand along the hard, firm curve of his backside and glide my finger lower, teasing him. "The things I want to do to you," I whisper against the shell of his ear.

"Hayes," he groans, gripping me tight, until I feel him, hard and thick, wedged right against every throbbing, rock-hard inch of me. I grit my teeth and breathe through the longing that barrels through my body. It's that or moan helplessly as he works himself against me, his cock rubbing mine with each grind of his hips. "I want you," he whispers.

"I want you, too," I admit, hating how breathless I sound, needy and desperate. "But we shouldn't."

"I know," he says quietly, sliding his hands up my back, kneading the web of stiff, sore muscles. "Doesn't mean I want it any less."

I set my hands back at his hips, holding him against me, as I kiss him, slow and soft. I shouldn't say it, shouldn't want it. But I'm weak beneath his touch, so fucking gone. I need him so badly, all sense flies right out of my head. "Unless . . ."

He leans in, kissing me back, chasing me for more. "Unless what?"

"We just . . . scratch the itch once. Get it out of our systems."

He hesitates for a moment, pulling back and holding my eyes. A rough swallow works along his throat. "When?"

"Tonight." I cup his jaw, slide my thumb along his mouth, tracing it. "Now."

He lowers his head, taking my thumb into his mouth and sucking it.

"Fuck." I squeeze his waist tight and hold him closer, crushing our chests together.

Oliver lets my thumb out with a pop, eyes holding mine. "Where?"

Sweet, heady relief rushes through me. "Anywhere. Whatever you want."

He smiles, smug and satisfied.

"Shut *up*," I growl at him, kissing him hard, pinning him against the sink.

"I didn't say anything!" he mutters into my mouth.

I thrust against him, hard and deliberate, sliding every inch of myself along every inch of him. His eyes flutter shut. "You were thinking it."

He grins as he cups my ass and squeezes. "Thinking what?"

"That I'm so fucking desperate to taste you and touch you and make you come so many ways and times until you can't even walk straight that I would get you off on the roof of an In-N-Out if you asked me."

"If it makes you feel any better," he says as I tug out his tiny ponytail and sink my fingers into his hair, "I'm just as desperate."

"Nothing makes me feel better," I tell him hoarsely, taking his hand and guiding it over my erection. He pants as I work his hand along me. "Nothing makes this better when you're around. You're a fucking nuisance. A maddening, infuriating temptation."

"Gav," he whispers, and it's my undoing. "Please."

"Anything," I tell him, slipping my hand along his stomach, beneath his shirt, grazing my knuckles over taut, warm skin. "Let me touch you."

"Yes," he pants. "Hell yes."

I slip my hand beneath his shorts, his boxer briefs, and feel him, silken smooth, hot, and throbbing hard. Fuck, he's beautiful. He's perfect.

"Oh, God," he groans.

"No God here," I tell him. "Tell me who's giving you pleasure."

"You are," he whispers, cupping my neck, pulling me in for a kiss as I slip my thumb along the sensitive underside of his cock, over the slit that's wet, leaking for me.

"Say my name," I tell him.

"Gavin," he says, then louder when my hand wanders lower, stroking, teasing, making him plead against my neck.

"That's it," I tell him, kissing his temple, breathing him in. "Fuck yeah. C'mon. Come for me."

"I'm so close," he groans. "Shit, I'm so close. I swear it's not usually this fast, I just—"

"Oliver," I mutter against his cheek, then kiss his mouth again and again. "I'm about to blow my fucking load, only from getting *you* off. You don't need to explain yourself."

"I want it to last," he says faintly, slipping his hands beneath my clothes and cupping my bare ass. "I don't want this to be it."

"It won't be," I promise him, tenderness flooding me as I touch him, as he clutches me and works himself against my hand, chasing release. "We have all night."

He sucks my earlobe, and my weak knee nearly gives out. "I want every minute."

I'm about to promise him the fucking world if he wants it, when suddenly Oliver's back porch floodlight bursts to life, pouring like high beams through my kitchen window.

We're both startled for only a moment before we crash back down on each other, kisses deepening, bodies moving, until the sound of a woman's voice shouting an expletive makes Oliver freeze, then whip around, facing his house.

I stand there, stunned.

He shields his eyes, squinting. "Oh shit!" He straightens his shorts, pats his pockets frantically. "I don't have my phone. Shit, I don't have my phone, and she's—"

He spins around, wide-eyed, breathing heavily. "I'm so sorry. I really have to go see if she's okay. I—" He clasps my face and kisses me one more time, hard and deep. I wrench away just as he lets go, as he slams his feet into his muddy sneakers and bolts out the back door toward his house.

I stand, foolishly watching him long enough to observe him wrap his arms around a woman nearly as tall as him, a waterfall of flame-colored hair spilling down her back as he hugs her tight and sways her. Comforts her. Kisses the crown of her head.

According to my doctors, I have a dangerously high pain threshold, but even this is too much for me. I can't watch a moment more.

So I turn away and lock the door behind me. Then I walk through my house, flicking off one light switch after the other, until, once again, everything is dark.

SEVENTEEN

Oliver

Playlist: "Slide to the Side," Beaty Heart

Pretty much the only thing potent enough to relieve me of the erection of my lifetime is the sight of my little sister in tears. "Ziggy," I whisper, swaying her tight. "I'm sorry. I left my phone…" I glance out at the yard, where my water bottle and phone lie abandoned near the pile of weeds I was pulling before Mitchell ambushed me. "I left it outside. I didn't mean to ignore you."

"It's okay," she whispers, dabbing her nose with the back of her hand. "I'm sorry I'm such a mess. I'm just so angry, and I needed to talk to you because you always make it make sense. I figured maybe you'd fallen asleep on the couch or you'd left your phone in the car, so I drove over and tried to use my key, but it didn't work, and I got even more upset, then—"

"Hey. It's okay." I hold her tight, how she likes, and keep swaying her. Ziggy's on the autism spectrum, and since she was diagnosed back when we were teens, I've learned how to give her comfort when she's upset like this. Hard pressure, rhythmic swaying, making a safe space for her to tell me whatever she needs to or, conversely, to let silence be enough when she can't seem to form words.

"You're always welcome here," I tell her. "I always want you to be comfortable showing up when you need to. I feel like a jerk for not having my phone and for not giving you a new key. Come on inside." I pull my keys from my pocket and open up the house for her before jogging across the lawn to grab my phone and water bottle.

As I run back, I glance toward Gavin's kitchen window, regret and guilt knotting inside me. His house is completely dark now. I can only imagine how it looked to him, seeing me practically jump out of his arms when I noticed a woman outside my house and run straight toward her. I have a feeling he's locked that door and shut me out. In more ways than one.

Worst part is, I know it's for the best. I know Gavin wanted me for only one night, and I know I shouldn't want him for a thousand more. But I do. I want him. And with every sliver of him that I see, of the person I'm starting to realize is the *real* Gavin, I only want more.

Acting on that wanting, encouraging it, even this little bit, is asking for trouble. If I indulged it and fell for him, then what? Pine for him for as long as he stays with the team? Watch him walk off into the sunset and retire somewhere warm and lovely to live in a big grayscale house with no one to fill it with color, or worse, with someone who agrees that black, charcoal, and heather gray are the be-all, end-all of interior design?

I'd be crushed.

No, it's for the best that Ziggy showed up, that our wild night was cut short, that Gavin and I stopped before acting on this attraction and ruining the tentative camaraderie we built during our trip for the preseason game.

I know I've likely done some damage, pulling away tonight. Gavin's pride may be hurt until he lets me explain myself and tell him it had nothing to do with him and everything to do with a family emergency. Worse, he might be relieved.

Worse yet, he might not actually care at all.

Just how much *I* care about that is deeply worrying.

"Ollie?" Ziggy peers out from the house and sees me standing outside my back door, lost in very unwise thoughts.

It's definitely for the best that my sister showed up.

"Sorry." I tear my gaze away from his house.

"Why were you next door?" she asks, glancing toward Gavin's house. "Do you need to go back? I can wait."

"Nah. Nope. All good . . . Just a . . . quick . . . little . . . neighborly visit. No big deal."

Stepping inside the house, I shut the door, then lock it. Ziggy flicks on the soft overhead recessed lights, then flicks them off.

"Too bright," she mutters, then flops onto my sofa, all long, lanky limbs. A groan leaves her.

"What's the matter, Zigs?" I squeeze her toe gently as I walk by into my kitchen. "Want some tea?"

"Yes, please," she says, massaging her temples.

I wait for her, because that's what Ziggy needs when she's upset—time and patience to let her formulate her thoughts, not pressure to spit them out. As I turn on the kettle and set out two mugs with peppermint sachets in them, Ziggy stares up at the ceiling, her socked feet bouncing rhythmically off the edge of my sofa.

Finally she says, "Nobody takes me seriously."

I close the distance between us, circling the dining table, then leaning against the back of the sofa. I peer down at her and ask, "What do you mean, 'nobody'?"

She doesn't meet my eyes. She just keeps staring up at the ceiling. "I mean nobody."

I sift through that, trying to think about what she needs from me, if anything, beyond a listening ear. Ziggy's struggled socially for a long time. It's part of why she ended up having a comprehensive psych eval and getting diagnosed with autism. She was depressed and anxious, had compulsions and panic attacks. So many of her needs and struggles weren't being met or understood, and trying to mask them had led her to the edge of a breakdown.

After being diagnosed, she took her time to process her diagnosis, learn her unmasked self, and finish high school through cyber school while spending a lot of time in therapy, playing soccer, keeping life simple, her social circle small. Surprising us all when it came time to decide between trying to go directly into professional soccer or playing for a college team, and she was hell-bent on going to UCLA.

She got in, of course, made the team, secured a full-ride scholarship, and she's seemed to be doing well so far. She's a senior now, and she's also on the US U-23 team, playing only for them now that UCLA's season is over. I thought she'd really hit her stride, been feeling more confident and acclimated since becoming an upperclassman on the UCLA team, since making U-23 and its starting lineup. She's *seemed* to be doing well.

Sure, she is a little weepy sometimes and wants to come over to watch rom-coms with me, make popcorn, and not really talk about anything. I can always tell something's on her mind when she does that, but usually just being with me, laughing, goofing off, seems to have her smiling and calm by the time she drives back to her studio apartment near campus.

What have I missed while I've been wrapped up in my life? Twisted up with Gavin lately, the pressures of the new season, the weight of responsibility since being named captain. When did I lose track of my little sister?

"Ziggy," I say quietly, reaching down and stroking her hair, which she always likes. "What's making you feel this way? Did something happen?"

She shrugs, dabs her nose, and blinks away the threat of tears in her eyes. "Not one specific thing, no. It's just . . ." Groaning, she scrubs her face. "In the family, I'm always going to be the baby. The one everyone just . . ."

"Adores?" I offer.

"Yes!" she yells, like this is the worst offense.

"You poor kid."

"Shut up." She punches my thigh without even looking and nails my quad perfectly.

"No dead-legging me. My legs are my livelihood." I lean down and poke her armpit, making her squeal. She sits up and wipes away tears from her cheeks.

I hand her a tissue and say, "You sure nothing specific happened?"

"No." She shakes her head, then blows loudly. "It feels like this everywhere. In the classroom. On the team. In study groups. I know I'm quiet until I'm not and then I'm blurting stuff. I know I can be awkward and I've got habits and behaviors that make me seem immature, but I'm an adult. I take care of myself, and I know my needs and my limits and how to advocate for myself, and I'm trying so hard to be perceived as independent and mature and I'm *not*."

She sucks in a breath and says, "I just want to feel like people respect me. Like they don't see me as this timid weird girl, but instead . . . as a woman who can do brave things and unexpected things, and be, like . . . cool."

"Ziggy." My heart twists. "You *are* cool."

She rolls her eyes. "You're my brother. You're obligated to say that."

"I mean it, though. You're cool. You're genuine and smart and have incredible deadpan humor. You have the most impressive vocabulary of anyone I have ever met. You're beautiful and a veritable fountain of random trivia knowledge. I always want you on my team when Trivial Pursuit time happens at the A-frame."

Laughing faintly, she stares down at her hands. "Thanks, Ollie." After a long stretch of silence, she says, "Do you ever just feel like . . . you're outgrowing yourself? Like there are these parts of yourself you thought would never change that are rearranging inside you? Like the things you thought you knew most about what you wanted from others, from yourself, are morphing you into a person you're not sure you're ready to be, but you can't stand for things to stay the way they are, either?"

I stare at her, feeling my pulse pound as her words reverberate in my heart and through my limbs. Not that losing our self-control and getting physical was objectively "good," but I think about how good it's *felt* since Gavin and I almost came to blows on the field—the relief it's been since the tension I'd compressed and compounded inside myself cracked my kill-him-with-kindness facade and spilled into pranks and honesty, trust and even a little laughter . . . and pleasure, even closeness. Just a bit of closeness. Somewhere we'd never have gotten if I'd just kept gritting my teeth and smiling my way through my misery.

I think about how long I've told myself I can't have those good things with someone if they so much as brush shoulders with soccer. And I think about how unsatisfying it's felt to live such a compartmentalized life. Because that's not who I am . . . or if it is, it's not who I always want to be. For a time, putting my head down, pursuing my goals with single-minded focus, served me, but that doesn't mean it always will or that what was right for one season is right forever. Ziggy's right. You outgrow parts of yourself, and maybe this way of dealing with my fear is something I've outgrown. That doesn't mean my fear—my very real reservations about mixing pleasure and my profession—has just evaporated, but it feels . . . freeing to acknowledge how I've been handling it might need to change, might bear reexamination.

Peering down at Ziggy, I tell her quietly, "Yeah, Zigs. I know how you feel."

The kettle starts to whistle, and while I fill our mugs, then carry them to my living room, Ziggy stares out my window at the moon, a heavy pearl, low and glowing in the sky.

"I've been feeling such . . . restlessness," she says as I sit close to her, set down our mugs of tea, then hold out my hand. She sets her hand in mine, and I clasp it firmly, reassuring her. "I've been so angry lately. But I didn't know who I was angry with, or even exactly why."

I squeeze her hand gently. "Do you feel like you've figured it out?"

She nods. "I'm angry with *myself.* I've been holding myself back, believing things about myself that aren't true, that make me feel frustrated and misunderstood and stuck. I *hate* feeling stuck."

Again, my stomach knots. I remember what our brothers told me in Freya and Aiden's backyard, that they didn't recognize me, that maybe all that anger I thought was caused by Gavin was caused by myself, too, because of what I'd been denying, hiding, suppressing, all in the name of doing what I thought would protect my dream of succeeding on the team, would keep me from ever experiencing the pain and mess that my relationship with Bryce wreaked on my college career.

"What are you going to do?" I ask her quietly.

Ziggy turns toward me, her sharp green eyes holding mine for a rare moment before they slide away again to the moon outside. "I'm going to make a change. *I'm* going to be brave and change. Somehow."

I sit with her in silence as we sip our tea, wrapped in the hush of night and a blanket woven by moonbeams. Mulling over our conversation, I'm grateful Ziggy came, even if not for the reasons I first thought.

In the span of one conversation, I'm on the other side of where I began. When she got here, I was relieved that it stopped Gavin and me from doing something that would irrevocably alter and potentially threaten the stability of our team, our play, our success as co-captains. Now I'm relieved to recognize how miserable following through on that thinking would make me once again.

Ziggy's wise words have, even more so than my brothers', reminded me that I'm going to be dissatisfied so long as I keep lying to myself, living only a sliver of my full life because I'm so focused on what I could lose that I'm not seeing everything I'll never gain if I keep living like this. What if there's a way to be intentional and, yes, cautious, but also honest and real and . . . alive to *all* of myself?

I don't know what that means for when I see Gavin tomorrow, but I do know we're not going back to what we were. I know that we're grown men who can talk about what's going on between us, about what we did tonight.

The memory of him touching me in the kitchen floods my brain, and heat rushes through me. I don't want to think about that when my sister's snuggled up next to me on my couch. Thankfully, Ziggy wrenches me from my thoughts before I can start to worry that I don't know how to escape them.

"Thanks for talking with me," she says, nuzzling her head against my shoulder. "I don't know what I'd do without you, Ollie."

I press a kiss to the crown of her head. "I'm always here for you, Zigs. But just so you know, everything you said tonight, everything you figured out, I only listened. The wisdom was all yours."

A smile lifts her cheek as she snuggles in and stares up at the moon. "It was, wasn't it?"

The last thing I expect to see when I walk out the door the next morning is Gavin Hayes leaning against my car, wearing a scowl, head-to-toe black, and a pair of matching Ray-Bans.

The old me would flash my widest smile and hide my unease with a cheeky, cheery salutation, mask my anxiety behind my gift for mindless, pithy chatter. But the new me, whom Gavin nearly made come undone, whose sister inadvertently whipped his existential ass into shape last night, can't seem to force any of that this morning.

Instead, I stop a few feet away and say, "About last night. I can explain—"

Gavin holds up a hand. "Don't."

I narrow my eyes in frustration, but the effect is lost on him since they're hidden behind my own pair of sunglasses. It is unearthly bright this morning, and after having lain in bed until three a.m., ceiling-gazing while trying to sort through all my feelings, I'm functioning on so little sleep, this much sunlight is too much for even me.

"It's tomorrow now," he explains. "We agreed it would be behind us."

I hike my bag higher on my shoulder. "Yeah, except *it* never progressed past *i*-, and leaving that much unresolved is making me uncomfortable."

Gavin stares at me, gaze hidden behind his sunglasses. I feel it all the same. "Unfortunately, Bergman, I don't see how your discomfort is my problem, given you're the one who left things so *unresolved*."

The innuendo is clear. And unless I'm way off, there's also a deeper subtext. I know he's a crank and a foulmouthed, often rude one at that, but there's a softness inside Gavin Hayes that, like any human, he hates to have poked, or worse, abandoned. I think he feels like I've done both. I left him last night, and here I am kicking up that fact this morning, when he just wants to move past it. I'm starting to theorize that his soft spot is even more tender than most, given how deeply he guards it. And I'm worried that behind all that scowling and snapping is someone who uses those defenses to protect a very raw, very vulnerable part of himself.

I understand, and yet there's so much that I don't. There's so much I don't know about Gavin, about why he is the way he is, about why I don't see any of his friends from England showing up for his games or on his doorstep. Why I've never heard a peep about a family in his entire career. I have no context to make sense of his behavior, his sky-high cold walls, his roughness and readiness to keep his distance from everyone except a few sweet old guys who play poker with pennies at his house, sing karaoke, and clear out his pantry every week.

Bottom line, I don't *know* Gavin. And in all my kill-him-with-kindness, always-be-fine-ness, I've made sure he doesn't know me, either.

I know I'm attracted to him. I know he's attracted to me. There's a stadium's worth of sexual tension between us. But there's I-want-to-smack-you-upside-the-head-because-you're-pissing-me -off tension, too. And I don't know how to even begin to go about sorting that out if Gavin's just going to shut me down and go back to being his grumpy, gruff self.

"Do you mind?" he says, pointing to the car. "I don't have all day for you to stand there, stewing in your unresolved feelings."

"Fine," I concede, popping open the trunk. "I'll just have to deal with those unresolved feelings myself, then. I mean, I already dealt with one of those unresolved feelings pretty thoroughly last night in the shower."

His head falls back. He rubs his eyes beneath his sunglasses. "You can't say shit like that."

"Why not? It's a fact. Just reporting information. Yesterday was a high of sixty-six degrees. Last night, the moon was a waxing gibbous. Before bed, I rubbed one out in the shower."

A low growl rumbles in his throat. "Fuck off."

"I just told you, I already did. And given the state of your pants last night, Hayes, I sincerely hope for your mental and physical well-being, you did, too."

Shaking his head, he slowly pushes off the car, then walks toward the trunk. "You're an utter pain in the ass," he mutters.

I watch him chuck his bag into my trunk, then round the car to the passenger side. "Given you feel that way, may I ask why I have the honor of driving your grumpy butt to practice? I know I strong-armed you into carpooling, but given how not pleased to see me you seem, I would have bet a lot of money on you driving yourself today."

"My knee," he says, easing into the passenger seat as I open my door and join him in the car. "It's still fucked. I can't put enough pressure on it to use the gas and brake pedals to drive."

Sympathy rushes through me, the impulse to offer him comfort and reassurance, but I tamp it down. That's not what's going on with us. He's made sure of it, with that gruff, *I don't want to know* nonsense when I tried to explain last night and clear the air like a rational adult.

Focusing instead on turning on the car and adjusting my mirrors, I ask, "And you plan on practicing today how, then?"

"I don't," he says, backing up his seat and extending his leg as much as possible. "I plan on getting sorted out by Dan and Maria, then standing on the sidelines and giving you hell while you run around all day."

"Sounds delightful." I pull out onto the road and make the turn for Deja Brew instead of the direct route to the sports complex.

Gavin notices. "Oh fuck, no. Not this again. I cannot endure another coffee-for-the-cast-of-thousands run."

I flash him a smile, a real one. "Don't worry, *sötis*. This run is just for us."

EIGHTEEN

Gavin

Playlist: "Wait for It," Usher

"What did you just call me?" I stare at Oliver as he hums to himself, changing lanes in preparation for his right turn into Deja Brew.

Either he's ignoring me or he can't hear me past his infuriating humming of "One Last Time."

"Bergman," I snap.

He glances my way. "What?"

"What did you just call me?"

Slowing, he makes the turn for the coffee drive-through. "I'm not sure I understand."

Jesus Christ. I'm going to wring his gorgeous neck. "Have you lost your command of the English language? What can't you understand?"

He grins, and fuck, I can't look. It's a real grin, soft and crooked, not that megawatt shit he shows the world. It feels intimate and personal and so impossibly lovely I want to wrap my hands around that smile and slip it inside my pocket, and fucking hell, I really, *really* need to stop reading poetry.

Oliver hits a pothole in the road. I grab the *oh shit* bar and suck in a breath as a bolt of white-hot pain racks my lower back. My stomach knots. I'm being hit on every front, this nightmare of a paved road, today's excruciating level of pain, once again being stuck in Oliver's car, bathed in his scent, the sight of him, flooded with memories of last night, touching him, wanting him, being words away from humiliating myself, confessing what I'd give for him, *do* for him—

Anything. Everything.

Shifting in my seat, I grunt out of the sheer agony that is moving. Today is a day colored by pain, stamped by pain, cut out by pain; there isn't a motion or movement or thought that isn't imprinted, shaded, or shaped by it. Blinking, breathing, turning, shifting—all of it hurts. It's consuming. And I wish for just a moment I could shut my eyes and escape it, float out of my body and into a space devoid of sensation, where I could exist without knowing where every fucking nerve ending is in my back and hips and knees and neck, where breathing didn't feel like knives in my spine and shifting didn't make my back send a dagger of pain through my leg until my molars clacked and bile crawled up my throat.

Mercifully oblivious to my misery, Oliver finally says, "I'll clarify. I understand the question. I just don't understand why you expect me to answer it, seeing as you went all grunting Neanderthal back there and shut me down when I was trying to communicate with you." He glances my way, a flash of genuine annoyance evident, even with those sharp pale eyes hidden by his sunglasses. "What if my explanation made you feel better about what happened last night?"

That's exactly my concern. I don't *want* to feel better about last night. I want to bury it and never revisit how raw and real and imperfect and hungry it was. How much I wanted not only to peel off his clothes and unwrap him like a fucking present, but to lay Oliver on my bed and learn every part of him—his pleasure, his pain, his wants, his fears.

Which is *absurd*. It's my years of abstinence that are to blame, confusing longing and love, desperation and deep intimacy. I was no more prepared for a one-time hookup last night than I was to walk onto the field today and kick a soccer ball. And I refuse to make an irrevocable mistake, on either of those fronts.

So I tell Oliver, with as little feeling and as much indifference as I can muster, "Bergman, I don't care about your explanation. It's over. Done. We agreed we'd move on."

His hands clutch the steering wheel so tight his knuckles whiten. "We also agreed to honesty and respect," he says.

"Ah," I tell him as he pulls up one car closer to the ordering window, "but only as it pertained to co-captaining and the team. This topic most certainly has *nothing* to do with that. Because we would never let anything personal jeopardize our professional lives—our captaincies or the team."

Oliver glances over at me, his expression hidden behind his sunglasses. I never realized how much he says with his eyes until I couldn't see them. I'm sorely tempted to rip off those aggravating polarized lenses right now and demand the truth.

Which would be the height of hypocrisy, of course.

"No," he says evenly, his voice calm and serious as he stares at me. "No, we wouldn't."

The car behind us honks, ending our stare-off. Oliver drives forward, relentlessly polite and cheerful as ever while he places our order, then pulls up to the payment window. It's a different person from last time, who's so busy making drinks in between making change they don't have time to bullshit with Oliver, thank God.

Oliver puts on *Hamilton* while we wait, seemingly incapable of existing in quiet—granted, extremely tense quiet—and I don't even have the willpower to tell him to turn it off. He's chosen "Wait for It," and that song has had me in all three minutes and thirteen seconds of its clutches since I first heard it.

"You know," Oliver begins, sounding dangerously philosophical. "This song's themes and subtext raise serious questions of—"

I groan. "Must you pontificate? Can't we just let Leslie Odom Jr. sing the shit out of this song and sound like sex in a voice box?"

His mouth quirks, but he quickly schools his expression into something frustratingly neutral. Is this what Oliver feels when looking at me, when everything I'm feeling and thinking is hidden behind the cool, inscrutable expression I've perfected—frustrated, shut out, infuriated?

If he does, then I have no idea how he hasn't burst a blood vessel. I'm about to rupture something when this is the first time I've ever been on the receiving end and it's been all of five seconds.

Oliver thanks the person at the window as they hand him our drinks. A small cup is set in my hand, again with *GG* written on top. I frown down at the lid, then up at the menu I just noticed inside the window, where I see *The Double G* advertised as a custom drink.

"What the hell." I point past him, toward the menu.

Oliver wrinkles his nose and leans closer. "Well, would you look at that."

"I'm looking. I noticed it, you menace. What is this about?"

I remember what he said when I asked him *last* time what *GG* stood for and he said it was between him, God, and Deja Brew's owner, Bhavna. There's some significance to this, and I'm frankly too pissed about too many things to be rational about it. "Goddammit, Bergman, stop being cryptic and tell me. If this has anything to do with me, I deserve to know."

Taking a long sip of what looks to be an iced matcha green tea latte, Oliver pulls out of Deja Brew and says, "Apparently, the drink I specially ordered for you was a big hit when Bhavna did a tasting of new specialty drinks. Now it's on the menu."

"What," I say between gritted teeth, "does the double *G* stand for?"

"Bhavna follows the team," he says, focused on merging into

traffic, ignoring me. "The first time I made a whole-team coffee run, I asked her to make you a little something special." He keeps his eyes on the road. "I was hoping she'd pick up on my sinister vibes toward you and throw in something rough, like pickle juice or Worcestershire sauce, but alas, she did not. Not that you acted like what was in that drink made a lick of difference anyway."

I remember his wide smile, the drink thrust in my face as he passed around coffees. How raw and empty I felt those first few weeks. Back in a country that I'd literally run away from, home only to sad or, at best, bittersweet memories. Here simply because my body was not capable of the caliber of play required in England, because here I could still be somebody, lead a team, keep playing the game.

"It was good," I admit. "Just not good enough to wash down the very bitter pill I was still trying to swallow."

The pill of leaving a world-class club that had been home to the height of my career. Leaving behind a town that had become familiar, an adoring—well, in times gone by, adoring—fan base, supposed friends, a lover, a whole life.

Oliver glances my way, then back to the road. "Was that just a genuine—albeit highly metaphorical—sentiment out of your mouth, Mr. Hayes? Did you just communicate your . . . *feelings?*"

I point with my breve cup at the speakers and tell him "It's Leslie Odom Jr.'s fault" before taking a sip of my drink. "Show me someone who can listen to Aaron Burr reflecting on indiscriminate suffering, the inevitability of death, the point of existence, and not even inadvertently say something genuine."

He cracks a smile.

I sip my coffee, watching him when I shouldn't. Just like last time, watching sunlight paint his face, burnish his beard, the tips of his lashes, flash off his wide grin. "Bergman."

"Hmm?"

"Tell me what the fucking Double G stands for."

"Oh, that. The Gorgeous Grump," he says breezily.

I nearly spit out my drink.

His smile widens. "As Bhavna says, just like you, the Gorgeous Grump is rich, dark, and bittersweet. Classic breve, half-and-half with espresso, and a splash of dark-chocolate syrup added."

My stomach somersaults. "You're fucking with me."

"I most certainly am not," he says, eyes on the road. "And don't get any ideas. *I* didn't come up with that drink—Bhavna did."

Oliver might think I didn't notice, but I did. He said Bhavna came up with the drink but not who decided on its name. I don't indulge myself in wondering, hoping he's responsible for that.

Instead, I indulge in my breve. In its warmth. Its rich semi-sweetness. Like most things in life—a small, fleeting pleasure.

———————

After our drive to the facility, my visit with our physical trainers is not encouraging. They know what not to say, because I've told them I already know what they'd tell me. They still say it, though, with worried expressions and careful hands.

I'm playing on borrowed time.

I don't need them or the specialists I see to tell me. I feel it. I feel the consequences of pushing my body brutally for over half of my life. And I know that every time I lace up and go back on the pitch, I'm tempting fate, that I'm one wrong turn or fifty-fifty ball away from it all being over.

I just refuse to think on that. I refuse to accept that the end of what has been the only good thing in my life draws closer.

Every athlete I know has struggled with the end of their career. It's only natural. We live and breathe the sport, perfect our bodies for it, devote our time, our healthiest, most energetic years, the so-called "prime of our lives" to the game, and then one day, whether because of chronic pain or injury or the understandable wish to avoid any more of either, it has to come to an end. And then there's this yawning expanse ahead, decades and decades—hopefully, at least—of life stretched before us that we're suddenly supposed to know what to do with, now that the thing that's shaped our lives since we were adolescents, often even younger, is gone.

It's hard enough for those with family, friends, a relationship, children, hobbies. I have hardly any of those. A man who literally saved my life by sticking a soccer ball at my feet and believing in me is dead. A slew of friends and a former long-term lover back in England whom I pissed off when I signed with the Galaxy, because I wouldn't listen to them and stay in England and retire when they thought I should. Maudlin poetry lining my shelves. Black-and-white photos lining my walls, taken places I only ever visited alone. The poker guys, with their half-hearted bickering and karaoke obsession. My next-door neighbor, co-captain, and irritating thorn in my backside . . .

Oliver.

I watch him from behind dark sunglasses, standing on the sidelines, even though I should be seated and elevating my sore knee. Problem is, I'm a prideful motherfucker, and I'm not sitting on the sidelines, and since Dan and Maria doctored me up, being in my body has been dialed down from nearly intolerable agony to familiar, exhausting pain.

Oliver stands beside Santi, talking with his hands, laughing when Santi makes a face, clearly telling some joke. The whistle blows, and like well-trained athletes, they split off, immediately in game mode. I watch Oliver fly across the field, envy coiling through me.

It's so easy to latch on: my jealousy of his whole, young body, my resentment that I have to spend the final chapter of my career enduring his presence as such a stark contrast to mine, salt in the wound of my reality. That's what I've clung to since I signed, and it burns through me, sharp and hot, as I watch him spin with the ball, rainbow it cheekily, then barrel toward the goal. With one flawless fake, then a cut, he nails it into the net, Amobi rolling after, diving and missing the ball entirely.

Rico whistles softly.

Jas shakes their head. "He just keeps getting better."

"Mm-hmm," Coach says, smiling into the sun, eyes hidden behind her sunglasses. "And he's just getting started."

It hits me like a punch to the gut, that reminder. I grit my teeth, watching him, waiting for the full power of my hatred for everything he has that I don't anymore, for everything ahead of him that's already behind me, to barrel through my system like it has so often since I met him.

But . . . it doesn't. And what I feel is so much worse. Sadness. Unbearable sadness.

Coach cuts her gaze my way, as if surprised I haven't mouthed off or said something tart. She arches her eyebrow. "You all right over there?"

I shrug, swallowing against the lump in my throat. "Fine."

Avoiding her, I watch Oliver, his easy smile, the way his eyes crinkle at the corners as he tugs his hair back, shifting his weight onto his back leg while Andre talks to him. My gut knots. Hot, feverish *something* scorches my insides, burrows in my chest.

I tear my gaze away from him, focus on the rest of the field, analyzing their ball movement, critiquing how fucking sloppy the midfield is without me.

Coach turns a little more fully to examine me. "What'd Maria and Dan say?"

"Nothing. Because they know what's good for them."

She's quiet for a moment. Then, "Hayes, I need you to be straight with me."

"I'll be fine to play our next game," I promise her.

She sighs. "That's not all I'm concerned about. I care about *you*. You know that."

I feel my disobedient gaze slide toward Oliver again, remembering how perfect he felt—the warm, wet pleasure of his mouth, his soft sighs and gasps, the glorious feel of his body against mine, hot in my hand.

The fucking irony is that the man who's been the constant source of my misery, whose life is becoming everything mine soon will no longer be, who's been such a bitter reminder of the painful truth that I can never get back those years that await him, is the one person who's given me the closest to respite from my misery in so long.

"Hayes," Coach presses.

I cross my arms tight over my chest, a shield against my aching heart, telling myself as much as her, "I'm fine."

NINETEEN

Oliver

Playlist: "September Fields," Frazey Ford

There are some choices I'll forever regret, choices I'd give anything to take back and do differently . . . Some of them involve pranks I took too far. Harsh words said in the heat of the moment. But the one that outstrips them all, at least right now, is eating my feelings in the form of a half-pound wedge of triple-cream brie.

I just got so frustrated with Gavin. It's been three weeks since the kitchen make-out and the next morning when he shut me down, demanding we leave it behind us, and the worst part is, I shouldn't even be mad. He's kept his promise—been civil, respectful on the field, in the locker room. On our carpool rides home, he's mostly quiet, but he'll make a dry quip here and there.

He's kept his promise; I've kept mine. No more pranks or innuendos or big-dick jokes, and I'm angry and horny and frustrated, and I can't even put my finger on exactly why, when we're doing exactly what we should: ignoring our attraction, treating each other decently, and kicking ass in preseason.

So when I got home after practice today, I ate my feelings and went way too hard on the cheese. And now my stomach's cramping, rumbling ominously. A fine sheen of sweat beads my temples.

I'm going to be violently ill soon. And it's the world's worst timing.

"Uncle Ollie, pay attention." My niece, Linnea, sits on the

couch behind me, her legs slung over my shoulders, while I'm
sprawled on the floor, my back slumped against the couch.

Clutching my stomach.

"What's up, bud?" I ask her tightly, trying to breathe through
the pain.

She leans in, her big ice-blue eyes meeting mine. "Daniel Tiger
is gonna meet his baby now. Like I met my Theo baby."

I smooth her dark wavy hair back from her face. It's wild,
thanks to the wrestling match we just had. The one I had to put an
abrupt stop to because my stomach started cramping.

"Okay, Linnie, I'm watching."

Sighing, she sets her chin on top of my head, her hands idly
tapping my shoulders. "Are Mommy and Daddy okay?" she whispers.

My heart clenches along with my stomach, but I do my best to
ignore the latter, pushing off the ground, sitting on the sofa, and
tugging Linnie onto my lap. "Linnie, what do you mean?"

"Last night, they were both making ouchy noises," she says. She
sniffles. Wipes her nose. Very much like her mother, Linnie's a
crier. A big feeler. An empath.

I frown. "Ouchy noises?"

Linnie shuts her eyes, scrunches her face, and wails, "*Ohhhhhh!
Ohhhhhh!* Like that."

Heat hits my cheeks. Sweet Lord.

Those noises.

It's really not something I want to think about, but I have some
vague recollection, from when I used to nerd out on the old med-
school texts Dad kept at the house, that it's around a month after
birth that you can safely resume sexual activity.

Theo was born five weeks ago today.

Which explains the "ouchy" noises Freya and Aiden were making, as well as Aiden's frantic text this evening along the lines of

"Can you please take Linnie for an overnight? We're desperate for a break."

I thought this meant like an *actually just have one child to contend with* break, a *nap when the baby naps* break, or hell, a *just not answer questions every hour the firstborn is awake* break, not a *sexcapade* break.

I thought kids murdered your sex life, yet here I am on babysitting duty during my longest no-sex streak in years, with a next-door neighbor I'd love nothing more than to bang into next week, who's decidedly avoiding me—as he should—while the parents of two kids under four are getting it on.

Life is cruel.

"Uncle Ollie?" Linnie whispers, sniffling again.

I'm brought back to the moment with a pinch of guilt. I should be reassuring her, not having a pity party for myself. Kissing her temple, I rub her back.

"I think Mommy and Daddy are fine, Linnea. Sometimes when adults are . . . in bed . . . they just kinda . . . groan and stretch?"

Linnie wrinkles her nose. "Hmm. But they were in the shower. I heard the water and, like, thumps. Daddy says no gymnastics in the shower 'cause I could get hurt. Sounds like *they* got hurt. They shouldn't do it either."

I bite my lip, trying so hard not to laugh. "Fair enough."

Sighing, she slumps against me. My stomach spasms, and it takes everything in me to bite back my own "ouchy noise" so I don't upset Linnie any more than she already is.

Why, *why* did I eat all that brie?

I'm lactose intolerant, which I realized years ago after a dare gone wrong with Viggo, involving the consumption of more cheese cubes than I care to admit. Now I know better. But I love cheese so much. I take a dairy digestive aid pill with the lactase enzyme, which helps when having, say, *a* slice of pizza, or *a few bites* of cheese.

Not half a damn pound of it.

I knew I was going to pay. I was prepared to. I just wasn't expecting to get a frantic text from Aiden, begging me to take Linnie.

My parents are on a romantic getaway in Napa. Viggo's God knows where, but his phone isn't even ringing, and the rest of my siblings are either in different states or traveling with their teams.

Which left me. The guy who can't say no and who's about to crap his pants after gorging on brie.

My stomach clenches again, the pain so sharp, I hiss out a breath. Covertly, I slip my phone from my pocket while stroking Linnie's hair with my other hand. She's stuck her thumb in her mouth, her head heavy against my chest as she watches *Daniel Tiger*. I can tell she's not tired yet, but she's starting to mellow out.

If it were her bedtime, I'd be set. I'd tuck her into the guest room that I turned into a safe space for her to sleep—a queen-sized bed pushed up against the wall with a mesh safety gate on the other side so she doesn't roll off the mattress, a night-light, soothing mint-green walls, and thick butter-yellow weighted curtains to block out light so she's not woken up by the sunrise—then I'd go pay on the toilet for my dairy hubris and collapse into bed afterward.

But it's not her bedtime yet. Not for another two hours. Which means I desperately need reinforcements.

Where the hell are you? I text Viggo. This time, the text shows as "delivered," meaning his phone is finally on.

He and I have mutually agreed upon phone tracking, so I look him up, then swear under my breath. He's two hours away, in Escondido *again*.

Jesus, he texts back. What did I miss? I have seventeen missed calls and five voicemails from you.

I have Linnie, I type. I took her spur of the moment because Aiden wants to boink Freya, little did I know, and I ate a ton of cheese before I knew I was going to be watching her.

Oh God, he texts. That poor child. She's going to be scarred. Also, never again refer to what Aiden does to our sister as boink-ing. In fact, just never refer to it.

You're not the boss of me, I write. So have you left Escon-dido? When can you get here?

Ashbury has a flat tire, he writes back.

I roll my eyes. The dork named his beat-up car after his favorite scarred duke from his endless historical-romance reading.

But you have a neighbor, he continues, next door, who you could ask for help. That's what coworker neighbors are for: a cup of sugar, carpooling, watching your niece while you shit your brains out . . .

I clench my teeth. You've done enough interfering on that front. I made it very clear I want you to stop, Viggo.

Oh, I remember, he texts. I'm still having nightmares about a bedful of fake tarantulas. You're sick, you know that?

You, I type, exhaling harshly as I breathe through another stomach spasm, need to mind your own damn business. I'd hoped a bedful of fake spiders might get it through your thick skull to keep your nose out of my love life, but here we are.

Fine, stubborn sibling. I can get there in a
couple hours if you really *really* need me.

I glare at my phone. Don't bother. I'll figure something out. NO THANKS TO YOU.

After chucking my phone at the sofa, I scrub my face. I'm not texting Gavin for help. Linnie and I will be fine. Haven't I been humiliated enough? He's shut me down, moved on from what happened. He doesn't care about what we did that night in the kitchen or why I brought it to a halt. He doesn't care about *me*.

And I don't need yet another person I'm drawn to making me feel inadequate and discardable. He's over it. So I am, too.

Well, I'm trying to be.

Involving him in my personal life, asking him for help, is not happening.

I breathe through my nose as another spasm racks my stomach. I'm not going to last much longer. In fact, I'm not going to last at all.

Gently, I lift Linnea off my lap and set her on the couch. I dash into her room for the baby monitor, then back, plugging it in, angling it on the entertainment center's shelf so I can see her.

"Be right back, okay? Linnie? I have to use the bathroom. I have the baby monitor here so you can talk to me and I'll hear you."

"'Kay," she says, her voice mellow, her eyes glued to the TV. I tuck a blanket around her and scooch her to the end of the sofa so her head is on its arm, visible on the monitor, then sprint to the bathroom down the hall with the other half of the baby monitor.

And then I pay dearly for eating my feelings.

I should feel better, but I don't. Sometimes it's as simple as a bathroom trip, but this time, the residual muscle spasms in my stomach make it so I can't even stand straight. Hunched over, I join Linnea on the couch again, rubbing her back as I draw up my knees against a sharp cramp in my gut.

"I'm hungry, Uncle Ollie," Linnie says.

I groan, both at the thought of food and the thought of getting up to make it for her. "Want to raid your snack cabinet?" I ask her weakly.

She frowns. "I want *dinner*, Uncle Ollie."

Man, she's right. I peer up at the clock, then down at my phone, racking my brain. I could order food, but everything will take at least half an hour to get here, and when Linnea tells you she's hungry, she's *hungry*. She's not going to happily eat snacks and wait through yet another *Daniel Tiger* episode for her dinner.

I have to think. I need someone who can make Linnea a dinner she'll eat while I curl up in the fetal position on the sofa, and I need them fast.

In short, I need a miracle.

Suddenly a light flicks on outside, pouring long, bright beams through the windows into my living room, which has turned dark with sunset. I glance toward their source and freeze.

Gavin stands on his back porch, hands on his knees, chest heaving, gray T-shirt drenched in sweat. He stands slowly, as if it pains him, then takes a ginger step, then another, before typing in the passcode to enter his house.

Wherever Viggo is, he's probably smiling deviously, drumming his romance-loving fingers together. Out of pure spite, I want to ignore the only real solution that I have, which is the same solution Viggo presented: Gavin.

I really, *really* don't want to ask him for a favor. If this were purely about me, I wouldn't do it. But this is about Linnie, who whines, "My belly is hungry, Uncle Ollie!"

Sighing, I unlock my phone and pull up Gavin's number. The last thing I want to do with the guy whom I'm still really horny for but am supposed to be avoiding is beg him to come over and feed my niece, but desperate times call for desperate measures.

Oliver: I have an emergency.

My phone buzzes almost immediately with his response.

Gavin: What's wrong?

Oliver: My stomach's upset. I'm not contagious, just indigestion. My niece is here and she's hungry and I need an adult who can

make her dinner while I'm a pathetic lump on
the couch. She goes to bed fairly soon, I just
need someone to fill in the gaps until then.
An hour, hour and a half, tops.

I hold my breath, truly unsure how this is going to play out. Gavin might just be a big enough dick to tell me this sounds like a personal problem and he can't help me. My phone buzzes.

Gavin: I smell foul. I went for a run and I'm
covered in sweat, so let me rinse off quickly,
then I'll be over.

I send him ten prayers-of-thanks emojis, then drop my phone and gently nudge my niece, pausing *Daniel Tiger* so she'll look at me. "Hey, Linnie. Remember Gavin, from Uncle Ollie's team?"

She frowns my way. "Uh-huh. Why?"

"He's my neighbor, and he's going to come make dinner for you and keep you company since I don't feel so good. I'll be right here, but I just need to stay lying down. Can you go unlock the back door so he can come in?"

"Why?" she says.

Why. Her favorite word.

"My belly hurts, and I need an adult to help me take care of you until it stops."

Her bottom lip sticks out, a thoughtful pout. "Is he gonna be grumpy to me?"

I swallow nervously, making a promise I hope Gavin doesn't make me regret. "No, he won't. He's not always grumpy." My heart does a weird flip-flop as I remember his hand clasping mine on the plane, cupping my neck before that first preseason game, his calming voice, low and steady, reassuring me. "He's just grumpy some-times. He won't be now."

"Why is he grumpy sometimes?" she asks.

"People are grumpy sometimes because they don't feel good, or they're unhappy, or it makes them feel protected. But most of the time grumps are like . . . Mormor's"—that's what Linnie calls my mom—"*kladdkaka*: hard on the outside, but soft and warm on the inside."

Linnie smiles. She *loves* kladdkaka, a thick, rich Swedish choc-olate cake that I love, too. "Okay, sounds good," she says, skipping over to the back door, flipping the lock, then running back to the couch to watch *Daniel Tiger*.

Five minutes later, my house security beeps right after my phone buzzes with a text.

Gavin: Coming in the back door.

I don't bother texting him back. Because he's here now, stand-ing in my house, and it's really weird.

Good weird. I think. Judging by the warm, fizzy sensation churning inside me that has nothing to do with lingering indiges-tion. Gavin's hair is wet and messy, like he literally just showered, toweled it, then hustled across the yard. He's wearing black sweats and a black shirt, and he toes off gray sneakers with black stripes as he stares straight at me.

"You all right?" he asks.

I smile gamely. "Never better."

He shuts the door behind him. "Food poisoning?"

"Nah. What I ate just isn't sitting right with me."

Gavin seems skeptical. "You look like hell."

"Heck," I tell him, jerking my head toward Linnea, who stares at *Daniel Tiger*.

He glances her way and frowns. "Ah. Right. No swearing around young impressionable minds."

"Exactly."

"Kladdkaka!" Linnie yells, having noticed him, then throws off her blanket and hops off the couch.

Gavin frowns down at her. "What did you call me?"

She crosses her arms and frowns up at him. "Uncle Ollie promised you weren't going to be grumpy."

Gavin crouches until he's at her eye level, making both of his knees audibly pop. "Perhaps Uncle Ollie shouldn't make promises he can't keep."

My niece stares at Gavin, then leans in. He leans back. "What the fuck are you doing?"

"Fudge," I correct him.

Linnie holds his eyes. "A staring context."

"Contest," he says. "And who says I'm participating? Staring contests have to be mutually agreed upon."

Her eyes cross as she leans closer. His mouth quirks at the corner, like he's fighting a smile.

"You blinked!" Linnie hops up and down, turning to me. "Kladd-kaka blinked."

"What is she calling me?" Gavin grumbles.

I smile as Linnie launches herself at me and immediately starts tugging at my hair, trying to wrangle it into a pigtail. "If you're extra nice the whole time you're here," I tell him, "maybe I'll explain afterward."

He scowls, strolling past us into the kitchen. "Well," he says, "the chef is in. What'll it be?"

Linnie peers up, wide-eyed, like she suddenly remembered how hungry she is. "Guac!" she yells. "Yogurt! Bean-and-cheese quesadilla!"

"Not together," Gavin says, opening the fridge.

"Yuck, no." Linnie scrunches up her nose as she tumbles off of me and follows him. "Yogurt. Then guac. Then quesadilla. Then ..." Linnie glances over her shoulder at me.

I'm in the process of angling myself on the sofa so I can watch them, biting my cheek so I won't groan when another sharp stab of pain cuts through my stomach.

She leans in and whispers something in Gavin's ear. He listens, then cups his hands around her ear and whispers back.

Linnie laughs. Hard.

Then Gavin does something I've never seen: he *really* smiles. A wide grin lifting that stern mouth. There's the tiniest sparkle in his eye. And then he stands and pulls out the stool I keep for her, sets her up at the counter with a big piece of paper and art supplies. Fiddling around the fridge, he pulls out her favorite strawberry-banana yogurt, then a few ripe avocados I stuck in there to make them last. My cheeks heat when I see him critically inspect that half-eaten wheel of triple-cream brie before he shoves it aside and helps himself to my vegetable crisper.

Linnea turns to me and points to the speakers on my kitchen counter. "'*Canto*, Uncle Ollie?"

I'm pretty useless right now, but I do have my phone on me and synced to the speakers. Ten seconds later, I've got *Encanto*'s soundtrack playing.

While the movie's upbeat opening number fills my kitchen, Gavin peels the lid off Linnie's yogurt, plops a spoon in it, then slides it her way. Shoveling yogurt into her mouth, she leans over her artwork, paintbrush in hand, tongue stuck out in concentration, her hair perilously close to falling into wet paint. Gavin steps beside her, and while I can't tell what's being said over the music, I'm pretty sure he asks her if he can pull up her hair, because she nods yes before his hands carefully brush back every fine dark strand obscuring her face.

Then he twists her hair into a soft little bun, big hands, like his big feet with a soccer ball, somehow so deft and dexterous, nimbly wrapping it into a hair tie without a single wince from Linnea, not one hair pulled or pinched, which is more than I can say for my uncle-doing-hair track record.

I watch them as they jam to *Encanto* in the kitchen, Gavin shaking his shoulders to the beat of the music a little, like he doesn't even know he's doing it, Linnie bouncing her knees and belting a high note.

My heart feels like the avocado Gavin's mashing up.

Linnie paints, sloppily eating her yogurt. Gavin makes guacamole, chopping cilantro, mincing onion and garlic, juicing a lime, his fingers sprinkling salt, cracking pepper. Then he dips a chip from the bag that he found in the pantry into the guac and offers it to Linnie.

She crunches on it thoughtfully, chews, swallows.

Then she bounces on her step stool, so happy with what's in her mouth, she nearly falls off.

Gavin catches her, then gently scoots the stool closer to the counter, a tight, worried expression on his face as she smiles up at him and offers him a high five for his amazing guacamole.

He high-fives her back. And that's when I know his fate is sealed.

Because the way to Linnea's heart is her stomach. And her stomach loves guacamole.

Over chips and guac, Gavin joins Linnie in her artistic efforts. Linnie's mouth moves like she's talking at him nonstop, though I can't hear her over the music, her butt bouncing to *Encanto*.

I could watch those two act like old friends in my kitchen forever, but then my stomach goes from bad to worse, making me speed-walk to the bathroom once again.

And then there's nothing pleasant to say or think for quite a while.

TWENTY

Gavin

Playlist: "I've Got You Under My Skin,"
Ben L'Oncle Soul

"One hug, Kladdkaka," Linnea says, big pale blue eyes blinking up at me. Wrestling free from underneath the sheets Oliver tucked her into, she opens her arms and says, "Pleeeease?"

I scowl at her from where I stand, arms crossed, leaning against the doorway of her room, or rather, the room Oliver clearly has set up for her. I push away the memories, the stark contrasts to my own history evoked by this scene, and tell her, "Don't push it. I blew a kiss, and that's all you're getting."

Her pout deepens.

I roll my eyes, pushing off the doorframe. "Fine. But do *not* tickle me."

She giggles. "I respect your boundaries."

"Now you do. *After* you tickled me."

She shrugs as she smiles, all wide-eyed innocence and dimples. "I didn't know you don't like tickles."

"No one likes tickles, rug rat," I grumble, bending over her and gently wrapping her in my arms. She's strong, a powerful little athlete already, but she's still so small, so vulnerable.

The old, sharp pain I've buried for so long slips through the cracks made by just one evening with her. My shitty childhood is a chapter of my life that I've done everything possible to leave behind me. But holding this little girl who's so trusting, so clearly loved, wrenches old, awful memories to the surface.

Living with those miserable excuses for family, my aunt and uncle. Realizing very early on I was better off living anywhere but with them. The backpack with all my possessions inside it that I took everywhere I went. The places I found to stay. To hide. Then, finally, Fred. And soccer. And never ever looking back.

"Good night, Kladdkaka," Linnea whispers before she plants a soft kiss on my cheek.

I swallow around the lump in my throat. "Good night, Linnea."

I have every intention of walking out of that room without so much as a glance over my shoulder, but like a fool, I stop in the doorway and turn around.

I'm rooted to the floor.

Oliver smooths Linnea's hair back from her face as she turns, curling up with a stuffed dolphin. He rubs her back in slow circles and sings softly in a language I don't understand but that I recognize from the many that I became familiar with while playing abroad. Swedish. I don't know much, just enough to recognize the words that matter. *Safe. Love.*

Something splinters inside me. Cracks clean in two.

And that's when I know I am in serious danger. In danger of wanting so much more from Oliver than just to make him come undone, to scratch this exhausting itch that I've been denying the past few weeks.

You've been denying it longer than that, says that unwelcome voice in my head.

I force myself to walk away, to remember this is what I'm good at, because it's walk away or be walked away from, and I choose to leave on my terms. To hold on with both hands to the control I ached for in my life for years and finally found in soccer. The control that's already slipping through my fingers. Here, in his house and in mine. On the pitch and on planes and in hotels and in the locker room. In my body. In the cold, jagged corners of my heart that have started to thaw and soften.

I'm halfway down the hall when I register the sound of Oliver's alarm system making the same alerting ding it did when I opened his back door. My pace quickens; my hand forms a fist. Just as a precaution, ingrained, long-ago-learned self-preservation.

A man walks in, quite tall, though not as tall as me, ball cap tugged low and obscuring his face. A thick, scraggly brown beard drifts down to his chest.

He walks in like he owns the fucking place, tossing a pair of keys absently onto the side table next to Oliver's sofa as he toes off his boots.

The world tints a furious, pulsing red. "Who the fuck are you?" I ask.

The man glances up, his face still hidden in the shadow cast by his ball cap's brim. His head dips down, as if he's raking his eyes over me. "I'd ask you the same."

I'm simply too stunned, too angry to make my mouth work. When he deduces I'm not going to answer him, he strolls past me. My pulse pounds in my fists as I stand, helpless, furious, watching this man walk through Oliver's home with such familiarity.

Wandering into the kitchen, he flicks on the lights and opens the refrigerator.

"Answer me," I growl.

He pauses, then turns, an open container of leftover quesadilla in his hands. I want to wrench it out of his grip and slap the lid on it, because that's for the little girl down the hall who begged for another quesadilla even when I knew she'd never have room for it, who is now determined to have her leftover quesadilla for breakfast.

"Put the food down," I tell him. "That's for Linnea."

He tips his head, then sets the container on the counter, snapping on the lid. Which is when Oliver strolls into the kitchen from the hallway, one hand on the baby monitor he's turning on. He comes up short, blinking at the man in his kitchen.

"Viggo?" Oliver stares at him, blinking in surprise, then glancing over at me.

Viggo. I remember that name. He's the one Oliver was yelling at, the one who'd somehow locked him out of the house. Were they lovers? Had they fought? Are they reconciled now?

Fuck, I feel sick at the thought.

"What are you doing here?" Oliver asks him.

"Hi, honeybunch." This man—*Viggo*—closes the distance between them and wraps his arms around Oliver, pulling him close, before he smacks a kiss on his cheek.

The world darkens. Blood roars in my ears. I want to rip his arms off. I want to yank him by the collar and throw him out the window and wipe every trace of his touch off Oliver's body.

Fuck. I'm shaking, rage and shock and possessive hurt slicing through me, revealing the raw, undeniable truth: I want Oliver. All of him.

I know I can't have him forever, but I want him for however long I can. Until whatever it is that finally finishes me off from professional play, and I disappear to lick my wounds and figure out what the hell to do with myself. I want him to myself. To drive him wild and hold him and give him hell and please and protect him from handsy, lanky, mangy-bearded fuckers with no respect for personal space.

"Get off," Oliver tells him, wiping his cheek as he scowls at this *Viggo*. "What are you *doing*?"

"I came to help," he says, shrugging and going back to raiding the fridge.

"He already has help," I growl, then turn toward Oliver. "Do you want him out?"

Oliver blinks my way, eyes wide. "What?"

"Do. You. Want. Him. Out?" I ask. "I will gladly remove him from your property."

The man glances over his shoulder as he tosses a handful of blueberries into his mouth. "Not very hospitable of you."

"Not the hospitable type," I tell him. "Especially if he doesn't want you here."

The man flashes a smile beneath that gnarly beard that makes the hair on my neck stand on end. It feels . . . vaguely familiar. "What's he to you?" the man asks.

"Viggo," Oliver says sharply. "This isn't funny. Get out."

The man shuts the fridge with his hip, glancing between us. "I take it I'm not needed, then."

"Absofuckinglutely not," I snap.

Oliver peers at me curiously before he turns back to Viggo and glares. "I know what you're doing, and it's messed up. I told you I was going to figure this out on my own, and I did. Now go. Raid someone else's fridge."

Viggo sighs. "Fine." Pushing off the fridge, he walks back through the living room, tugging on his shoes. He flashes another wide smile Oliver's way, then at me. "Enjoy your evening, gents."

With a salute, he swipes his keys off the table and slips out the door, shutting it quietly behind him.

I turn back toward Oliver. "What the hell was that?"

Oliver crumples onto a stool at his kitchen island and buries his face in his hands. "A man trying to make a horse wear swimming trunks."

"What the fuck does that mean? Are you delirious? Dehydrated?"

His laugh echoes inside the space of his hands. "I'm going to throttle him," he mutters.

"Oliver," I growl, making his head snap up. "What was that? Who the hell was that?"

Silence hangs in the space between us. Too late do I realize how . . . intense I sounded. How much I've just revealed.

Slowly, Oliver spins on the stool and cocks his head. "What does it matter?"

I glance away, dragging a hand through my hair, racking my brain for how to salvage this and cover my ass. "A man just . . . walked into your house and raided your fucking refrigerator."

He stares at me, then finally says, "So?"

"So?" I throw up my hands. "That's weird, invasive shit."

Oliver snorts. "Viggo to a T."

My jaw clenches. "Why . . . was he here, just walking into your house like that . . ." I try to hold back the words, but they force their way out. "Touching you like that?"

His fingertips drum softly across the counter. He stares at me. "I'm going to ask you again: Why does it matter?"

"It doesn't," I lie, anger and panic knotting inside me. I can't stay. I can't care. I try to find that place inside myself that I slip into every day—cold, contained, detached. But it's like the lights are out inside me and I can't find that familiar door, that escape I so desperately need as Oliver pushes off his stool and walks toward me, hands in his pockets.

"Fine, then," he says, shrugging. "If it doesn't matter, then you don't need to know."

"Goddammit, Bergman."

He rolls his shoulders back, chin high and proud, holding my eyes. "What, Hayes?"

I hear the air sawing out of my lungs, feel my heartbeat pounding in my ears, in my limbs. "Don't push me."

He takes another step closer. "*Now* you want answers. What happened to 'We agreed we'd move on'?"

My hands are tight, aching fists. I don't trust them not to wrap their fingers around him, pin him against me, hold him tight while I give that tart mouth what it deserves: a deep, punishing kiss. Many of them.

"This is different," I finally manage.

He tips his head. "How? You've made it clear you're past what happened. What does it matter to you who's in my house or what goes on with them?"

I don't have an answer for that. I can't explain myself. I can't admit how the past three weeks have been the worst kind of torture.

Sighing, he scrubs his face. "I know I asked you for help tonight, that I very briefly transgressed the 'strictly coworkers, only professional' truce we've stuck with the past few weeks, but that was for my niece's sake. You helped, and I appreciate it—" He closes his eyes briefly, takes a deep breath, then says, "And now I need you to go."

It knocks the air out of me, hearing him say that. I'm the one who's pushed back, created distance, ordered him to leave, booted his ass out my door. Oliver telling me to go, wishing me gone . . . fuck, it's not right.

And that's exactly what you're avoiding, the voice inside me warns.

Correct. That's exactly what I'm preemptively sparing myself— the pain of being unwanted when my allure fades with my career, when I'm nothing but a tired, sore, washed-up former athlete with more aches and pains than the poker guys combined, and *his* career takes off, drawing him to better clubs, luxurious places, the eager touch and attention given by those who'll be even more drawn to his looks and charm as he becomes more accomplished, earns more fame.

But, another voice whispers. *There's still a way, isn't there? To get what you want without risking any of that?*

I stare at Oliver as he holds my eyes, a muscle in his jaw flexing, arms crossed. Fuck, he's aggravating. And gorgeous. And I want him so damn much.

Could I do it? I have before—fucked and kept my feelings squarely out of it. With Elliot, I did it for years. When he reacted precisely how I knew he would to the news that I was leaving England, signing with the Galaxy, I felt nothing. Not disappointment, not loss, not surprise. I knew what I was to him—a means to the lifestyle he enjoyed, a famous guy to be seen with, a damn good lay with absolutely no emotional attachments required.

What if Oliver and I could have that, too? A mutually agreed upon "all fucks, no feels" understanding. I have no idea if he'd want that. And yet my desperation tells me I'm going to lose my fucking mind if I don't at least try to find out.

"It matters," I croak.

Oliver's eyes widen. "What?"

I close the distance between us, clasp his face, my thumb sliding along his cheekbone, the very place that fucker kissed him. "I wanted to tear his limbs off when he touched you."

Oliver's arms fall to his sides, and now his hands are fists like mine were, like he's struggling as much as I was a moment ago to keep them to himself. "Why?" he says quietly.

I lean in, our chests brushing, air rushing out of his lungs. "Because I want you like a sickness eating away at me, Oliver, and seeing him . . ." My jaw clenches. Words are lost.

"I want you, too," he admits, shutting his eyes, like he can't look at me and say it. "To the point of distraction. I'm so miserable. But . . . I told myself I'd never do this again. I can't."

I slide my thumb down to his jaw, slip my other hand through his hair, knead his scalp, making his eyes drift open. "What are you talking about?"

His eyes search mine for a long minute. He swallows roughly, his expression guarded. "I told myself I'm not getting involved with anyone I work with. It . . . blew up in my face badly when I was younger. And this—the team, my focus on the season and on my career—I can't risk that again. I won't let feelings complicate or compromise any of it."

Anger pulses through me as I see the pain he holds in his eyes—pain that he tries to hide. "Fucking Bryce Burrows," I growl. "That piece of diving shit."

Oliver's mouth quirks. "In retrospect, he's highly underwhelming and definitely wasn't worth all the angst, but . . ." He sighs. "That's not how I felt back then. I'm not the most rational person when I fall for someone. And I fell for him. Hard."

Ugly, potent jealousy sours my stomach.

"I want nothing more than to give in to this," he says quietly. "And I'm having a very hard time dealing with how frustrated I am denying it. But you could be very, very bad news for me, Gavin Hayes. And I didn't come this far to let another person blow up everything I've worked for."

I sift through what he's said, hunger and need making me lean into his touch, feast on the way his pupils dilate, the way his chest rises and falls unsteadily, like mine. "It doesn't have to blow up," I tell him, a plan formulating in my head.

He laughs emptily. "It doesn't, but it likely will, and then I will be screwed."

I shake my head, sliding my hands down, rounding his shoulders, holding him tight. "Just fucks. No feels."

He stares at me. "What?"

"We're both losing our minds not acting on this." I nudge my hips against his, making us both suck in a breath. Oliver's grip tightens on my pockets, holding me there when I try to pull away because it feels so good I can barely form sentences while we're touching like this. "If we scratch the itch, keep it strictly physical, feelings out of it, then you risk none of that."

He stares at me, breathing unevenly. "You'd want that?"

A groan rolls out of me. "Fuck yes." I nudge my hips against his, showing him exactly how much I want.

"You just . . ." He shakes his head. "The past few weeks, I'd swear you couldn't care less."

My hands move against my will, down his arms, threading through his fingers, stroking his palms. "That is because I am very, very good at hiding what I want and feel and need." I lean closer, my mouth a whisper from his. "I've seemed my usual surly self."

He nods.

"But I have been in hell," I admit to him. "Watching you when I shouldn't. Wanting you when I shouldn't. The things I've done to you in my mind, when I'm alone. In the shower. In my bed. Fuck, it's a madness, how much I want you."

Air rushes out of him as he wrenches his hands from mine and steps back, breathing roughly. "You promise?"

"Promise what?"

"That you're not doing this to sabotage me. That you're not going to mess with me, turn this against me somehow."

Cold fury ices my veins. "Bergman."

"Promise me," he says.

I search his eyes. "You piss me the fuck off. You are aggravatingly cheerful and much too polite on and off the pitch. You choke on set pieces and you pass the ball too readily when you should shoot instead. You are much too attractive for your own good, and your wardrobe is an affront to the eyes, but I have never, nor will I ever, do anything to sabotage your career or your happiness. You have my word."

He blinks at me. "But you . . . you used to hate me. Sometimes I still think you do."

Here's where I have to tread very, very carefully. If I admit to him—to myself—the truth, this arrangement I'm proposing will be entirely off the table. If I admit how damn much I feel about Oliver Bergman when I'm promising to fuck him senseless and satisfy this ravenous craving between us with not a drop of emotion involved, he will shut this down and for very good reason.

Because if he knows what I feel, it would give him permission to feel that, too. And that's exactly what he's asked me to promise not to do to him, what I will not do, when I know how this ends. Me leaving. Him living. Happily. Without me.

"I have never hated you," I tell him quietly, keeping my hands to myself, needing him to hear me, to understand, to believe me.

"Then, if not hate, what was the past two years, Hayes?"

I stare at him, knowing I can't tell him what I'm thinking: *That was doing everything in my power not to end up exactly where we are—loathing you for what you have while longing for who you are, aching for the person who's gained everything I'm about to lose, wanting you more than I want my next breath.*

"I hated how I felt around you." It's an incomplete truth, but it isn't a lie.

"Likewise," he fires back. "But you didn't see me being an asshole."

"Not overtly, but you found plenty of ways to get under my skin. You just did it with a smile."

He shifts uncomfortably. "I had to give it back to you *somehow*."

"Yes, well, I'm not the warm-and-fuzzy type to begin with. Having to rub shoulders with you was not going to bring out my nonexistent friendly side, especially when I was attracted to you."

His mouth parts. "Wait, you've been attracted to me—"

"Since I fucking saw you? Yes."

And I resented you for it, I almost admit. *I resented how happy you were, how gorgeous and young and promising. How content you were, when I was anything but.*

"It was irritating as fuck," I gruff. "It still is."

His mouth quirks. A faint blush stains his cheeks. "But you wanted me. You couldn't stand me, but you wanted me. You still do."

I hold his eyes. "Yes."

He bites his lip, staring at me. "So . . . it wouldn't change anything. Same dynamic as always, professional at work. And when we're home—"

"Very unprofessional," I promise him.

A smile lights up his face. His blush deepens. Then he schools his expression and offers his hand. "Deal."

I stare at his hand, then glance up, meeting his eyes. I slap away his hand, wrench him by the shirt, and drag him into my arms. "I'm going to kiss you."

He nods. "I'm good with that."

"But first, you're going to tell me who the fuck walked into your house like he owned it and kissed you first."

"My cheek," Oliver says. "He kissed my *cheek*."

I growl as I walk him backward until he's up against the wall and I'm pressing him there. "Tell me."

Oliver rolls his lips between his teeth, then says, "Don't get mad."

"Bergman," I warn.

"It was my brother."

I stare at him, feeling like the floor has dropped out from underneath me. "Your *brother*?"

Oliver's trying very hard not to smile. "Also, that night when we were in the kitchen and a woman showed up outside my place? That was my sister."

"Jesus." I rake a hand through my hair, setting distance between us. "How many fucking siblings do you have?"

His smile wins, brightening his face. "Six."

"Six!" I blink. "There are six more of you running around? God help us."

"Shut up." He grips my shirt and pulls me close. "Now do you feel like an ass?"

I stare at his mouth, at that smile that won't leave, that I want to kiss until it's a gasp of dizzied pleasure, wide with wild abandon. "A little," I admit.

"Hayes."

"Hmm," I tell his mouth.

"Up here."

Reluctantly, I tear my gaze from his lips to his eyes. "What?"

His eyes search mine. "Now that you know it was my brother and your little territorial display was unnecessary, do you still want m—"

"Don't bother finishing that question, Oliver Bergman."

He swallows. "Okay."

I slip my hands around his ribs, the powerful, lithe muscles knit to his torso. "I want you. And don't you dare ask me again."

"Okay," he whispers. And then he undoes me.

So simply, so easily, totally unaware of the power he holds. Pushing off the wall, Oliver clasps my face, then presses the softest, slowest kiss to my mouth. His fingertips work along my scalp, his thumbs slipping into the divots of my face where, not that I've been beardless once in over a decade, dimples form on the rare occasion that I smile.

"I really wish we could get this started right now," he says.

I groan as he kisses the corner of my mouth, the sensitive space behind my ear. "That's exactly what we're doing."

He sighs against my skin, making me shiver. "There's just one small hiccup in that plan."

I slip my hands beneath his shirt, touch his skin, his body, because I have to. "What hiccup is that?" I pull away, holding his eyes, seeing the smudges beneath them, the fatigue he hid so well with Linnea. "Do you feel ill again?"

Just as I say that, I notice the monitor that connects to Linnea's room is bright, lit up as she mutters something in her sleep.

I glare at the monitor, then back at Oliver. We definitely can't do what I want with a kid down the hall. "Mother *fuck*."

He smiles tightly, then leans in for one more of those slow, soft kisses that make my aching legs turn boneless. "Get some sleep, Hayes." Stepping back, he looks so infuriatingly pleased, I nearly tackle him to the wall. "You'll need it for when I get my hands on you."

I snort while stepping into my shoes, opening his back door. "That's precious. You think *I* need a warning."

"Generally, I consider it polite to give someone a heads-up when they're about to be demolished by so many orgasms, so many ways, they'll forget their own birthday, but—" He shrugs. "What do I know?"

Spinning, I face him as we stand on his threshold. Oliver stares at me, looking much too smug.

"Demolished, hmm?" I close the distance between us, tucking a hair behind his ear, my mouth lowered there. "When I'm done with you," I whisper, "you're going to have forgotten much more than that, Oliver Bergman. Every moment of pleasure another soul has given you, even pleasure at your own fucking hand, will be *gone*. I will obliterate it and ruin you for anything but my touch and my mouth and my cock. *That's* a promise."

Oliver glares at me. "Is that a challenge, Hayes?"

"It's whatever you want to call it, sweetheart. It's all going to end the same. You. Wrecked."

He tips his chin, looking me over. "Then it's on. Pistols at dawn."

I frown. "What the fuck are you talking about?"

"You clearly haven't read enough historical romances."

"Fucking correct. I've never read one. And I have no clue what you're talking about."

"That's how you threw down the gauntlet, challenged a man to a duel. And *I* challenge *you* tomorrow morning. Your place or mine. One of us will come out the victor."

I bite my lip. "Is this your deeply nerdy way of saying you want to fuck first thing in the morning?"

"Yep. Linnie gets up at the butt crack of dawn in the morning. I'll be back by seven and very, very ready to take you down. Or go down on you. Or both."

Heat rushes through me. I drag him close again, kiss him, battling his tongue, drinking in his ragged breaths. Part of me wants to tell him no. I know how I feel when I wake up, how everything fucking hurts, how slow and sore I am.

But the thought of telling him no feels physically impossible. I want him too badly. I'll . . . set an alarm. Wake myself up in time. Take a hot shower, limber up in time for when he shows up.

With one last kiss, a slow tug of his bottom lip, I pull away. "I'll text you the code. Just let yourself in."

Oliver stands there, flushed, breathless. "Okay."

I turn away, slip out of his house before I'm tempted to kiss him again, to torture us any further.

As I stroll from his yard to mine, for the first time in so, so long, I feel the buoyant pleasure of having something to look forward to. Peering up at the stars, full of rare, real joy, I smile.

TWENTY-ONE

Gavin

Playlist: "Die for You," LÉON

After a night of shit sleep, riddled with filthy fantasies starring Oliver, I wake up in a foul mood to the sound of my alarm. The world's bright as my eyes blink open. Every fucking thing, including my deeply unsatisfied, aching-stiff cock, hurts like hell. My body's in its usual agony. I feel every vertebra in my spine. The knot tightening my neck, tension banding around my temples. The first bend of my knee makes an unstoppable groan creak out of me.

I feel deeply entitled to the sour outlook with which I greet the day.

I'm too sore and miserable to go all the way into the kitchen and make myself a coffee. Instead, I piss, brush my teeth, splash my face, then stand at the sink, groaning at my reflection, the lines etched by pain, the dark circles under my eyes. "Fuck."

Swearing under my breath, I amble back toward bed, then crawl in. God, lying down feels good.

The next thing I know is my house alarm's beep, then the door falling shut. I hear his steps, brisk, familiar. A ridiculous smile tips the corner of my mouth. I'm half-asleep, telling myself to wake up, look sharp, but there's something so . . . right about lying here like a lump, knowing he's coming—his kisses, his touch, his everything.

I groan at that thought, right as Oliver's weight depresses the far side of my mattress.

Blinking open my eyes, I meet his. His smile lights up his whole face. "Hi," he says.

I don't have words for how good it feels, seeing him here—how much I need him. I take his hand, bring it to the aching muscles knitting my shoulders to my neck. "Hi," I finally tell him, my voice hoarse and gravelly from sleep.

Oliver rubs my shoulder gently before his hand slips into my hair, along my scalp. Fuck, I could just lie here, basking in his touch. Except that's not what this morning is. This morning is me obliterating him with orgasms and stunning him with my sexual prowess.

Though Oliver seems to have forgotten the challenge he issued, because when I turn, about to give him a hard, crushing kiss, he smiles, the morning lighting up his face. And then he just stares down at me before bending close, pressing a deep kiss to my mouth. Velvet hot, wet, teasing. My mouth falls open as he clasps my jaw, his thumb stroking my bottom lip, his tongue finding mine. He kisses without restraint, with as much confidence and uninhibited joy as he does everything. I love how he kisses.

His clothes come off, fast, efficient, down to his boxer briefs. I whip back the sheet, and he slides inside, mouth finding mine again, hands in my hair. All I can do is moan at the pleasure. Of his mouth and mine; of long, heavy muscles plastered against me; of his erection jutting against my hip.

Fuck, it feels good. Every morning, I wake up in pain, but now pain's sharpest edges are blunted just a little by the pleasure of his hand sliding down my body, his leg tangled with mine.

As I stare at him, he smiles a faint, lopsided smile that warms his face, brighter than the sun lighting up my room. And my heart cracks, spilling its fatal poison through my body, flooding my limbs, taking control.

No feelings, you fool. You promised yourself and him.

My hand drifts down the powerful, lean muscles of his arms, across his back. Sparks dance in my fingertips.

"You're so fucking cute in the morning," he says quietly.

I nip his throat, lave it with my tongue. "I am not *cute*."

His smile widens as he rakes his fingers through my hair. "Your hair's sticking straight up. You have a pillow crease on your cheek. You, Gavin Hayes, are unfairly cute right now. I say so."

That's it. No more pillow talk. Time for fucking. I try to reach behind me, going slow because it's as fast as I can move when I first wake up, but a sharp pain pulses in my back. Groaning, I drop back into bed.

Oliver props himself on his elbow, glancing at the nightstand drawer. Reaching past me, he opens it. "Lube. Condoms. That what you wanted?"

I nod tightly.

He smiles. "Just jumping right in, are we?"

"Damn right. Now lie down."

He flops back, lube and condoms in hand, and grins wickedly. "Bossy."

Easing onto my side, trying my best to ignore the fresh pain pulsing in my lower back, I run my hand over his pecs, tease his nipples with my thumb, first one, then the other. His eyes go hazy, and he brings a hand to my hair, playing with it as he looks at me. "Tell me," he says.

"Tell you what?" I growl, pulling him in for a kiss.

He sighs against my mouth, threads his leg tighter with mine and gently drifts his hand down my back. "What hurts."

"It's fine," I lie, holding in that truth and everything else I'm thinking. How beautiful he is in daylight, sun dancing off that halo of golden hair spread on my pillow, gilded hairs sparkling along his legs and arms and chest, arrowing down his flat, chiseled stomach. How perfect it feels, holding him, feeling him holding *me*.

My palm slides down his stomach, my knuckles teasing his hips, the edge of his underwear.

He's not amused. "Gavin."

A thrill dances through me, hearing my name on his lips. Then he presses up on his elbow, eye to eye with me. "I don't want to hurt you."

"You won't."

He frowns, searching my eyes. "You're in pain. We don't have to—"

"Fucking touch me," I beg, taking his hand, lacing my fingers with his. "I'll tell you if something hurts, but just fucking touch me, Oliver. Now."

His gaze intensifies, his thumb circling my palm. Silently, he presses into my shoulder, until I'm rolled onto my back, his eyes searching mine. "Okay?" he asks.

I nod. "Yes."

He slides his leg farther over mine, propped on his elbow, looming over me.

Historically, when I've been intimate with others, I've been in charge. It's always felt natural, given my . . . leadership-oriented nature, my propensity to control and see strategy and boss people around. But with Oliver, there's something clear as he slides his thigh higher over mine, his hand sinking into my hair as he stares down at me. He's comfortable taking charge, too. Which I knew. I've seen it on the pitch, in training, during games. His is the kind of strength and self-possession that's not wrapped in fury or aggression or acute impatience. It's poise and calm, sureness in what he's capable of, in what he wants.

And for the first time in so fucking long, I feel safe enough to give it up, to hand it to him—to let him carry everything for once.

How this will happen, the ways we'll learn each other and find pleasure.

"And this?" he asks, holding my eyes as he massages my neck gently, then my shoulder.

I nod. My voice is a croak as I tell him, "Yes."

He smiles faintly, bending, kissing me. "Good."

My arm curls around his back, pulling him close as he drifts his hand across my chest. He bends, licks my nipples, first one, then the other. My head rolls back as he kisses my throat, soft lips, warm breath, his hand drifting down my stomach, kneading sore muscles at my sides, then gently teasing along my waistband.

I grit my teeth as he bypasses my cock entirely and rubs my thighs, one at a time, ignoring how much I'm arching my hips, hungry for touch.

"Don't tease," I growl.

He smiles. "Me? Tease?"

I'm about to say something rude and demanding when he puts me out of my misery, stroking my cock through my briefs, making air rush out of me. "Yeah."

Deftly, he hooks his fingers inside my briefs and drags them down, slowly, carefully, as if he knows how fucking sore I am. He stares not at my newly exposed body, but into my eyes. "I haven't had any partners since the last time I was tested," he says. "No STIs."

I slide a hand up his arm, holding his eyes, too. "Same for me."

He drifts his hand along my thigh, then finally looks down. "Fuck," he groans, staring at my cock, hard and throbbing, jutting straight toward him.

I can't take another moment. I wrench him down, whipping the sheet around him, cocooning us in. He laughs quietly. "You're so damn impatient."

"Yes," I admit, slipping my hand inside his underwear. "Take these off, Oliver."

He does, readily, quickly, kicking them away. Part of me wants to throw back the sheets and lay him flat and stare at him, but I don't honestly have the courage to do that. Not this time. I'm already so overwhelmed that he's finally here, touching me, so close, his body perfectly nestled against mine.

I drag him closer, kiss him deeply, clasping his jaw, tangling my tongue with his. A moan leaves me as he wraps his hand around the base of my cock and strokes it, so fucking perfect. His thumb slides over the tip, working where I'm wet for him along the sensitive slit.

My balls are tight and drawn up, which Oliver feels when he slides his hand back down, cups them and grins. "Someone's close."

"Shut up," I growl.

He smiles against our kiss. "I am, too."

Pulling back, he helps himself to the lube, warms it in his hand, before he brings it back to my cock, working it harder with tight, fisting tugs that make air rush out of me.

"Fuck, Oliver. Oh fuck." I crush him against me into a deep, desperate kiss, reach for him without breaking our kiss, and find him, so hard and hot, weeping at his tip, grinding against my waist. "Don't stop," I tell him, hearing him pant as I take him in hand.

He laughs tightly. "I couldn't stop if I wanted to. Gav, easy. I'm so close."

I feel every inch of him, every inch of myself in his hand, the sweet, torturous ache thickening me in his grip as he jerks me off, pumps my cock and stares into my eyes.

"Come here," he tells me, breaking his grip only long enough to ease me toward him, lying on my side.

"Yeah," I beg, knowing what he's doing, throwing his leg over my hip as he fists both our cocks in his hand.

We groan into each other's mouths with the first pump of his hand, working us on each other, the tips of our cocks rubbing, making air rush out of me again. I clutch his hip, rutting into his fist. I have never been this desperate, this close, this fast.

Then again, I've been hard for this man for two years. I could argue this is actually the longest I've ever lasted. "Gonna come," I warn, my voice hoarse and tight.

He nods, breathless as I crush my mouth to his, gripping him hard as the first juts of my release paint his hand, his cock, which stiffens even more.

He groans my name, his release pulsing from him as he works himself against me.

I gasp, my hands frantic, holding him against me, needing to feel him come everywhere, in his legs as they lock around mine, his hips punching against mine, his chest brushing mine, his lips chasing mine eagerly as my hips jerk again with another desperate rush of release.

I groan his name, too, pleasure flooding my body as I watch him roll his hips once more and shudder another hot ribbon of release along my stomach.

Our breaths saw out of our lungs as I look at him, stroking his hair, as his hand still touches us, even as we soften, holding us close, our pleasure a glorious, long-awaited mess that makes him smile.

Leaning in, I press a slow, hungry kiss to his mouth, then ease onto my back. My eyes feel heavy. My body feels heavier. I tuck Oliver against me, feeling sleep weigh me down. I tell myself I won't sleep, just . . . rest my eyes for a few. Because soon it'll be time to get up and get ready for our game . . .

Time dissolves, warm as the cloth he uses to wipe us clean, gentle as his body tucked against mine.

The next thing I know is Oliver's voice, as if coming from the end of a tunnel. He sounds so far away. Relief washes through me as I realize I still feel his body close. "Gavin," he says.

"Hmm?" I nuzzle the crown of his head, sigh contentedly. "Give me ten minutes," I tell him, "and then I'm going to wreck you."

He laughs against our kiss, then pulls away on a sigh. "I wish. But we have to get up and get moving. We've got a game today . . . Wait . . ." Oliver blinks, props himself up on his shoulder. "Did we fall asleep?"

Like in a screwball comedy, our eyes widen in tandem, then snap to the digital clock I keep on my dresser.

We were supposed to be at the stadium fifteen minutes ago.

That's when we both yell, "Fuck!"

TWENTY-TWO

Oliver

Playlist: "Everything Moves," Bronze Radio Return

Gavin drives like a bat out of hell and gets us to the stadium in record time.

"Flat tire," he tells Coach, who sits in her office with Rico and Jas, before she can ask where we've been and why we're forty-five minutes late. "Very sorry," he says, double-tapping her door. "Hasn't happened before, won't happen again."

I nod. "Sorry, Coach."

She glances between us and sucks her teeth. "Uh-huh. Get your asses in there."

"Yes, Coach." I salute her as Gavin drags me past the door, down the hall.

"You good?" he asks.

He's favoring his left leg, limping slightly. I watch him walk, concern tightening those anxious bands around my chest.

"Bergman," he barks.

I snap my head up. "Yeah, I'm good. You?"

He glances over his shoulder, something fierce in his gaze, a fire that's doused as soon as we make eye contact. "I'm fine."

It's said with finality. A tone that says, *Do not cross me on this*. Like he knows I'm aware of every sore spot on him that I touched, every movement as he eased out of bed that made him wince and hiss a breath before he threw back a handful of ibuprofen, swallowed them dry, and forced himself to move faster than I knew he wanted to.

I don't understand how someone whose body is so clearly hurting and hurt goes out on that field and runs through that kind of pain, collides bodies, takes tackles, forces himself into bursts of vicious speed up the midfield.

I'm worried about him. And judging by the angry look he gives me as he catches me staring at him, Gavin knows it.

"Eyes up," he says sharply, opening the door to the locker room. "Focus."

"I don't need you to tell me to focus on my fucking job, Hayes."

The faintest smirk tips his mouth. "Good."

He follows me into the room. I glance back. "Aren't you supposed to go see Dan and Maria? Get your pregame tune-up?"

His lip curls as he brushes by, ignoring me. Santi's on him, asking questions—Ethan, too. They so obviously look up to him, even though he scares the shit out of them. He's got this instant magnetic force of authority. I watch him listen, answer questions, set them at ease in his terse, no-bullshit way.

When he catches me watching him, he arches an eyebrow. I look away. And then I tell myself it's time to suit up and kick some ass out on that field.

———

I'm playing the best soccer of my life. Despite being nearly constantly double-teamed by my opponent's defenders, I have two goals and an assist, and my legs feel lighter than air.

Clearly, I should get laid before a game more often.

We're at the eighty-five-minute mark when that thought crosses my mind, the first time I've thought of Gavin in that way since we went out on the field. I haven't been distracted, haven't felt myself pulled toward him or fixating on him or this morning, on anything except the game unfolding around me and my responsibility to make it a winner.

Not yet, that voice inside me whispers. *But it's only a matter of time until it blows up in your face.*

For the first time, I glance back at the midfield, spotting Gavin instantly. The wind snaps his hair back, revealing his stern features—severe brows, neat beard, dark eyes tinged with gold as the sun bathes him in its rays. He looks pissed—he always looks pissed during games—but I know he's just ruthlessly focused.

I am, too.

I know exactly where my wingers are, where the goalie is behind me, as I cut across the field and Gavin snaps the perfect pass my way. God, his precision is freakish. The ball flies right past my feet as I seal off my defender, then take off, catching the ball in stride and barreling toward the goal.

I feel him before I see him in my peripheral vision, powering down the field, forcing his way past a defender who throws an ineffectual shoulder his way. The guy bounces off of him as Gavin cuts right, open for the pass that I send his way, then one-touches it into the back of the goal.

Relief soars through me. We've earned a lot of goals today, but unfortunately so has our opponent. With this one, we've narrowed the deficit. Now we're down only one.

I can't help but crack the widest smile as the stadium explodes, as the team piles up on Gavin. He shoves them off, one by one, but he ruffles their hair, shoves good-naturedly. And when he looks at me, he smiles.

"Fucking brilliant," he says, tugging me toward him, forehead to forehead, before he shoves me off. A gesture of pride, connection, that makes my heart pound in my chest.

I keep my eyes down on my cleats as he walks past me, deeper on our side, in preparation for kickoff, but I can't wipe away the happiness inside me, lighting me up. It's the kind of joy that fills me from the top of my head to the tips of my toes, that makes my fingertips hum and sends a kick of jittery, giddy adrenaline flooding my veins. I feel on top of the world.

Which is why it's all the more jarring when, just thirty seconds later, as I step up to challenge our opponent's defense, a vile slur cuts through the air and punctures that happy aura. It's not the first time I've heard the word. And, unfortunately, in all likelihood it won't be the last. Being reconciled to the fact doesn't make it easier, though. The defender who said it throws his shoulder into me sharply after he passes the ball, sneering as he jogs past me and glances back.

Unfortunately for him, looking back at me leaves him entirely unprepared for a six-foot-four, livid co-captain shoving him violently to the ground.

"Hayes!" I sprint forward, stepping in front of Gavin, hands on his chest. "Hayes. Stop."

Gavin's not looking at me. He's glaring murder at the defender, chest heaving, that vein in his temple throbbing. "I'll fucking kill him."

"Shut up," I tell him, grabbing his face. "Don't say that."

He lunges forward, and I have to shove him back. "I don't fucking care."

"*I* care." I grab his shoulders again. "Stop."

The ref jogs over, whistling and halting play. I'm about to open my mouth and defuse things, when Gavin turns, shoves me behind him, and proceeds to tell the ref in a shockingly calm tone what happened.

"Get him the fu—" Gavin catches himself, his jaw clenching. "Get him off this pitch," he says, pointing at the defender. "Or this game is over. We'll walk right off."

Coach is out on the field now, walking as fast as her extremely pregnant body allows her, followed by Rico and Jas. The other team's coach comes out, too.

The refs turn toward me. Ask me to corroborate. I won't say the word. I won't dignify that hatred by repeating it. But I nod when they say it, asking if that's what was directed at me.

And then I feel it. Those bands narrowing around my ribs. My hands turning numb. My heart rate accelerating faster than Gavin's car as he gunned it down the road this morning and got us to the stadium. I sway as I start to lose feeling in my legs.

"Hey." Gavin's there, gripping my arm, tugging me toward him. "You're all right."

I shake my head. My knees buckle.

"Fuck, Oliver. Breathe." He tugs me closer, holding me tight. "You're okay. You're safe." His head snaps up as he looks toward the team. "Oy!"

The world's swimming, its sounds reduced to my too-fast tugs of air, my heart pounding in my ears, but I see them—first Santi, then Ben, Ethan, Carlo, Andre, even Amobi, who bolts down the field—everyone circling around us, boxing us in.

You'd think being swarmed by the team roster when I'm hyperventilating would make things worse. But it's just like the tight embrace Gavin wraps me in, pinning my head against his shoulder—it grounds me, comforts me, shields me.

"Breathe," he says quietly, his hand heavy on my back.

As my breaths become less frantic, I hear what I couldn't before, Santi muttering under his breath, praying maybe, encouraging me, perhaps both—soft, whispered Spanish. Carlo's Portuguese drifts on the air, blending with Andre's French. Ben wraps an arm around Ethan, another around Amobi, shouldering out a videographer, sealing us off.

"You got this, Oliver."

"We're here."

The team's words, some in English, some not, are quiet, peaceful, their presence steadying. "Gav," I whisper.

"What do you need?" he says, hand pressing on my back.

I can't answer him. I just need to know he's there, to feel him grounding me to earth.

"Focus on my breaths, Oliver. Breathe when I do."

"Trying." I lick my dry lips. "Talk?"

He clears his throat. "Coach is going to murder someone. She is an eight-and-a-half-months-pregnant fury, and the ref is about to shit himself."

I feel a faint smile tug at my mouth. I suck in a breath of air that feels deeper, a little slower, not shallow and dizzying. "More."

"Listen," he says. "You can hear her."

"I don't give a *damn* what that playback video does or does not show you," Coach growls at the other team's coach. "Your player used a slur on one of mine, which means he's out. You're better than this and your team should be, too. Zero tolerance."

As we both listen to Coach obliterating the weak placations of our opponent's coach, I feel Gavin's anger, like a banked fire waiting for fresh oxygen to send it roaring to life. I feel his control, the way he steadies himself for me, holding me tight.

"Damn right," Coach says after a stretch of conversation between the refs and the other coach that I couldn't hear. "Hayes!"

Gavin hesitates.

"I'm okay," I tell him, shakily stepping back. I can feel my hands. My legs aren't solid, but I can stand on my own. The team's there for me to turn to, still reassuringly close.

Gavin glances from me to Coach, torn.

"Go," I tell him.

He strides off, furious yet controlled. He exchanges brief words with the ref and both teams' coaches, then watches the defender, who's walked off the field after being given his red card. And then, with a blank expression and a curt nod, Gavin receives a yellow for the well-deserved shove he doled out.

I lower to a crouch, feeling blood flow back into my brain, dispelling the dizziness, the punching stars in my vision. Jas steps in, crouching, too, their dark eyes meeting mine, tight with concern. "Okay, Bergman?"

Drawing in a deep breath, I realize that I am, somehow. That what just happened for the first time in front of my teammates somehow feels like it had less power over me *because* it happened in front of them, because they stood by me and protected me when I was at my most vulnerable.

I knuckle away a single tear that's formed in the corner of my eye, nodding.

Jas stands and offers their hand, which I clasp and let them use to haul me upright. "Yeah," I tell them, feeling sureness fill me up and strengthen my voice. "I am."

"Bergman." Coach sets her hand gently on my back, looking up at me, her eyes tight with fury and hurt. "I'm sorry."

I force a smile. "You have nothing to apologize for."

Gavin's beside me, his shoulder brushing mine. I wish so badly right in this moment I could slip my hand inside his, that he could hold it tight.

"We don't have to finish this game," he says, looking at Coach but saying this for my benefit. Clearly they've discussed this. "We can walk off this field right now."

I glance out at the clock, seeing it dwindle toward the ninety-minute mark, mentally adding at least five minutes of stoppage time. Then I look out at my teammates, at that wide-open goal calling my name.

"I want to finish it," I tell them. "I feel a little shaky, but it'll feel good to move again, run through it, end strong. He got kicked off." I nod toward the other end of the field, where the defender walked out. "That's enough for me."

"And he'll be getting slapped with a fine," Coach tells me.

Gavin's staring at me, eyes tight. "You sure?"

I nod, glancing out across the field. I want to get out there and score, not just tie it up, but win. Not because I have anything to prove in light of the hatred I experienced today; their bigotry isn't my burden to bear. I want to win this game because I believe it's possible, because I believe in myself, because right here, right now, pouring everything I have into this game, is exactly where I want to be.

After convening with the refs, Gavin and I pull the team together. I glance up at the clock, seeing five minutes of added stoppage time, just like I thought. As the ref walks toward me with the ball, Gavin stares past me, eyes dark, expression unreadable. I feel anger rolling off him in waves. Following his line of sight, I catch another player on the team giving me a nasty look. Clearly, he thinks his teammate was treated unfairly.

I flash him my widest smile, then happily accept the ball from the ref.

The next four minutes are an exercise in frustration. My opponent's defenders double-team me like they have all through the game, and now they're trying to rough me up—emphasis on *trying to*. There's a real upside to being six three and a hundred and eighty pounds of pure muscle; I don't really budge.

We're still down one, and I'm so hungry to score, it's like a fire in my blood.

As a foul's called on the other team, I run up as high on the field as I can while staying onside, watching the clock, knowing at any minute they might blow the whistle.

That's when I feel it, the weight of Gavin's gaze on me. Peering up, I meet his eyes and try to make some kind of sense of his thunderous expression. I can see that vein in his temple pulsing from here, and as the whistle blows, as he takes that very first touch on the ball, I know something's different. It's like traveling back in time, seeing a player I haven't since before I became a professional myself. Gavin *flies*. Moving with the ball in a burst of speed, footwork so fast it's a blur, he burns through the midfield. I drop deep and wide, clearing space for him, mindful to stay onside.

Tearing down the field, he heads straight for the defender who gave me the nasty look when we resumed play, who's kept his mouth shut but made it clear with how many times he keeps stepping on my foot and throwing an elbow that he's trying to make me miserable.

The guy lunges as Gavin cuts with the ball, leaving his legs splayed, and Gavin deftly slips the ball right through his legs. He's nutmegged him. The stadium's chanting, screaming, losing their collective shit at what they're seeing.

My heart's in my throat, my pulse pounding, as Gavin steps around the defender he's just embarrassed and made fall on his ass. On his first touch, he sends the ball arcing through the air straight to me. I sprint toward it, knowing it's perfect—that I'm as fast as he needs, that he's sent the ball exactly where it needs to go.

My head connects with the ball, which flies into the corner of the net.

Goal!

I'm screaming, elated, smiling so wide my face hurts, as the team piles on top of me, shouting, thrilled. We're tied. Which is good. Fine. But not great.

Not enough.

My eyes lock with Gavin's in understanding. He glances toward the dwindling time. Thirty seconds left. I know exactly how we're going to use it.

To win.

TWENTY-THREE

Gavin

Playlist: "You'll Never Walk Alone," Penny and Sparrow

Endorphins pump through my body. I stare out at the field, feeling energy, fire, in my limbs like the game I loved never left me, like everything I have is at my fingertips, in my feet, about to pour out onto the grass until it seeps into its soil. I feel the strength in my body, even knowing it's ebbed. I feel my voice, hoarse and sharp, cutting up my throat from my place in the middle of the field, from the center of this place that's the center of my world.

I see Oliver, drink him in. Chest heaving. Flushed. Dripping in sweat. Hair half out of that infuriating spurt-of-gold ponytail.

Fucking perfect.

The whistle blows. There's no time to tell him what I want to do. Our opponent has the kickoff, and they're already sending it deep into our end. Ben's fucking useful for once, winning it off their offense, dropping it to Amobi, who works it over to Carlo.

Carlo sends it up the wing to Ethan. Cutting in, Ethan sees me ahead, higher in the midfield, and sends the ball my way. I wait for him, toying easily with my defender, faking him out and breezing by. I hear the stadium noise tick up, feel the hairs on the back of my neck stand on end.

Reading my tactic, Ethan cuts toward midfield as I stretch the field, deep toward the sideline, drawing out the defense until the box is exactly how I want it, wide open, with Oliver running in to fill it.

I trust Ethan to know I want a give-and-go, having screamed at him since preseason started to see those triangulations quicker. I send the ball his way, and he reads me perfectly, a straight shot down the field.

But farther than it should be.

Cursing under my breath, I explode, a hot warning pain radiating through my back, slicing down my leg. I ignore it, sprint toward the ball as it darts dangerously close to the goal line.

My defender's hot on my heels. Too close for me to get a foot on the ball and keep it inbounds. At least, for me to get an *upright* foot on the ball. At the last moment, I slide in across the goal line and nudge the ball to safety when it's inches from the paint.

The stadium erupts as my defender trips and stumbles past me, as I crawl upright and sprint back onto the field. The next defender's barreling toward me. I fake right, as if going for the goal, then tap the ball left, making him stumble, too.

And then I see him, tall, lightning fast, that golden head of hair heralding his arrival. As Oliver sprints toward the goal, I flick the ball off the outside of my right foot. It's one step in front of him. Then he's there with a one-touch to the back of the net.

Goal!

Arms raised, I feel triumph singing through my veins.

But then a body slams into me, wrenching my back. There's a pop, and a burn blazes through me, chased by pain like I've never known, swallowing up the world in darkness.

I know it's a dream. No, a nightmare. And yet I can't make myself wake up.

My pain is dulled, thank God, my steps measured, as I walk

into the locker room and drink it in. The polished wood of each player's cubby glinting under the lights. The funk of soccer gear and body sweat. The sound of my bag dropping at my feet like it has for seventeen years. The creak of my cubby's bench beneath my weight as I stare down at my bag, the tools of my trade: a ball, a few scraps of flimsy fabric, a pair of cleats.

My armor against the world. The armor that *became* my world. When no one wanted me, when I hated everything, when I felt helpless and hopeless. Soccer was everything.

I want to wake up. I don't want this dream to be reality. But somehow I know reality isn't what I want either, so I stay, just a little longer. Instead of waking, I walk out of the tunnel as I have so many games, the lights flooding my vision when I step onto the grass.

I can't leave it without saying goodbye.

And that's when I know the truth.

It's over. Done.

All that's left is to say goodbye.

With the wind in my hair, the give of the grass beneath my feet, a silent, empty stadium, I stand. And feel it.

An end. A loss.

I suck in a breath. Then another. My chest aches. My eyes burn. My breathing turns tighter as I drop to the grass, crush it in my hands. My heart pounds, a pain in my chest that intensifies until I swear it's going to split me apart—

"Hayes."

A warm hand clasps mine, wrenching me awake to a familiar presence. Sympathetic dark brown eyes. Calm, even voice.

"Coach," I croak.

Her mouth lifts with a small smile. Her hand squeezes mine. "Lexi."

Just one word. It carries a world in it. She's not my coach anymore. Because I don't play for her. Because it's over. I'm done. I knew it when I ran down that field, when I poured everything I had left in me into that last play and pain knocked me unconscious.

I swallow thickly, blinking away tears. "Lexi."

Coach swallows, too, and dabs the corner of her eye. "Damn pregnancy hormones," she mutters.

Our gazes hold. Gently, she lets go of my hand and sits back in the chair beside my hospital bed. "You're gonna be okay," she says quietly, her eyes not leaving mine.

"Am I?"

She nods. Confident, reassuring. A coach, through and through. "Dr. Chen said so. Though I don't mean just your body. I'm talking about this—" She taps over her heart. "This, too."

I sniff as I clench my jaw, resenting her faith in me. "I don't have what you do. This was everything. This was all I had."

"It was. It *was*." Sitting up, she leans in and clasps my hand again. "And it was beautiful. But that doesn't mean it's all you *can* have. I've been there, Hayes. I know. I know right now it doesn't feel believable, it feels like an insurmountable loss. That's grief, and it's yours to feel.

"And yet I'm going to tell you as your friend, as someone who's been where you are, there is more. There is friendship, there is love, there is community, there is a beautiful world out there, yours to know and be known by."

I blink up, staring at the ceiling. "I don't know how . . ." My words die off.

She's quiet, her hand holding mine. "You will. You're going to figure it out. How to recognize and receive the people who love you, the life waiting for you. And until you're ready to reach for that, I have one last directive for you, Hayes."

I force myself to meet her eyes. "What?"

"I want you to stay. I want you to lead. I want you back on that field."

"I can't," I tell her thickly.

"You can." She leans in. "You will." Her hand clasps mine the tightest it has yet. "Only from the other side of that white line." Her warm smile sparks something small and fragile, the faintest flicker of hope. "Who knows. With some new perspective, you might just find exactly what you're looking for."

TWENTY-FOUR

Gavin

Playlist: "I Do," Susie Suh

Being hospitalized, poked, and scanned until I'm practically radio-active buys me twenty-four hours of reprieve. Twenty-four hours before I have to face Oliver. Before I have to put an end to what barely ever began.

When I hear banging on my back door, dread fills me. Slowly, I walk my way to the door and unlock it.

Like it's a normal week in his life, that he's often verbally harassed and I'm regularly stretchered off a field, Oliver whistles as he breezes by me, carrying a baking sheet stacked high with containers.

"What the fuck is that?" I shove the door shut behind him.

He slides the tray onto my kitchen island. "You changed the code."

"Intentionally."

"Honestly, at this point I should just have a key."

"Hell no." I walk gingerly toward him, then ease onto a stool because everything hurts too much for me to stay standing, let alone help him. "I'd come home to a rainbow-confetti-blitzed house."

"That would require you to *leave* your house in the first place," he says, throwing me a look.

I flip him off.

He grins.

"As for your suspicions," he says, "I'll concede, it's not outside the realm of possibility or my existing repertoire."

"I pity your parents."

"Oh, me too. God bless them. They're getting *all* the jewels in their heavenly crown."

I frown as I watch him unload container after container of food into my refrigerator. "What is all this?"

"It's this stuff called food, Hayes. You need it to stay alive. Heal. Feel good. Ring a bell?"

"I'm eating," I grumble.

He cocks an eyebrow, then goes back to rapidly transferring dishes from the tray to my refrigerator. "Peanut butter protein bars and Gatorade do not a complete meal make."

"I was going to get to the store."

My refrigerator, which was indeed virtually empty before this, is now filled. I stare at all the containers in disbelief. "This is obscene."

"Don't look at me," he says. "Well. That's not quite true. Look at me for those, those, and those." He points to a row of wide Pyrex containers. "I made those, but the rest is the poker guys, my mom, and a few folks from the team whose culinary capability I trusted. I started a meal sign-up, and these dishes were volunteered in no time. All of them can be frozen once you figure out what you want to eat in the next few days and what you'd like to save. Even Linnie whipped something up, with Mom's help. She made you your namesake dish—"

"Kladdkaka." I stare, speechless, as he lifts the lid on a cake carrier, revealing what looks like a rich chocolate cake. "Why does she call me that?" I ask hoarsely.

Oliver clears his throat, avoiding my eyes as he inspects the cake. "Before you came over, she was nervous you'd be grumpy with her. I reassured her you wouldn't by comparing you to kladd-kaka: hard on the outside, but warm and gooey on the inside."

Carefully, he puts the lid back on.

My heart knots. "These . . ." I swallow thickly. "People cooked for me?"

Oliver shuts the fridge door behind him, looking at me carefully, like an X-ray down to my soul. "Of course. They love you, Gavin."

He pushes off the fridge, then walks around the island. Careful not to knock any of my throbbing limbs, he steps in between my spread thighs and cups my face. I flinch, but he doesn't. His thumbs just sweep along my cheekbones. "Why is that so hard to believe?"

I shut my eyes.

I'm trying so hard to be strong. To pull away. To keep that vital distance between us. And Oliver is so fucking good at blasting right through it. I want to lean into his touch. I want to beg him to make me feel anything besides hurt from the marrow of my bones to where I swear I can feel it pulsing in my fingertips.

"Hmm." Gently, he tips up my chin, examining me. "You haven't shaved."

I haven't had a steady enough hand. The pain in my back is so sharp, my hand shakes when I've tried. But I don't tell him that. Instead, I say, "Haven't felt like it."

He leans a little closer, presses his nose to my hair. "You need a shower, too."

Equally daunting, when my legs and back have hurt so bad, I haven't felt confident I could handle the agony caused by the movement necessary to wash myself. I've been worried that I'd black out from it and knock my head.

I shrug, which, of fucking course, hurts.

"Good thing I'm here," he says.

I glare up at him. "Fuck. No."

He smiles, glides his hands through my filthy hair. A groan rolls out of me. Damn, that feels good. "You sure about that?" he says. "I could wash your hair for you. Give you a fresh shave. Change those stinky sheets on your bed."

A moan sneaks out before I can bite it back and instead say something cutting, cold, anything to push him away.

"Just imagine," he says, still massaging my scalp. "Cool, crisp sheets. Your skin smelling like soap instead of sweat. No prickly scruff on your neck. Your hair wet and clean."

"Shit," I groan.

His smile widens. "Better than dirty talk, isn't it?"

"Go away," I beg.

He smooths back my hair, which clings to my sweaty forehead. I glare at him, hating how exposed I feel, how defenseless I am—sensation, pain, need, fear flooding me, overwhelming me. I don't want him to see me like this. And yet he has. He's here still. He's not gone.

But he will be, that warning voice whispers.

He shakes his head. "You're so darn hypocritical."

"What the fuck are you talking about?"

"You held me, rounded up the team to shield me after I was verbally harassed, while I had a panic attack in front of twenty-five thousand people."

"I should have knocked his fucking lights out," I growl, hating the memory, seeing it again, the word leaving that piece of shit, then hitting its mark with Oliver, whose eyes widened, then dimmed.

I long ago learned to harden myself against people's bigotry, the disapproving looks and homophobic comments, sometimes in other languages that weren't hard to translate. I got stronger, bigger, more intimidating, until most people were too scared to insult me, at least to my face. I built my walls higher, made myself colder, froze them out until I felt nothing when ignorant words came my way.

But that's not who Oliver is—no chilly detachment, no thick skin or sky-high boundaries, nothing shielding his heart when that word struck its blow. I wanted to disembowel that piece of queerphobic shit for putting a stricken look on Oliver's face.

"Hayes."

"Hmm?"

Oliver slips his finger down my forehead, my nose, tracing my mouth. "I didn't mean for you to go down crappy memory lane. My point is, you helped me. You took care of me. Now I'm going to help and take care of you."

"The fuck you are." I stare at him, a knot in my throat. Angry. Relieved. Scared. "I don't have an easy way to get clean," I admit. "Don't like baths, so no tubs. No bench in my shower, either. I never thought . . ."

I never thought I'd *need* a shower with a bench. Because I've been living in fucking denial. How else did I think it would end? I always knew I wouldn't walk off the pitch for the last time. I knew nothing could tear me away from this game other than my body being rendered irrevocably unfit to return to it.

"I don't know how to do it," I finally manage.

Oliver searches my eyes before an easy smile returns. "Well, then you are in luck, my friend. Because I have a shower chair. I'll go grab it and bring it right over."

"Why do you have that?"

"My dad had most of his leg amputated and uses a prosthetic limb; he finds it much easier to sit while showering. My soon-to-be sister-in-law has rheumatoid arthritis, uses a cane for stability, so I made the leap that she'd value that option, too. They both live close; the chances that they'd need my shower are slim, but I didn't want them to ever be here and need a rinse-off and for that basic function of my bathroom to be inaccessible to them." He shrugs. "It's not hard to keep a shower chair in my closet, ready for when they might need it, or hell, when *I* might need it. Statistically, it's only a matter of time until I bust something and need the thing myself. When I've saved up enough, I'm gonna redo that shower, build a bench, but for now, this is what I've got."

Not that I'm surprised by this confession, knowing what an obscenely considerate, kind person Oliver is, but it makes a difference, hearing it from him, anyway—that he's grown up loving and admiring someone whose body knows pain and hardship, that not only his own flesh and blood but also the woman his brother loves struggle with pain and mobility, and it's so . . . fucking natural to him to see them, to consider them.

To love them.

Maybe it's because I'm so damn desperate to feel clean. Maybe it's because I'm lonely and in so much pain, I can barely think about anything besides that. But rather than tell him to fuck off and, with what strength I have left, not so politely shove his ass out of my house, I hold Oliver's eyes and tell him, "All right."

"Fuck. Shit. Fucking shit," I growl as I ease onto the shower chair and set the hand towel that Oliver left draped on it across my lap for modesty's sake.

"How's it going?" he asks on the other side of the door.

"Fucking peachy," I call.

"All clear?"

"I'm decent, if that's what you mean." I peer down at the towel. "Well, decent-ish."

The bathroom door whips open. Through the fogged-up glass, Oliver is visible, walking in, wearing the shortest, tightest pair of swim trunks I have ever seen.

And of fucking course, they're the most heinously vibrant multi-colored floral print.

"I know," he says, stepping in, sliding the shower door closed behind him. "They look amazing on me."

I shake my head as he steps closer, inspecting the bottles, finding the shampoo, and squirting it into his palm. "You did it just to torture me," I tell him. "I have to sit here literally at eye level with—" I make the mistake of glancing at his groin and swallow roughly.

Oliver's got a flush to his cheeks as he starts lathering shampoo into my hair. "Well, then I guess you'll just have to shut your eyes and focus on relaxing if you can't appreciate the beauty of my psychedelic hibiscus swim trunks."

"The print's seared into my retinas." I shut my eyes, tip my head back. "Like fireworks, when you see them on the backs of your eyelids."

"Man, I love fireworks," he says. "That boom that just rattles your chest, colors splashing across the sky like a big flick of the cosmic paintbrush."

I sigh as he steps behind me and scrubs my scalp. He takes his time, deep circular motions with his fingertips, before his touch eases down my scalp to the base of my skull, which throbs with a headache. Next he scrubs near my temples, massaging there, too. Then he detaches the showerhead to rinse it, his hands capable and steady, running through my hair.

"Next," he says, stepping around me, dropping to his knees, and organizing his tools to the right. Shaving cream. My razor. A small bowl that's collected shower water to rinse it.

I shut my eyes, suddenly panicked, overwhelmed. It's too much, too intimate.

But right as I open my eyes, as I'm about to tell him I can't do this, Oliver pushes up on his knees and faces me with a beard of shaving cream, thick white gloop pasted across his eyebrows, too.

I snort an involuntary laugh that echoes around the shower. He looks ridiculous.

"Hey, now," he says, striking a pose. "No laughing. I look good. Like Santa Claus who got Botox."

"Stop," I say hoarsely. "Stop making me laugh. It hurts."

My back does hate to laugh. But my heart loves it, this moment that he's here at my feet, being ridiculous for my sake.

"Oh damn." He squints. "Shaving cream in my eye."

"Come here." I wipe the shave cream that's dripped over his eye, cup my hand into the shower water overhead until it's full, then gently rinse his eye, half washing away his ridiculous shaving cream beard, too. "There."

His eyes crack open, then meet mine.

I tell myself to let go, my hand to stop cupping his face, my thumb to stop sliding along the sharp plane of his cheekbone.

But I can't.

I just . . . can't. I can't fight it any longer. I feel . . . broken. My body, my resolve. I've built my walls so many fucking times, only for Oliver to crash through them over and over again, and I simply cannot turn him away again.

I lean closer. Oliver leans in, too, until our mouths are so close. Until I realize I'd get a mouthful of shaving cream if I did what I want. Oliver seems to realize this, too. He jerks away, looking self-conscious. Like some freakish contortionist, he arches back deeply under the water and rinses his face.

If I attempted that right now, I'd die. Just die of pain.

I wait for the familiar envy, resentment, anger to flood my body, to wipe away my desire for him.

But it doesn't come.

Instead, this horrible, awful ache settles in my heart, a knot slipping around it, tightening. I have the most terrifying thought—no, vision?—that this knot, insistent and tight, is the end of a tether, and that tether, gossamer fine yet tensile strong, stretches from my heart, through the air and space and, fuck, even time, and its other end, its home, is a knot like mine, around another's heart.

Around his.

Oblivious to my world-upending thoughts, Oliver straightens and shakes like a wet dog, sprinkling me.

"Oy." I scowl at him.

"Like you weren't wet already." He grins, back to his playful self as he pushes up on his knees again, shaving cream in hand.

Eyes on his task, he lathers it on my neck, along my beard.

"Nice and steady," he says as he grips the razor in one hand, my chin in the other.

I swallow. Oliver smiles a wicked sort of grin, eyes on his task. "Do you know how much self-control it's taking not to sing *Sweeney Todd* right now?"

"Just what I want to hear with a blade at my neck: you're feeling inspired by a murderous singing barber."

His grin widens, eyes on his task still, his grip on my jaw firm and steady as he drags the blade up my neck. "For someone who 'doesn't like musicals,' you know an awful lot about them."

I fight the urge to swallow but can't help it. The nervous need overwhelms me. "After that first game, when we watched *Hamilton* ..."

Oliver pauses shaving me, meeting my eyes. "After *Hamilton* ...?"

"I . . ." Another nervous swallow. "You said Lin-Manuel Miranda was Sondheim and Shakespeare. High praise. I love poetry, love Shakespeare's sonnets. So . . . I started poking around Sondheim musicals. Found a few I liked."

His hand falters. Now it's his turn to swallow thickly. "Which ones?"

"*Sweeney Todd*. Such a bizarre story, but 'Johanna,' that first stanza, the lyricism ... Then *Into the Woods*. Weird but rather deliciously dark and catchy. *Company*. Delightfully irreverent. *A Funny*

Thing Happened on the Way to the Forum. Fucking hilarious. And, of course, *West Side Story*. Which definitely did not, as the youths say, 'get me in my feels.'"

Oliver bites his lip. "You cried like a baby when Tony sang 'Maria,' didn't you?"

"I did no such thing."

He rolls his eyes, returning to shaving my neck.

"I may have shed a few brief, manly tears."

He snorts. "*Manly tears*. As if our masculinity's threatened when we weep freely and feel feelings, or worse, learn how to articulate them. The horror!"

I laugh quietly. "It's horseshit."

"That it is," he says, gently tipping my chin down, starting on the edge of my beard along my cheek.

"Your dad didn't raise you that way?" I ask.

He shakes his head. "Nope. My dad hugs me just as much as he hugs my sisters, just as hard and long as my mom does. Actually, often longer." He laughs quietly. "Kisses my head still every time he says goodbye. Wouldn't change it for the world."

I stare at him, recognizing another yawning gap, another world of difference between us. "You're very lucky."

Oliver nods, eyes on his task. "Don't I know it. I mean, don't get me wrong—he's scary as hell when he's mad, but that has lots more to do with him being my height, broad as a house, than with him getting particularly loud, and never rough physically. He's a giant teddy bear, really, who I've always been desperately afraid to disappoint."

I roll my eyes. "Like you ever disappointed him."

Oliver glances up. His face guarded. "Hayes, the pranks I played on you, that's nothing compared to what I was capable of when I was younger. I mean, I was a mischief-making pain in the ass. That halo over my head?" He points to the head in question. "A recent turn of events. Just since I signed with the Galaxy. Figured I better clean up my act."

"Hmm." I peer down at him. "Well, for what it's worth, I've liked it when your halo slipped a little. It's good, you know. To not care quite so much, to not please *everyone*, *all* the time."

He shrugs, dipping the razor in the water, rinsing it. "Yeah. I'm starting to figure that out. It just feels . . . safer to be what people need, to keep things positive rather than sharing the messy stuff. I hide behind that upbeat front. It's not all purely good intentions."

"Everyone hides," I tell him. "One way or another. At least your way is kind. You see people in a way others don't. You see the good in them. You make them feel special and appreciated. You hold on to hope in moments that are so easy to be cynical about. If that's not bravery, nothing fucking is. Don't discredit yourself."

Oliver stares at me, eyes wide, a faint, warm pink on his cheeks. The razor clatters from his hand to the water bowl. He swallows thickly. "Hayes."

Heat fills me, until I'm sure I'm as flushed as he is. I don't regret what I said. But I do regret how exposed I feel. How aware I am that but for a few square inches of terry cloth covering the essential bits, I am naked, Oliver wedged between my thighs. "Bergman."

He pushes up on his knees. Sets his hands gently on the edge of my seat. His eyes hold mine. "I'm having very unprofessional thoughts right now," he admits.

Biting back a groan, I cup his neck. "Likewise."

God, I'm desperate for him. To touch him, to make him feel and see in himself what I do, to move past pain and distance to share pleasure and closeness.

"You sure?" he whispers, his hand settling on my thigh, warm and heavy, his thumb tracing a circle that makes my heart pound, desire flood my body.

I nod, drawing him close. "Come here."

He does. So gently, so slowly. He slides his other hand up my throat, cups my jaw, kisses me. I exhale into his mouth, sweet relief. There is nothing righter than kissing him.

Warmth, pleasure fizz through my veins. That ache, that tight, furious knot, squeezes my heart, shortens its lead, draws us close, until he's leaning into me, his mouth hot and silken, his tongue lazily stroking mine.

I moan into his mouth as he works his hand higher up my leg.

"Let me touch you?" he asks.

I nod.

Holding my eyes, he drags away the towel. His touch glides over my hips, my stomach, tenderly between my thighs, before he wraps his hand around my cock and strokes, tight, slow, just how I like it.

"Touch you," I mumble into his mouth.

He nods against our kiss, dropping his hand from my face only long enough to shove down those ridiculous swim trunks and free his cock. I hold him, touch him as he touches me, as we kiss, slow and deep.

I'm washed in pleasure. God, the pleasure, the joy of not feeling only pain, radiating out to my fingertips, sparking across my skin.

Oliver pants into my mouth, pumping himself into my hand, but then he pulls away abruptly, starts kissing his way down my chest. "I want to taste you," he says roughly.

My hand sinks into his hair. "Fuck, yes."

His mouth wraps around me, makes my hips lurch, agony shear through my back. I force my body to grow still, to simply receive what he's giving me, pleasure blunting the sharpest edges of my pain. His mouth, wet and hot, his tongue gliding along the tip. He's slow and teasing, his touch wandering my body as he takes me into his throat and groans.

I watch his shoulders roll, his hips shift.

"Touch yourself, Oliver."

Air rushes out of him. He drops his hand.

I brush his hair back off his face, slide my fingers through the wet, silky locks, guiding him, praising him. "That's it. That's perfect. So, so good."

Need pounds through me, coiling tighter, hotter, an intensifying ache that demands I move, thrust, fuck. "Close," I whisper.

He smiles, pops off long enough to look at me, his hand sliding slow and firm, fisted around my cock as he thumbs the slit and makes me gasp. "You think I don't know?"

"Get over here." I tug him by the shoulder, kissing him hard, desperate.

I love you. I kiss those words, say them with my hands as I touch him. I'm too taken with pleasure, heat, euphoria to panic as the word pounds in my head in time with my heart.

Love. Love. Love.

I'm too focused on the sweet warmth of his mouth, the little sounds he makes, pants and pleas, as we kiss.

I slide to the edge of the chair, and Oliver leans in. Our bodies meet, chests, stomachs, hips. Our hands find each other, the water pouring overhead easing our way.

"Yeah," I whisper as he fists me in one hand, sinks his other into my hair. Our kisses are our mouths making love, deep and slow.

"Gav," he groans. "God. I lo—"

I kiss the word away. More terrified to hear it from his lips than from mine. While there is no one more worthy of being loved than Oliver, do I deserve his love, his loyalty? Do I deserve his future, the best years of his life, meant to be faced head-on, instead spent glancing over his shoulder for me?

I feel him thicken in my hand as his breathing grows jagged. He buries his face in the crook of my neck, bites me, chases it with a deep, hot kiss that makes my hips lurch, makes me come, hard and long, frantic in his hand as he works me, the water and thick ropes of release wetting his hand as he pumps me hard. I slide my hand lower, rub him behind his balls, which are tight and heavy.

"Oh, God," he yells, crushing his mouth to mine. "I have to—"

"Come for me. That's it."

He shouts hoarsely into our kiss, hips punching as he spills into my hand again and again. I clutch him to me, crushed against my chest, the pain in my back a shadow to the bliss of holding him. Lazily, he wraps his arms around me, our kisses turning slow, gentle, between gasps of air.

Nothing but the steady pound of water, our rough, fast breaths. I drift my fingers through his hair, kiss his forehead.

Oliver sighs, content, nuzzling my neck, pressing a kiss to the base of my throat.

Slowly, he pulls away. His hands slide gently along my thighs.

I smooth back his hair, feeling a ridiculous smile lighting up my face. Oliver leans in, gives me another savoring kiss. He frowns and bites his lip, examining me.

"What is it?" I ask.

A guilty smile lifts his mouth. His thumb swipes down my neck. "I gave you a hickey."

I roll my eyes. "I don't fucking care."

"Well, good, 'cause I can't do anything about that." Our eyes meet and his smile softens, shifts, tender and vulnerable. So fucking beautiful. "What I can do something about"—he reaches for the razor, squirts shaving cream into his hand, his eyes meeting mine, familiar and sparkling, a new precious closeness as he kisses me once more—"is that spot I missed."

The smell of breakfast fare greets me when I finally emerge from my room, the pop and snap of food cooking over high heat.

I catch my reflection in the glass of a photograph framed in the hallway. Dark circles. Lines of pain bracketing my mouth, lining my brow.

I stare down at my aching legs, strained muscles, compromised, swollen joints, swallowing thickly. Dr. Chen's debrief in the hospital said it all. There's no chance I can make a meaningful comeback after this. At my age, with my injury history, the prognosis with my herniated discs, and the likelihood that I'll need surgery . . . it's over.

I'm done.

And he's only just beginning.

Can I endure it? Can I be happy for him? Celebrate his triumphs without constantly mourning my own? Will I feel lost? Defeated? Will I resent him?

Until I know that, what business do I have asking Oliver for more? What do I risk saddling him with—a sore, sour fucker with a handful of grandpas for friends who have better social lives than me, an ornery cat who pisses in my shoes, and, barring some unforeseen early death, another forty-some years of me twiddling my fucking thumbs?

I watch him standing in my kitchen, tall, shoulders back, whistling quietly to himself as he slides bacon and eggs onto a platter that already holds a massive stack of thin pancakes that smell like heaven.

"Gotta tell you, Hayes," he says, sliding one last over-easy egg onto the platter. "I feel your eyes on me like an X-ray, so if you're trying to be subtle about staring at my ass, I have news for you: you're not."

Heat fills my cheeks. I clear my throat. "You should go home and get some sleep."

"And you should be resting in bed," he says, flashing me one of those dizzying smiles that make me want to crush my mouth to his. "But you can't always get what you want."

"Do *not* start singing."

The smile deepens. "Who, me?"

I glare at him as he finds the loophole and starts *humming* the Rolling Stones song, trying very hard to resolve myself to find some way to get him to go without scaring him off for good. What do I say? *Hey, Oliver. Mind just waiting in the wings while I figure out if I can be with you without feeling like my heart's being ripped out of my chest? If I could love you the way you deserve, if I'm worthy of even asking you for everything I want?*

But Oliver's holding my gaze with that same quiet, sure confidence he had the first time he ripped off my clothes and made me come undone, and again when he strolled in tonight with his arms full of food and looked into my eyes and told me with his body and his touch that he is not always the easygoing man he often seems to be.

"I was going to bring you breakfast for dinner in bed, but here you are, so let's eat outside," Oliver says, pointing to my outdoor dining table out back.

I peer out the glass panes of my back door, seeing a bright starry sky, a mellow spring breeze swaying the first blossoms in Oliver's colorful garden. Sighing, resigned, I tell him, "Fine."

TWENTY-FIVE

Oliver

Playlist: "Yellow," Frankie Orella

Gavin's grumbling under his breath as I slip a pillow behind him when he eases down to his chair and leans back. There's something wrong with me, wires crossed in my brain, because his foul-mood muttering just makes me smile.

I'm not happy he's in pain or struggling with me seeing him like this. I *am* relieved that he's okay enough to get clean and shave, to grumble and gruff; that he's hungry and willing to indulge me as I set our places, light a few votives, then sit across from him.

I know he wants me gone. I know he thinks he's safe to hurt and heal only on his own.

But I can't leave. I can't stop replaying that moment when I realized he was on the ground, writhing in pain. I can't stop the panic that tightens my throat again, that makes my heart fly in my chest all over as I remember how scared I was. How it felt like the world was collapsing and all that mattered was reaching Gavin, holding his hand, feeling how hard he squeezed back, his eyes screwed shut against the agony making him writhe on the field.

I stare at him, lit by candlelight as he peers down at his food, his frown tinged with confusion and vulnerability. I look at his dark hair flopping into his face, his beard, which is neat and sharp once more, because he let me in, let me close enough to do that for him.

I look at this man whom I held on a pedestal for so many years, idolizing—the man who became a reality rather than a myth and shattered the illusion I'd created, whom I vilified for disappointing me so deeply. Now I don't see my idol or my enemy. I see *him*. Scared, hurting, angry, lost, a man who clings to those jagged edges and wields his sharp tongue, who's so practiced at pushing away anyone who wants to be close.

And I see someone who's shown me, in so many ways, that it isn't the heart of who he is; it's his protection, his survival. His armor, shielding his heart.

I stare at him, so damn scared yet oddly relieved to admit it: how much Gavin matters to me—not the soccer legend or the sullen captain of my team, but the man. The man who makes my niece guacamole and colors with her. The man who holds me when I'm panicking, who believes in me when I have belief enough for everyone but too little for myself, who sees through every happy-go-lucky layer of my bullshit straight to the heart of my own aching fears and wants.

I promised myself I wouldn't end up here again, falling for someone whose life is tangled with mine, whose world and career I share. And yet here I am, worse off than I ever was back in college.

I stare at Gavin, begging him with my mind: *Show me. Show me how you're different from him. Show me how this can work.*

I don't know what to do. Does Gavin want me the way I want him? Is he just as scared of this as I am? Or maybe all he's ever wanted was to bang my lights out, then send me on my way. In which case—

"Bergman."

I blink, forcing myself to give him an easy smile. "Hmm?"

He examines me, brow furrowed. "What's the matter?"

"Nothing." I sit back, picking up a strip of turkey bacon and biting into it.

His eyes narrow. "You had an awfully funny look on your face for it being *nothing*."

I throw him a glance, pointing his way with the turkey bacon. "I was remembering your caveman beard, may it rest in peace."

"Piss off," he growls, stabbing another neatly cut bite of pancake, which he drags through egg yolk. "If it still looks like shit, you've got no one to blame but yourself."

"Excuse me, I am an expert barber. And cook." I reach for his plate, pinching a piece of turkey bacon and pancake together, then popping them in my mouth.

"Oy!" He looks at me, wide-eyed, deeply offended. "Eat your own!"

"Yours looks better. That bite." I point to my mouth and roll my eyes with pleasure. "Too perfect to pass up."

"My sentiments exactly," he grumbles, "considering I'd assembled it and *was* planning on enjoying it."

"Oh, cool your gym shorts. I'll get you more if you run out. For being excited about that bite, you left it there an awfully long time."

He throws me a glare, which softens as I smile at him, until he's looking at me like he wants to kiss me instead of throw me off his porch. My heart sprints inside my chest.

Finally, he refocuses on his plate. "Oliver."

"Oh, boy. I'm being Oliver-ed."

His jaw clenches. He doesn't look up. "Thank you . . . for . . . this. For everything."

Now my heart's decelerating, stuttering. Anxiety spins its web, tangles my thoughts with familiar worries.

"But?" I ask quietly. "There's a *but* coming, isn't there? And not the fun kind."

Gavin sighs, dropping his fork and rubbing his temple. "You need to focus on your captaincy, the team, the season. I need to . . . I've got a lot to tackle, myself."

My heart collapses, and in rushes sadness, chased by bitter disappointment.

See how quickly he's ready to move on? How little being together meant?

Is it that simple, though? Or is . . . is Gavin waging the same war that I am? Is pulling back protection rather than dismissal? Does his caution signal that he sees me or us not as something easily thrown away, but rather as something precious and fragile that deserves going slow, the gentlest handling?

Or am I just hopelessly falling for this man and trying to convince myself he could possibly fall for me, too?

Oh, God. I *have* fallen for him. So hard. And I have to figure out what to do with that. I have to discern if my heart's got the best of me all over again or if it's made the best choice despite all my efforts to deny it.

I don't know how to figure that out except . . . to wait. To see if he'll let me in, if this distance he's already creating has a purpose that I simply don't understand yet.

Swallowing against the lump in my throat, I tell him, "Okay."

His head snaps up, eyes locking on mine. He looks suspicious. "You're not going to bicker with me about this? Give me hell? Throw a bizarre anecdote in my face and try to talk me out of it?"

"Nope."

His hand wraps tight around his fork. He realizes what he's doing, stares down at his hand, and seems to have to will it to loosen, then let go. "Right," he says, frowning at his food. "Well. That's . . . refreshing."

I force a smile, even though inside it feels like my heart's blistered and breaking. "See? I can be agreeable."

"Sure you can." He eyes me sharply, takes a bite of bacon. "I'll just be waiting for a water balloon to explode over my head. Another glitter bomb in my car."

He's so quick to fall back on who we were. On what we've been. A part of me wants to grip his shirt and shake him and make him tell me what this means. But the bigger part of me knows that I'm scared to hear his answer, that he's hurting and vulnerable and pushing him right now is unwise.

My heart hurts. I peer up at the stars, swallowing around that lump in my throat again, hiding my face so I don't risk giving myself away. I take a deep breath and do what I've done for years— wrap my sadness in the blanket of cheerfulness, force the topic toward an easier, happier place.

I've always loved stargazing. Being reminded how vast the world is, how small I am in its grand scheme, yet how inextricably linked I am to those stars, being made of the very thing burning in the sky—bright, beautiful stardust.

"Ursa Major." I point. "Ursa Minor. The Big and Little Dippers."

"I'm familiar," he says dryly without looking up, having another bite of food.

"Do you know their story, those constellations?"

He watches me warily, chewing coming to a stop. "No, I don't."

I nod, looking back at the sky. "So, the story goes, Zeus—who really did not keep it in his pants—and Callisto got down to business, had a kid named Arcas. Hera, Zeus's main squeeze, who allegedly had a fierce jealous streak, got wind of this and was *not* pleased. Though I'm not exactly sure why we act like that's some kind of character flaw, jealousy, when her husband was about as faithful to her as I am to my commitment to go easy on the dairy."

Gavin rolls his eyes, but his mouth quirks in amusement.

"Anyway," I tell him, studying the stars, which, with the city's light pollution, twinkle only faintly in the night sky. "Zeus decided that in order to protect Callisto and Arcas, he was going to change them into bears, grab them by their nubby little tails, and chuck

them up into the night sky. That's why their tails are stretched out."
I point to the row of stars, one after the other. "See?"

Gavin doesn't answer me. He's looking at me with this blank
expression. His throat works in a swallow. "What the hell is the
point of this?"

I glance back up at the stars, lacing my hands together behind
my head. "I'm getting there. These ancient stories—myths—have
lasted so long, these bizarre explanations for burning balls of gas,
because there's something that resonates. Maybe they don't make
much sense in literal terms. They're definitely far-fetched efforts to
understand our existence, our surroundings, when none of what
we know now existed to demystify the vast, complicated workings
of the world, but I do think there's still some nugget of wisdom in
them."

"And what nugget is that?" Gavin asks.

"That sometimes life takes a turn we didn't see coming. That a
single choice can irrevocably alter the path of our lives, and we
have no idea what choice that might be and where it might take us.
I mean, I'm pretty sure Callisto didn't think her life would end up
how it did simply because of her choice to be with Zeus. And poor
Arcas, that kid was born into this world at the whim of a whole
family drama that completely upturned his life. Zeus—I'm gonna
hazard a guess here—his 'let's make them bears to keep them safe'
was a fairly impulsive solution, because it protected his lover and
son, but at what cost? They were lost to him forever, their lives irrevocably altered, likely not in any way they'd have wanted or hoped.

"So, I think . . ." I tip my head, examining the constellations
stretched across the sky. "I think it's a reminder that there's a lot we
can't control in life, that sometimes we get dealt a real shit-kicker,
but . . . in ending up where we never meant to, even in bodies we
don't recognize, situations we didn't ask for, there's still a little

beauty to be found. Purpose. Meaning." I point to the bears, side by side. "Maybe even love."

Gavin stares at me, throat working roughly. "I think that's easy for the bystanders to say. That there's a redeeming significance to be found in others' suffering."

Tearing my gaze from the stars, I search his eyes. "But we all take turns, don't we? Being the bystanders and the ones who suffer. What if we're meant to be counterpoints to each other—not to diminish each other's pain, not to overstate the silver linings of hardship, but instead to stand in witness to it, to help each other see that little bit of light and hope that keeps us going, that reminds us life is some hard shit, but the people who love us through it . . . they make it bearable?"

He arches an eyebrow. "*Bear*able?"

I grin. "Pun intended."

Our gazes hold as his sardonic expression softens, as my grin begins to slip. Gavin swallows and stares down at his plate, pushing his food around. "Well, when you get too old for footie, be sure to call American Greetings. They can put you to work."

I throw a piece of bacon at him. "Shut up."

He grins down at his plate but hides it quickly. After a heavy exhale, he says, "Oliver . . ."

My heartbeat slows with dread. I feel my hands clasp beneath the table until my knuckles ache.

"I . . ." He lets out another slow breath, scoots his food across his plate. "I know I said it already, but . . . thank you."

I don't know what he's thanking me for. The shower. This meal. Being here with him. Understanding his need to step back. Again.

I don't know. And I'm so tired of not knowing. But I've been the one so many times showing up at his door, barging my way in, and look where it's gotten me. This time, I can't chase him down. I can't shoulder my way in. Much as I hate it, it's my turn to wait. To see if he thinks I'm someone worth chasing down, too.

"You're welcome," I finally manage.

Gavin meets my eyes, but only briefly, like he won't allow his gaze to linger. Glancing up at the stars, he's quiet for a while before he says, "Dammit. Now every time I look up at night, all I'm going to be able to think about are bears with stretched-out tails and . . ." His voice dies off. He peers down, spears his food, then fills his mouth as if to shut himself up.

He doesn't finish that sentence, doesn't say what else he'll think about, looking up into a sparkling nighttime sky. But foolishly, I let myself finish that sentence, let hope glitter, like a star in my heart.

Me.

TWENTY-SIX

Gavin

Playlist: "Cold Cold Man," Saint Motel

It's been only three weeks, but it feels like three years. I've spent them watching Oliver step fully into his role as sole captain now that I'm out of commission, though the team doesn't know it's for good. Three weeks I've watched him take command, lead by word and example. Three weeks I've warred with how deeply I want him, how badly I want to let him want me, fearing my baggage will overshadow us, worrying I have no business asking Oliver Bergman for anything except that recipe for the soup he brought and maybe, perhaps, any other musicals worth adding to my playlist, because I have all of Sondheim stuck in my head and all it does is make me think of him.

Which is torture. I already think about him, see him, ache for him enough as it is.

Standing at the sidelines, I watch him, observing the tiniest things I never used to allow myself to before, when all I wanted was to avoid noticing him, being drawn toward him, actually liking him.

Now I soak up everything. The way he listens with his whole body, eyes on whoever's come to him, fully turned their way, brow furrowed in concentration, a comforting hand on their shoulder. His joy in the tiniest moments—when he tips his face toward the sun as it guts the clouds and pours across the field, the way he breathes deep and fills his lungs when a breeze picks up, his slow satisfied smile when he savors a bite of food.

Like pressing a bruise, leaning into a stiff joint, I force myself to see him. All of him. Young. Healthy. Happy. Team captain. Easily ten years left in his career. And to tell myself who I am now. Injured. Weary. Retired. Finished.

I stand and watch him, no longer his sneering, resentful enemy. I watch him with my heart in my throat, unfairly proud of every step he takes on his path toward greatness.

Though he'd be a step further already if he stopped being so damn generous with the ball.

I scowl as he dumps it off to Santi, even though with a simple step over, he'd have Stefan's ass on the grass, the ball in the back of the net. It's the pregame warm-up, so nothing's exactly on the line, but it's the principle that's the problem.

"Bergman!" I bellow.

He glances my way, pale eyes narrowed against the glaring spring sun. My misbehaving heart drums behind my ribs.

"What?" he yells back.

I jerk my head, signaling I want him to come my way.

He arches an eyebrow, then, on a sigh, turns and jogs toward me.

"Hayes?" Assistant Coach Jas turns their head my way. "What happened to convene with the coaching staff first?"

"He needs to be more selfish."

Jas nods. "Agreed. But Coach Lexi said protocol is you run it by Rico and me first."

I roll my shoulders, chafing at the restriction. "Apologies, Coach Jas."

Rico glances our way from where he stands at the edge of the box, talking with our goalie coach and Amobi. Knowing something's up.

"Coaching comes naturally to you," Jas says diplomatically, their eyes hidden behind the usual polarized lenses. "Lexi said it would."

And of course she was right. She knew, when she visited me in the hospital after my injury, exactly what to say, how to nudge me toward this role. Because she knows me. Better than I'd like.

She knew I'd use this opportunity to fill in the gap left in her absence while on maternity leave, to expose myself to the full disparity between Oliver's and my lives. To see if I can prove to myself and him that I can do this. Because I have a sneaking suspicion Coach Lexi Carrington is a giant matchmaking meddler, and she's rooting for us. She has been since the first moment she dragged us into her office after naming us co-captains and told us to play nice *or else*.

I've waited for the moment she'd be proven wrong, that my hopes would be proven false, too—for some revelation to come that the hurt would be too great, the juxtaposition of our situations too painful.

Well, I've hurt. And I've ached. And I've wanted. And yes, some of it's been for soccer, but more than anything, it's been for him. Oliver.

I watch him jog my way, draw closer, eyes on his cleats, brow furrowed in thought. The sun glints off his golden hair, kisses his jaw the way I have.

My heart pounds in tempo with his feet as they strike the grass. *Love. Love. Love.*

God, it's horrible. It's like an infection. A sickness. A fist around my guts. It's so much more than wanting to sleep with him, to cook with him and watch musicals together and grumble about how *my* cat pisses in *my* shoes but does nothing but twine around Oliver's legs and purr in his lap.

Just as my spiraling thoughts reach a fever pitch, Oliver arrives, scooping up a water bottle and squirting a long stream into his mouth. He smacks it shut and sets it down.

"Cap'n Coach," he says with a salute.

I roll my eyes.

Jas's mouth quirks. They stroll off toward the field, giving us privacy.

"You gotta admit, it's got a ring to it," Oliver says. "Cap'n Crunch. Cap'n Coach."

"I'm neither a captain right now nor your coach."

The music Oliver's got everyone in the habit of playing to keep up morale switches to upbeat electric funk with rib-rattling bass. He spins and two-steps past me to the beat of the music. "And yet here you are, gearing up to boss me around."

"You need to take those shots," I tell him. "And don't give me that 'it's only practice' bullshit. You're warming up for a fucking game. What you do now, you'll do then."

He stops dancing, as if I've taken the wind out of his sails. Frowning, he glances over his shoulder toward the net. "My side scored, did we not?"

"Yes, but *you* didn't. And you could have."

He shrugs. "That's not what matters most."

"Wrong." I step closer. "You have years ahead of you, a decade if you're lucky, and you're going to spend them underperforming unless you push yourself to step up, win fifty-fifties, and take the fucking shot."

His expression hardens; that relentless smile dissolves. "Just because you've done it that way doesn't mean it's right for me."

"Yes, and I'm such a terrible example. What an underwhelming career I've had."

His eyes flash as he stares at me, then glances out to the field, where Jas hollers at Ethan and Stefan as they scramble back on defense. "You're thirty-four and your musculoskeletal system is wrecked," he says. "You're in pain all the time. Respectfully, there are more important things to me than scoring every goal I possibly could when someone else can do it without it costing me my body."

"Careful," I warn him.

"You started it," he says, scrubbing a hand through his hair, exhaling roughly as he glares at the ground. "Is that all? 'Cause if so, I've got a game to get ready for."

I'm taken aback by his sharpness. The agitation in his body language and tone.

"No," I tell him calmly, hands in my suit pants' pockets, dropping my voice as I stare out at the field. "You're wise to be cautious. I'm not telling you to do what I've done. Believe it or not, Bergman, there is a happy medium and I fully support it. All I ask is next time you're in scoring range, push yourself to hold on to it rather than give it away. You might be surprised to discover what exactly is motivating you to give up something you deserve. Maybe that impulse isn't as good as you think."

His eyes meet mine again with an intensity I haven't seen in three weeks. I drink in his gaze, careful to keep my expression neutral.

"Fine," he mutters before storming off.

A few seconds later, Rico joins me, watching Oliver. "What was that about?"

I watch Oliver as he runs, doing my best—and failing—not to smile. "Putting a fire under his ass."

Even not on the field, I'm still in pain. My back is wicked tight; my neck throbs; my knee audibly cracks every time I lunge on it, yelling. I'd rather be out there, doing it fucking right, but having carte blanche to scream at Ben is decent consolation.

"Benjamin, get your ass *back*. Get fucking *central*!"

I tug at my tie and loosen it, scowling at the field as the team does what I want but slower. It's so goddamn frustrating, when my legs ache to run, knowing where to go, when my mind sees the pass Ben misses, the run Andre should have made.

"Fucking hell," I growl.

Jas is quiet. Rico hollers at Ethan to tighten up on his mark.

I have a love-hate relationship with this fucking getup that I'm wearing. Crisp white cotton shirt, lightweight dark-blue Italian wool suit, yellow-and-blue diagonal-striped tie that honors the team's colors. I hate it because of what it means I've lost. And I love it because it feels right. It feels like possibility. Like what might come next.

I didn't use to want *next*. I wanted *now* to last forever. But now that *next* is here, all I can think is I want tomorrow and the next day and forever; I want life to move forward for the first time in so long. And I want it with Oliver.

Even if he's poised to piss me off right now. I'm not holding my breath for him to take my advice and do what I told him to during the pregame warm-up. But as I watch him streak up the field, ball at his feet, that kernel of hope in my chest blossoms, small and delicate. Walking along the sideline, I track his progress. My heart pounds.

He's closing in on the goal. His defenders collapse on him. I hold my breath, hands turned to fists.

"C'mon," I mutter. "Fucking do it."

I see the moment Oliver would typically make a gorgeous pass to one of our midfielders, even if they weren't wide open, so long as they were more open than him. And then I realize that moment is history. He's kept going.

As a defender closes in on him, Oliver executes a perfect inside step over, his man committing to the opposite direction and tipping to the ground.

"He's wide open." I clutch Rico's arm. "He's wide fucking open."

Oliver takes one touch past his defender and cracks it into the net, wide and low, far beyond the goalie's reach.

Goal!

"Fuck yes!" I pump my arm as Rico yells inside his cupped hands, as Jas claps and smiles.

Oliver beams, elated, sparkling eyes crinkled at the corners. I watch the team swarm him, leap onto his back, ruffle his hair, before they break apart and leave him to walk in long, smooth strides toward center field for kickoff. I shouldn't stare at him, shouldn't feel my heart trip in my chest as something powerful and petrifying floods my veins. Something that makes the world stand still as Oliver glances my way.

Our eyes hold.

And for the first time in my entire life, I can say there's something as incredible as being out on that pitch, scoring the perfect goal.

Watching the man who holds my heart in his hands do it, too.

It feels like a lifetime, but it's been only a week since that moment. Apparently therapy can do that to you—warp time, mess with your head. I know it's good, but right now it just feels exhausting, as exhausting as the meeting I just had, the papers I just signed, to formally end my playing tenure with the Galaxy.

Setting a gentle hand on my back, Mitch smiles up at me, eyes tight with concern and, hell, if it's not a bit of fondness, too.

"Proud of you," Mitch says.

I sniff and blink away the wetness in my eyes, shutting my front door, doing the visualization my fucking therapist, whom I started seeing two weeks ago, taught me, a trick to tell my mind it doesn't have to fixate on painful things, that it can focus instead on what makes it happy.

Load of shit is what that is. Worse, it works. At least sometimes. It's helped me focus on concrete plans, a to-do list of positive, forward-thinking tasks to complete before I felt I could in any
good conscience ask Oliver to give me a chance—plans to show
him I'm capable of being a supportive partner, when the natural
tension between our positions in our careers, our health, our ages,
could threaten to draw us apart.

"Thank you," I mutter, letting Mitch hug me. "This feeling-my-
feelings shit is shit."

He laughs his wet ex-smoker's laugh and pats my face gently.
"It's hard, but you're doing it. And it's not done being hard either,
but it's still worth it. *He's* worth it. So are you, Gav."

I dab my nose and make myself straighten up to my full height,
like a soldier readying for battle. "Right. Well. Here goes." I throw
a thumb over my shoulder toward Oliver's house.

Mitch scratches the side of his head. "Yeah. About that."

"About what?"

He eases onto a stool at the kitchen island with a groan. "He,
uh . . . left."

"Left," I growl. "And you know this *how*? You were going to tell
me *when*?"

"Easy." He lifts his hands placatingly. "I know because *I* am
Oliver's friend. We take a brisk sunrise neighborhood walk every
Wednesday morning before lazy asses like you roll out of bed."

I pinch the bridge of my nose and sigh heavily. "Of fucking
course you do."

Mitch doesn't acknowledge me. "On our walk this past Wednesday, he told me where he'd be while you fellas have your bye week."

"And," I say between clenched teeth, "you didn't think I'd
value being told that little tidbit, given what I just fucking did?
Given what I have planned for tomorrow? Given everything I've

been trying to do for the past fucking month so I have a goddamn chance with him?"

He arches a silvery eyebrow. "I'll be honest, Gav—I wasn't sure you'd follow through just yet, and frankly, you didn't deserve him if you didn't. So I waited."

"Excellent." I throw him a sour, sarcastic smile. "I appreciate your faith in me."

"I do have faith in you. I knew you'd do it. I just wasn't sure *when*. And until I was, I had to think of him, too." He leans in, sets his hand on mine, which is splayed on the counter, my knuckles white. "I meant it, what I said. I am proud of you."

I stare down at his hand, resting over mine. "I hope it's enough."

After a few reassuring pats, he says, "I hope so, too."

"Where is he, Mitch? Please."

"A wedding. His sister's? No, his brother's. I can't remember."

"Doesn't matter. There's loads of them. One of them is getting married. Fine." I tug my hand away, pacing, thinking. "Where is it? When is it?"

"The *when*, I'm not sure. But the *where*, I can tell you." He sits back and grins. "Better get packing and book a flight. There's an A-frame in Washington State calling your name."

TWENTY-SEVEN

Oliver

Playlist: "Elephant Gun," Beirut

I watch the sunrise crest over the horizon, spilling faint pearly light across lush spring-green grass. Leaning on the railing of the A-frame's back deck, coffee cup in hand, I shift on my feet, breathe in the fragrance of the crushed rose petals and straggling evergreen boughs strewn across the deck's wide varnished planks.

A beautiful wood arch still stands where it framed Willa and Ryder two days ago, home to those roses and evergreen boughs before the wind whipped them away. I smile, remembering it—my brothers and me standing behind Ryder, knuckling away tears. Rooney, Frankie, and my sisters behind Willa, doing the same.

It was a quiet ceremony, small and intimate. Mostly family, a few friends, including a special appearance from Tucker and Becks, Ryder's college roommates, whom I hadn't seen in years and who were close with Willa, too.

Mom and Dad walked Willa down the aisle. Ryder and Willa recited their personalized vows. We ate Swedish fare by candlelight because Willa loves Mom's family recipes, then danced on the deck until the lovebirds drove off in their trusty Subaru and the rest of us collapsed into our beds, happy and exhausted. Yesterday, we lounged around, played soccer and board games, then went on a long springtime walk.

It was as close to perfect as it could get, but for that nagging ache in my heart that I did my best to ignore. Another wedding here. Another "happily ever after" that wasn't mine.

I take a sip of coffee, gulping it even though I know it's hot, that it will hurt. There's a sharp, hot pain already knifing down my sternum. What difference will it make?

It's been a month. A month since Gavin and I were as intimate in that shower as I felt two people could be, since we sat outside afterward and once again he pushed me away until I was at emotional arm's length.

The way he touched me, brought me to orgasm, kissed me, the intimacy he gave me in letting me care for him, see him at his most vulnerable, keeps gnawing at my gut, twisting my heart into a knot. What do you feel for someone when you let them see you like that, touch and comfort and care for you? How do you push them away afterward, like he did?

In a way, I understand. I know his life is in limbo, his pain unimaginable. I know he's all but allergic to feelings and even more terrified of feeling them.

But it hurts to be pushed away. It still *really* hurts.

"Good morning, sunshine."

I glance over my shoulder at the sound of Willa's voice, and frown. I'm surprised to see her here, given she and Ryder aren't staying at the A-frame. Their house isn't far, so they've slept at their place, then showed up to visit during the day. It's wildly early for her to have gotten up and driven this way. "What are you doing here?" I ask.

Feisty light brown eyes, curly waves tangled up in a bun, she smiles. "Forgot my phone."

"Ryder come with?"

She shakes her head. "Nah. He's still sleeping. I was going to drive back home now, but then I got a whiff of freshly brewed coffee." Lifting a small mug, she says, "Mind if I join you?"

"Of course not." I scooch a little, making room for her to lean on the deck, too.

We watch the sunrise in silence for a few minutes before she says, "So, how you doing?"

I shrug and force a smile. "Okay. You?"

She narrows her eyes at me. "Perhaps I should rephrase. How are things with you and the gorgeous grump next door?"

Dammit. My brothers never keep their mouths shut. "You heard about that, huh?"

"I also have eyeballs. I watch your games on TV. I saw that last match you two played together. He was about to rip that fucker's throat out for you, and deservedly so. Then the way he played afterward until he went down, pouring everything onto the field until you got the win . . ." She shrugs. "Pretty clear what's going on."

I turn and face her. "How so?"

She smiles softly, leaning her elbow on the deck, facing me, too. "Let's just say I have walked more than a mile in his shoes."

While both Gavin and Willa are elite-level professional soccer players, I have a hunch that commonality isn't what she's referring to. "What do you mean?" I ask.

"I mean I'd bet my favorite pair of cleats that after he laid everything on that pitch for you, he made your life miserable pretty much the moment you two were off it."

I eye her warily. "Uhhh, yes. And you know this how?"

"You may not remember. You were kinda young and oblivious when Ryder and I were first working out what we were," she says, glancing out at the land. "But I did not make things easy for him."

I was in high school when they met in college, and Willa's right—I was pretty oblivious, but not entirely out of the loop. "I remember you were going through a lot. Your mom had just passed."

She nods, staring out at the sunrise. "Yeah. But it wasn't just that. I didn't grow up like you all did. Not many people do," she says, throwing me a wry glance. "I was so scared. To love someone the way I loved Ryder. To be loved by him, by all of you. So fully and unconditionally."

I swallow, my heart aching, thinking of Gavin, how painful it seems for him to accept affection or care . . . any sort of loving relationship. I still know so little about his past, and I wish I knew more—his family, the years that formed him and led him to where he is now, to how and why he operates the way he does.

"I get Gavin. Like recognizes like," she continues. "I've met him, too. Did you know that?"

I shake my head. "When?"

"He founded a support program for kids in state care all along the West Coast. Volunteer athletes receive training and go through a crapload of vetting. Come in at the same time, same days each week, and play sports. Give the kids encouragement, quality time, a sense of community and belonging while they're dealing with so much uncertainty."

I blink at her, stunned. "What?"

"Technically, I'm not supposed to tell. Professional athletes who are recruited to participate in advertisements, volunteer time for special events and fundraising, meet directly with Gavin. They asked me to film a commercial for it—"

"I've seen the commercials." I shake my head, struggling to process this. "That's *his* organization?"

She nods. "Anyway, when I agreed, I was made to sign an NDA that I wouldn't disclose his relationship to it."

"And so you're telling me because . . . life's boring, so why not get yourself sued?"

She smiles wide, dimples popping in her cheeks. "Because I'm not scared of him. Because I know you'll protect his privacy. Because we emotionally constipated loners have to help each other out, and I have a hunch that next time Gavin Hayes comes knocking on your door, you're going to be understandably wary that this cycle of him letting you close then pushing you away is never going to end, and I want you to know there's more to him than what you've seen, that if he works hard in therapy, if he has a partner who knows his struggles and his past, who understands he's making his way but maybe progress won't always be as fast or straightforward as either of you would like, he *can* choose you and stay with you and let you get close." She lifts her left hand, which bears a sparkling diamond ring and matching wedding band on her fourth finger. "I'm proof."

I stare at her, at a loss for words.

"You know," she says, leaning against the deck again, sipping her coffee. "This was supposed to happen years ago."

"What was?"

She gestures around us, the half-stripped wooden arch, rose petals and remnants of evergreens carpeting the deck. "This. The wedding."

"Oh." I scrub my neck. "That. Yeah."

She rolls her eyes. "Ollie. You don't have to act like you don't know. Like we weren't engaged for three years and it took me that long to work up the courage to go through with the wedding, not because I had a single doubt about the man I love more than my own life, but because I couldn't figure out how to face that day without my mom."

Her smile fades as she glances out at the woods around us, eyes darting up to the treetops. "Even though she's been gone for years, it felt like a new grief when I realized I'd walk down that aisle without being on her arm, without her teasing me to make me laugh when I got nervous beforehand, without her nagging me to put curl cream in my hair so it wasn't a frizz ball on my wedding day."

She sighs heavily, tapping her ring against her coffee cup. "It was just . . . this raw, terrible loss, all over again. Then, once I felt like I'd gotten my bearings, wrapped my head around it enough to be able to set a date, I started worrying that my sadness, missing her, would ruin the happiness of the day, that I'd disappoint Ryder, the family. I kept waiting to finally feel *okay* enough to do it."

"Did you?" I ask quietly.

She shakes her head. "No. The okay-ness never came. I just realized I'd been missing the whole fucking point."

"What point was that?"

Her gaze slides my way; her eyes hold mine. "I was waiting for it to get easier. Thinking I should be able to handle my grief better, at Christmas, at New Year's. On her birthday. On mine. On my wedding day. But grief doesn't get easier. It just gets familiar. You learn to live with it, and if you're lucky, you find people who'll love you while you do.

"Ryder has loved me every step of the way for exactly who and where I am. Delaying our wedding day, fearing my sadness would somehow diminish the joy of our wedding, did a disservice to the depth of his love and mine. Our whole relationship, our love for each other, has grown and deepened *through* the hard moments, not because we haven't faced any.

"You and Gavin have both been hurt in the past. You have wounds and fears, and there's no getting around them. If you choose each other, you'll choose to see those parts of each other and treat them gently and try to understand them. Maybe you feel ready to do that. But if I had to guess, Gavin's still figuring out how it works, whether he thinks he's capable of entrusting that to you. I know it took me a while to wrap my stubborn head around it."

I swallow roughly. "I do think I understand how it works, but the readiness part . . . understanding it doesn't make the thought of doing it any less scary."

"It's okay to be scared," she says. "If you feel ready, if he comes to you, tell him what you're afraid of. That's intimacy. Being brave in trusting him with your truth."

Gently, she wraps an arm around me and sets her head on my shoulder. "You got this, Ollie. And remember: you are enough, just as you are. If Gavin does it right, he won't leave you in a bit of doubt about that." She taps the space over my heart. "And you need to do your part, too. Believe in yourself, in your worth, that you're enough. Because you are."

I nod, dabbing my eyes on my shirtsleeve.

Smiling, Willa pushes away from the deck and drains the last of her coffee. "Well, I'd say my work is done. Off I go."

"You don't want to stay for the goodbye brunch?"

She shakes her head. "Nah. I've got a husband I plan to go home to, wake up the fun way—"

"Ay!" I scrunch my eyes shut. "None of those details. Get out of here."

She's still laughing when she shuts the door behind her.

Cleaning up from the goodbye brunch is the usual chaos—all of us in an assembly line of interweaving duties to clean up the remnants of coffee cups and juice glasses, platters and plates and left-over food.

Theo cries as Freya tries to nurse him to sleep. Linnea continues to tantrum from the middle of the great room floor because she wasn't allowed to eat wedding cake for breakfast. Viggo's hungover, scrolling moodily through his phone with the volume on too loud while scraping dishes clean, then handing them to me to rinse. Rooney scrubs dishes alongside Aiden, who rinses them clean, while Ziggy dries them, her noise-canceling headphones blocking out the world. Ren puts away clean dishes while Frankie wipes down the table and kitchen surfaces. Mom and Dad smile at each other tiredly as they tidy up the living room.

"Viggo," Axel snaps, strolling in from his garbage-hauling trek outside and setting a fresh bag in the bin. "Turn that down."

Viggo glares at Axel. "Would it kill you to ask nicely?"

"Yes," Ax says. "Now turn it down."

Viggo grumbles, picking up his phone from the counter, just as the clear voice of a news announcer says, "And now, highlights from the press conference given early this morning announcing soccer legend Gavin Hayes's retirement."

I nearly drop the plate I'm rinsing, before setting it hastily in the sink, madly drying my hands on my shirt. "Don't. Don't turn it down."

Lunging for Viggo's phone, I grab it and have grand plans to run somewhere private to watch, but the moment I see Gavin, my legs stop working. I sink to the nearest chair at the table with a clumsy flop.

My heart splinters as I look at him, drinking him in. Blue suit. Blue-and-gold tie. His beard neat, hair neater. He stands tall, stoic, clutching a piece of paper.

". . . Playing this game has been the greatest privilege, the richest joy. And for years, the prospect of saying goodbye to it has been my deepest fear and sadness." He swallows thickly, sets the paper down, and runs his hand flat across it. "But I cannot sustain this level of play. My body has reached its limit, and as much as I wish it were not the case, I have had to listen to it, to respect it, after it brought me this . . . incredible opportunity—" He swallows thickly again, bites his cheek. "And so it is with gratitude for the journey that I have been fortunate enough to know, the players I've called teammates, the coaches who have shaped and directed me, that I announce my retirement from professional soccer."

I wipe away tears, my chest aching. A hankie appears in my peripheral vision. I don't question it, just accept it and loudly blow my nose. How long has he known? Why haven't *I* known? I could have been there for him, comforted him—

He didn't want you there, did he? that despairing voice whispers. *He hasn't wanted you for weeks, since he knew he was done here. You were just an insignificant pit stop, and now he's moving on.*

I shake my head, willing away those hopeless thoughts, reminding myself what Willa said—*You need to do your part, too. Believe in yourself, in your worth, that you're enough.*

I watch Gavin on the screen as he folds up his paper, dabs the corner of his eye. So composed and calm, even though I know his heart is breaking. I want so badly to be right there beside him, to be the arms he turns to when the lights go out and he clears out his cubby and he comes home.

When he falls apart. I want to be what he's been for me: safe, strong, comforting.

I love him.

The words drift through me, natural and gentle as a breeze whispering over my skin, the sun warming my face. I *love* him.

I love Gavin whether or not he'll love me back. I love him if he comes out of retirement or walks away from the game forever. I love him, and I don't know when it happened. When annoyance gave way to affection, when bickering became foreplay and lust's grip became love's fist wrapped around my heart until its every beat was just for him.

He's retiring, leaving the game, exiting my world, and yet nothing's clearer, safer, easier simply because he won't do drills with me or bark at me across the field. The old me would have been relieved, convinced this separation of our careers would be all we needed, and voilà!

What a fool I was to think it could be as simple as drawing a line between the person I'd allow myself to love and the game I

loved, too. What a bogus idea that I could open my heart to someone safely, cautiously—that with the right person and the right
boundaries, falling in love wouldn't scare me just as badly as, or
worse than, it did the first time, that it wouldn't make me feel like
I was hovering on the edge of a cliff, no guarantee that the person I
was falling for would be there to catch me.

I still don't know if he'll be there. But now I know the truth:
the nature of my heart, the fullness with which I love and live,
means that to love is to risk deep pain.

And it also opens my world to incredible, intimate love.

I want that with him. I want Gavin.

I just . . . don't know if he wants me. But I'm ready to be brave
and find out.

Staring at his image, contained on a phone screen as the press
turns unsurprisingly feral, I start to plan, dream, hope. The flight
home I'll try to move up to today instead of lingering here alone
for a few days, how I'd planned; the words I'll say, the way I'll say
them.

But for now, I watch him, because I have to do this, to stand
witness to what I wish I could have witnessed in person—his bravery, his pain, his dignity as the press shout his name, begging to be
called on.

Clearing his throat, Gavin rolls his shoulders and straightens,
then points to a man in back whom the camera pans to, slim, wiry,
with thick glasses. The man says, "Colin Woodruff with ESPN.
Mr. Hayes, first, please let me express what a beautiful statement
that was. We're all sad to see the end of this era in your life, and yet
so much is still ahead of you. What's next?"

Gavin nods, stares down at the paper on the podium. "Taking
care of myself, finding ways to give back to the community. Hopefully settling down."

"Where?" Colin asks, shouting over new voices.

Gavin glances up at the camera. "That depends."

"On?" Colin prompts.

Before Gavin can answer him, a bang on the front door startles me so badly, I nearly drop Viggo's phone. A dozen hands dart my way, collectively steadying it.

That's when I realize my entire family has congregated behind my chair, looking moved and curious.

Two more rapid thuds shake the front door, ringing through the great room and the silence they've created. Then a single ring of the doorbell, like whoever went to town on the door only just realized that a more modern method of announcing themselves was available.

"I got it!" Linnie yells, scrambling up from her tantrum spot on the floor.

"Hold up." Viggo runs toward the door. "Adults answer the door, Linnie."

"Rules you out," Freya mutters, burping Theo on her shoulder.

Viggo flips her off.

"I saw that," Linnie yells.

Aiden, ever the strategic one, simply leans back and glances out through the window with a clear view to whoever stands outside. "Shit. Shoot, I mean."

He runs toward the door, bodychecks Viggo out of the way, then scoops up Linnie. "Oliver." He jerks his head. "You should get that."

Viggo's just righted himself and is reaching for the door again when I get there and shove him away. I peer through the peephole. My knees nearly give out.

"Who is it?" Viggo asks, shoving me aside, trying to see through the peephole. "Ack!"

Ren's got him by the shirt collar, dragging Viggo away, as he tells him, "Chill out, V. Ollie can handle himself."

"Okay, let's go!" Mom says, clapping her hands at everyone, shooing them to move. "Come on, hurry!"

It's like *Home Alone* when the family realizes they're running late for their flight, a mad dash of people crossing the hall, running upstairs, running downstairs. Bags land in the foyer. Sheets fall in piles outside rooms. Doors slam shut as footsteps thunder across the house.

I stand at the door, my hand shaking as I reach for the doorknob, my heart pounding in my chest.

Why is he here?

There's only one way to find out. Breathing deeply, finding my courage, I wrench open the door and step onto the porch.

TWENTY-EIGHT

Oliver

Playlist: "Wildfire," Cautious Clay

I shut the door behind me. My heart swoops, then soars.

Gavin's in the suit he wore at the press conference this morning. Except now it's a little rumpled, his tie is loose, there are a few wrinkles in his jacket, a scuff on his polished shoes. He holds a very fancy bottle of champagne and a breathtaking bouquet of flowers.

"I . . ." He clears his throat. "I was told there was a wedding. And on the off chance it was happening when I showed up, I wanted to be prepared."

"The wedding was two days ago." I swallow around the lump in my throat. "You're a little late."

"Ah." He searches my eyes. "But I hope . . . not entirely *too* late?"

I bite my cheek, scared to hear a double meaning in that, scared to hope. And yet I can't stop myself from saying, "No. Not too late."

Slowly, Gavin crouches, knees popping as he sets down the champagne and flowers. He straightens, walks toward me. "Oliver—"

"I watched the press conference," I tell him, backing up instinctively.

He stops, holding my eyes, searching them. "You saw it already?"

I nod. My throat feels thick with the threat of tears. "I'm sorry."

He stares at me, looking suddenly very wary. "For what?"

"Your retirement. I know this game is . . . everything to you. Saying goodbye to it, the finality of announcing to the world that it's over . . ."

My words trail off as something like relief smooths his expression. He takes another step closer, and this time, I hold my ground, too confused by his response to give in to fear and step away.

His knuckles brush mine.

"That's just it, though," he says. "It isn't over. This part of my career is, yes. But my life isn't. This is just the beginning." He wraps his hand around mine, warm and dry, strong and steady. "That is, if you—"

The door flies open, startling us apart.

"Hello!" my mother says brightly. Wrapping Gavin in a sudden hug, she says, "Welcome! Go on inside. Get comfortable. We were just leaving."

"Mom," I say, voice strangled.

Gavin hugs her back, giving me a perplexed look over her shoulder. "Thank you."

Mom lets him go and then hugs me next. "Be brave, *älskling*," she whispers. "I love you."

When she slips away, I see Dad's filled her place, gently clasping Gavin's shoulder. "Beautiful speech, son."

Gavin looks stricken, then moved. "Thank you, sir."

"Don't be a stranger," Dad says as he tugs me in for a hug and a kiss to my hair before throwing us a wink and following Mom toward their car.

My siblings spill out of the house, first Ax, who nods politely, then Rooney, who flashes us a wide, sunny smile before slipping her arm inside Axel's while they start toward their house, which is settled deeper in the woods.

Aiden exits next, hustling the rest of my siblings out like the house is on fire. Freya blows us a kiss, baby Theo tucked in her arm.

Linnea throws herself at Gavin's legs and earns his hug before Freya scoops her up, too, and she dissolves into overtired, too-much-party tears. Then comes Ren, smiling wide, and Frankie, wiggling her eyebrows as she smirks. Ziggy throws me a coy smile, takes one look at Gavin, and turns bright red, then hustles down the stairs. Viggo's last, of course. Gavin doesn't recognize him at first without the mangy beard that he shaved for the wedding, but when he does, his eyes narrow.

Viggo sizes him up, then offers a hand, which Gavin takes. A very intense staredown ensues. Their knuckles turn white as they try to squeeze the life out of each other's palms. "Just remember, I know where you live," Viggo tells him.

"Good grief," I mutter.

"Okay, that's enough *Godfather* antics from you," Aiden says, taking him by the shoulder and giving us a knowing grin as he drags Viggo down the steps with him.

Gavin glances over his shoulder, watching the mass exodus of cars happily honking as they pull out. "That was . . ."

"Embarrassing?"

"Intense," he mutters, frowning thoughtfully. "Sweet. Funny. Weird." He turns back and sets his gaze on me. "Sort of like you."

"That's it," I tell him, shoving the door open behind me. "You've crossed a line. And now we're gonna take this inside."

Gavin smirks and follows me in, drinking in the space as he shuts the door.

A wave of nervousness crests through me. "Will you . . . I mean, were you . . ." I clear my throat. "Did you want to stay?"

Gavin turns and looks at me curiously. "I mean . . . I thought . . . Yeah. Do you *want* me to stay?"

My heart pounds. "Yes. I do. If you want to. Stay, that is."

Reaching up, he loosens his tie. Heat rushes through me as I stare at the hollow of his throat revealed when he yanks open the top two buttons, then drags his tie through his collar with a *snap*.

He looks agitated, confused. "I want to stay, yes."

"Good. Great." My voice cracks on the word as my cheeks heat. "Excellent."

"My bag's in the rental," he says, pulling a key from his suit jacket's pocket. "I'll get it—"

"Let me." I close the distance between us, pluck the key from his fingers. Backtracking, I tell him, "Explore, if you want. Just don't look too close at the family photos. I had an awkward phase that started in first grade and didn't end until sophomore year of high school."

His mouth quirks in a faint smile. "I doubt that highly."

"Believe it." I nod my chin toward the wall of family photos before darting out to his car to grab his bag.

My heart bangs inside my ribs. I have a thousand thoughts, a million questions.

Why is he here? What does he want?

Does he want *me*?

By the time I walk back inside with his bag, Gavin's got his suit jacket off, his shirtsleeves rolled up. I try not to stare at his bare forearms, sculpted muscles, tendons, and veins visible as he rests his hands in his pockets and walks leisurely down the hall, taking in the photos. "You are a nauseatingly photogenic bunch, aren't you?"

"Blame Mom and Dad."

He huffs a soft laugh, glancing my way. When he sees me with his bag, he strolls forward. "I'll take that—"

"Wait." I clutch it, searching his eyes. "I . . ."

I want you to stay in my room. I want you in my bed, cuddling and holding me.

I can't admit that. Not when I don't even know what the hell is going on. What if he's here to do some official, formal, in-person passing of the captain baton? What if he just stopped by for a little R & R?

God, listen to me. I'm grasping at straws. Why else would he be here if he didn't want me somehow? The truth is, I'm too afraid to admit what I want, what I hope, as I stand there, staring at him, tongue-tied.

"What is it?" he asks.

"I . . ." Swallowing thickly, I lick my lips. "Do you want to go for a walk?"

His brow furrows. He answers slowly, "Sure. Yeah. That'd be good. Just nothing too technical. No hills." He throws a thumb over his shoulder. "My back's still shit. I'm only moving like this because Dr. Chen gave me an injection, but if I push too hard, I'll pay for it."

I try to keep my expression neutral, to not betray how surprised and touched I am that he's confided in me about his pain, his needs, his limits. "Of course."

"I should change, then," he says, nodding at his bag, which I still hold.

"Right. Sure. Um . . ." I deliberate. There's the first-floor suite, which my parents use when they're here. Then there's my room upstairs. Maybe, for now, as much as I don't want to, I should take him to my parents' room. Easier on his body. Accessible bathroom, including a shower bench. "This way," I tell him.

Gavin follows me to the room, a faint frown tugging at his mouth as he inspects the space.

I glance around, too. The curtains are open, letting daylight spill in, revealing nature's springtime masterpiece outside. Balmy wind whipping the trees, carrying blossoms with it in a colorful dance through the air. Tall evergreens. Tufts of lime-green grass dappling dark earth.

I notice the bed's been stripped, the sheets changed, a different color than they were when we got here and I helped Mom make beds throughout the house. I try not to think too hard about what my parents were intending when they made a point of preparing this room for someone else.

"Something wrong?" I ask.

"No." He shakes his head, taking his bag from me. "I'll just change."

"Okay. Sure. Right." I back away, turn, and walk right into the wall. Mortified, I don't even look over my shoulder to see if Gavin caught that; I just scramble to escape the room.

As soon as I've shut his door behind me, I sprint down the hall, take the stairs three at a time. Frantically, I brush my teeth, brush my hair, yank off the shirt and sweats I slept in, swipe on deodorant, tug on fresh clothes, stomp into my sneakers, then run downstairs. I've just managed to artfully lean against the banister as Gavin walks out of his room, wearing black sneakers, black joggers, and a charcoal-gray long-sleeved shirt that hugs his massive arms.

His mouth tips as he drinks me in, a soft smile that makes my heart beat double time.

"Can I help you?" I ask.

The smile deepens. He tugs on his Ray-Bans. "You look like a fucking Funfetti cake."

I glance down at my outfit. My favorite yellow sneaks. Watermelon-pink joggers. A pale blue T-shirt that brings out my eyes. Lifting my chin, I stroll toward the front door and throw it open. "I'll have you know I *like* Funfetti cake."

I feel Gavin's eyes on me from behind. "So do I."

After yanking the door shut behind us, I lock it, then pocket the key. He's still watching me behind the Ray-Bans, his stare intense. I clear my throat and point ahead. "This way's a nice, even walk. No hills. A one-mile loop. That work?"

He glances in the direction I've pointed, then nods. "Yeah."

"Fine! I mean, good. Excellent. Great. Here we go." God, I'm a nervous wreck.

Starting ahead of Gavin, I look for a tree to bang my head into and knock myself out before I can open my mouth again and make a bigger fool of myself.

But something about his silent, steady presence as we start to walk begins to settle me. He's quiet as we make our way, remaining half a step behind me. I keep my stride slow and leisurely, hoping I've set a comfortable pace for him, drinking in the view. It's my favorite time of year here—warm, golden sunshine, glossy green grass, a cool blue sky dappled with cotton-ball clouds.

A canopy of blossoms clusters the trees overhead, and the wind makes them rain a gale of petals. Snow white, lemon yellow, palest pink, they float from the sky, swirling around us.

As I gaze up, drinking in the sight, I feel Gavin's hand wrap around mine. "Oliver."

I turn and face him, heart jackhammering in my chest. "You okay? Need to go back? Gotta pee?"

He steps closer, his eyes searching mine. "No. But I *do* need to ask you something."

I nod. Too fast. Too many times. My heart's pounding right out of my chest. Gently, Gavin sets his hand over my heart, soothing it. "Take a breath," he says quietly.

I nod again, forcing myself to take a deep, slow breath in, then out.

"Good." He steps closer still, drifting his hand up my chest, to my neck, until he cups my face. "Now, stop running off."

My eyes widen. "I . . . I'm not. Not that you have any place to lecture me on that."

His eyes search mine. His throat works with a swallow. "That's fair. But I'm here to change that."

"You are?"

"Oliver . . ." He frowns. Suspicion seems to tighten his expression. "Wait . . . you don't . . . you don't know why I'm here."

I shake my head. "I'm so confused—"

"Jesus." He drops his head and sighs heavily. "You didn't watch all of it, did you?"

"All of what?" I ask.

"The press conference." He lifts his head and meets my eyes, his thumb gentling my cheek. "All of the press conference. You said you watched it."

I blink, racking my brain. "You'd just opened it up to questions—that's when I stopped. Because . . . you were here. You were banging on my door. That mattered more."

"Fuck," he groans. Now he looks both relieved and also deeply nervous. "Okay. Yeah. Well, that helps. I feel a little better."

"Gavin." I grab him by the shirt. "Please just tell me what the hell is going on."

He smiles softly, his expression tinged with nerves as he runs his hands through my hair, along my temple, ghosts his thumb over the shell of my ear. "I pictured you being more off-the-grid here, unable to watch the press conference, so I thought I'd beat you to the punch. I'd planned to say it myself, but then I got here and you said that you'd seen it, and then I was relieved. Because I'm a fucking coward. And now you're saying you haven't seen it—"

"For the love of God, Gavin Hayes, tell me what the hell you're talking about!"

He yanks me close, until our mouths are inches away from each other, our chests heaving. Like that day in the locker room, heat billowing between us, intensity flashing in his eyes. His gaze drifts down to my mouth, then drifts back up, holding mine. "I love you."

I grip his shirt tighter, leaning into him. "What?"

He walks us back, slowly, like a dance, until I'm pressed against the trunk of a massive old tree, until Gavin's pinning me against it. "I said, I love you. And I know I haven't done much to inspire your confidence in those words coming from me. I don't have experience with this. I don't know what I'm doing. And I'm fucking scared as shit, because I don't know how it will end or if we'll come out winners, and I fucking hate even the *thought* of losing, let alone losing something so precious, losing *you*.

"I know I might be too late. I might not even have you to lose in the first place, but if I let one more day go by without taking a chance, telling you what you mean to me—that I love you more than a ball beneath my feet or the heart in my chest—that would be the greatest loss of all."

Once again he brings his hand to my heart and says, quiet, reverent, as he searches my eyes, "This past month, all I've wanted is to wrap you in my arms, drag you to bed, and never let you go. To cook with you and watch you sing along to musicals and give you hell for your eyeball-singeing wardrobe, but I had to do this first, Oliver. I had to face what will be: the end for me and the beginning for you. I had to watch you have everything that I'd lost and know I could do it, to prove to us both that while I loved soccer, I love you better, best, beyond.

"This past month has been agony, wanting you, feeling nothing but love and pride, but it's shown me what I can do—that I can share this world with you, be happy for you, cheer you on, that it will never come between us like I once let it."

Oh, God. The pieces fall into place, that night when we were so close and yet he once again pushed me away, the weeks following, full of only professionalism and politeness. They were all for this moment. For us.

I cup his face; my voice is unsteady. "You're sure? I don't want to hurt you. I never want my life, my world, to hurt you. I couldn't take it."

He leans into my touch. "You won't have to. I told you how I spent the past month, and I've spent the past two years confronting it then, too. Two years facing what you are and will be, what I have been and never will be again."

"But you didn't love me all that time," I point out.

His mouth tips in a wry smile as he drifts his knuckles along my cheek. "Didn't I?"

Thank God I'm leaning against a tree. I'd fall on my ass otherwise. "What?"

"Oliver. It was distance myself or drop to my knees and fall at your feet," he says roughly as he leans into me, as our bodies touch and ache. "I saw you and felt like you'd blasted a hole in my chest. I couldn't let myself feel how much I wanted you, admired you, *longed* for you. Not when you had everything in your clutches that was slipping through my fingers."

Tears blur my vision. I stare at him, stunned, thrilled, disbelieving. "I didn't know," I whisper.

"I didn't either," he admits. "Not at first. Not for a good while. I knew you made me feel like my blood was on fire and my heart was incinerating my chest, like I was battling this consuming feverish *something* that I felt only for you. It was so easy to call it hatred for your gain while I lost, to fixate on my resentment and envy of you, to never look too close or too long. When I finally had to, when Coach shoved us together and forced me to face you head-on, and I realized, God help me, what I was up against, I buried those feelings like I've always buried uncomfortable, unclear shit."

I remember what he said that night in my house, when both of us admitted how badly we wanted each other, when I was almost as stunned and surprised by his admission as I am now.

I am very, very good at hiding what I want and feel and need.

"I wanted you, too," I tell him quietly, twirling a soft, dark lock of his hair around my finger, spinning it, savoring how close he is, not just his body, but his heart, all of him. "I have. For so long."

His eyes search mine, cautious, hopeful. "Yeah?"

"Yeah," I say through the knot in my throat.

"I know I've given you reason to doubt me, Oliver, but I promise that's behind us. I'm here. I'm yours." He brings my hand to his chest. "I promise it all—my body, my soul, my life, for you, *everything* for you, to care for you and love you, if you'll let me. You're the fucking sunrise of my heart, love. All I need is to wake up beside you, to hold your hand and keep you steady when you need me, to watch you with pride and admiration, to give you hell for not being more selfish on the field and too generous off of it. I love you. Do you believe me?"

Nodding, frantic, I tell him, "Yes."

I pull him close, kiss him soft and slow, and he kisses me, too, his mouth firm, smooth, so gentle, remembering mine. "I love you," I tell him. "I love you so much."

Air rushes from his lungs as he wraps me in his arms. "God, Oliver, I want you. I want to make you happy. And I want to be happy, too, or at least, not completely miserable."

I smile against our kiss, running my hands through his hair. A groan tears out of his throat as he presses me against the tree. "I've missed you," I whisper.

"I've missed you, too," he growls. "After that awful press conference nonsense, I couldn't get here fast enough."

A contented sigh falls out of me as he kisses me again, the corner of my mouth, my cheek. "You're really here."

"I'm really here." Dragging his hands down my waist, he clutches my hips.

I bury my hands in his hair, kiss him, feverish, hungry. "I love you," I tell him. "And I'm terrified."

He pulls back only enough to meet my eyes and search them. "Of what, love?"

I swallow roughly. "Of how much."

His eyes soften. He nods. "Me too. I'm rubbish at this. But I'm learning. I'll be better. You'll be able to count on me, Oliver. I'm not going anywhere. Do you trust me?"

"I trust you." And I do. I trust him. I believe in him. Because when Gavin Hayes sets his mind and heart to something, he does it without reservation, pouring out everything he has. Somehow, I became what he set his mind and heart to. Somehow, I'm the one he loves.

Gavin smiles, tender, adoring, a rare spark of light in those dark eyes, only for me. "Now, what do you say we go back," he says. "And this time, you show me *your* bed?"

TWENTY-NINE

Oliver

Playlist: "Young and Beautiful," Glass Animals

Standing at the threshold of my room, Gavin frowns at the twin bed. "Hmm."

I laugh, biting my lip. "Yeah."

"Never mind." Taking my hand, he drags me out of the room, down the hall. He's slow down the stairs, careful. It makes my heart pinch, worry collapsing my chest.

"Stop fretting," he says. "I'm fine. Well, I will be."

"You're hurting."

He glances over his shoulder, still holding my hand as he walks us down the hall to the first-floor bedroom. "I'm always hurting. I probably always will be." Slowing to a stop, he turns and looks at me, guarded, concerned. "If that's—"

"Don't finish that sentence," I tell him, bringing his hand to my mouth, kissing it, holding it to my cheek. "That's not coming between us, not going to scare me off. It hasn't before, and it's not going to, now or ever."

Gavin swallows roughly. "Okay."

I search his eyes. "Do you believe me?"

His mouth tips faintly with a new, tender smile. "Strangely . . . yes. Seems I do."

"Good." Clasping his hand tight, I take the lead and guide him through the bedroom to the bathroom.

I tear off my shirt, lean into the shower, and yank on the water. Before I can turn, I feel him behind me, the firm, warm skin of his chest pressed to my back. His mouth drifts along my neck, my shoulder as his hands trail down my sides, twine up my torso, until they rest over my heart. "You're perfect."

I lean back and steal a kiss. "So are you."

He smiles against my mouth, turning me toward him. My hands cradle his face as our mouths meet, slow and decadent. A quiet groan rolls from his throat. "Get naked, damn you."

I laugh, stepping out of my shoes and clothes. Gavin stares at me, eyes dark, pupils blown wide as he drinks me in. "Fuck."

I stand, proud and still, letting him look, soaking up the desire and appreciation heating his gaze. This is his first time fully seeing me. I had a full glorious view of him that morning at his house, in his bed, but *I* stripped underneath the blankets, depriving him of the same pleasure.

Staring at me still, Gavin yanks off his clothes, then walks us right into the shower. His mouth parts mine; his tongue glides slick and hot. Our breaths are rough, loud enough to be heard over the rush of water as I run my hands over his broad chest, the fine dark hairs dusting hard muscles. I kiss the scar on his collarbone, the birthmark on his neck, the freckle at his temple.

He wrenches me close, hand on my jaw, crushing our mouths together, wet, warm, hungry. I wrap my arms around his neck, press our chests together, our bodies where we're hard, throbbing, pinned together. Our mouths fall open as he moves against me, the water smoothing our way.

"Come here," he gruffs.

"I'm here," I laugh.

He walks us farther back until we hit the shower wall, his hand tight around my waist.

"I want you," I whisper as he runs his hand over my ass, rubbing it appreciatively.

He groans against my neck, kissing the hollow of my throat. "I'm yours."

I take his hand that's still massaging my butt affectionately and guide it lower until he feels me, a grunt punching out of him. "You want me here?" he says.

"So bad. I don't always, but that night in the kitchen, when your hand went wandering, I almost died, almost came so close to begging you for it. I've gotten myself off so many times since then, imagining that."

"Shit," he mutters, pressing himself into me, kissing me deep and slow. "I haven't in so long. I'll come the moment I'm inside you."

"That's okay," I tell him gently.

He shakes his head. "No, it's not. I'm going to take my time and make it good, and you're going to be patient."

I stare after him as he steps out of the shower and quickly dries his feet on the mat before prowling into the bedroom. I'm too distracted by the sight of him, warm, suntanned skin rippling with the flex of his muscles as he moves, to process what he has until he's stepping back into the shower, tossing a bottle of lube on the bench, then kissing me.

When he tears his mouth away from mine, he reaches past me, pumps bodywash from the dispenser mounted to the tiles, and works it between his hands. A grin lifts the corner of his mouth. "My turn to wash you."

I smile as he runs his hands over my neck, massaging gently over the curves of my shoulders, down my arms, chest, back, hips. He strokes my cock next, from base to tip, cleaning me, teasing me, before gliding his touch into the cleft of my ass, cleaning me there, too. His kisses are tender, exploring, reverent. I steal soap from my body, bring it to his, and wash him, too, until the air smells like herbs and steam and our warm bodies.

Backing up toward the built-in shower bench, Gavin pulls me with him. Once he's lowered himself down, he leans in, kisses my hip, my stomach. He wraps his hand around the base of my cock and pumps me, firm and leisurely.

"Shit," I mutter.

He smiles, sucks the tip, takes me deep, then deeper still. I sink my hands into his hair, throwing my head back as he sucks me off expertly, his mouth tight and hot and wet, his hand teasing me lower, sliding back, farther back, until I feel him rubbing me where a thousand nerve endings spark to life.

I gasp as time becomes as hazy as the air around us, as he swirls and strokes with his fingers, as his mouth's grip grows hotter, tighter. I feel my knees about to buckle, orgasm tingling low at the base of my spine, tightening my balls, swelling my cock. "Gonna come," I whisper.

He pops off his mouth, making me moan helplessly. Grinning, he spins me around so I face away from him. "Hands on the wall," he commands, pressing my lower back until I bend forward, showing me what he wants.

"Yeah," I beg, realizing what's coming, splaying my hands on the tile walls, looking at him over my shoulder. "Please. Now."

"Easy." He kisses my hip, one ass cheek, then the other, before he splays me wide, blows a soft warm breath over where I'm so sensitive, exposed fully for him. It makes a shiver run up my spine, threatens to make my legs buckle again. "Fuck," he groans. "Look at you. What a lucky man I am."

Sitting on the bench, he can easily set his mouth exactly where I need him. And he does.

A shout bursts out of me as I feel his tongue, a thousand times better than his finger, stroking, flicking, making my hips roll, need tighten my body. I hear the snap of a cap being opened before his finger breaches my body's resistance, his tongue coaxing me still. Then another finger. It burns but only faintly in the wake of all this pleasure. I reach for my cock, needing to give myself relief, but his hand lands softly on my ass, a teasing, gloriously pleasurable swat that warms my skin. "Not yet," he says.

"I need it," I groan.

"I know what you need. Be patient."

I nod, leaning into it, sighing as he adds a third finger, as his other hand slides up my back, comforting me, then wraps around my chest and teases the small sensitive peaks of my nipples, before it lowers to my stomach, which dances under his touch, lower still, until he's working me in his hand again, water making it glide, frictionless and blissful.

"There you are," he says quietly, kissing my ass, biting it softly. "The bed," he growls. "Now."

I wrench open the shower door and stumble forward, then reach for the towels. I throw one at him, hastily drag one down my body, too. Gavin pushes off the bench, stiff and careful, and stalks toward me with a slow, hungry smile as he bites his lip and grips me by the arm, pulling me close.

He kisses me deeply with a slick, wicked tease of his tongue. Breathing harshly, he wraps the towel around my back and dries my skin. I dry him, too, between kisses, quick, half-assed in my efforts to actually get us dry, before we drop the towels and kiss our way into the room, until the backs of my knees hit the mattress.

Smiling coyly, Gavin gently shoves me until I flop back on the bed. I stare up at him, breathing unsteadily, and feel a smile that matches his warm my face.

"You." Shaking his head, he rakes a hand through his hair. "You are going to be the death of me."

"I better not be. Then who would I torture with my incredible dance moves and Technicolor wardrobe?"

I watch him as he strolls toward his bag, which sits on the dresser. He unzips it, slaps it wide open from the inside. I stare at his gorgeous, powerful body. Big round shoulders, sculpted arms, broad chest. That round, hard ass and deep divots at his hips. Thick, chiseled thighs and sturdy calves. "Enjoying the view?" he throws over his shoulder.

I set my hands behind my head, propping myself on a pillow. "Immensely. Your ass needs its own zip code."

"Oy. It's proportional to the rest of me." He tosses a bottle of lube my way.

I catch it and blush. "Someone was confident he'd get a warm reception."

"I'll be getting a warm reception all right," he says, condoms landing in a gold-foil heap on my lap next. Slowly, he eases onto the bed beside me. I turn and face him as he tugs me close.

Our eyes search each other as he runs his hand down my arm, my ass, and pulls me tighter against him. We kiss, his hand wandering me, touching me *there*, coaxing me, making me ache until I'm begging nonsensical things.

Suddenly, he winces. I set my hand on his arm, stroking his warm skin. "We can stop anytime. I don't want it to hurt."

He holds my eyes, quiet as he grips my hand, brings it to his mouth, and kisses my knuckles. "I know you don't."

He swallows thickly, holding my hand to his mouth. That's when I feel the first warm, wet tear.

Moving even closer, I wrap my arms around him. "Talk to me," I tell him.

He buries his face in my neck, breathing unsteadily. When he pulls back and holds my eyes, his are wet, glistening. "I never . . . I've never been . . ."

Safe. Seen. Loved. Not like this.

I feel the words he struggles to say, mirrored in my heart. "Me neither." I kiss him softly. "But you are now. We both are."

He nods, kissing my temple, my cheek, my mouth.

"How about you lie back?" I tell him between kisses. "Is that comfortable for you?"

He pauses, searches my eyes as he swallows roughly. "Yeah. You don't mind that?"

"Mind that?" I whisper against our kiss before a laugh jumps out of me. "Oh, damn, I'm gonna have to pin you down and take your amazing cock while I look into your eyes. Poor me."

He laughs, rusty and warm. It makes goose bumps dance over my skin. When he smiles at me, I see what I hoped to: relief and deep, desperate desire.

Easing onto his back, Gavin holds my eyes. I straddle his waist, touch his chest, his hips, as he warms lube in his hand, then glides his fingers between my legs and touches me where I need him to, breaches that tight, aching space that's still relaxed, warm from the shower, from his touch and his tongue, taking each new finger until he's found that spot inside my body that makes my back arch, my breath hitch in my throat.

"Yeah," I whisper.

Gavin's smile is cocky, handsome, as he sets the condom packet in his teeth and tears it open, spits the wrapper's edge away.

"Could you look any more self-satisfied?" I ask him.

He wiggles his eyebrows. "Let me enjoy myself. I've waited a long time to see you this desperate."

"Shut up and do me dirty, Hayes."

He laughs hard as he rolls on the condom, then coats it with lube, too. Lifting up, I position him beneath me, my breathing shaky as I guide him inside me, the blunt, thick tip of him easing in just a little before I stop and let my body adjust.

My eyes roll back as he glides his hand along my thigh, my stomach, as he mutters naughty, toe-curling praise when I sink down on him and each patient nudge of his hips seats him deeper inside me.

"Oh, God," I groan.

"What have I told you?" he growls. "God's not here giving you this cock. Tell me who is."

"You," I tell him hoarsely, bracing my hands on the bed as I lean forward and move, guided by the bliss of his body inside mine, already stroking my prostate.

"Fuck," he grits out.

I clasp his hands and pin them against the mattress, lacing our fingers together. "Feel okay?"

He nods, fast, jerky, eyes hazy as he watches me move over him. A soft smile tips his mouth.

Minutes spill into minutes, time reduced to simply this—quiet words, patient touch, learning each other this new way. I have never felt so loved, so safe.

"Come here," he pleads, and I do, leaning in until I'm braced over him, sighing as our chests meet.

His hands roam my body, and a groan of relief rumbles in his throat. His eyes search mine, and I smile at him, nuzzling his nose.

"I love you," he whispers.

I slip my fingers through his hair, drift my fingertip over the shell of his ear. "I know. I love you, too."

He lifts his head, kissing me, slow, luxuriously, his tongue gliding with mine. I gasp, working my hips against him, chasing such intense pleasure I can barely hold my eyes open. Gavin's right there with me.

"Oliver." My name is an ache, an absolution, tearing out of him.

I pause as I peer down at him and cup his face. "Am I hurting you? Do you need me to stop?"

"No," he growls. "Don't you dare fucking stop."

He grips my ass, moving me, showing me what he wants until I take over. With each roll of my hips, his cock works that spot, the one he found so expertly in the shower and just as brilliantly as soon as we were in bed, too.

It's a white-hot wave building inside me, until it's seismic pleasure cascading through my limbs, my legs, my ass, my chest, everywhere his body moves with mine. I swear under my breath, kiss him with total abandon. Gavin's breathing is jagged and fast, broken heaves of air between wicked, foulmouthed praise for how good I feel, how perfect I am, how perfect this is.

I'm loud, panting, as my hips turn frantic, Gavin's arms around me tight. He crushes our mouths together and I grind down on him, rubbing that spot mercilessly, chasing a deep, gnawing ache.

I bury my face in his neck, not even knowing what to do with this, how intense it is, how it's seizing my body in shaking need.

"Look at me, Oliver. Please, love."

I force my eyes open as it happens, the first crest of my release that rips through me, all of me that's wrapped tight around him, in every inch of my cock rubbing against him as it swells and spills, wet and hot between our bodies.

I gasp his name, shout it as I come and come.

Clutching my hand so tight my knuckles ache, he kisses me wildly, tongue and teeth. His eyes find mine, hold them as his mouth parts, as his hips jerk, as he pulses inside me and groans my name.

A shudder runs through him as he buries his face in my neck and gasps, holding me so tight, I can barely breathe. And I love it. I love him. I love this moment that I already know I'll always remember—the world collapsed to soft sunlight and ragged breaths, cool sheets and hot, sweat-soaked skin.

And love. So much love.

Gently, Gavin cups my face, his thumb tracing my lower lip. "God*damn*."

With a soft kiss, I earn his groan, his hard-won smile. "I love you, too, sötis."

"Oliver," he whispers against my neck before pressing a kiss to my skin.

I run my hand along his arm, sighing happily. "Hmm?"

"You never told me. What does *sötis* mean?"

I smile. "Sweetie."

He arches an eyebrow. "*Sweetie?*"

"Mm-hmm. And there's a new one now. *Hjärtanskär.*"

"And what's that?" he says, knuckles stroking my cheek.

"My heart's love."

I watch his smile unfurl like the dawn, glowing, soft, unrepeatable. I remember what he called me: the sunrise of his heart. I feel, in the deepest, most secret place of my soul, exactly what he means.

THIRTY

Gavin

Playlist: "Tonight—acoustic version," Lie Ning

"How's the view?"

Shifting in the hot tub, I watch Oliver drag the glass door shut behind him. My heart trips. I still can't believe he wants me, loves me, as much as I want and love him.

"Well," I tell him, "it's no textured ceiling. But I suppose a crystal-clear sky of stars will have to do. How about you?" I lift my chin toward his phone.

He grins. "Oh, I'm just still watching you on repeat, telling everyone at that press conference that you're gone for me."

I snort. "I said no such thing."

"You implied it." He smiles at the screen, hitting play, listening to me answer Colin from ESPN.

Following up on my answer, when I told him I'd be settling down, Colin shouts over the rest of the press, "Where?"

"That depends," I hear my voice say.

"On?" Colin prompts.

"Wherever the man I love goes next, if he'll have me . . . If he will, I'll be following him."

Oliver sighs and sets down his phone. "It's better every time. Though awfully bold of you."

"I'm nothing if not determined. I had a plan to win you back."

I grab his hand and kiss it. "And don't you know, I was victorious after all. It's almost like I have an incredible record for wins or something . . ."

"You and that ego," Oliver mutters. Leaning on the edge of the hot tub, he sinks a hand into my hair and tips up my face for a deep, slow kiss. "Need anything?"

I pull away and give him a proper once-over, finally processing what he's wearing. "Christ."

"Sorry. Word is that God guy works in his own way and time. Which frankly has always ticked me off. Point is, I cannot fulfill your request."

I roll my eyes but clasp his jaw for another hard kiss. "Your swim shorts are heinous."

"Aren't they?" He smiles against my mouth. "I wore them especially to tick you off. Things have been much too amicable the past twenty-four hours."

"That's because I fucked the sass right out of you."

A blush heats his cheeks as he sits back and folds his arms across his chest. "While there may be *some* truth to that statement, I would like to jog your rather selective memory and remind you that since I had you in my mouth and sucked you off so good, they heard you begging to come all the way in Seattle, all you've done is smile and look at me with hearts in your eyes."

Except now.

For the first time since we tumbled into bed yesterday afternoon, there's been something weighing me down. And Oliver knows it.

"You okay?" he asks.

I sniff, stretch my arm across the hot tub, toying with the string at his swim trunks.

Deviously tight and short, they're an obnoxious highlighter yellow, covered in silk-screen-print bananas. I squint. "It's like looking into the sun."

Oliver barks a laugh as he brings his hands to his waistband. "Well, I guess I'll just have to take them off."

My hand lands on top of his, stopping him. "Not yet. I have . . . something I want to say first."

"Okay." He turns his hand, lacing our fingers together. "What's up?"

I jerk my head, beckoning him into the tub, which has felt incredible on my back.

Oliver swings his legs around and sinks down beside me, sliding one hand along my thigh under the water, threading his fingers through my hair with the other. "All ears," he tells me.

I stare up at the sky, those stars shining infinitely brighter since we're miles from the nearest city. I smile, remembering that night in LA, the last time I studied the stars with Oliver by my side—the shower, our meal outside, his weird, lovely story about the Big and Little Dippers, telling me in his anecdotal way that I wasn't alone, that there was something salvageable in what felt like the absolute wreckage of my life.

I wrap my arm around his neck and tug him close, pressing a kiss to his temple, breathing him in. "I love you," I tell him.

Gently, he rubs my thigh. "I know."

"I want to watch Rodgers and Hammerstein musicals made into movies and fold your garishly bright clothes and kiss you everywhere and do dishes with you and tell you when I'm hurt and trust you not to think I'm a worthless piece of shit without a ball at my feet."

His hand freezes. "Gavin, I would never think that."

Tearing my gaze from the stars, I meet his eyes and turn my hand until it's clutching his beneath the water, our fingers interlaced. "I know. But . . . it's hard for me. To really *know* it, deep inside myself."

"Why?" He searches my eyes. "Why do you think of yourself like that? I don't understand."

"I know you don't. Because you grew up learning that you were lovable whether or not you were worth millions of dollars or if you'd scored the most goals. I didn't. Thank God you don't understand that."

Oliver slides his fingertips along my palm, head bent as he studies our hands touching. "You're right—I grew up being affirmed and protected. But I want you to know I still have insecurities. I'm the youngest boy of five, the sixth kid of seven. I've battled feelings of inadequacy plenty. My anxiety, it messes with my head, makes me worry about things I shouldn't, beat myself up, overanalyze moments in the past that I can't change but that my brain insists on obsessing over anyway."

"You're perfect," I tell him fiercely. "I'll crush anything that makes you feel otherwise."

Peering up, he meets my eyes and smiles wryly. "I'm not perfect. And I didn't say this to make it about me or diminish what you went through—I just . . . want you to know I might understand a little, what it's like to know something up here"—he points to his head—"but not down here." He sets his hand on my chest, over my heart.

I clasp his hand in mine and press a kiss to his palm, then hold it tight, tracing its lines.

He presses a kiss to my shoulder, then sets his head there. "You have more you need to tell me, don't you?"

"Yes. And I hate talking about it. Thinking about it. Remembering it. But my fucking therapist said it's an important exercise in vulnerability to trust you with my past. Or some shit like that."

He smiles up at me and it sets my heart afire, glowing. "You're in therapy," he says. "I'm proud of you."

"It's fucking horseshit, is what it is."

"It's hard."

"Hard." I snort. "My dick gets hard. My abs are hard. Therapy is a Herculean fucking labor. God, it's the hardest thing I've ever done. But apparently Pauline knows what she's talking about. She fucking better, for how much I'm paying her. And she says this is where I start, so . . . here goes."

Clearing my throat, I clutch his hand, feel him, remind myself he's here, holding me. Still wanting me.

"There's no one from my past that I miss, no one I ever let close," I tell him. "Except one person. Fred."

Oliver smiles. "Fred's a good name."

I nod. "When I met Fred, I was not in a great place. In fact, I was beating the shit out of someone who'd thought that being older than me was a good reason to try to beat the shit out of *me*. We were brawling in the park across from his convenience store. Fred came out, dragged me by the collar out of the fray. I was filthy and hungry and very, very angry."

Oliver holds my hand tight, watches me, waits.

"He brought me inside his store. Gave me a granola bar and a juice and told me to sit my ass down and cool off. Then he went in back and brought out a soccer ball, set it in my hands, and said, 'Next time you want to kick the crap out of something, you put that ball in front of your feet and kick it instead.' He took me by the shoulder, pointed up to the television anchored to the wall, to some Prem game replaying on the TV. 'See that?' he said, 'That's a game of control.' Then he tapped my chest. 'That's what you're gonna do. Control that anger inside you and do something with it.'

"Then he walked me through his store, out to the back. It was this dead-end alley, the sun pouring down on it. It felt like walking into church, or what I imagined church was supposed to be: somewhere safe, somewhere you felt peace. Sanctuary.

"He pointed to a small net at the end of the alley, said, 'You come here anytime, shoot, dribble, get your anger out.' I was skeptical. I'd already dealt with my fair share of men trying to take advantage of me, a neglected, unsupervised boy. I said something to that effect, all piss and malice. He got very quiet, searching my eyes, putting the pieces together.

"Then he said, 'This place was my grandson's. He's gone now, and I just . . . haven't had the heart to put it away. He told me not to, said someone else would need it.' And then he just looked at me . . . like no one ever had before. Like he didn't see a dirty, hungry kid too big for his clothes, too angry for his own good, and he said, 'Now I know he was right.'"

I blink so the wetness pooling in my eyes won't spill into tears. Oliver dabs the corners of his eyes.

"I barely ever went 'home.' My aunt and uncle were my legal guardians, but they . . . they were not good people." I shudder, pushing away terrible memories, memories I'm not yet ready to talk about or deal with in therapy, though I know I will one day. "I wasn't safe there."

"Your parents?" he asks quietly.

"Never knew them. My dad was never in the picture, far as I know. My mom passed when I was a baby. I don't even know what of. My aunt just reminded me she resented it."

He squeezes my hand, presses a gentle kiss to my shoulder before resting his head there again. "I'm sorry."

"Me too, but I can't change the past. That's what Fred taught me. All I could change was my future. And so I did, thanks to him."

We sit in silence for a long time as I stare up at the stars, unburdened, relieved to have told Oliver everything Pauline said I needed to. Damn her, she was right.

His voice soft and gentle, Oliver breaks the silence as he says, "I know you already have the world's admiration. You know you have mine. But for what it's worth, knowing what I do now, I admire you so much more for *this*, Gavin: for having found something to hold on to when a lot of people would have understandably given up, for letting a stranger love you when the people who should have loved you best failed you most. That's a greater courage, a deeper strength, than anything you have or will ever show on a field."

My heart aches, love stretching it at the seams as I press my forehead to his. "Thank you."

Tipping his head, Oliver brushes noses with me, then presses a kiss to my lips.

When he sits back, fingers threading through my hair, he says, "Fred inspired your support program for kids, didn't he?"

"How do you know about that?"

He shrugs, smiling coyly. "I have my resources." Scooting closer, he says, "Fred gave you more than soccer. He gave you hope, and you were brave enough to take it and run. That's what you want to give kids."

I grumble something noncommittal, feigning deep interest in retying my swim trunks' drawstring.

Oliver kisses my cheek. "I'm sure he's so proud of you, Gavin."

"He *was*."

"What do you mean by that?"

The words rush out of me, angry, unstoppable. "That . . . *fucker* didn't tell me he was dying. He didn't tell me. He kept it from me, until he was on death's doorstep."

"Oh, Gavin." Oliver sits up straight in the water and faces me fully. "God, I'm sorry."

"He said he was protecting me, that I had no business sitting around, pissing away a season, watching him die," I growl, roughly wiping my eyes. "It's been fifteen fucking years, and I'm still so angry with him."

Oliver pulls me into his arms, until my head hits his shoulder, buried in the crook of his neck. "Of course you are."

"He was the *one* person who was supposed to love me and not fuck it up, and he did it anyway. He kept his sickness from me. Because my career was what mattered more to him. My career was what made *me* matter. All anyone's ever seen or cared about me is my brilliance in fucking soccer. My career ending, it's so much more than just losing something I poured my heart into for decades. It's taking away the one thing I've ever been able to count on. Except . . ."

I pull away, just enough to meet his eyes, to clasp his face as I tell him, "Except you. I need you to know this. I will fuck up. I will get growly and freaked out, and I will panic as I adjust to this next part of my life. But I love you. I choose you. I choose us. I will fight with everything I have for us. And maybe knowing this shit that is my past will make it a little easier when I'm a fuckup. That's . . . that's what I wanted you to know."

Gently, Oliver eases through the water, straddles my waist, legs bent on either side of my hips. Now it's his turn to cup my face. "I don't scare so easily. I'm not going to dip the first time you bite my head off—news flash: you already have plenty the past two years, and here I am."

I grumble miserably and drop my forehead to his shoulder. Oliver presses a kiss to the crown of my head and says, "I love you, Gavin Hayes. Soccer or not. Fifty million bucks to your name or a five-dollar bill. And Fred loved you, too."

"Some way of showing it."

Oliver nods. "He messed up. Sometimes people do very foolish things when they love someone. It doesn't mean he loved you less. It means he loved you imperfectly. I'm going to mess up sometimes and love you imperfectly, too. I don't want to, but hard as it is to believe, I am a mere mortal."

I lift my head, eyebrow arched. "I've seen your set piece execution; I remember."

A smile lifts his mouth. "We're both going to mess up. And that's scary. But I think it's okay to be a little scared—maybe it's even good. It means we know what's in our hands, how precious it is." He sets his hand over my chest, his palm warm and heavy. "Our hearts."

I swallow roughly, jaw clenched, eyes wet. "I'll keep you safe," I tell him. "I'll love you with everything I have."

"I know. And I'll keep you safe, too. And I'll make sure you never doubt what you mean to me. I'll tell you loud and often, as free as the wind on my skin, the sun and the stars lighting up the sky. I'll tell you that I love you, your tired legs and your aching back. That I love you when you walk off that field for good and when you step onto it in a new way because you simply can't walk away from it, not yet, maybe not ever.

"I'll tell you that I love you when I'm old and you're older. That I love how you hate color but you love it on me. That I love how you love the ones most people overlook: the incontinent cats, the lonely grandpas, the curious, chatty kids. I'll tell you that I love how deeply you love others even when you are afraid to. That I love you for bravely showing me love when you didn't know what it was, but you knew I needed it, and you needed it, too.

"I will never let you doubt, Gavin Hayes, that no matter what life brings us, I love that you exist, in all the slim chances of time and space, that you are here, now, with me. I will spend as long as we have so unbelievably thankful that I found you."

My eyes well. Slowly, I pull Oliver close. Our mouths brush, soft, warm. I breathe him in, hold him close, breathing out, slow and unsteady.

Brushing back my hair from my eyes, he traces my beard along my neck, my cheekbones. Then he wraps his arms around my neck and kisses me, hard and promising. I groan as my body hardens and burns awake for him.

"What hurts?" he asks.

I smile at him, drifting my hands down his back. "You tell me." I move my hips so he feels me, ready beneath him.

"Here?" Oliver asks.

I shake my head. "Inside."

We stand, both a bit unsteady, and step out of the tub. I wince as I take my first step across the deck. God, my back's a mess. Suddenly, that surgery I've been dreading, the one that Dr. Chen told me is absolutely necessary for the multiple disc herniations in my lower vertebrae, sounds incredibly appealing.

Towels around our waists, we enter the house through the sliding glass doors. I stop almost immediately, noticing the fire Oliver built.

"Not that your butt was out of bed long enough to notice yesterday," he says, "but the nights are still cool here, even though it's warm in the daytime. I figured a fire might feel nice."

I take in the great room of the A-frame—well, really it's a massive cabin with an A-frame at its heart that's been updated and sprawled into much more, cozy and comfortable, rustic simplicity. The great room is lined with bookshelves, gorgeous modern art that Oliver's explained is his brother Axel's, and lots of family photos. The fire in the hearth snaps and illuminates a plush sofa that could easily hold a dozen people.

"It's perfect," I tell him, tugging him close, giving him a kiss. "Thank you."

Walking past a long reclaimed-wood table and mismatched chairs separating the living area from the kitchen, I stare at the rug in front of the fire, the couch's many cushions.

"Come on," Oliver says, bringing me back to the moment, hooking his finger into the towel at my waist and dragging me toward the bedroom.

"No." I jerk my head toward the fire. "Here."

"The floor, though. It'll hurt—"

"Those couch cushions look removable," I tell him, grinning. "I'll take care of it. You get what we need. That small bag I packed, please."

"All right. But if you break something else because you insisted on doing the deed on a hardwood floor, I am not answering to Dr. Chen. You are."

I bite back a smile. "Fair enough."

"So this bag," he says, backtracking toward the bedroom. "How do I know which one it is? Let me guess. It's black."

"It's dove gray, thank you very much."

While he strolls down the hall, I tug off my towel and wet swim trunks, then yank off the cushions and stiffly toss them in front of the fire.

I sense Oliver's back, bag in hand, before I glance over my shoulder and catch him staring at my naked form. "Stop ogling me and get over here."

Dropping his towel, Oliver peels off his swim shorts and closes the distance between us. I cup his neck, draw him close. He gasps in pleasure, as if this is all he needs, our bodies touching, hot from the water, even hotter in front of the roaring fire.

"Lie down," I tell him.

He groans, running his hand over my cock. "Or I could get on my knees."

I shake my head. "Go on. I've got plans."

Sighing, Oliver flops back on the cushions like a starfish and pouts.

"I'm going to remind you when this is done that you *sulked*. And you're going to feel very foolish."

"Yeah, yeah."

Slowly, I ease onto the cushions, too, then push him onto his side, so his back is to my front, my back to the fire as I curl around him. Oliver hears me rustling in the bag and glances back right as I'm sliding on the cock ring, tight down my length.

His eyes widen as he says, "Oh *shit*."

"You good with this?"

"Um, is the California condor a critically endangered species?"

I shake my head and kiss him. "Such a weirdo. I'm going to take that as a yes."

"That's a deeply affirmative yes."

"Good," I tell him. "Now turn back."

He does what I say, resting his head on my arm, sighing with pleasure as I kiss his neck, then his shoulder. He reaches back and runs his fingers through my hair, meeting my mouth for a slow, hot kiss as I drift my hand up his body, teasing his chest and nipples, then down his stomach and hips to the hard muscles of his thighs, pulling him close. "You want this cock, Oliver?"

He nods quickly, rubbing himself against me. "Yeah."

It's quiet but for the pop and snap of the fire, until I turn on the cock ring, eliciting a low, steady hum. Oliver jolts when I rub against him, making sure he feels it vibrating against his ass.

I can picture it already, burying myself in him, that vibrating half-moon at the cock ring's base rubbing behind his balls, making him wild. "You want this, still?" I ask.

"Hell, yes," he pants.

Teasing him, I turn it off just as quickly as I turned it on. He groans in frustration. "Be patient."

I grip his jaw and kiss him, tongue and teeth, rhythmic plunges, hungry give and take, how our bodies will soon move. Slipping my hand down his ass, I touch him there, rub and tease him.

Oliver kisses me back just as hard, gliding his hand over my body, the simplest yet satisfying touches that make me sigh. Panting, the ache inside me at a fever pitch, I roll on the condom, warm him up more with lube and my fingers. I press soft kisses along his shoulder as I lube up the condom, too, and stare down at his gorgeous body—golden skin, long, strong muscles, that sweet, tight ass.

"Please," he whispers. "I need it."

"I know you do, love." Gently, I ease in, groaning as I breach that tight place and feel him, so incredibly snug around me. "Fuck, you feel good."

Oliver moans in pleasure as I rock my hips and fill him, slow and steady.

"So good," he mutters, reaching back, kissing me.

"And it's about to get better." As I turn on the cock ring, a gasp tears out of him.

"Shit," I hiss, easing back, then pumping into him, my hand teasing his cock, holding it tight at the base like the cock ring holds mine.

Oliver writhes, arches his back. "More. Please."

"Easy," I whisper. "Don't chase it. Just let it come. Let me give it to you."

He groans and reaches back, clutches my neck, kisses me, hot and slick, his tongue gliding with mine. "It feels so good."

I nod, breathless, the sensation building in my body so powerful, I can barely form words.

As we move, the fire warms us, hands wandering, breaths ragged, pleas and praises filling the air. Time fades to the nighttime darkness, the glow of the fire, the sounds of our bodies together.

Moving so little, it's gentle on my back, that heat from the fire soothing the insistent ache. I draw Oliver tighter against me, kiss his throat as he throws his head back and I breathe him in, his sweat, the scent of his skin. I pump his cock, then move lower, cupping his balls as they're teased by the vibration, down his thighs, up his stomach. He reaches back and rubs my ass, my hip, holding me against him as I stroke into that spot that makes him shout my name, makes him start to shake and gulp air.

"That's it," I growl, feeling his body tense, his release build. Sliding my hand up his chest, I hold his throat softly, guiding his head back. "Look at me. Look at me when you come."

Oliver stares into my eyes as I lose myself in his eyes, too. I feel the strength of his body, the strength of mine, power and need and heat, as I pump into him, as he holds me tight.

Clasping his jaw, I take his mouth, hold his eyes as he comes and calls my name against my mouth. He clings to my body as another wave of his orgasm hits him, so intense, it wrenches my release from me, makes me shout his name, too. My hips jerk as I grip his cock and pump him hard, earning hot, thick ropes that paint his stomach and my hand as he gasps my name.

Dazed, limbs heavy, I paw at the button for the vibrating cock ring, ending its overwhelming sensation.

"Holy *shit*," I groan. Oliver laughs faintly, making a hoarse laugh rumble out of me, too.

"You," he pants, "were right. I feel very foolish for pouting. Then again, if that's what pouting gets me every time, I may need to starfish on the floor and sulk more often."

I smile against his kiss, soak up his slow, contented sigh. "I'm glad you liked it."

"Liked it? I loved it." Reaching up, he slips his fingers through my hair and kisses me again. "Got anything else fun in that little dove-gray bag that you want to share, Hayes?"

"Oh, Bergman," I whisper, grinning wickedly, "just you wait."

THIRTY-ONE

Gavin

Playlist: "You're the One I Want," Chris and Thomas

I have an unobstructed view of the Pacific Ocean at dusk, but my gaze is fastened on a far better sight.

Oliver stands in line beside his brothers, suntanned and striking in a black tux, laughing as he palms away a tear. In my peripheral vision, I see Ren cup Frankie's face as they kiss to an eruption of applause. But my eyes don't leave Oliver. They hardly ever manage to.

As the bride and groom walk out to more applause, I stare at Oliver and feel peace crest like a wave in my soul.

There are plenty of big names here, but there are no frantic camera flashes, no probing questions or enthusiastic fans. By some feat of money or connections or some combination of both, the beach is protected this evening, away from prying eyes and press. Here, we're simply family and friends, celebrating two people promising each other forever.

I'm starting to get used to that. Being simply Gavin. Little by little, I'm learning to embrace the relief that comes with not waking up having to prove my worth to myself or to the world, the serenity of accepting myself as I am, believing that's enough.

I have someone reminding me of that every day, too, which certainly helps—the man who comes bounding toward me and slips his hand around my waist. "You owe me fifty bucks."

"Piss off," I tell him.

"I didn't cry!" Oliver yells. "You bet I would. I bet I wouldn't. Fifty bucks. Now hand it over."

I kiss him even though he's full of shit and earn his satisfied smile as he pulls away. "I watched you, you mendacious pain in my ass. You cried."

"I swiped away a bit of moisture at the *corner* of my eyes when the wind picked up," he says loftily, hand out. "Let's go. Cough it up."

I slap his open palm. "Fuck no. Besides, I'm not the one raking in the dough now. You're the breadwinner."

He rolls his eyes. "This again."

"I've got a long retirement to plan for. A budget to respect."

"Kladdkaka!" Linnea runs into my legs and smiles up at me, cheeks flushed, her fluttery yellow dress already smudged with something that looks suspiciously like chocolate cake. At least, that's what I hope it is.

"Hello, rug rat." Crouching, I smile and meet her eyes. "You look very lovely, Linnea. And you did an excellent job throwing your flower petals."

"Thank you!" she says, plopping herself on one of my thighs. Pain pulses in my knee, but it's not unbearable, more tiring and familiar than excruciating. I'll ice it tonight. Then Oliver will massage it for me. Then his hand will wander higher, higher and—

"Remember, Linnie," Oliver says gently, brushing her cheek with his knuckles. "Take it easy with Kladdkaka's body."

"She's fine."

He sighs and just smiles.

"Kladdkaka." Linnea sets her hand on my cheek. "Can I come over soon?"

"Absolutely. I have lots of free time nowadays."

A smile lights her face. "And I want your guac."

"You got it."

"Yay!" Pressing a kiss to my cheek, she throws her arms around my neck and says, "I'm so glad Uncle Ollie loves you, Kladdkaka. I love you, too."

Swallowing roughly, I hug her back. "I'm glad he loves me, too. And I love *you*, Linnea. Very much."

She laughs, a bright, bubbly child's laugh. Then she hops off my lap and skips away, barefoot and twirling in her dress.

"You're worse than all of us," Oliver says.

Easing upright, I throw him a glare and tug him close by the waist. "How so exactly?"

"She's got you wrapped around her finger so bad."

"I can't say no to a face like that. How can you?"

He smiles, stealing a kiss. "You're such a softie. But don't worry. You keep wearing that scowl and your grayscale clothes to scare away the world. Your secret's safe with me. I'll just keep you all to myself."

"Not if your brother has anything to say about that," I mutter, noticing the brother in question coming our way.

"Huh?"

"Ren wants me to go public with the support program and merge with his nonprofit. Says with both our faces on it, we'll get so much more financial backing and even stronger publicity, which then of course means—"

"More money to help more kids." Oliver nods. "It's smart."

"Smart, yes. But it requires things like talking to people and leaving the house and not swearing as much."

Oliver smiles wide. "Let me guess. This plan was hatched at the not-so-secret Shakespeare club of his that you joined."

"That," I tell him primly, "is none of your business."

His smile widens. "I think it's great—the club that we pretend I don't know about but also merging organizations with Ren's to reach and help more kids."

Just as he says that, his brother breaks in, a hand on each of our shoulders. "Family picture time," Ren says. "Come on!"

"Sure thing," Oliver tells him, following in his wake, my hand in his. I try to extract myself. I'm not a part of that.

Ren and Oliver turn in unison, looking uncharacteristically serious, with their sharp black tuxes and twin deep frowns. "Gavin," Ren says. "Come on. Family photos."

My mouth opens. Shuts. "I don't . . . That is—"

"Sötis, I told you." Oliver threads his fingers through mine again, tugging until I start walking with him.

Reassured that I'm coming after all, Ren turns and disappears into the small crowd, presumably to round up the rest of the family.

"You Bergmans put the poker guys and their pushiness to shame," I grumble.

"Speaking of." Oliver's eyes find Mitch, who stands nearby with his arm around a petite bespectacled woman with short silver-white hair. "I still can't believe it."

Millie, a former administrator for Ren's team, turned out to be Mitch's pen pal, and they're now dating. When I mentioned her name and we realized the connection over a recent Sunday family dinner, Ren nearly fell out of his chair.

"Our lives were destined to entwine," Oliver says dreamily. "And you're stuck with me forever, so you're in the family pictures. Don't be a grump about it."

It's a moment I'm learning to work through, to loosen the grip of fear and accept an outstretched hand like the one firmly clasping mine, its thumb sweeping soothingly over my skin. "You're just as stuck with me, I'll have you know," I growl against his neck before pressing a kiss above his shirt collar, breathing him in.

Oliver smiles as a blush warms his cheeks. "I do know. You're just not used to being manhandled by a dozen oversized half Swedes and their equally assertive partners and offspring, let alone being reminded you're now one of theirs."

"Precisely."

Oliver's smile deepens. He tugs me close and kisses me soft and slow, for all the world to see. "Good thing you've got the rest of your life to get used to it."

———

"Oh, sweet God," I groan, stretching out my aching legs on the chaise in the backyard. My knees pop. My ankle cracks. Fuck, it feels good to put my feet up.

"Your ice pack, sir." Oliver sets it on my aggravated knee. "And your heating pad." He wedges that between my lower back and the chaise. "And my favorite spot." He eases onto the chaise, then shimmies my way until he's leaning his back against my chest, wrapping my arms around him.

Then and only then do I feel his body relax, a long, contented sigh leave him. I press a kiss to his temple and stare up at the stars, my heart so impossibly full. "I love the fuck out of you, Oliver Bergman."

I feel his smile as he nuzzles his temple against my jaw. "I love the fuck out of you, too, Gavin Hayes." Peering up at me, he slips his hand along my neck, into my hair, scratching affectionately along my scalp. "That was a good wedding."

I grunt in agreement, running my hand over his chest, kissing his temple again. "Great food, great music and dancing, didn't run too late. The trifecta of party perfection."

"Mm-hmm." He presses a kiss to my jaw, then settles in against me. "You're a good dancer."

"Damn right, I am."

He snorts a laugh. "And humble as always."

"You are, too. And if you think I missed those rainbow argyle socks you snuck on, I didn't."

"Damn," he says. "How'd you spot them?"

"Your Electric Slide moves. A sartorial Technicolor eyesore is what those were. You couldn't for once do what you were told and wear a tux and appropriate dress socks."

He grins. "You like my sartorial Technicolor eyesores."

I grin, too. "I do. I love them, actually. I could find you in the blink of an eye all the way across the dance floor."

Sighing happily, Oliver glides his hand down the nape of my neck, rubbing those tight, sore muscles. "Your place or mine tonight?" he asks.

"Mine. Wilde is going to start pissing in more than my shoes if I don't show my face soon."

Oliver grimaces. "Sorry. I've been hogging you at my place."

I swallow the threat of nerves, threading our hands together, sliding our fingers along each other's. "We could . . . have one place together. Someday."

Oliver's head snaps up, his eyes meeting mine. A new, precious smile that I've never seen before warms his face. "Seriously?"

I feel a ridiculous smile lighting up my face, too. "Seriously. I know it's fast. And I don't . . . I mean, it's not like hugely pressing if you didn't want, but if you *did* want, I may have hired an architect to scope out various options for merging our bungalows into one home. For us."

Oliver sits up, then spins and faces me. "You did?"

"I mean, they're just rough plans—"

His kiss silences me as he whispers against my mouth, "I already know I'll love them."

I pull back, searching his eyes. "Really?"

"Yes." His smile is soft and tender, his eyes holding mine. "Really."

I kiss him under the glittering night sky, brimming with possibility. For the first time in so long, hope fills me, bright as the stars above. Holding the man I love, heart of my heart, I tell him the truth.

I can't wait for what comes next.

Gavin

Playlist: "Yellow," Vitamin String Quartet

Six months later

Four hours into my birthday, and I'm reminded why I've never cared for celebrating it. My birthday so far has involved sleeping like shit, an aching back, and an early-morning massage therapy appointment that barely took the edge off my pain. If I cared about my birthday, gave a fuck about it being a day that went *my* way, I'd already be thoroughly disappointed. I'm exhausted, sore, walking stiffly from my car up my walkway, beneath a sky that's been a moody overcast gray since I finally snuck out of bed, leaving my deeply asleep boyfriend to rest peacefully. And that's fine. I have no expectations, no hopes for this day to be anything special.

Just another day waking up, another year older. Except . . .

I stop at my front door, glancing toward Oliver's house beside mine, the construction underway to join our houses, forming one big home. *Our* home. I stare at that tangible proof of Oliver's commitment to me, his love for me, and I feel a swell of . . . something. Something bubbly and warm and so fucking good.

What do I have to be morose about? Yes, I'm still battling pain. Yes, I'm still a little lost in the wake of my retirement, finding my new routine, sorting out how I want to meaningfully fill my days. But I still have so much to be thankful for. Breath in my lungs; the privilege of financial security, giving me the means for the upcoming surgery to mitigate my pain, which I've been dragging my feet about, nervous to incur even *more* pain; and most of all, a man who loves me. So, so much.

As if in agreement with my stern self-talking-to, the gloomy sky cracks open, golden light spilling out. Bold and bright, it bathes my face, warms my skin, and seeps right in, straight to my heart.

I smile faintly as I turn, leaving my front porch, strolling over to Oliver's.

I let myself in, calling his name, then walk through the rarely used front room, down the hall, past the bedrooms, to the kitchen and living area. "Oliver?" I call again.

Soon as I catch sight of the kitchen, I freeze, wide-eyed. Sound and color explode around me.

"Happy birthday!" Linnea hollers, a half second ahead of Oliver's boisterous voice.

They're wearing rainbow polka dot party hats, and through the multicolored confetti that's begun to drift around me, I watch them bring kazoos to their lips, then blow loudly.

I blink, stunned, taking in the sight. A tall, listing birthday cake—homemade, by the looks of it, with its Tower of Pisa lean, wobbly iced letters, and lopsided frosting flowers. A colorful hand-painted sign taped to the rafters, complete with a backward *B* in *Birthday*.

"It's your birthday, Kladdkaka!" Linnie yells, running toward me, barreling into my legs.

Slowly, I bring my hands to her shoulders and squeeze gently. "So it is."

My gaze fixes on Oliver, who holds my eyes, his smile bright, even as anxiety makes it tight at the edges, lacking the free, wide warmth it has when he's truly at ease, truly happy.

I swallow roughly, blinking. Fucking hell, I'm going to cry.

Oliver reads it all, the anxiety draining from his expression as he rushes toward me and wraps me in a gentle hug, careful of my sore back. One hand still clutching Linnea's shoulder, I wrap an arm around his neck and draw him close, bury my face in his neck, exhaling unsteadily as I dab my wet eyes against his shirt.

"Thank you," I whisper, my voice hoarse.

Linnea squeezes my leg in a hard hug. "Are you happy, Kladd-kaka? About our surprise?"

I pull back enough to peer down at her and gently drag a knuckle against her round, rosy cheek. "So happy."

Oliver watches me closely, quiet, tender concern painted on his face. He threads his fingers through mine and squeezes. I squeeze back.

Leaping away, Linnea bounds back toward the kitchen island. "Come on, then! Time for candles and wishes!"

"I thought we were doing presents first," Oliver says, smiling at her.

Linnie frowns. "Well, we were. But I'm hungry for cake."

A laugh jumps out of me. "That makes two of us, but I *would* love to see my presents first."

"Remember," Oliver says to his niece sweetly, scooping her off the stool she's climbed onto and into his arms. "I promised Mommy that I wouldn't just feed you cake. We said we'd eat a healthy lunch while Kladdkaka opened presents, *then* we'd have cake."

Linnea sighs wearily. "But then I won't have *all* the room for cake."

Oliver laughs now, shaking his head. "I feel you, Linnie, but that's for the best. Take it from someone who periodically does not make choices in his stomach's best interest—your tummy will thank you for eating a quesadilla before you tackle birthday cake."

"I'm not hungry for a quesadilla, though," she says, pouting. "I'm hungry for cake."

"Hmm." I frown thoughtfully, strolling into the kitchen. "What about quesadillas with a big dollop of Kladdkaka's famous home-made guacamole?"

Linnea's eyes light up. "Oh, yes! I'm very hungry for that!"

————

I'm never going to recover from this. The love, the sweetness, over-flowing my heart, spread across the table. I stare at Linnea's art made just for me, so many drawings of us, two dark-haired stick figures on the beach, on the soccer field, cooking in the kitchen, one shorter and smiling wide, the other with a beard and a soft smile that feels so like me, and with us, always Oliver, too, big, bright smile, blond squiggly hair and beard. Wearing a hot-pink birthday crown, I reach carefully across her art, past the stuffed animal cat in my lap that looks just like Wilde, which Linnea explained I can snuggle when I miss him, and give Linnea a big, long hug.

"I love all of it, Linnea," I tell her. "It makes me feel . . . very celebrated."

She beams up at me. "Good. That's what birthdays are for!"

Oliver sets his hand on my thigh beneath the table and squeezes gently. I wrap my hand around his and smile over at him. "Thank you. This is . . . not what I was expecting, and I mean that in the very best way."

Oliver gifts me a soft, sweet smile. "First, I was going to rope in the whole Bergman brood, but then I realized we should probably ease you into all this—being the center of attention in the family, on the receiving end of all that love."

I huff a laugh. "That was wise."

"You like the cat?" Linnie asks, scooping it up from my lap. "Isn't he so cute?"

"Very cute. And very thoughtful of you. Though in a few months, Uncle Ollie's and my houses are going to be one big home, and

Wilde will get to roam all around, so hopefully I won't have to miss him too much longer. Then maybe you can borrow Wilde's twin to have at your house, when *you* miss him."

Linnea's eyes light up. "Really?"

"Of course."

Linnea hugs the stuffed cat to her chest. I smile down at her. "Well," I say to both her and Oliver, "thank you for all my gifts, and for lunch—"

"Wait!" Linnea yells. "One more thing!" She lunges for a bag that I hadn't noticed in all the colorful chaos strewn across the table and sets it in my hands. "Open it!"

I tug away the tissue paper, unearthing a hot-pink T-shirt that reads *FUC*, handwritten in fabric paint.

I have to try very hard not to laugh. "Thank you, Linnea. This is—"

"Favorite Uncle Club!" she yells. "FUC."

Oliver's trying hard not to laugh, too. "I told Linnea you'd need to wear that just around the house, so it wouldn't make the others jealous."

"And here I was so looking forward to gloating in front of Viggo," I say with a sigh.

"Don't worry," Linnea says. She pats my shoulder gently, her face the portrait of seriousness. "I'm making one for every aunt and uncle on their birthdays. Soon everyone will have a FAC or FUC shirt, and you can all wear them everywhere!"

I crack a wide smile and accept another hard hug from her. "That sounds perfect."

"Cake now!" Linnea yells, rushing over to the island for rainbow polka dot paper plates that match her and Oliver's hats.

Turning toward Oliver, I tell him, "Let's just hope Viggo will let himself in here on a night I'm wearing my FUC shirt. *Then* I can gloat."

Oliver snorts. "He'd lose it."

"Thus the appeal." I glance Linnea's way, see she's absorbed in sorting candles by color, then lean in, cupping Oliver's neck and stealing a quick kiss. "I love you. Thank you again for this."

Oliver smiles, leaning in for another kiss. "I love you, too. I'm glad you're happy. You deserve to be. Both today, on your birthday, and every day."

"Thanks to you," I whisper, "I am."

"Here we go!" Linnie yells.

Oliver and I glance up, eyes wide as we process Linnea teetering on the edge of the stool, the cake about to topple out of her hands.

We both lunge for it, but Oliver's more agile, faster, thankfully, catching the plate just as it starts to slip from her grasp.

"Phew!" Linnea says, hopping off the stool. "Good catch, Uncle Ollie."

Oliver blows out a calming breath as she skips past him. "*Phew* is right."

"Time for wishes!" Linnea hops up and down impatiently, candles in hand, as Oliver gingerly lowers the cake on its platter to the table, then slides it toward me. It leans ominously, swaying like a Jenga tower about to topple.

Oliver and I lunge again, but it settles.

"Candles!" Linnea yells. "One for every year!"

Oliver and I meet each other's eyes. There's no way this cake will survive us sticking candles in it. It'll tumble if we even try.

"How about one candle?" I offer. "A big one to make one big wish."

Linnea frowns. "Just one?"

Oliver seems to deliberate, then bends, whispering something in her ear. Linnea's frown flips to a beaming grin. "Just one's fine. *Today.*"

My gaze flicks up to Oliver. I stare at him, suspicious.

Oliver just smiles, then carefully takes the hot-pink candle Linnea holds up for him before he eases it into the cake.

I pray, even though I haven't prayed in so long, that the cake doesn't fall. Linnea would be crushed—I know it.

Physics is defied, or perhaps my prayer is answered, because the cake stays steady. Oliver has the candle wick burning with just one click of the lighter. Just one little flame, but its warmth spills across the table, brightens Oliver's and Linnea's faces as they smile at me.

"Make a wish, Kladdkaka," Linnea whispers. "And make it a *big* one."

I smile at her, and then my gaze slides to Oliver, who watches me, love and candlelight shining in his eyes. I stare at the man I love. The man I want to love forever.

I shut my eyes. Draw in a breath. And make the biggest wish of my heart.

Oliver

"That," Gavin says quietly, "was the loveliest birthday I've ever had."

I smile at him as we walk hand in hand from his car, back from driving Linnea home. Leaning in, I press a kiss to his cheek. "And it's not even over yet."

"What's that supposed to mean? And what's this about Linnea's promise of just one candle *today*?" he asks. It flashes before me, that moment he shut his eyes, drew in a breath, hot-pink birthday crown nestled lopsided in his dark brown hair, his brow drawn tight, like every drop of his will was distilled in that moment into the wish he made as he blew the candle out. "I feel this implies the promise of more candles in the future."

"Better be more candles in the future." I grin.

Gavin narrows his eyes playfully. "You're being evasive."

"Who, me?" I scoff. "I would never."

"I promise you, Oliver, I'll get it out of you by whatever means necessary," he growls, tugging me close, making our chests bump and earning a pained grunt from him.

Worry cuts through me. "Gavin—"

"Hush." He cups my neck and kisses me, hard and deep. I melt into his touch, his mouth expertly moving with mine. "I'm fine."

"You're hurting."

"I'm all right," he says gently, between kisses. "I promise. I'm soaring on a high of cake and a very large dose of naproxen sodium and so much love."

I smile against our kiss. "You sure?"

"Very sure." After one more kiss, he asks quietly, "Your place or mine?"

I glance between our two homes, and Gavin's gaze follows mine, to the construction between them, the beginnings of what will open and bridge our houses into a home that's all ours.

"Pretty soon," I tell him, "we won't be having this conversation."

"You're right."

I glance his way. "I can't wait for that. For . . . so much of what lies ahead for us."

Gavin smiles softly. "Me neither. I think about it all the time."

"You do?"

"Fucking hell, yes, Oliver, it's all I can do not to dream and think about life with you, everything I want from you, to give you, to share with you." He draws me in for a kiss, drags my bottom lip between his teeth. "Now, your answer, please. Your place or mine?"

I picture my soaker tub, something that Gavin, my once anti-tub kind of guy, has come around to, now that I've shown him the benefits beyond cleanliness that can be found there.

Smiling wider, I kiss his cheek, his jaw, that spot right behind his ear that makes him shiver. "Mine."

———

Turning the corner of my bathroom, I tell Gavin, "Found the sea salt, mint, and lavender bubble bath . . ." My voice drifts to silence as I stare at him, his arm stretched wide across the tub, a wicked grin on his face, the hot-pink birthday crown perched on his head.

"Wow," I whisper.

"My sentiments exactly." Gavin bites his lip, staring at me. There are no bubbles yet—he sent me searching the closet for a very particular bubble bath—so I can see everything. His knee drawn up, the other leg stretched out the length of my massive soaker tub. His hand beneath the water, stroking himself as his gaze rakes down my body.

"Come here," he says roughly.

I set the bubble bath on the tub's ledge, then yank off my towel. I'm not coy about it, no delay, no teasing. I need him. I need to feel close. After a day filled with tiny anxieties, worries, fears that I wouldn't get it right, my first time celebrating his birthday, I need that touch and reassurance that he's as happy as he says he is, that how I planned this day was really just what he wanted.

Careful not to step on him, I ease into the tub at the opposite end, bracketing my legs over his. Gavin frowns, then grumbles, "I said come *here*."

"I am here," I tell him, smiling.

He shakes his head, then jerks it toward his arm, stretched across the tub. A blush hits my cheeks. I smile wider. "Oh, *that* here. My mistake."

"I'll say." He shifts a little, making more room for me, and I crawl toward him, then sink into the crook of his arm.

Gavin wraps his arm around me, tucking me against his side. My hand lands on his chest, right over his steadily beating heart. His lips meet my forehead, a soft, reverent kiss. "That's better," he whispers.

I smile. So at peace. So in love. "It's perfect."

He glides his hand down my shoulder, my arm, to my hand. "You really feel that way?"

I peer up at him, surprised by the insecurity in his voice. "Of course I do. Gavin, I'm so happy, it feels like a crime, like no one has any business being as happy as I am every day when I wake up beside you."

A wobbly smile lifts his mouth. "Well . . . that's good, then."

I cup his cheek, then kiss him, slow and soft. "I love you."

He sighs into our kiss, opens his mouth. Our tongues flick and dance, the kiss growing hotter, hungrier. "I love you."

My hand skates down his stomach, gripping his cock, stroking firm and slow, just how he likes. His head falls back. The crown tumbles off and lands on the tub ledge with a clatter. "This okay?" I ask.

He moans as I start to rub him with my other hand, teasing that tight bunch of muscles and nerves. "Very okay," he whispers hoarsely.

His hand finds me, hard and aching, and he strokes me, too, smooth and firm, the way he's learned I love. I wrap my thigh over his, reach for a kiss that he meets fiercely, teeth clacking, rough breaths.

That's all it is for minutes, the quiet splash of water, the sounds of our bodies rolling, arching beneath its surface, harsh tugs of air, muttered curses, pleas for more.

Gavin draws me tight inside his arm, crushing my chest to his, making our hands fumble before they regain their grip. He wraps his hand around mine, brings our cocks tight against each other, and moves, fast, urgent.

I stare at him, panting, gasping, feeling my body climb higher and higher, white-hot need spiraling through my limbs.

"I love you," he grits out, holding my eyes. "I love you so fucking much."

"I love you," I tell him, my voice breaking, the threat of release too much to breathe properly, let alone manage a sentence.

"Look at me, Oliver," he begs. "Let me see you fall apart, love."

I do. I fall apart in his arms, crying out his name, shaking in his firm grip. And then I watch him, too, the satisfaction, the peace roll across his face as he comes, as he falls back against the tub and sighs, drawing me in for a kiss.

"Good way to wrap up your birthday?" I ask between tugs of air.

He grins, breathing harshly, too, and kisses me. "The best."

I smile into his kiss. "Excellent."

"I never want it to end," he admits, his face bashful, sweet, so rare for him.

"Thankfully, it doesn't have to. Tomorrow, it's still your birthday weekend. We've got more birthday celebrating, more birthday sex ahead of us—"

"What now?" He sits up slowly. "*More* celebrating?"

I smile sheepishly. "And more birthday sex? Did I mention that?"

He narrows his eyes. "Oliver."

"It's just . . . a little cake and song for you tomorrow, at Sunday family dinner. That's all. Unless . . ." I swallow nervously. "Unless you really don't want that."

Gavin stares at me, his stern expression softening. "I won't have the first idea what to do with it, but . . . I think I do want that."

Relief spills through me. "That's okay. You've got years and years, decades, to get used to Bergman birthday celebrations. And Mom's even making kladdkaka. Linnie said it's the only thing you'd want."

Gavin swallows roughly. "That sounds . . . perfect."

"Good, because Mom already baked the cake—"

"No." He shakes his head. "Not the cake—well, not *just* the cake." Gently, he leans in, cupping my face, his thumb tracing my bottom lip. "The 'years and years, decades' part. With you . . ." He presses his forehead to mine. "*That* is what sounds perfect."

Tenderness fills me. "I hope you know that's what I want, what these dreams and plans and hopes are for—everything for you, every moment with you. To build a life we both love and want to share."

He nods, kisses me, slow and sweet. "I know. And I hope *you* know that is exactly what I want, too. That this . . ." He lifts my hand, sets it right over his heart. "Is yours. That its every beat is for you."

"Well." I blink away tears. "Damn."

"What is it?" he asks, a furrow in his brow.

"There goes *my* birthday wish."

He smiles, wide and beaming, so rare, so lovely. "I suppose you'll just have to find lots of other beautiful things to wish for with me, for years and years, decades, even. Think you can manage that?"

I smile, too, as his mouth meets mine, as we kiss and sink into the tub, the warmth of our bodies close, our hearts even closer. "I think I'd love that. Almost as much as I love you."

ACKNOWLEDGMENTS

Like many people, once I gave in to the hype and watched *Ted Lasso*, I fell hard and fast. As someone who's a sucker for any character unpacking their embedded patriarchy and eschewing toxic masculinity, and who grew up playing soccer and deeply missed playing during the pandemic, when games were canceled and seasons postponed due to safety precautions, watching *Ted Lasso* was a balm to my soul. When I finished the first two seasons, I felt this aching need to stay in a world that felt like Ted's, to linger in rowdy locker rooms and shenanigans during practice, to see teammates being there for each other, rising to the occasion as they faced challenges both on and off the field.

And thus was born an idea for Oliver's book: a player whose heart echoes Ted Lasso's, someone who's always chipper, friendly, playful, yet who's also privately contending with loneliness and anxiety; and another player, who, like Roy Kent, grumpy, growly, and foulmouthed, fears the end—like we all do—of what's given his life purpose, validity, and meaning. And then, because I am in the business of writing happily ever afters, I thought, let's make them fall in love!

To say writing Gavin and Oliver's story brought me joy is a wild understatement. It was cathartic and healing and beautiful and challenging in the best ways, like one of those magical runs when your legs feel loose and strong and the sun's out but not too bright and the wind moves just enough to cool your skin without knocking you over: hard but satisfying, peaceful yet invigorating. It wouldn't have been possible without some incredible people who worked with me to ensure that, in addition to my own lived experience, some of which is portrayed in these characters, their lived experience of this story's representation was authentically, sensitively portrayed. Jess, Tim, Ellie, thank you. Your wisdom, honesty, and dedication to helping me make this book inclusive, thoughtful, authentic, and respectful means the world to me.

I hope this story has brought you joy and affirmation, that even if you wear that sunshine smile, you realize you don't have to hide when the storm clouds roll in, that you can be loved even—no, *especially*—when you're anxious and scared; that if you feel grief and pain, those worthy of your love will love you through those hard moments, make you laugh and hold your hand and remind you that, as the song beloved by soccer and musical fans alike reminds us, "you'll never walk alone."

The Bergman Brothers series, continuing with this book, portrays a big messy family, found family, and friends—imperfect people trying exceptionally hard to love each other well. There are rough patches and plenty of struggles along the way, but ultimately, their love is accepting, affirming, and profoundly safe. Some might say this isn't very realistic. To which I say, I'd like it to be, and this is why I write. As Oscar Wilde said, "Life imitates Art far more than Art imitates Life." I believe stories affirming everyone's worthiness of love and belonging have life-changing power—to touch us, heal us, and deepen our empathy for ourselves and others. Stories have the power to reshape our hearts and minds, our relationships, and ultimately the world we live in.

I hope by now that, as it has been for me, this Bergman world is a haven for you, reader, where these intimate relationships with oneself and others, platonic, familial, romantic, and beyond, affirm the hope for all of us—that we can be curious, not judgmental; be open-minded and open-hearted; welcome and embrace one another, just as we are; and become better, wiser, kinder, for having experienced all that is possible when we do.